Praise for the Scottish Bookshop Mysteries

"Shelton stocks her tale with appealing characters and intriguing Nessie lore. Cozy fans will be rewarded."
—*Publishers Weekly* on *The Loch Ness Papers*

"A complex plot . . . and an enchanting Scottish setting combine to create a clever entry in a capital series."
—*Richmond Times-Dispatch* on *Lost Books and Old Bones*

"A complicated mystery with plenty of historically based characters and whose ending provides more than one kind of surprise."
—*Kirkus Reviews* on *Lost Books and Old Bones*

"This spotlessly clean, fun-filled read takes plenty of twists and turns on the way to the satisfying ending."
—*Publishers Weekly* on *The Cracked Spine*

"Shelton's breezy cozy series may interest readers who enjoy Sheila Connolly's 'County Cork' mysteries."
—*Library Journal* on *Of Books and Bag Pipes*

"Move over Claire Fraser; American bibliophile Delaney Nichols is about to take Scotland . . . by storm!"   —Ellery Adams

"Full of wit and whimsy . . . delightful characters . . . fantastic!"
—Jenn McKinlay

"A sleuth who'll delight book lovers."   —*Kirkus Reviews*

"Endearing characters, and prose that immediately transports readers to enchanting Edinburgh . . . and leaves them eager for a return trip." —Lucy Arlington

"For book lovers, mystery seekers, and anyone who enjoys a determined new heroine. Sure to be a winning series." —Erika Chase

"[For] readers who appreciate bookseller sleuths such as Marianne Macdonald's Dido Hoare or Joan Hess's Claire Malloy . . . The feisty Delaney is an appealing protagonist and the secondary characters are charming as well." —*Library Journal*

"Shelton's lovely depictions of Edinburgh, its denizens, and its bookshops will enchant lovers of cozies with a Scottish setting." —*Publishers Weekly*

THE
STOLEN
LETTER

Paige Shelton

St. Martin's Paperbacks

Published in the United States by St. Martin's Paperbacks, an imprint of St. Martin's Publishing Group.

THE STOLEN LETTER

Copyright © 2020 by Paige Shelton-Ferrell.
Excerpt from *Deadly Editions* copyright © 2021 by Paige Shelton-Ferrell.

For information, address St. Martin's Publishing Group, 120 Broadway, New York, NY 10271.

www.stmartins.com

ISBN: 978-1-250-20389-2

Our books may be purchased in bulk for promotional, educational, or business use. Please contact your local bookseller or the Macmillan Corporate and Premium Sales Department at 1-800-221-7945, ext. 5442, or by email at MacmillanSpecialMarkets@macmillan.com.

Printed in the United States of America

Minotaur Books edition published 2020
St. Martin's Paperbacks edition published 2021

10 9 8 7 6 5 4 3 2 1

For my sweet dad

ONE

I must really love my job. There was no other explanation for my happy, hurried footsteps. I couldn't wait to get to work.

I hadn't been inside the most wonderful bookshop in the entire world for the last two weeks. Instead, I'd been with the most perfect man on the most perfect honeymoon. We'd seen more of Europe than I ever thought I'd see when I first moved to Scotland just over a year ago. Of course, I also hadn't planned to meet Tom Shannon, Scottish pub owner, and then marry him. Sometimes, it's all about the surprises. Maybe it's always about surprises, but it takes a few big ones for us to notice. And, boy have there been some *big* surprises along the way. It's been better than I could have ever anticipated.

I leapt off the bus and set out in a quick pace. But then I skidded to a stop and took a deep breath. I'd quit having moments of staggering awe, moments when I wondered if it was all really . . . well, real, a while ago. I had accepted that it was okay to be so happy, to be grateful for all the amazing moments that had happened since I'd answered an online ad about a job in an Edinburgh bookshop. Was I up for an adventure? A secretive sort of job in a bookshop with a coveted place behind a desk that had seen the likes of kings and queens? Oh, yes, it seemed I had been. And here I was.

As I stood there in Grassmarket, I looked toward the shop, The Cracked Spine. Nothing about its façade had changed since Tom and I had had our wedding inside. The awning above was still there, and I could see a couple stacks of books on the other side of the window. I'd put those stacks there, and I'd been the one to organize them. I always did the window displays, and this one had been about a color. None of the books in the window were part of our rare or valuable collections. They were used books, some of them I'd read, some I'd never heard of; only a few of them spoke to me. I'd used books with blue covers, and from this vantage point I thought the stacks were still exactly as I'd arranged. If that was the case, none of the books had sold, and though the shop seemed never to have any financial challenges, I decided I needed to redo the display, create something that would better sell a book or two. I could do that.

The owner of the shop and my boss, Edwin MacAlister, had plenty of money. There really was no need to worry about the financial future of the Cracked Spine, but, still, we were there to sell things.

The Tudors hated to be wrong, and therefore never were.

I blinked at the bookish voice. I looked around. It was a strange comment, coming to me from some place I didn't understand.

The Tudors? The royals?

Had that really been my intuition speaking to me as it did sometimes, through the books I'd read? If so, I didn't remember the book, and I didn't have a sense that I needed to be listening to my intuition. All was well, or so I thought. Maybe someone had actually spoken to me, or I'd overheard the words.

I looked around. Nope, that didn't seem likely.

I plunked my hands on my hips and looked toward the bookshop again. I didn't know what exactly had just happened, but I didn't dwell on it long.

My eyes scanned over to the bakery, its front window fogged around the perimeter from the early morning baking. I could imagine the delicious smells, and I decided to pick up breakfast. I didn't know if everyone would be in this morning, but Rosie would be there, with Hector, the miniature Yorkie she cared for but was worshiped and waited on by all of us. A thrill zipped through me at the prospect of seeing them both.

Hamlet might have class, but he'd be in at some point, even if only for a little while. A student at the University of Edinburgh, he was a young man, and had become much like a younger brother to me now. He'd been gifted with an old soul and named appropriately. If reincarnation was a real thing, there was no doubt in my mind that Hamlet had hung out with Shakespeare himself, had probably given the old bard a run for his money, maybe even did some editing.

It was doubtful Edwin would be there. He didn't come in as much as the rest of us, and since he'd started dating a restaurant owner from Ireland, Vanessa Morgan, he'd been around even less.

I decide to see who was inside the bookshop first, and then get breakfast accordingly.

I set out again, forgetting about the strange bookish voice and enjoying the temporarily clear skies above the lively morning crowd. Old Town Edinburgh and Grassmarket drew tourists from all over the world, and this morning the square seemed busier than usual. I was back to doing fine in my fog of happy. Until I ran into someone else who'd probably been enjoying her own version of a beautiful morning.

"Lass, watch where you're goin'," she said.

"I'm so sorry," I said.

The woman had dropped the books she'd been carrying. We both got to work picking them up.

Books, lots of books. I was curious about the titles, but we had too many to retrieve to take the time to look closely. There were no dustcovers, no protection on any of them, and the old, hard bindings all seemed to have damaged spines and worn corners. In all, we gathered thirteen well-worn books. It was quite a load.

"Can I help you carry these somewhere?" I said as I balanced five of the books on my hip.

My voice fell off as I looked at her. It couldn't be possible. For an instant I wondered if I was looking at an older version of myself; had this person I was looking at traveled back through time just to give her younger self a stack of old books?

The woman might have been twenty years older than my thirty-one, but her hair was identical to mine, both the bright red color and the frizzy texture; it rained far too much in Scotland to worry about trying to tame it.

But the similarities went even further. Our blue eyes were the same tint of diluted sky, and we both had too many freckles.

"Goodness, are you seeing what I'm seeing?" she asked, her accent as light at Edwin's—or I'd just become so used to the range of accents that I no longer really noticed the lighter ones anymore. "If I'd had a daughter, I'd wonder if you were her."

I smiled. "The resemblance is . . . uncanny. I'm Delaney Nichols."

We both held too many books to shake hands.

"Mary Stewart," the woman said with a nod. "At least we don't have the same name. That would have been quite the conundrum."

"I agree."

For a few seconds, we just looked at each other. There was no denying the resemblance, but we stared long enough that it was almost weird.

"Can I help you get these somewhere?" I said.

"I'm looking for a bookshop. I was on my way to it." She looked behind her, down the longer part of the Grassmarket square, the area toward Tom's pub. The Cracked Spine was at the other end, along a shorter street.

"The Cracked Spine?" I said.

"Aye, that's the one." She smiled. "Do you know it?"

"In fact, I do. Come with me."

Mary walked next to me, and I wondered if we looked odd, the two of us, with matching flaming hair and freckled skin, both carrying books as we made our way toward the bookshop. At least I was in slacks and she was in a dress. Chances were that everyone was in their own world, but I couldn't stop glancing over at her. She kept glancing at me too. We smiled curiously at each other.

The sign on the bookshop's door had been turned to Open. I peered in through the window as I balanced the books and reached for the door handle. Rosie was at the front desk, and I was suddenly struck by two things: I was once again infused with excitement to be back, but even with only that brief look at my grandmotherly coworker, I knew something was wrong. Maybe something just wasn't as right as it needed to be, but the pinch at the corners of Rosie's eyes and mouth told me that at least something wasn't normal. She was upset, but I'd have to wait until we were alone to ask for details. I pulled the door and the bell above jingled.

"Lass!" Rosie said as she smiled big and came around the desk. "Ye're back!"

"Rosie, Hector." I placed my stack of books on the table that held the blue-book window display. I wasn't going to ignore Hector's quick approach, no matter what else was going on. I picked up the small dog and let him whine happily at me as he licked my cheek. It was so good to see them that, momentarily, tears burned behind my eyes. As I still held onto Hector, Rosie and I hugged tightly.

"Hello there," Rosie said to Mary when we disengaged. "Are ye a relative of our dear Delaney?"

"No," Mary said.

"Rosie, this is Mary Stewart," I said. "We ran into each other out in Grassmarket. She was looking for the bookshop. Mary, this is Rosie."

"Aye?" Rosie said. "Nice tae meet ye. And the two of ye ken ye look alike?"

"Aye," Mary said.

"Yes, we noticed."

"Well, that's . . . interesting." She stared at Mary a moment and then turned back to me. "How was the honeymoon? Was it . . . romantic?"

"The most romantic," I said with an exaggerated dreamy tone. But then I remembered we had a guest and cleared my throat.

"Oh, that's lovely," Rosie said.

"Congratulations!" Mary said, still holding books and smiling at the happy reunion she witnessed.

"Thank you." Reluctantly, I handed Hector back to Rosie and turned to Mary. "Here, let me take those. You were on your way here to see if we want to purchase the books?"

"I was." She handed over her stack.

I carried the books to Rosie's front desk and then retrieved the ones I'd brought in.

"You work here, and you just got married?" Mary said as she followed me.

"Yes, and yes."

"You're from America though? That's what I'm hearing in your voice."

"I am. I moved here a year ago for this job, and it looks like it all . . . stuck, I guess." I smiled as I placed the second stack next to the first one on Rosie's desk and put a hand on top. "Are you from around here?"

She hesitated a long beat before she answered. "Aye, in a way."

"Born somewhere else?"

Mary smiled and lifted her eyebrows. "Many times."

In matching perplexed, and frozen poses, Rosie and I looked at her and blinked.

Mary waved off her comment and laughed. "I was born in Scotland, but spent a lot of time in France."

"Aye," Rosie said doubtfully, still probably caught back at Mary's strange comment.

I jumped in. "Is Hamlet here?"

"No, he'll be in later today though," Rosie said.

"Okay." I turned back to Mary. "Well, tell me about the books. I'd love for Hamlet to see them too, but Rosie and I can take a look."

"That's lovely. Thank you," Mary said. She glanced at the

book on the top of the stack. "They're not overly valuable, but I think they're worth a little something. And they're all about Elizabeth I."

"Elizabeth I of England? Elizabeth *Tudor*?" I said.

"Aye," Mary replied.

I listened for the bookish voice again. It didn't speak, but I looked at the book under my hand. It was titled *His Last Letter: Elizabeth I and the Earl of Leicester*.

I would bet that the words I'd heard were inside this book. I must have read it at some point. I must have somehow seen Mary before I ran into her. My eyes could have skimmed over her and maybe even the spine of the book, so my subconscious could push it all to the surface. I *had* been in a haze of excitement and happiness, post-honeymoon bliss.

"Delaney?" Rosie said.

I looked at her and then at Mary. "Yes. Well, let's have a look."

All thirteen of the books had been published since 2000 and they were all in less than ideal shape. But there were people who might be interested in them. I had reshelved all the books in the shop, making specific sections. There were some Tudor shelves. I could easily make a subsection, a sub-shelf of books specifically about Elizabeth I. In fact, as I looked at the books Mary brought in, I wondered if I already had and just didn't remember doing it. Surely, I had seen and read at least one of these at some point—I couldn't let go of the voice. But things *had* been busy. The wedding . . . everything.

"I think we'd be interested," I said. "I'd like Hamlet to price them. Would you like to leave them here or bring them back when he's here?"

"No, no, I'll leave them. Just let me know. I'm not selling

them for the money. I just needed to clean off some shelves, make room for more, pass them onto other interested readers." Mary smiled. "Anything will be fine."

Even our smiles were similar.

"Do ye have time for a cuppa, some coffee?" Rosie asked.

She was curious about Mary. Though Rosie was generally welcoming to all our customers, it took someone special for her to offer refreshments.

"I would love some coffee," Mary said.

"I'll go," I said, meaning I would step over to the other side, the dark side, where the attached building held our dingy kitchenette, a few offices, and the warehouse. It had been Edwin's warehouse, the place he kept his assortment of collections, but it was mine now too. We shared equally when he was around, but when it was just me, it was all mine. It was the place that also held the desk that had been mentioned in the ad, the desk that had seen the likes of the kings and queens. Even on my honeymoon with the most amazing man, I'd missed that desk. I'd missed my job, my coworkers. I'd missed the warehouse.

"All right. Ta, lass," Rosie said. She eyed Mary as if she was glad she was going to have her to herself for a few minutes.

I set off up this side of the stairs, and moved through the door separating the sides, opening it and then closing it behind me. We never left it open. The warehouse was no longer the secret it had been for decades, but we didn't advertise its existence. The dark side wasn't as cared for as the light side, and we didn't want curious customers exploring on their own. It wasn't well lit, and the stairs on this side weren't swept often. The police knew about the warehouse, and my family had been given a tour. Tom and my landlords, Elias and Aggie, had seen it, but we didn't broadcast the fact that there was a big room at the back of the building containing lots of stuff, at least a smattering of which were priceless items.

I'd become so accustomed to the cooler air on the dark side, the dusty smells, that I didn't always notice them. But, today, after being gone for two weeks, they seemed obvious. I rubbed my hands over my arms and shivered once.

The bare lightbulb didn't illuminate when I flipped the switch. I stood on the landing a long moment, flipping it up and down and looking perplexed up at the bulb. It hung from the high ceiling at the bottom of the stairs. A tall ladder would be needed to change it, and I wondered how long it had been out.

With only a few lines of natural light coming in through the dirty windows in the front and the one on the back wall, my eyes took a few seconds to adjust as I made my way down the stairs.

I bypassed the kitchenette and grabbed the keyring holding the oversize blue key from my pocket. With three adept turns to the left I unlocked the heavy, ornate, red door and pushed through.

Home. The warehouse. These lights came on when I flipped the switch. My desk and a worktable took up most of the middle of the space, shelves extended up all the way to short, wide windows at the top. These windows weren't grimy and gave me great sunlight and moonlight when the clouds weren't thick, and kept me semi-aware of the time of day.

Mostly, I did research, cleaning, archiving. But strange things had happened inside the warehouse too—not often enough to worry about, but I'd lived moments of confusion and wonder inside the small, jam-packed space. And, today, I sensed . . . something wasn't right. Something was off about the whole day so far, Maybe this was just normal back-at-it anxiety.

I looked around more slowly and with some extra focus. It appeared that nothing had been disturbed in the last two weeks. The shelves were still loaded with books as well as all the items Edwin had collected over the years. My life and work had been interrupted by Nessie herself before the wedding and the two weeks away, but before all that had happened, I'd been researching the origin of three small tapestries. Edwin had thought they'd been in Queen Elizabeth I of England's bed-chambers.

The theme of the day was only continuing. I paid close attention, in case any of the bookish voices wanted to pipe up. They remained quiet.

The tapestries were on one of the shelves—I'd cleared off the shelf and placed each individual tapestry inside its own protective and chemical-free archive folder. I squinted toward them. They looked to still be there, undisturbed.

A cursory glance told me the desk and worktable were fine, and my chair seemed to be tucked in exactly as I'd left it. It took a second, slower inspection to notice what was different.

My desk wasn't ever messy, but it usually had a few books or folders atop it. I'd left two books on a corner so I would remember to show them to Edwin when I returned. They weren't valuable but were both written in the old Scottish language, Gaelic. I knew Vanessa was intrigued by everything Gaelic, and I thought she might enjoy them. A note had been placed on top of the books.

"Oh," I said aloud as I reached for it.

Delaney—When you return, remind me to tell you all about the Burgess Tickets. Hope the honeymoon was as perfect as the lovely wedding. Always—Edwin

"Burgess Tickets," I said. "Sounds good. I can't wait to hear the details."

I placed the note back on the books and looked around one more time satisfied there was nothing else out of place or noticeably wrong. I sniffed in the dusty, old smells and wished I hadn't offered to get the coffee. It was good to be back, and I just wanted to stay right where I was.

Nevertheless . . .

I flipped off the light, closed and locked the door, and hurried to the kitchenette. Thankfully, the light in there was working too.

Balancing the tray back on the light side, I veered around a half wall that separated the front of the bookshop from a back corner that held a table. This was where Hamlet did most of his work, and where we had meetings or visited with customers. The walls in the corner were lined with wood file cabinets packed with documents Edwin had purchased or collected, or customers had sold to us. Hamlet did most of the document work, but I did a little.

As I caught Rosie's eye, I remembered the last time we'd been gathered around that table. It had been at the wedding. We'd had the reception at Tom's small pub, but we'd exchanged vows and had cake in the bookshop. It had been some back and forth parading along Grassmarket, but it had been fun. And my parents and brother had been in town for the special day. They were now back in the States, and I missed them.

Rosie's expression garnered my full attention. She was sending me some sort of unspoken communication. Her eyes grew wide with what I thought might be disbelief. She didn't look at me long enough for me to understand what might be going on, but she spoke up quickly.

"Delaney, Mary here, though she spells her name S-T-E-W-A-R-T, has the same name as a woman she thinks she used tae be."

I put the tray on the table. "I don't understand."

Rosie smiled patiently at Mary as Hector sat on Rosie's lap. Even the dog's attention was firmly and curiously aimed toward our guest.

Mary looked at me. "I was just telling Rosie about . . . well, I'm certain I've lived many lives."

"Oh. That's interesting," I said as I sat too.

"Aye, and . . ." she looked at Rosie and then back at me, "well, I believe that I lived one of my lives as a Scottish queen."

The facts came together quickly in my mind, once I zeroed in on a few things.

"Mary Stewart," I muttered. "Sounds just like Mary Stuart. Mary, Queen of Scots!"

Rosie and Mary nodded.

I sat forward and leaned my arms on the table. "You think you were once Mary, Queen of Scots?"

I didn't know if she was impressed by my apparent knowledge of the once and martyred queen, or if she was just satisfied that I now knew, that she'd shared the part of her that was the most difficult part to share.

"That's correct," she said admirably. "In fact, I'm certain of it. No doubt in my mind."

I meant no disrespect, but my response was not that of a polite Kansas farm girl. It wasn't polite no matter where I'd come from. Even across land and sea, I could sense my mother's disapproval when all I did for a good long few moments was laugh.

TWO

"I am so sorry," I said, horrified by my behavior but unable to rein it in as quickly as I should. "Please consider this embarrassing reaction a nervous laugh, not a laugh-laugh."

Mary smiled. "It's okay. I'm fully aware that my circumstances are difficult to believe and understand. Imagine my own surprise when I realized I'd lived more than one life. I didn't go searching for past lives, but they found me anyway."

"And how did that happen?" Rosie asked.

I looked at Rosie. She was someone who believed in the Loch Ness Monster, had believed even before . . . well, before we found things that *might* convince even the most skeptical of doubters. With Mary, she seemed both surprised and interested in what she had to say, but perhaps disbelieving, doubtful. Maybe I wasn't reading her correctly.

"Oh, it's a long story," Mary said. "But it started with dreams. I dreamt things I knew I'd never heard or read about before, so I started studying. There came a time when I became educated enough about some particulars that I couldn't trust the dreams anymore, but my beliefs built from there. Dreams and self-education led to things I can only describe as memories." She put her fist to her chest. "It all became a certainty, but I can't pinpoint exactly when. I understand how that can be difficult for anyone who hasn't been through it to believe."

"Sometimes people can become certain of things that are-nae real anyway, sometimes they've convinced themselves," Rosie said.

"Of course." She looked at Rosie. "I'm one hundred percent certain though, and I can prove it."

"Aye?" Rosie said.

The bell above the front door jingled.

"Please give me a moment," Rosie said. She stood, and with Hector in tow, they went to help a couple customers.

It was just us two doppelgängers at the table now. Mary looked at me a long moment. I had questions, plenty of them, but they weren't organized in my mind.

"Look at us," she said filling the silence before I could. "I mean, any other day, had I stopped by, you and I might not have met. Your coworkers might have made some comment about how I looked like you, asked me to come back in to meet you, but who knows?"

I sat forward. "Do you think it's fate that we met today, or maybe something to do with how you're tuned into your past life? It's more than one past life?" I said.

"I think it's more than one, but the only one I really remember is the queen's. To answer your question though, I think me coming here today is an example of how some mysteries aren't solvable, but happen all the time anyway, forcing us to pay attention to something we might have missed. I do think it was probably destined for the two of us to meet, Delaney. I've been thinking about taking the books to a used bookshop for almost two years. What if I'd brought them in before you arrived?"

"I have been here a year."

"Except for the last two weeks, or when you might have been out briefly for something else." Mary shrugged. "We ran into each other. Literally. It's a mystery that we may never quite understand. Consider this too—what if, and this is a doozy so I'm not saying I believe it but since anything is possible—what if my desire to take these books to a bookshop set the cosmos in motion to bring you here a year ago. We really do look alike. Perhaps the universe wanted us to meet, and since I was procrastinating, those universal powers sought you out?"

"Uh, that's pretty far-fetched."

"Aye, but don't you think that the notion of past lives is just as far-fetched?"

"Yes, but in a different way."

"Have you seen pictures of the queen?" Mary asked.

"Mary, Queen of Scots? I think so, but I'm not sure I've paid much attention."

Mary pulled out her phone and searched. A moment later, she held it up for me to see. "Look at her. Look at me, at you. See the similarities?"

There were similarities. The red hair, the pale skin, though I didn't notice as many freckles on the portrait Mary held up. The three of us did have somewhat pointy chins.

"Okay," I said. "But I don't have any past life memories."

"I'm not saying you also once lived as the queen, I'm just saying there must be something between the three of us. We might never understand it, but we were destined to meet, Delaney, I'm sure of it. Today, we might not understand why, but I suspect we might someday."

I smiled, my manners coming back. "Well, I think that's lovely."

"What if I could convince you that what I'm saying is real, that there is evidence that I am a reincarnation of Mary, Queen of Scots, Mary Stuart?"

"The proof you mentioned?"

"Aye."

I squinted at her. "I'm listening."

Mary laughed. "Not here. At my house. I'd like to invite you and your new husband for dinner. Rosie too. My husband and I would love to have all of you over. He's going to be just as surprised as you and I are, more maybe." She paused. "Your husband isn't tall and bald is he?"

I laughed. "Dark, curly hair. Blue eyes."

"Phew, Henry has brown eyes. Would have been even more bizarre if they'd looked alike, huh?"

I didn't know what to make of Mary. She was delightful. She was weird. But she wasn't weirdly delightful, which is a description unto itself. I was pretty good at quickly reading people, but I couldn't get a read on her. I listened for the bookish voices to come back and nudge me the right direction. Nothing. Maybe what they'd said before we'd run into each other was all they meant to tell me.

"That's very kind," I said. "I think we would enjoy that."

Rosie and Hector rejoined us after the other customers left the shop.

"We've been invited over to Mary's for dinner," I said. "She will show us her proof that she was once Mary, Queen of Scots."

"Aye? Sounds intriguing."

"How about tonight?" Mary said.

"Oh," I said as Rosie shrugged and nodded. "Well, I think that should be fine."

"Excellent. We'll continue this tonight. I look forward to meeting your husband."

Mary wrote down her address and phone number on a scrap piece of paper and gave it to me. In an oddly formal gesture, we shook hands. So did she and Rosie.

"Thanks for taking the books. I hope they sell," she said.

"I think they will," Rosie said as we all walked toward the front door.

"Rosie, please feel free to bring a plus one if you'd like."

Rosie nodded. "Ta, but it will just be me."

"I'm looking forward to the evening. Thank you again." Mary pulled open the door, and with one last smile she exited the shop.

Rosie and I looked at each other with equal uncertainty.

"She's an odd one," Rosie said.

"Yes. I'm looking forward to dinner."

"Aye, I think I am too."

"No Regg tonight?" I asked.

Regg and Rosie were an on-again, off-again couple. They were on again as of the few minutes before Tom and I left for our honeymoon.

"He'll be busy tonight." Rosie looked at me. "But, we're getting along verra well."

"Good. Okay, Tom and I will pick you up."

"Ye ken he's available?"

"If he isn't, he'll want to clear his schedule. I don't think he'll want to miss this."

"We might all be chopped up and thrown in her cooker."

I laughed, but then sobered when I saw Rosie wasn't smiling. "Really?"

"She's an odd one." Rosie repeated, but smiled now. "But I like the odd ones. I used to be one myself, I suppose."

"How's that?"

"Ah, maybe I'll share that story with ye soon." She reached down and picked up Hector.

I looked at the scrap of paper Mary had written her address on. Rosie slipped on her reading glasses and looked too.

"A lovely neighborhood." She squinted. "Look at the M in her name."

Mary had printed the words, all the letters legible and ordinary, except for the M in Mary. The two straight lines had extra lines added at their bottoms, perpendicular dash-like marks. It made the M fancier than the rest of the note.

"Hmm," Rosie said as she looked again. "321 *Leven* Court. That's interesting."

"Why?"

"Can we call up some internet information on Mary—the real Queen of Scots' version?"

"Sure." I pulled out my phone and quickly found the Wikipedia site. I handed the phone to Rosie; she scrolled and read.

"I thought I remembered that. The queen once escaped from Loch Leven castle," Rosie said.

"That's either a coincidence or she moved there on purpose," I said. "I can see forcing the similarities to prove a story."

"Lass, can ye see if there are samples of the queen's handwriting online?"

"Absolutely." It took only another second to find several examples.

Together Rosie and I inspected. The handwriting was identical, even down to the extra lines on the Ms. Not all of them, but many of the queen's Ms had those dash-like lines.

"I can't find this spooky yet," I said. "It could all be forced, on purpose. Googled," I said. "None of this is evidence."

"No."

I bit my lip and looked out the front window. There was no sign of Mary, and Grassmarket had become much less busy now that the morning rush had mellowed.

"Should we go or should we cancel?" I asked.

"Och, lass, I'm going. Some of yer adventures are simply too much for me, but I'll not miss this one. I'm intrigued."

"Sounds good." I plunked my hands on my hips. "Okay, I think it's time to either go get some breakfast or get back to work. Did I miss much? You looked deep in thought when Mary and I first came in."

"We missed ye, lass, and I'm glad ye're back. It would be verra unladylike of me tae ask any personal questions, but I do hope ye and Tom had a good time." She smiled.

"We had a great time." I winked.

"Oh, tae be young and in love." Rosie smiled and Hector barked.

Then Rosie's demeanor transformed, as if she'd lowered a curtain or turned down the lights. "But, aye, ye missed some . . . drama."

"I'm listening."

"I think we should sit down."

"Rosie?" I put my hand on her arm. "Tell me. What's up?"

We didn't sit down, but there's a chance we should have. I couldn't have been less prepared for what Rosie had to tell me.

"Lass, it seems as if . . . as if the bookshop is tae be shut down. We're going tae close."

Surely, I hadn't heard her correctly. I shook my head, once, twice. "Rosie. What?"

"Aye, t'is verra bad news."

It was almost the worst news possible.

THREE

"I don't . . . I don't understand," I said after my stomach returned from the plummet it took. "That's simply not possible. The bookshop can't close—not permanently. That can't be what you mean."

"Lass, that's preceese what I mean."

"Precesse?" I asked, hoping it was the Scots word for *not even close to*.

"Och. Precisely."

"I was afraid of that. Why?" I said. My muddled and shocked mind searched for a solution and the problem that might go with it. "I mean, if it's a matter of Edwin not wanting to work anymore, I can do whatever he needs me to do."

Rosie put her hand on my arm. "Lass, it isnae that t'all. Edwin would never choose to close the bookshop. There are apparently some issues with building codes."

"Building codes?"

Rosie frowned. "I should have let Edwin tell you. He has the details, and I'm afraid I'll tell it wrong. I'm sorry, lass, I've been thinking about it for a few days now. I should not have just dropped the news so inconsiderately." She smiled weakly. "At least I asked if you wanted tae sit down first."

"Oh, Rosie, the bookshop just can't close." I grabbed my phone. "I'm calling a meeting."

That's exactly what I did. I texted Edwin and Hamlet, requesting their presence as soon as possible—demanding it, actually. I didn't care if I interrupted important meetings or classes. I needed everyone there. I needed to understand what was going on. They greeted me with hugs and kisses on my cheek, but I didn't have time for such frivolity. I told everyone to sit at the back table, and I even turned the sign on the front door to Closed.

I began by asking what in the world was going on. In bits and pieces, they said the same thing Rosie had said, however, with more detail.

"We have structural issues, problems," Edwin said.

"Structural issues?" I said to Edwin. "What are the specific problems?"

"I'm still trying to understand," Edwin said. "I received a phone message a few days ago. It was a strange recording that said we were to be out of the building by the end of next month, that the inspector's findings regarding our building's structural integrity issues were ironclad. The final vote will set everything in motion."

"Final vote?" I asked. "Who's voting?"

Hamlet sat forward, placing his arms on the table. "The city is governed by a Lord Provost, similar, I believe, to an American mayor. Under that position is the City of Edinburgh Council. Councilors vote and make the sorts of decisions regarding building codes, et cetera. There is also a Parliament, but they are more involved with things like foreign policy and defense.

We have done some research regarding specific people and times, but don't have the answers yet. We are certain it's a council matter. The vote is scheduled to take place one week from today, next Monday."

I relaxed a little. "This can't be real. It's a scam or something. A phone scam. They happen all the time."

"We thought so too at first, but I looked online, and there *is* a final vote scheduled for one week from now," Hamlet said. "And, the agenda item lists The Cracked Spine specifically."

"What does it say?" I asked, my panic zipping back up to high alert.

"The Cracked Spine failed its building inspection and is deemed unsafe to continue operating within the city limits of Edinburgh. The vote will finalize the decision, or maybe it was formalize. Well, something like that. I can show you," Hamlet said as he began to scroll over his phone.

"Are there other buildings at risk? How many others?" I asked.

"Not that I could see."

"But, this building is fine," I said. "And Edinburgh—Scotland—is filled with older buildings, for goodness' sake!"

"Aye," Edwin said. "That's why I'm not too worried. I think we'll be fine. I am trying tae figure out the best approach tae get this taken care of. If all else fails, we'll be at the meeting, all of us."

"I can't find it right off," Hamlet said. "I will at some point."

I nodded at him and looked back at Edwin. "Do you know the Lord Provost?"

"I do, but he and I don't see eye to eye on a few things. We've not gotten along as of late."

"What's happened?"

"Some particularly old and lovely trees were taken out in Princes Street Gardens. The council voted, in the most secretive way possible to remove the trees, and they were gone soon afterward. Something to do with museum renovations not being possible without first removing the trees. I, along with many others, wasn't pleased. We've been vocal, and I'm afraid I overspoke my disapproval when I complained about the trees being removed. I used my friendship—well, acquaintanceship—with the Lord Provost to more effectively—at least in my opinion—vent my and the others' anger. I should have probably handled it better."

"Huh," I said. Edwin was all about the history of his country, his city. Trees would be just as important as buildings to him. But our building should be the most important to all of us.

"Aye," Edwin said. "Trees. They were around for hundreds of years, along the walkway to an oft-visited museum."

"By the gardens? Which museum?"

"Scottish transportation over the centuries. Fascinating."

"I haven't been there, but it does sound fascinating."

"Aye."

"Are we going to have to move the shop?" I asked, more whine to my voice that I would have liked.

Edwin and Rosie looked at each other quickly before they both looked at me again. Neither of them spoke. In fact, it seemed they pursed their lips more tightly.

"What?" I looked at Hamlet.

He said, "Delaney, this building is as important to the bookshop as the books inside it, almost as important as we are. The time, the history, the things it has been and seen. It's a whole being. This is where the bookshop was born, and this is where it will die—though, hopefully, not at the end of next month."

I got what Hamlet was saying, but I wasn't going to give up on the idea of relocation quite yet—if only to give myself *something* to hang onto. They'd had more time than me to process this information, but I wondered if they'd been as rocked at first as I felt now. I wanted to throw a temper tantrum.

Hamlet read my mind. "We're all upset, but we're trying to figure out the best approach."

"Does the council have regular meetings, something before the vote?" I asked.

"We couldnae find one scheduled earlier than the vote," Rosie said.

"That seems convenient, that they contacted you with no other chance to make our case." I shook my head. "Hang on. There was a building inspector's report? When was an inspector in here?"

"None of us remember an inspector," Edwin said.

"Then this just *can't* be real."

"We hope not," Rosie said. "We are proceeding as if it's something we need to fix though, or at least clear up."

"Of course. Me too. What should I do?"

"Delaney," Edwin said. "I left you a note in the warehouse . . ."

"Yes, I saw it. Something-tickets."

"Burgess Tickets. Aye. I wondered if you might have come across The Cracked Spine's. Historically, it was a certificate that was once used as a way of giving someone permission to do business in a burgh. It gave the holder the right to other things too; to vote, attend church service, and be an important part of the community. It's not something that's used any longer, but back when I opened the shop, I did receive one. By then it was more honorary, but nevertheless I'd like to find it."

"Will it keep us open?" I asked.

"I doubt it, but it might give me more ammunition, at least historically speaking. I'd like to have it."

"I'm not sure I would recognize something like that, but I don't think I've seen it."

"I haven't either." Hamlet looked toward his file cabinets and then back at the rest of us. "If we do have it, I think ours might be somewhere in my files, but I'm sure I haven't seen it. I've seen my fair share over the years."

"Well," Edwin said. "Everyone keep looking please. It might not trump a questionable building inspection, but it can't hurt."

"I'll look today," I said.

Edwin smiled and reached over the table to put his hand over mine. "I really do think it will be all right."

I looked at Rosie—she forced a smile. I looked at Hamlet—he frowned uncertainly.

"I hope so," I said.

What I didn't say, but what they certainly knew was that this bookshop was my life. Yes, I was now happily married to the most amazing guy ever, but my life was still *my* life. This bookshop was a big part of what made me the person I was, the person I liked the best, and it was probably the place that made me the best person I could be to everyone else around me. I loved these people. I loved Scotland. I loved this old building too. This had to be fixed.

"Lass, I do have money. If that's what it takes, I'll spend it." Edwin sat back again.

"Bribery?" I said. "That's a good idea."

"Well, I was thinking that maybe the building just needed reinforcement, some work done, but I won't rule out bribery."

"Good. Good plan."

I was willing to do anything, including spend Edwin's money.

"We will work on it," Hamlet said.

I sat back too and tried to think clearly. I wasn't there quite yet. I'd still need some time to get over the shock.

"Okay," I said. "Okay. That's good. I'm going to try to get to work, but if anyone comes up with any ideas, please let me know."

They all nodded.

"Very good. We will all work on it." Edwin pushed himself up from the chair. "I'm afraid I have to go for now though. I will be available on my mobile though."

"We'll keep looking for the ticket," Hamlet said.

"Aye," Rosie said halfheartedly.

I was the only one who seemed to notice her tone. I looked at her. She sent me a weary, quick smile that looked more like she was simply trying not to frown. I was glad I'd be with her this evening. If there was more to this that she wasn't saying in front of everybody else, I'd do my best to get it out of her.

We told Edwin we'd see him later, and the rest of us got to work.

I'd already noticed that other than Edwin's note, the warehouse didn't seem to have been disturbed while I'd been gone. Everyone who worked at the bookshop had a key, but it was a rare moment that Rosie or Hamlet visited. Rosie had been around for so many years that the walk over two flights of stairs didn't warrant the harassment to her knees unless she was also grabbing some tea or coffee from the kitchenette. Hamlet would stop by when he had a few extra minutes to chat, but those few minutes would usually grow to more; we could spend hours in discussion. Our last conversation had been speculation about space travel. It had been lively and we both decided we'd probably pass on a visit to Mars, no matter how curious we were about its inhabitants.

I did a cursory search for the Burgess Ticket, but I didn't find it, still wasn't sure what it might look like, even after I did some quick internet research. There wasn't one style, other than they all looked like official certificates, even the handwritten ones. I'd searched the file drawers in the warehouse enough times to be fairly certain there wasn't a Burgess Ticket inside one.

I was too wound up, too freaked out. I needed to channel my energy into something else for a bit, if only so I could think more clearly about our predicament.

I'd brought Mary's books over with me. I glanced at the stack and realized I was curious about her motives. All the books were, indeed, about Queen Elizabeth I, but none of them were specifically about Elizabeth's relationship with Mary, Queen of Scots. Mary *had* been the queen of Scotland, even as she lived some of her younger days in France, for twenty-five years, but Elizabeth had been the queen of England for a much longer time.

Elizabeth had been so influential that her name gave birth to an era—the Elizabethan era. It was when her sister died that Elizabeth was crowned queen. Her sister had been a "legitimate" child of Henry VIII, but because Elizabeth's mother's, Anne Boleyn's, marriage to Henry VIII had been annulled,

Elizabeth was considered illegitimate, though Elizabeth reigned anyway, for forty-four years.

Her status as illegitimate was what many held onto as the reason Mary Stuart should be the ruler of England, but, ultimately, most of the problems came down to their strong ties to their religions. One of the first things Elizabeth did as queen was to establish the English Protestant Church, dissing the old Catholic ways. Mary stuck with the Catholic church to the end. The internal and external struggles, indeed deadly battles included, because of the different religions and their ties to the rulers of the nations caused constant turmoil back then.

It was a volatile time. I shook my head as I thumbed through the last of Mary's books and skimmed the interesting fact that after Elizabeth's rule, it was Mary, Queen of Scots' son, James VI, who became the king of England. He turned out to be a well-liked king.

It was a sad, violent history, but part of what made the countries what they were today.

I set the books aside, gathered the tapestries I'd been working on pre-wedding, and brought them over to the worktable. They were small pieces, which wasn't the norm. Tapestries had served as castles' wall coverings, wallpaper, as well as insulation. Decorative in nature, they sometimes also depicted a story. The one I placed in front of me first seemed to be a story from the Bible, the story of Abraham. I knew that because Hamlet had somehow recognized the scene.

I was close to zeroing in on the approximate date it had been created. The stitches weren't even and identical, therefore, I'd determined that this one had been handmade. That determination had been as simple as looking through a magnifying glass at the stitches.

I counted the colors. Older tapestries could only be made using about twenty different colors, inks that dyed the thread being made from plant and insect dyes. With the magnifying glass again, I determined that there were only about twenty colors used on the tapestry, and some of the light blues were a little different than the other light blues. That sort of thing happened when dye ingredients weren't always consistent.

In my studies, I'd also learned that some dyes were still created using insects to this day. Most interesting to me, the cochineal, an insect that liked to live on cactus, was used to make dye that was still found today in some foods and lipsticks. The more I learned about certain things, the more I became concerned about what we consumed. I tried not to let it bother me too much.

As I now moved the magnifying glass over the top of the tapestry, two things happened at once. I thought I saw something that needed extra attention, and a bookish voice spoke.

Magesty, there is less danger in fearing too much than too little.

I stood up straight.

I had an inkling of an idea that I'd just read those words as I'd thumbed through Mary's books, but my looks had been cursory and tinged with the still overriding anxiety about the bookshop's fate. I wasn't sure I could find those words again. I blinked and wondered what the voice may be trying to tell me.

I had no idea. But I knew that I had also come upon something on the tapestry that wanted my attention.

I looked at it again and zoned in on a coat of arms. It was small. I leaned closer and put the glass over just the bottom right corner. Yellow, blue, and red, the coat of arms depicted three lions, though one looked like a dragon to me, guarding a

crown. Semper Eadem adorned the bottom. *Always the same.*
I ran over to my computer and googled everything to confirm
that yes, this was Elizabeth I's coat of arms. Did that mean this
tapestry belonged to her? Maybe. The time frame might work.
Not machine made, handsewn, and simple ink. The elements
were there to make me wonder enough to know I needed more
research.

I put the glass down and tried to figure out what the universe, via the things and the voices, was trying to tell me.

And I had an idea of something. It was faded and far away,
but the idea was filled with the news of the closing of the bookshop as well as the woman I'd met who looked so much like me
and who thought she was once Mary, Queen of Scots. Were
they all tied together? Working together? I was grasping for
straws, *but there some something there,* I thought. I hoped.

Maybe Mary really had been onto something when she
thought it was destined that she and I meet. Maybe she, the
bookish voices, and the tapestries were all part of the equation
to keep the bookshop open for business.

Something about the timing made me think I needed to pay
close attention, put that universal equation together correctly.
I would do my best.

Hopefully, dinner that evening would tell me more.

FOUR

Tom had spiffed himself up. After a day at the pub and a number of soccer (football) match crowds, their attention on the television as they cheered and sloshed their drinks incessantly, he'd come home and given me a fly-by kiss before hitting the shower.

"You clean up so nicely," I looked up from the papers I was reading as he joined me in the front room.

"Ta, my love," he said with a small head bow. "You're lovely tonight, as always."

I'd put on a dress and a little eye makeup. It was more than I usually did. "I'm probably wrinkling sitting here, but I got so interested in this article. It's about some Mary, Queen of Scots' documents found tucked away in a box in the museum. Joshua hasn't said a word about them, but, of course, he has no way of knowing about today's turn of events."

Joshua was a good friend, a young and brilliant post doc who worked at the National Museum of Scotland. We shared a love of old things and both enjoyed walking slowly through museums; really slowly.

Earlier in the day, I'd called Tom from the warehouse, and told him about meeting Mary, the strange possibility that the bookshop might be closing, and the tapestry discovery. He thought Mary and the tapestries sounded intriguing, but he'd mostly had questions and concerns about the bookshop. Along with the rest of us, he couldn't quite understand what was happening, couldn't believe it might happen while being so very afraid that it could.

"Mary, Queen of Scots' documents? About her?" Tom said.

"No, written *by* her. Journal entries, things about collecting taxes, tasks that went along with being the queen," I said.

"Aye?" he said. "In a box, in the museum cellar?"

"I don't know where the box was in the museum, but isn't it weird that it's in today's, of all days, paper?"

"Aye."

"It's astounding that any of her papers survived."

"It really is," Tom said. "How did they not disintegrate, or fall apart?"

"They weren't bothered, I guess, by humans or the environment," I said. "I'm really not sure. Maybe Joshua will let me look at them."

"You might not want to tell Mary that you know someone at the museum who could show you real Queen of Scots' papers. She might bother you to come along."

"Maybe she can tell me what they say before I even look at them," I said with a half smile.

"If she's telling the truth, maybe." He glanced at his watch. "Time to gather Rosie?"

"Let's go."

We were living in my cottage, not Tom's house as we'd expected to do. The electrical system in the old blue house by the sea had gone on the fritz, so Tom and I'd had to move out before we'd even moved in, just so the issues could be fixed. It was too cold in Edinburgh to live someplace where there wasn't heat, especially when there was a place that had plenty of heat—as long as we remembered to feed the machine on the wall that regulated the electricity with the proper amount of coins. But, that wasn't necessarily true either. My landlords and friends, Elias and Aggie, made sure the machine was always topped off. They didn't know I knew, but I knew.

We were enjoying the cottage, but it was a small space. I wondered if Tom would quickly grow impatient with the tight quarters, but he seemed fine so far.

We were newlyweds; we still hadn't quite figured out the timing of some of our routines, like getting ready for our days, cooking, cleaning, relaxing. Those things that come with time were still to be figured out some. They would be for a while, but I was enjoying every moment. It seemed Tom was too. Not once had he behaved as if the walls were closing in. Not once had I sensed that he regretted committing himself to one person.

We knew each other well, had almost lived together before we were married. But married and actually living together with that piece of paper were different, not by much, but it was sometimes noticeable. So far so good.

Elias and Aggie were thrilled we were there, no matter how temporarily. I half-wondered if maybe they'd sabotaged the blue house's electrical system just so we'd have to stick close by. They denied doing as much when I'd teased them about it, but I'd caught the quick look they'd shared: *not a bad idea.*

I hoisted myself up off the couch and smoothed my dress. I felt particularly girly.

Tom didn't hesitate but immediately pulled me close. "You are the loveliest woman I've ever seen. I can't believe how lucky I am that you're mine."

I pulled away slightly and looked up at him. "Well, this is probably all a dream and soon I'm going to wake up in my parents' house in Kansas. I'm going to be highly disappointed that none of this was real, but it's made a wonderful dream. Maybe a wizard and a tornado will be involved."

Tom smiled. "You're also adorable."

"Thank you, sir. You are not so bad yourself."

For a small moment, there was a good chance we'd miss the dinner, but we moved past it. We'd made the commitment and we'd told Rosie.

Tom sighed. "Shall we go meet the queen?"

"We shall."

Rosie lived in a flat not too far away from the bookshop. She and Hector could walk to work or jump on a bus for a quick ride. She preferred walking, but the bus was a good option for rainy days.

Tom parked in a spot directly in front of Rosie's building and joined me as we went to gather her. There were only two apartments above what was most recently a souvenir shop. From what we could discern, it looked like it was about to become a hair salon. Rosie said it had been many different things over the years, but the owner of the building, her landlord, had been very fair as rents had increased throughout the city.

Rosie had worn a lovely new dress for our wedding, but other than that day, I'd never seen her so dressed up as she was tonight.

"Och, Tom, marriage looks good on you," she said as she opened her door.

"Thank you, and you look lovely, Rosie."

"Ta. Come in, say good evening tae Hector, and then we'll be on our way." She turned and the pleated skirt of her purple dress puffed as if it wanted badly to twirl. I would have bet she had already twirled, at least once.

Rosie's flat was made just for her. A small front room, a small kitchen, two small bedrooms, and one small loo. Her fluffy furniture was covered with bright fabrics and a mish-mash of brightly colored pillows. More brightly colored throw rugs decorated the wooden floors. Edwin liked to call Rosie's flat, the most colorful place in Scotland. Though packed with stuff, it was always clean, tidy, and smelled like she'd just washed dishes—there were never any dishes in sight.

Hector was napping on his favorite pillow on the couch; a red one with gold fringe. He sat up lazily and looked perplexed at Tom and me. Once he recognized me, he jumped off the couch and ran into my outstretched hands.

"Hello," I said. "You don't see me here very often, do you?"

He seemed pleased. Once he was done greeting me with his signature cheek kisses, he looked over at Tom. Hector had become used to seeing Tom but hadn't quite accepted him into the family yet.

Tom reached over and scratched behind Hector's ears.

"Ye ken his weakness," Rosie said.

"He and I are going to be grand friends one day, but I don't think that day has come quite yet. I'm ready, but I think he's still wondering," Tom said.

"Soon," Rosie said.

I tried not to laugh at her doubtful tone as Tom and I shared quick smiles.

Once in the car, I asked her, "Rosie, is there something

more going on with the shop? I've told Tom all about it, but it seemed like you were trying to tell me something more with your eyes today."

"No, lass, there isnae anything more really, but I was trying tae tell ye something maybe." She paused a long thoughtful moment. Tom and I glanced at each other but didn't interrupt. "It's that, I dinnae think that Edwin's got the fight in him anymore. He kens how much we all love the bookshop, but he's old, lass. Maybe it's time for him to retire, at least that's what he might think. He also has Vanessa now. They seem tae be getting along verra well. I think they might want tae travel."

"We'll let them travel." I turned around in my seat and looked at Rosie. "We'll even let him retire. That bookshop can't close, Rosie, but not just because I don't want it to. I've thought about this all day, and the shop is so much more than Edwin, so much more than all of us. It's a part of the lifeblood of the city. Edwin knows that, he just might need to be reminded."

Rosie smiled a little with her mouth but fully with her eyes. "I was hoping you'd see it that way. It'll be up tae ye tae figure it out, lass. I'll help in any way I can, but ye will have tae do the legwork. Hamlet will help too, but he's so busy with school. Are ye up for the fight?"

Tom laughed once and looked at Rosie in the rearview mirror. "She's up for the fight."

"I am," I said. "I've never been up for a fight so much in my life."

And I was. *I would fight to the end,* I thought as I turned back around.

As Tom drove toward Mary's house, Rosie regaled us with a story about the "old days" with Edwin, one that she'd just remembered today for reasons she would soon illuminate. Apparently, there was a time when Edwin unknowingly befriended a bank robber. There were no cell phones in the 1970s and a storm had taken out the bookshop's phone. The "friend"—*let's call him Joe*—showed up one evening as Rosie was getting ready to close for the day because of the terrible storm and the flickering electricity.

Joe, drenched and seemingly bothered by something, hurried into the shop with a bag over his shoulder. He asked Rosie if he could keep the bag in Edwin's secret room. But, though Rosie knew Edwin and Joe were unquestionably friends, Rosie knew Edwin hadn't confirmed to him about the warehouse's existance. Back then, Edwin hadn't told anyone but Rosie about the warehouse.

When Rosie told Joe no and indicated that he had to go, he became agitated. Rosie, much younger *those years anon*, didn't have any patience for Joe and she became firm in her request that he get out of the shop immediately.

Their confrontation became physical, but even though Joe was bigger, Rosie was a "tough lass" and she punched him in the nose. He dropped the bag and ran out of the shop.

"Aye?" Tom said as he looked at Rosie in the rearview mirror.

"Aye, but the rest of the story is even better. I kept the wee bag. Well, I had Edwin put it in the warehouse."

Tom and I shared another look. "Was there money in the bag?" I asked.

"Och, aye. The bag was full of coins with Mary, Queen of Scots, on them. They're verra valuable, I would guess."

"Really?" I said. "What happened to the bag of coins?"

"Last I heard Edwin put them in the warehouse. He told Joe tae leave town, leave the country, and he wouldnae turn him in."

"Why didn't he just call the police or return them anonymously?"

Rosie shrugged. "Sometimes Edwin thinks he kens better than the law, than anyone. When he was younger, he was even surer of himself. I do remember we couldnae figure out where they'd come from, and then at some point we just quit wondering, moved onto other things."

"Do you think we could find the coins?" I asked.

"Depends on if Edwin kept them. He might have later returned them and just didnae tell me, and this is why I wanted tae tell the story. Edwin would want the coins returned, even after all these years have passed. Ye and Edwin need tae discuss it. Our visitor and our host this evening made me remember them. If they havenae been returned, Edwin would want that done, as soon as possible."

"They must be worth a fortune," I said.

"Again, that's yer job tae figure oot, lass. I've done my part," Rosie said.

I smiled. "I'm glad you remembered. And thanks for sharing."

"Ye're welcome."

Tom turned onto a dark street. "This is Leven."

I sat forward and peered out the windshield. "I can barely see the houses."

Most of the homes were set back from the road, each of them up a hill or behind a full front garden of trees and bushes.

"It should be about four or five up, on the left side," Tom said.

"Look up ahead. Do ye suppose that's it?" Rosie said.

It didn't take long to figure out which one she meant. Down a bit, along the road, there was something I hadn't ever seen in a city; torches. Fire torches stood on each side of what I guessed was a driveway.

"Those can't be real," I said.

When we were closer, Tom said, "No, they're just made to look like flames."

Inside glass cases, fanned material was lit from the bottom, giving the illusion that flames burned inside. The lights were two of the infrequent lights on the street and unquestionably marked the entrance to a driveway.

"There's the number," Rosie said. "That's the hoose."

The driveway was paved with varying sizes of smooth stones. Tom turned in and proceeded slowly.

"Careful of the moat," Rosie said.

"Moat?" Tom stopped the car.

"I wouldnae be surprised if there's one up ahead," Rosie said.

"Okay, I'll keep my eyes open." Tom continued along the driveway.

The path sloped up and toward the right, and just when I wondered if we'd taken the correct turn, the house came into view.

Correction, the castle came into view.

"Ye must be coddin," Rosie said.

My Scots translator, Hamlet, wasn't nearby, but I didn't think this one was too difficult. "Kidding?"

"Aye, something like that. That's quite the place," Rosie said.

"Wow," Tom said.

It wasn't the most beautiful castle I'd ever seen—in fact, it might not have been a castle so much as it was a replica of a castle.

"Hang on," I said. Tom had already stopped the car.

It was probably rude to remain parked there for long, but I had to know. On my phone I searched for Castle Loch Leven, and was quickly rewarded. "I thought it looked familiar. It's a replica of the castle Mary, Queen of Scots, was imprisoned in for a year or so. Well, it's smaller, but the structure seems to be the same shape."

The home before us was made with stone walls and did look like Castle Loch Leven in that it had a tall main building, rectangular with squared off corners, and lower walls surrounding what would have been the keep, if it had actually been a real castle.

"Weel, if she's not the auld, dead queen herself, she's certainly obsessed with her," Rosie said.

"Aye," Tom said.

"And look, there *is* a moat." I pointed.

A small stream of water ran along the front of the house but didn't seem to go all the way around. Technically, it was probably just a water feature, but it had been created to look like a moat.

"I'll be," Tom said. "I'm looking forward to meeting her."

"She looks just like yer new wife," Rosie said. "Only older."

"That's what Delaney said. If her husband is an older version of me, I think we'll have to wonder about more than reincarnation in the works."

"Believe it or not, she mentioned that he was bald. The thought came to her too," I said.

"Good news. Well, you know what I mean," Tom said.

We sat there way too long, but I didn't push Tom to continue up to the top. A moment later, he did though, slowly and with a few extra glances outside his side window to make sure we didn't drive over and into any "moat."

There were windows on the front of the house—small, as they would have been on the castle, but curtain sheers were on the inside over these. If I'd seen animal skins, I would have rolled my eyes, but I still wouldn't have been deterred.

Tom stopped in a paved spot that seemed to have been made specifically for visitors to park their vehicles. I didn't see a spot to tether horses, but even back in the day, the real castle might not have offered such accommodation. There were three other cars parked in the miniature parking strip.

"We might not be the only guests," I said.

"Or, all of the autos are theirs," Rosie said. "We will soon see."

Tom opened the back door for Rosie, but I was out before he could come around. Tom and I brought flowers, Rosie brought some whisky. Considering Tom owned the pub, it seemed like we should be carrying the whisky and Rosie the flowers, but it worked this way too.

"Och, I'm so excited tae see her proof," Rosie said as she led the way to the tall door, her purple pleats poofing again.

Tom and I smiled at each other and followed behind.

FIVE

"Welcome!" Mary said with an arm flourish. She wore a red gown that was tied at the waist, something a queen might wear as a robe back in the day, but of all the things I'd researched over the years, clothing hadn't been one of my strong interests.

"Thank ye for inviting us," Rosie said as she led the way inside and handed Mary the whisky. "Och, t'is a lovely place."

"Thank you," Mary said, but her eyes had stalled on Tom. "Goodness, you look *nothing* like my husband."

"Tom Shannon." Tom extended his hand. They shook and then he handed her the flowers. "Pleasure to meet you."

Mary took the flowers, all the while keeping her eyes locked on him. Lots of people stared at Tom.

"My goodness, you are . . . something," Mary said.

"And you look extremely familiar." Tom smiled at Mary and then at me, breaking Mary's locked gaze. "Delaney told me about the resemblance, but I must admit, I'm a wee bit surprised. You two could be related."

"I know," Mary said as she batted her eyelashes at him. I

didn't hold it against her. "It's uncanny! Did Delaney tell you the other part?"

"I believe she did," Tom said. "You were once someone else."

He didn't sound doubtful in the least, but I knew he was. Tom wasn't one for any sort of unexplained or unusual phenomena. I'd lived through a strange Christmas, having been visited by what my bookshop friends were sure was a ghost. Tom was still trying to find a reasonable explanation for what had happened, but he didn't like to talk about it much. I knew he didn't believe in past lives or reincarnation, but he would be a polite guest. And he was certainly intrigued by someone who claimed to have lived before.

"I *was* someone else," Mary said. "Thank you for the flowers and the whisky. How lovely."

"You're welcome," Tom and Rosie said together.

Mary set the gifts on a side table. "In fact, I have lived many lives, but only one other than this one that I remember very clearly." She winked at Tom. I thought it was interesting to see what I would look like in twenty years when I winked at my husband. Not bad.

"Mary, Queen of Scots," I said.

"Aye. We just call her *the queen* around here; it saves any confusion regarding which Mary is being discussed." She waved her hand once through the air. She moved her hands a lot, talked with them, as if they were extra punctuation. It worked for her.

I looked around the entryway, my eyes growing wider at every blink. The home was set up in a boring square, but there was nothing boring about the rest of it. The bottom floor had high ceilings and a stairway along the right wall. Other than in castles, I'd never seen a stone stairway. Stone used in buildings in Scotland was cold, and never did warm up much. A thick, red carpet moved down the middle of these stairs. Tapestries, much bigger than the ones I'd been looking at in the warehouse, filled the wall along the staircase. If the carpet and the tapestries didn't actually warm the space, they gave the illusion that they did.

The floor we stood on was also made of stone—or probably just concrete—but I didn't crouch to investigate. It was well covered in throw rugs, similar to Rosie's flat but with fewer colors. Here, there were lots of golds and reds, but not many blues or greens. A large, ornate, dark-wood secretary stood to our side next to the table where Mary had placed the flowers and whisky. A round table took up the middle space. Atop that table, a vase of fresh flowers filled the air with pleasant and surprisingly mellow scents. But it was the fireplace in the middle of the wall on the other side that was the true showpiece. Massive, with high flames inside, the heat reached all the way over to us. But I was most interested in the secretary.

"That desk is beautiful," I said as I peered at it more closely.

Made of what I thought was cherrywood, dragons had been carved onto the closed drop-section. Three drawers, with ornate, brass pulls, lined up perfectly underneath. I knew it was an old piece of furniture, but it was in mint condition.

"Thank you. My niece, Dina, gave it to me. She's an expert on such things. She's upstairs. You'll meet her in a moment."

I stood straight again and looked at the fireplace. "Is that your only source of heat in the house?"

"No," Mary said. "We have a newfangled furnace, but this just . . . felt right."

I translated in my mind: It's what she "remembered" from her days as the queen.

"Well, helloo there," a man said from the top of the stairway. He was bald and just on the verge of having a belly. Mary had already told me she was fifty-one; the man seemed around the same age. "Are you all joining the rest of us for dinner, or shall we come down there and bring some marshmallows, so we might actually do something productive with all that fire?"

He was dressed like Hugh Hefner, in a paisley robe, with a pipe in one hand. His accent was British—nothing Scottish about it, I realized; I was pleased with myself that I could tell the difference. It seemed as if he was teasing, but I wasn't sure.

"We'll be up momentarily, dear," Mary said. "My husband, Henry. Henry, this is Rosie, Delaney, and Tom. I'm sure you all are entertaining yourselves just fine up there."

From above, Henry's pleasant twinkling eyes stopped twinkling when they landed on me. He moved down the stairs and toward me so quickly that Tom sidled closer, and I thought I heard Rosie make a surprised noise.

"Good gracious me!" Henry said as he stopped in front of me. He put the pipe next to the whisky and then took hold of my arms. "Is this really you?"

"Um," I said. "Hello, I'm Delaney Nichols," I looked at Tom. We'd already talked about me keeping my name as it had always been. He hadn't protested, but I still wondered if it bothered him that I hadn't taken his.

"No, I don't think so. I think you are someone else entirely," Henry said.

"Henry," Mary said as she stepped next to him and put her hand on his arm. "You're behaving inappropriately."

"I'm . . ." Henry blinked at Mary and then looked at me,

letting go of my arms. "I'm so sorry, Ms. Nichols. That *was* inappropriate. I was struck by your resemblance to . . ."

"His wife," Mary said conclusively. She cleared her throat.

"You both look so much like the queen. Are you aware of that?" Henry asked.

"That has come to my attention," I said, finding his overbite and friendly smile very charming.

"Henry, I told you I met Delaney and Rosie today, at that wonderful bookshop. I told you Delaney and I looked alike. We discussed it, as well as our resemblance to the queen."

"Love, you didn't say the two of you looked so much alike it was uncanny. You used the word 'resemblance.'"

"All right," Mary said as she hooked her arm through his. "We do look alike. Although," she glanced around at the rest of us, "I'm afraid I've ruined poor Henry seeing the queen for what she truly might have looked like. To him, I am she. Perhaps, it's because in his eyes I *am* his only queen."

Henry was struggling. Thoughts he wasn't vocalizing were filling his eyes with something that, to me, looked like emotional pain. Was our resemblance really that bothersome to him or was something else going on?

His wife's words finally filtered through and he looked at Mary and smiled, but the odd sparkle of emotional disruption didn't leave his eyes. "That is ever so true, my dear, ever so true."

Now, a speck of sadness lined his words and I inspected his face more closely. I was probably trying too hard to understand something I might be imagining, but I couldn't ignore it.

"Well then," Henry said. "Because our house is a bit strange, we have our family room, dining room, and kitchen up on the next floor. Shall we go up?"

"We shall!" Mary said.

Mary gathered the whisky, flowers, as well as Henry's pipe and followed the rest of us up. The second level was more about comfort than castle. And it was the place where the others waited.

Four people were there, standing as if they'd been posed. That's what it felt like, as if the scene had been choreographed. One woman, probably in her sixties or so, lounged on a big-pillowed sofa. With pleasantly round features and short, gray hair cut severely at her jawline, she held a cigarette holder that didn't have a cigarette in it. Her long silk dress added to Henry's and Mary's flowing clothing, and I wondered if pajamas were the costume of the evening. But the other three changed my mind.

A man and woman who appeared to be close to my and Tom's ages sat next to each other on stools this side of a kitchen island. They turned with matching poses—their hands on their thighs—and smiled at us. They were both dressed casually in jeans and sweaters—almost matching, but not quite. The woman's red sweater also had some sort of blue design woven through, but the man's was just red. The man looked familiar to me, but I couldn't place how I knew him.

Probably in their thirties, the man's long face was topped off with a very short haircut. There was no sign of a beard over his pale skin, making his blue eyes extra-bright. The woman's brown curls fell to her shoulders, but there wasn't any frizz in sight. I wondered about her hair products and made a mental note to ask her later if the moment presented itself. Her smile and blue eyes were less electric than the man she sat next to, but they drew me in a little more.

The fourth person, a woman, also probably in her sixties,

stood closest to the landing. She inspected us, one hand on her hip, a scowl pulling her features into a deep frown. She wore jeans and a denim shirt, and might have decided not to like us. At least that's what her scrutiny felt like. Her gray hair was drawn back in a tight bun and her glasses were so thick that her eyes seemed to almost disappear behind the lenses.

"Let me introduce everyone," Mary said. She nodded toward the woman on the couch. "This is Eloise Hansen, a friend from forever." Eloise nodded and Mary turned to the woman who appeared not to like us. "And Gretchen Lovell. Gretchen and Eloise are a couple." Mary looked at us as if to gauge our reaction. It didn't seem necessary for any of us to mention that same-sex couples were or weren't novelties in our lives, so Mary continued, "Dina," she looked at the woman on the stool, "is my niece. Mikey is her husband, but there are days we like him so much more than we do Dina." She smiled at the couple, who took the teasing with their own smiles and mini eye rolls.

"It's nice tae meet all of ye," Rosie said.

Tom and I said the same, but I added, "Mikey, have we met?"

"Not that I recall, and considering how much you look like Mary, I think I would remember," Mikey said.

He reminded me a little of my friend Joshua, who worked at the history museum, but Mikey didn't wear glasses.

"The rain?" I said, somehow remembering him in a bright yellow raincoat, but unable to place where the storm had been. I was sure I'd seen those striking blue eyes before. "It was raining when we met."

"I'm sorry. I truly don't remember," Mikey said.

I decided it must be his resemblance to Joshua. Once the greetings were over, I took a better look around the cozy space.

The floor up here was once again made of cold stone or concrete, but was covered with even more throw rugs. The couch and chairs, including the dining chairs were all cushioned and inviting. The large space held all three rooms, divided by the long kitchen island. The kitchen wasn't modern, but adorned with old-fashioned appliances—not old-fashioned enough to be considered from the queen's lifetime though. In fact, I realized that the kitchen appliances weren't, in fact, old things, but new things made to look old. Retro.

I immediately loved it—the atmosphere and time-warped sense of place—but no matter the décor, it was still cool up here.

Both the temperature as well as the atmosphere. I tried to hide a shiver with a smile, but Rosie saw me. Furtively, she raised an eyebrow my direction. I nodded that I was okay. She nodded. She'd keyed in on the ambiance too. There was a distinct bump in the air, as if we'd either interrupted something we shouldn't have known about or something that was about us.

No one here really knew us, so I decided we must have interrupted a personal discussion. Maybe they didn't like new people joining their dinner parties.

Then I realized that Rosie was in her element. She wasn't one to jump in on other adventures I'd had, but this one had her full attention and she was intrigued and curious and didn't mind the icy atmosphere. I hoped it would be a fun evening for her.

"Sorry to be so abrupt, but dinner is already ready, so please take a seat, everyone. We'll eat and make merry and get to know each other over some of the best food you have ever consumed," Henry said.

With the ease of a comfortable host, Mary directed everyone where to sit. Rosie was on one end of the long table. Tom,

Mary, and I sat on one side. Henry sat at the other end, in the chair closest to the kitchen. And the other two couples filled in the other side. The table was so long that we weren't crowded, and Henry used a corner of it to set down dishes as he served. He was both the cook and the wait staff, as it were. Mary didn't offer to assist him. None of us did, though I felt like we should. Rosie picked up on that too and then shook her head once. Maybe Henry just liked to do it this way. He was in his element too.

"Soup to begin," Henry said as he carried a large pot and ladle toward the table. He ladled, and we passed the bowls down and around.

"Delaney, it is uncanny how much you look like my aunt," Dina said as she picked up her soup spoon. "I mean, you two both have the same hair even, frizz and all."

"Dina," Mary said.

"I noticed the hair too," I said hurriedly. I'd still wait to ask her about hers. Being offended by my frizz or the mention of it would make for a long life of offense. It wasn't worth the time. "It's even uncannier that we ran into each other. Well, I ran into her."

"Must have been meant to be," Mikey said.

I realized they were all staring at me. I felt my cheeks heat, but it was more just a reaction than embarrassment. I shouldn't have expected anything different. They'd get over it eventually. I smiled at each of them.

"I saw the secretary downstairs," I said to Dina. "It's beautiful."

Dina smiled. "It is, isn't it? I have an antique shop and I know my desks. The one downstairs was surely around back in the queen's day."

"Really?" I said. "That's . . ." I had much more I wanted to say to Dina, but Eloise jumped in.

"Are you sure you're not related?" she asked.

"I haven't done much genealogy, but I grew up in Kansas in America. I don't know of any connection, but I've thought about it since meeting Mary today. Is there some crossover in our family trees? I don't know," I said.

"Do you remember your past lives?" Gretchen asked. Her tone friendly, which was a contrast to the stink eye she'd been giving us.

"I don't remember any past lives," I said.

"Are you a believer?" Eloise asked, her tone also friendly.

"I'm not a nonbeliever," I said, having come up with that line after my recent run in with the Loch Ness legend. I'd become *not* a nonbeliever, but that was the best I could do.

"I see," Eloise said as she and Gretchen shared a "told you so" look.

I dipped my spoon into the soup. I didn't want to offend anyone and their beliefs, but I also didn't want someone to bring out a Ouija Board or call on some old spirits for a séance.

However, Rosie had other plans. "Och, how could ye not believe? Have ye never had a moment, a déjà vu that was so much more than a déjà vu?"

"I have had déjà vus, but they've never felt like a past life sneaking in," I said honestly. I didn't want to offend Rosie either.

"Tell us about *your* past lives," Mary said to Rosie.

Rosie swallowed a spoonful of soup. "Delicious," she said as she patted her napkin on the corners of her mouth. "I dinnae have any clear recollections anymore, but when I was a wee-un,

I would tell my dear mother, may she rest, about my time on the *Titanic*. I'm sure one of my past lives was lost during that awful tragedy."

"Really?" Henry stood and made his way back to the kitchen. He grabbed a loaf of sourdough. "Sorry, friends, I forgot the bread. Tell us more about the *Titanic*, Rosie."

I wanted to say the same, but I just looked at her, wondering if she was sharing a true story or something she'd made up to get Mary to talk more about the queen.

Rosie nodded. "As a wee-un, I would talk about things that no bairn would ken. Mother and Da never talked about the *Titanic*, so they thought it was odd. But mother was intrigued by my ramblings, and she asked me tae sketch things I remembered."

The entire table was enthralled. Rosie managed another spoonful of soup, giving dramatic pause as we waited. After she took a piece of bread from the basket, she continued.

"I sketched some dishes, and I sketched some cabin details. Back then, we lived oot in the country, my mother didnae have a way to research those details, but she kept the sketches and years later, she found pictures." Rosie shrugged. "My sketches were spot-on."

"I believe you," Gretchen said and pushed up her thick glasses.

"The *Titanic* tragedy was in the early 1900s, aye?" Tom said.

"Aye, and I drew the sketches when I was a child, and I ken what ye're going tae say—that I could have seen pictures or something. Anything is possible, but Mother was certain there was no way."

Tom nodded. He probably wondered the same thing I did; was this real?

"Aye," Gretchen said before she looked at Tom. "Anything *is* possible."

"And it's more than possible that Rosie was there, on that sinking ship," Eloise said as she smiled at my coworker.

Tom smiled and nodded too. "I would never doubt anything Rosie said. Never. I wonder though if there was a possibility that . . . well, that something happened in your life that gave you the opportunity to be . . . influenced."

"I used tae wonder about that," Rosie said. "But it was all so long ago. I remember making the sketches, but I dinnae remember their inspiration. I haven't thought aboot it for a long time. When Mary came in today, I wondered again. Some of it came back tae me. I can't tell ye, Tom. I have no idea. All I ken is what it was—a strange thing that seemed verra real at the time."

Tom smiled at Rosie. "If it was real tae you, it was real. I have no doubt."

"Aye," Rosie said.

"Henry, this honey butter!" Dina said. "It's to die for."

"Thank you," Henry said, but I saw him eye a bowl of jam he'd put on the table too.

I reached for the jam and spooned some on my bread as the others continued to talk about the *Titanic*. No one had tried the jam yet, but I could tell Henry wanted someone to.

"Delicious," I said after I took a bite.

Henry smiled knowingly and leaned toward me. "Ta, lass. I made it myself just this afternoon."

And then he smiled sadly at me. The moment stretched too long, and I even thought I saw tears come to his eyes. I smiled at him, hopefully inviting him to tell me what might be bothering him, if that's what I was picking up on. My cheeks reddened again, but I didn't break the moment. However, Henry did. He pushed his chair back from the table. He stood, but before he turned to head back to the kitchen, he looked at Mikey.

In a few brief beats I witnessed a silent exchange between the two of them. Mikey was looking at his wife's uncle with what seemed like irritation, or maybe anger. Henry stared at Mikey a long moment, but without a smile. In fact, I was surprised there were no heated words exchanged. Henry broke that stare too and hurried to the kitchen.

I blinked at the quick exchange, even more curious about what might be causing the problem but knowing it was none of my business.

I turned to Mary as a lull hit the *Titanic* conversation. "You said you have proof of your past life as Mary, Queen of Scots. I'd love to see it."

"Oh, no, Aunt Mary, you didn't say it was *proof,* did you?" Dina said.

"I did. And it is. At least I believe it is."

Henry came back to the table with the most un-Scottish pot roast, potatoes, and carrots I'd ever seen. It was just like a Kansas dinner.

"Oh, I have no doubt that it is proof," Henry said. "There's no doubt in my mind that my wife was once Mary, Queen of Scots, though. I don't need any extra proof."

"I'd love to see it," I repeated.

"Me too!" Rosie added. That was the whole reason she'd come tonight, the whole reason for the purple skirt probably.

"And I will show it to you all after dinner," Mary said.

"Ah, that's the dessert!" Rosie said with a smile.

"No, no. Dessert will be even more to die for than the honey butter," Henry said. "Mary will be the cherry on top, like she always is." He lifted his wineglass toward his wife.

The rest of us did the same as everyone chimed in with "To Mary."

"Your highness," Henry said.

And, in the most regal of ways, Mary Stewart gave us all a slightly tilted nod. I wouldn't have been surprised if she'd lifted her hand and gave a royal wave too, but she didn't.

"Oh, boy," Tom muttered so quietly that I was the only one who heard him. I hope.

SIX

Dessert was most definitely to die for. A strawberry and banana trifle, Henry had not only included a sponge cake in the delicious mix, but he'd also stirred in bits of a shortbread he'd baked himself. It was the most Scottish part of the meal, excluding the shots of whisky that were served with the trifle. Rosie's whisky.

Henry's shortbread couldn't compete with Rosie's—I secretly made sure she knew that—but the whipped cream he'd whipped himself was unlike anything I'd ever tasted.

"What is that extra flavor in there?" I asked after I'd swooned.

"I'll never tell, but it's something you wouldn't expect," Henry said. "Tell you what, think about it. If you don't come up with it by our next meeting, I will happily share the recipe."

"Goodness," Mary said. "You must be special, Delaney. Henry never tells anyone his secrets."

"I'm honored," I said.

"I think he's having a hard time telling the two of you

apart," Gretchen shook her head. "Do you two realize that you have some of the same mannerisms too? Mary moves her hands more than Delaney, but you both have the same sort of tilt to your chins. I've been trying not to stare too much, but you'll have to forgive me if I do. It's bizarre."

Mary and I looked at each other. She was probably thinking the same thing I was. Did we want to become self-conscious that way?

Mary came to the same conclusion I did. "Oh, don't point out those things, or we'll be avoiding them the rest of the evening. It will all become awkward."

"Henry, what do you do?" Tom asked.

Henry took a long moment. He seemed to chew his dessert longer than necessary as he formulated an answer. "I'm mostly retired."

"Mostly?" Tom asked.

"Yes, it's too long a story to tell, and not very interesting," he said. "I used to be in banking, but that's all so boring."

"What do you do, Tom?" Dina asked.

Tom explained he was the owner of the smallest pub in Scotland, the one located in Grassmarket. Every person there had been inside it at one time or another and seemed excited that they now knew the owner. I suspected Tom would be seeing them all again soon.

Eloise was a doctor, and Gretchen an artist, a sculptor, specializing in African wildlife. We'd been invited to tour her studio and I was excited about the prospect.

But the most interesting of the group, in my opinion, were Mikey and Dina. I finally learned that Dina's antique shop was in Cowgate, her place full of old things that she restored and sold. She and I had more in common than I would point out until we got to know each other much better. Later I would realize that we never did talk about Mikey's job, because Dina's was so interesting.

"Please visit any time," Dina said. "I love to show off my things."

"Thank you, I will. Soon," I said.

"I look forward to it." Dina smiled.

Mary volunteered. Everywhere, apparently. She'd worked at the castle on the hill, as well as a docent in several museums throughout Edinburgh. A few years earlier, she'd worked at the National Museum of Scotland, where Joshua worked. I didn't bring up knowing him. She'd recently been spending most of her time at the Writers' Museum, just off of the Royal Mile.

"I love that place. The books talk to me," she said with a laugh.

I looked at her to see if she meant it as literally as they spoke to me, but I didn't think she did.

She continued, "Museums bring back so many things from my past lives. I can't tell if they're memories or distractions. I can't work in many of the old places with old things anymore. It's just too much heartache, but I'm so drawn to museums. The Writers' Museum is safe for me, not much about the queen inside."

"Oh, are you volunteering there again?" Dina asked Mary.

Mary blinked at her. "Aye, Dina, I am. They welcomed me."

"Good to hear," Dina said.

"Seems sensible," Rosie added, filling the uncomfortable and heavy silence that came after their cryptic words. "I mean, sensible that you like being at that museum."

From the beginning of the dinner to the end, my sense of Mary had changed some, but I knew that was only because of my own interpretation. I'd first thought she'd be interesting, but she was more than that; she was consumed by her "past life." *It was both interesting and,* I thought, *somewhat sad.*

"Did you see the article about the Mary, Queen of Scots' papers that have recently been found?" I said, still not sharing my friendship with the young post doc who worked at the museum.

Everyone had read the article though, and couldn't wait to see the papers exhibited.

"Do ye feel any ties tae such things?" Rosie asked Mary.

"Not at this point," Mary said. "When I see them, I might, but I have no sense of them at the moment."

Rosie nodded.

"Come along," Henry said. "Everyone's finished. Let's move over to the comfortable chairs and I'll have coffee or more adult beverages ready momentarily. I know you're here to see Mary's proof."

We all moved to the other side of the space, the living room. Tom, Rosie, and I all sat on the couch. My senses were tuned to high alert, both because we were about to see Mary's proof and because I couldn't let go of the silent exchange I'd seen between Henry and Mikey. As furtively as possible, I tried to watch them both. Mikey fed my curiosity, but this time it was with a look between him and his wife.

And I was sure I saw fear. Mikey looked at Dina with stern eyes and pursed lips. Dina's eyes got wide before she looked away from his and pasted on a fake smile. I was sure I was the only one who noticed it, but I'd ask Rosie and Tom later.

"Oh, I look forward to showing you the Writers' Museum," Mary said to me. "And, frankly, I look forward to showing you to the people I work with. Everyone will be very surprised to see there are two of us." She quirked a half smile. "Or three of us, if you will. They all know who I used to be."

"Do they all believe ye?" Rosie asked.

"Oh, yes." Mary laughed. "Well, they say they do. Anyway, you're here for proof." She plunked her hands on her hips.

"In fact, it has been a lovely evening," Tom said. "Please don't feel obligated to show us any proof. It has been fun to get to know you all."

I looked at him. His graciousness was poorly timed, and I held back the urge to nudge him with my elbow. He looked at me and smiled.

"Although, I might be speaking out of turn." He laughed. "I think my lovely bride would be disappointed if we left without knowing . . ."

"Aye," Rosie added as she sent Tom a frown. "Aye."

Mary smiled. "Very well." She turned and spoke back over her shoulder. "You might want to come closer for a look."

Mary reached back and to the neckline of her dress. She pulled the material over about two inches, exposing a mark.

"Oh, that's not a tattoo," I said. "That's a birthmark."

"Aye," she said. "In the shape of a crown. The queen herself had one identical. That's how I knew. Like Rosie, the memories were stronger when I was a little girl. I sketched faces of people I knew and could give them first names. Some of the sketches matched some of the pictures of those people that we now have access to, though all of that is iffy I know. However, this birthmark confirmed it for me."

I didn't remember knowing anything about a birthmark on the queen. It seemed hokey, frankly, but the mark on Mary's back *did* look like a small crown.

"I don't remember reading anything aboot a birthmark," Rosie said.

Mary released the fabric and then turned around to face us again.

"It's a rare known fact, but she did have one, I'm sure," she said.

"There's documentation?" Tom asked, but then he cleared his throat. "I don't mean to be rude."

Mary smiled at him. "I understand your doubts. It is documented. In my memory. Since a girl, I have had a clear memory of having the mark, and having it in another setting, castles and other places too. Mirrors weren't common in that time, but I remember a reflection in a stream. Though over the years, the memories of the people, the faces, have faded, the memories of the mark have not. I am sure of it."

A part of me wanted to confirm with her that this was really the "proof" she'd been talking about sharing with us, because as proof went, this was pretty shaky. But I didn't express my doubts. Tom wasn't the only one who knew how to be gracious.

"That's completely fascinating," I said.

"I believe you totally," Rosie said. "I can relate tae what ye're saying. I ken those sorts of memories. I don't remember them much now, but I remember remembering them those first times. They are real."

Mary smiled at Rosie and then at me. I knew she could see my doubt, but she couldn't possibly have known that at that moment, more than all the other moments, I was looking at something else—our differences. We did look alike, but there was something in the set of her mouth, the corners of her eyes that were different than mine.

Then, everything changed again, her mouth and those eyes

were, in fact, very similar to mine—when I wasn't telling the whole truth, when I was lying.

She and I were very much alike.

The queen wasn't mentioned the rest of the evening. We learned that Eloise had been Mary's doctor for twenty years, that they'd met in Glasgow, at a clothing shop that was no longer there. Gretchen and Eloise had met at university thirty years earlier and had been together ever since. Dina and Mikey had also met at university, but only ten years earlier.

As the enjoyable evening continued, I got no sense that Mikey was angry with anyone, and Dina didn't seem afraid of him. I realized I'd probably jumped to conclusions that weren't real. I'd been rattled by the news about the bookshop, so I knew I wasn't quite in my normal headspace. We didn't mention the bad news to our new friends. I wasn't sure if that was because we didn't know them well enough yet, or if we didn't want to say the news out loud again, making it that much more real.

I thought Tom might see Henry at the pub very soon. They talked football in that way that only true fans could. Henry liked the idea of catching a match on the telly at the pub.

As we said goodbye, Mary grabbed my hands. "Oh, Delaney, it is so lovely to know you. Please, let's not be strangers. It would be a shame, and possibly an affront to the universe if we don't become friends. I will visit you at the bookshop but come see me at the museum too. Please."

"I will. I look forward to seeing you again," I said.

"Me too!"

Truth be told though, and for reasons I didn't quite understand, I couldn't wait to see her again.

SEVEN

"Well, that's disappointing," Hamlet said. "A birthmark? I've heard of such legends, fictional only, but I don't know anything about such a mark on the real Mary, Queen of Scots."

"Me either," I said.

"I still believe her," Rosie said as she walked by the back table where Hamlet and I had settled.

"I don't disbelieve her," I said. "It was an . . . interesting evening."

In fact, Rosie had been quiet on the way home the night before, lost either in the queen's world, or maybe the *Titanic*'s. Both Tom and I had tried to start conversations, but she hadn't been interested. We'd walked her to her door, given her hugs, gave some love to Hector, and then told them goodnight.

I'd been thinking about both the bookshop and Rosie all night, worried mostly about my worker. So had Tom. I'd texted him first thing this morning when she'd come in and seemed fine, if maybe still somewhat distracted.

Hamlet watched Rosie make her way to a bookshelf against the far wall. "Why are you so sure?" he asked her.

Hamlet hadn't heard the *Titanic* story.

"Here," I stood as the bell above the door jingled, "tell Hamlet about your past life. I'll help the customers."

Rosie joined Hamlet as I walked toward the front of the shop.

Life can only be understood backwards, but it must be lived forwards.

Hello, Kierkegard, I said in my head. Though a philosopher who was more interested in talking about religion, it seemed only reasonable that the bookish voice was talking about the past life experiences of the last couple of days. I didn't take the bookish voice for more than just an extra voice to reinforce that things were off kilter.

The woman who came into the shop didn't need anything specific, so I didn't hover as she browsed. Instead, I grabbed Hector as he trotted toward me. We found a spot in the middle of the other side of the shop, not far from where Rosie had been pretending to look for something herself.

"How about you, have you had other lives?" I said quietly.

Hector looked at me like he wanted to answer correctly.

"Good dog," I said as he kissed my cheek.

All of a sudden and in a stretched out beat of time, everything changed. In the blink of an eye, a boom sounded somewhere in the distance. There was a pop in the noise, but I wouldn't remember if it came at the beginning or the end of the deep bass rumble mixed with a tinny percussion. It didn't seem close enough to cause damage, but, nevertheless, my instinct was to put my arm up to protect my head. The glass in the windows rattled, Hector barked, and a solitary book fell from a shelf. When the noise stopped—I couldn't be sure how long it lasted because every time I thought about it, it expanded, Rosie and Hamlet hurried to the front. The customer froze in place, supporting herself by placing a hand on a shelf. With wide eyes, we all looked at each other, wondering if what we all thought had happened, had actually just happened.

It had.

EIGHT

A bomb—something homemade according to the first reports—had exploded a car. It was made clear that it hadn't been what we typically called a car bomb, something made to murder a large number of people when a car with an explosive device was driven into a populated location, but something with the power that would surely kill or maim the person or people only inside the car. There was one fatality, a man in his early fifties. But that was all the information the newscasters shared yesterday.

We'd spent the rest of the day walking around in a confused daze with emotions that ran the gamut. Rosie closed the bookshop and Hamlet found an old, small television in one of the offices. He'd brought it and some old-fashioned rabbit ears up to the front of the shop. I didn't even know it was possible to view television that way anymore, but that's what we did, watching the repeating, vague news over and over again.

Because the explosion took place at the bottom of the Royal Mile, it was discussed that perhaps a political figure had been targeted. With not many facts, the newspeople speculated that maybe the explosion, something the police immediately labeled a murder, had something to do with a recent scandal, one I hadn't heard about, but that sounded uncomfortably relevant when I learned some of the facts.

As I'd heard from Edwin, Burgess Tickets were once granted to merchants giving them the right to do business in a specific burgh, or geographical area, as well as offering the recipients community perks. Back in the day, the tickets were delivered in miniature coffin-like containers called Freedom Caskets. The Freedom Caskets were sometimes silver or gold and ornately decorated. When the newscasters ran out of new information to share with the public, they talked about the tickets, the caskets, and their recent revival. Granting the tickets was an old tradition and one that the Lord Provost wanted to bring back, just because it was something nostalgic and gave a nod to Scottish history. The idea had gone over poorly—as something antiquated and "coffins are weird," but it had given life to something else.

Some citizens thought that all the old Burgess Tickets should at least be tracked down. If a business didn't have one, they should have to apply for one, or at least go through the same sort of motions businesses used to have to go through, and in doing so only be allowed to continue to do business if they were able to earn one. None of the newspeople seemed to know what all the specific requirements or qualifications used to be.

However, some of the citizens of Edinburgh wanted the standards raised to a point that included the potential for lots and lots of remodeling. The circumstances sounded eerily similar to what was going on with the bookshop, but Edwin assured me that Burgess Tickets had never once been brought up in the phone message he'd received the previous week, that it had been solely his idea to try to find The Cracked Spine's. He also claimed not to have heard about the recent idea of bringing the tickets back with even higher standards, though he didn't rule out that he might not have paid close attention to the news. Perhaps something had seeped into his subconscious; he just couldn't be sure.

And because of the murder, of course we all felt some confusion.

As we all came back to work the next morning, Edwin kept the bookshop closed and Hamlet again switched on the old television. It was as if the newscasters were still in repeat mode.

"Och," Rosie said when the Burgess Tickets were brought up again. "They have no idea who was kil't. They are making things up just tae fill time now."

"I think so too," Hamlet said. "But what if the bomber was someone who wouldn't meet the new ticket standards, if those standards ever came into effect? Maybe that's what they're thinking."

"We need more information," Edwin said. "Aye, the newspeople just want something to talk about."

What we did know was that it was a miracle that only one person had been killed. The explosion had taken place in a populated area. It seemed that there was no damage to any other buildings in the area and the only other injury was an elderly man who'd been so surprised by the noise that he'd fallen and hurt his knees. I wondered how there was so little other damage and yet we'd heard and felt the explosion as if it was right next to us.

Tom had run down to the bookshop from his pub seconds after the noise. Once we knew each other was okay, we called everyone else. Edwin and my landlords, Elias and Aggie, were fine. In fact, they were far enough away from the explosion that they hadn't heard or felt it. Tom's father, Artair, was also fine, though he'd felt the explosion from his office inside the University of Edinburgh's library, which was even farther from the bombing location than we were.

Then we called my family in Kansas to let them know all was well if they heard news of the explosion. They were happy to know we were okay.

Tom had headed back to the pub. He'd left it unattended, trusting a well-known customer to make sure no one robbed the place, either of the liquor or the money in the till. He'd dropped me off at the bookshop again this morning before heading back to work. He could have remained closed like Edwin had chosen to do, but Tom thought some of his regulars might miss their routine.

Once again, the newscaster began to say that the name of the victim hadn't been released yet, but she stopped speaking suddenly and held her hand to her ear. She continued, "We've just received word. The name of the victim has now been released. We have confirmed that he was a councilor to the Lord Provost. At one time the victim had been in banking, but he was retired from that profession, devoting all his time to helping govern our fair and beautiful city. The name of the victim is Henry Stewart."

And then a picture popped up on the screen. Even in grainy black and white, the man on the screen was familiar, too familiar.

I didn't hear the next few sentences because my ears had closed as my mind swirled. What the hell?

I looked at Rosie. She put her fist to her chest and sat down hard in a chair. Oh, no.

Suddenly, nothing was as important as my friend and co-worker. With my ears still closed and my mind still swirling, I jumped up and ran to her.

Edwin, Hamlet, and Hector joined me just as she went down.

NINE

Rosie was okay. It took a few minutes for her to come back from the faint, but she did. Hamlet made it to her first and, with quick thinking, he managed to get a hand under her head before it hit the hard floor. Once she was lucid, she was able to move all parts and the color came back to her face.

"Och, I'm so sorry," she said.

"No need to apologize," Edwin said as he reached across the table for her hand. "We're glad you're all right."

"Aye." She squeezed Edwin's hand. "I'm fine, but, Edwin, we just met that poor man two nights anon. He cooked us dinner."

Edwin looked at me. It hadn't even occurred to any of us to tell Edwin about the dinner. I nodded.

"Oh dear," he said when I gave him a quick summary. "I'm so sorry."

Rosie shook her head and then looked at me. "Do ye think one of the people from the dinner kil't him? Do you think we were in the same hoose as the killer?"

I had no idea. "No, no, Rosie, he worked for the government. It's something political, I'm sure."

I wasn't sure about anything, of course, and more questions were filling my head. Was there something else going on, or was meeting Mary and attending the dinner all a coincidence?

After dropping off Rosie that night, Tom and I had discussed the party. I told him what I'd noticed about Mikey and Henry and Mikey and Dina. He hadn't seen any of that and then I'd quickly forgotten about it. Mostly, we'd both just been intrigued by the birthmark and its label of "proof."

"I dinnae ken," Rosie said. "There was tension in the air. I couldnae understand why, and it felt like none of my business anyway, but there was strain there. Did ye sense it?"

"I did, but I couldn't figure it out either. We were the strangers though. They all knew each other. Who knows what's going on in their lives?"

"And now that lovely man is dead." More tears came to Rosie's eyes, but she didn't swoon.

"Hang on," Hamlet said suddenly.

We all looked at him.

"Oh, no," he said, but he'd fallen into his own thoughts. He looked up a moment later. "Rosie, I don't want to upset you further, but something just occurred to me."

"It's all right, lad. G'on."

"The queen. Mary, Queen of Scots. Her second husband was killed—in an explosion. His name was Henry Stuart. I believe his title was Lord Darnley."

"Oh, my," Rosie said. "That's . . . unbelievable."

"His name was Henry?" I said.

"Aye," Hamlet said. "I think so."

"Gracious. Wait, wasn't it alleged that the queen's lover killed him?" Edwin said.

"It was," Hamlet said. "I think . . . well, I haven't read about Mary Stuart in quite a few years,"

As Hamlet reached for a laptop he kept perched on a back shelf, I had another thought.

"Rosie, do you think we should call Inspector Winters and tell him about the dinner party?" I said.

"I do, lass. I dinnae ken if it will do any good, but I think we should talk tae the police."

"I'll call him right now."

I found my phone and pulled up the favorites screen. I kept thinking a day might come when I wouldn't need to keep the police inspector toward the top of my call list. However, that day wasn't today.

TEN

Unfortunately, I ran into an immediate roadblock. I'd called Inspector Winters's personal number, because that was the one he'd given me. It seemed he was on holiday. As his greeting continued, stating that he'd be away for a week or so, I debated whether or not to leave a message. Ultimately, I decided not to.

"Ye didnae leave a message," Rosie said when I disconnected the call.

"He's on vacation," I said. "I didn't want to bother him."

For a moment Rosie looked bothered, but shortly she nodded. "Aye, I understand. Should we call another officer, perhaps just the police's number?"

"Should we?" I said.

The four of us sat and thought about it a moment. Did we want to tell the police that we'd gotten weird vibes at a dinner Henry had cooked for us the night before he was killed? Also, Henry was a councilor and it seemed feasible that there might be a councilor or two out to make sure the bookshop was shut down, though none of us were sure who those particular councilors were. Our unspoken, but surely shared insights and concerns, suddenly seemed threadbare and potentially shone a suspicious light on all of us.

"Maybe not yet," Rosie said. "We have no proof of anything. I might be jumping to conclusions."

"We should let the police do their jobs," Edwin said.

"Aye," Hamlet added.

"I agree," I said.

For now.

I stood and made my way to the front of the store. I needed to gather my thoughts, calm down, something. I turned and looked back toward my friends. They had each fallen into their own thoughts, but they were going to be okay.

It had been a tragic couple of days, not just for Henry and his loved ones, but for the city of Edinburgh too. A bomb set off in a public place left sadness, anger, and fear behind. I'd always been one not to let fear rule my behavior, but as I looked out the window, I was grateful for the sense of security I felt inside the shop. It was all an illusion, I knew that. Anything can happen at any time. Bad things happened all the time, and usually when you least expected them. But I refused to live my life being worried about those sorts of things.

Nevertheless, I didn't push away the sadness and anger. Someone was messing with my bookshop, and now with my adopted city.

A shiver ran up my spine. Perhaps I was experiencing some sort of shock or coping mechanism. Or maybe the dreary rain outside made me cold. There were no bookish voices speaking—in fact, as I listened for them, I sensed they were too sad to speak.

Maybe I didn't want to focus on the fact that a man who had cooked me dinner two nights ago was now dead, brutally murdered. I grabbed an umbrella from the shelf and turned around. "I'm going out for a bit. I'll be back."

Edwin, Rosie, and Hamlet all looked at me with questioning eyes.

"Of course," Edwin said. "Take whatever time you need."

"Be safe," Rosie said.

"Do you want company?" Hamlet asked, but he knew the answer. He was just being polite.

I shook my head. "No. I'll be back."

I pushed through the door as I slid open the umbrella. It *was* cold and I hadn't grabbed my jacket. At least I'd worn a sweater, and I sensed I would warm up quickly.

The Royal Mile had been blocked off until just a couple hours earlier. The newscasters had announced that other than a small area, foot and vehicle traffic was being allowed back in.

I could have walked up Victoria Street and then down to the bottom of the Royal Mile; that route would have taken me past Tom's pub. Instead, I glanced toward it briefly before I hurried over the market square to where I knew a bus would be coming shortly. My timing was good and I didn't have to wait even a full minute before I boarded the bus that would at least get me up to the top of the Royal Mile.

"Hello," a voice said from behind me as I sat down. "Delaney, is it?"

I turned quickly. "Oh. Hello!"

"Fancy meeting you here," Eloise said.

I nodded and frowned. "I'm . . ."

"Going to look at where it happened?" She said without much of a question to her tone. "Me too. Mary called me a couple hours ago with the news that Henry had been identified. I'm gutted."

I nodded again. "I'm so sorry."

"I canceled patients. I've never done that. I had to get some air. It's so awful."

"May I join you?"

"Certainly."

I moved to the seat next to her. If we knew each other even just a tiny bit better I would have put my arm around her or hugged her once quickly.

Instead, Eloise nodded at me once sadly as the bus made it to the top of Victoria and waited to turn onto the Royal Mile.

"Is Mary okay?" I asked.

"Oh, no, not at all. I stopped by her house first and gave her something to calm her down. She's not one for medication but she's distraught. She's probably still sleeping."

"I'm sure it's terrible for her."

"It's so very bizarre and unreal."

"He was a lovely man," I said, mostly because I couldn't think of anything else to say. I had a million questions about Henry Stewart, but this wasn't the time or the way to ask them.

"He was," she said. She grimaced and hit her thigh with her fist. "He's made enemies though. I kept telling him to quit wanting to change so many things."

"Do you mean in his position as councilor?"

"Aye. He kept wanting to make the city a better place, at least better in his eyes. He was so used to running the show. Used to spend his days at the bank telling everyone else what to do, and they had to listen to him there. He never learned how to tread lightly because he didn't have to. Gracious, he angered some people."

I waited a good long few beats with the hopes that she'd continue. She didn't.

"Like who?" I finally asked.

"So many! That strange thing with the Burgess Tickets. What in the world was he doing, trying to bring back that old antiquated idea? And trees! He spearheaded cutting down some old trees to make a walking path easier. He knew how to work the system and the vote on those trees was sneaky, I tell you. I told him too."

Over the last couple of days, Edwin had mentioned both of the contentious items Eloise was talking about. Henry had been shaking things up. I'd been in a wedding haze and then on a honeymoon. Maybe all of this had come to a head while I was gone. I didn't quite understand the timing of everything, and I wasn't ready to tell her about the bookshop's predicament.

"Eloise, how long had he been a councilor?"

"He was starting his second year."

"What were his political aspirations?"

"Nothing beyond what he was doing. He didn't want to be Lord Provost. He didn't want a higher position. He knew he could get things done at his level."

"Sounds like it."

"Well, he certainly must have gotten under someone's skin," she said. Her fist clenched again, but she didn't pound it this time.

"Did you talk to the police?" I asked.

"Did I? No. Mary has, of course, but there's no reason I should."

I shrugged. "I don't know. Maybe you can remember something that might help them with a lead, if they don't have one, or some, already."

"Hmm. You might be right." She sat up straighter. "Here's our stop."

We exited the bus together. I was glad I was there—I was glad she was there.

Though there was no vehicle or body in the vicinity, the crime scene was buzzing. Officials were walking around in their white coveralls, some taking pictures, some taking measurements, some just looking at the destruction. The road and a streetlight had been damaged but it seemed the surrounding buildings were intact. Traffic was getting through, but slowly and as a police officer directed. We weren't far from Inspector Winters's police station and I thought again about leaving him a message.

Despite what had already been removed, the destruction and disruption at the scene was still shocking.

"Oh, my," I said quietly to myself.

"It's terrible," Eloise said. "I'm glad the auto is gone, but it's so . . ."

"Unreal," I said.

"Aye, and traumatic."

From behind a widely cordoned off area and for a long few minutes, we silently watched the police and the technicians work.

"Maybe it had something to do with Mary," Eloise said, breaking the silence.

"Mary? Why?"

She looked at me. "People either love or hate her, Delaney. She's sure she's a reincarnation of the queen. She doesn't keep it a secret. And then she goes around telling people she has proof and it's no more than a silly birthmark. People find her strange."

I shook my head. "Why would anyone care about any of that enough to kill Henry?"

"I don't know. Maybe this was to get back at her. The queen's second husband was killed in an explosion, did you know that?"

"Yes."

"Maybe this was some sort of sick act from someone who thinks Mary deserved it. *If she's the queen, she should experience the same tragedies* and such."

I blinked at Eloise. So far, she'd mentioned that both Mary and Henry had enemies. It seemed the suspect list could be long. "Well, her husband being killed in an explosion is only one of her many tragedies. I hope you're not onto something."

"Aye, it would be a terrible tragedy to see Mary beheaded."

I blinked at her again.

Eloise put her fist to her mouth. "I honestly can't believe I just said such a thing. Please forgive me."

"Of course," I said.

But it would have been impossible for me not to hear a thin thread of sarcasm in her voice. No, I would have to just let that go. She hadn't meant it.

"Wasn't it the queen's next husband, her third, the person ultimately accused of killing her second husband?"

"Something like that. Conspiring to and such."

"Is there someone out there who might fit the role as our Mary's next husband?"

"Is she having an affair? I don't think so," Eloise said. "I really and truly don't think so."

Of course, Mary, Queen of Scots, also denied an affair.

I caught the eye of someone looking at us. She was very tall and dressed in the white crime-scene coveralls, and even though her head was hooded and she was a good distance away, I could see the scrutiny in her gaze.

"I think I'm done here," Eloise said. "I should get back to my patients."

"Do you want me to go with you?"

Eloise smiled at me and suddenly her severe haircut didn't seem so severe. "You're lovely, Delaney, but no, I think I can handle it. I'm pleased we ran into each other on the bus though."

"Me too."

"I suspect we'll be in touch. Once you've befriended Mary, you've befriended all her circle. Don't fight it, that's just the way it is."

"I hope so."

"Me too. Goodbye, dear."

I watched her walk up the hill a half block before she caught another bus. I turned back around to look for the tall woman in the coveralls, but she wasn't in the same spot.

I only stayed another few minutes as I thought about the strange royal history and my new friends. Other than martyr, I didn't think I'd heard any word about the queen mentioned as much as "tragedy." There had been so much of it for her. But it had been a tragic, violent time. What the queen experienced went with the territory, I supposed.

The rain stopped and I decided to walk back to work, maybe stop by the pub for a moment on the way.

I wasn't sure why I had needed to see where the car had exploded, but Eloise hadn't asked for an explanation. I was glad, and I understood her curiosity too. It had been an unreal sequence of events, but even though Henry's car was no longer there, seeing where the explosion had occurred hadn't left me with any doubts. I wished it hadn't happened, but if it had, I needed to make sure it was real. It was.

On the way back to the bookshop, a twinge of curiosity about the tall woman came to mind, but only briefly. I forgot all about her by the time I made it down Victoria.

ELEVEN

"She mentioned the beheading and everything?" Tom said.

"Yes, but she apologized for bringing it up."

"These sorts of tragedies can cause stress." Tom was working hard at being sympathetic, but the circumstances of me running into Eloise bothered him.

There was a murder, after all.

"I chalked it up to stress."

We sat on the couch of our small cottage. It was a rare evening that Tom wasn't at the pub. He'd come home early because of the upsetting days, leaving his employee Rodger in charge. Rodger, a sworn bachelor, had demanded that Tom go and spend time with me. It hadn't taken much convincing.

"One of my customers follows the council votes closely. He mentioned that he liked Henry, admired him, but he had been pushing hard to bring back the Burgess Tickets and that the old-fashioned notion was creating some strife within the ranks, but it wasn't anything that should have led to murder."

"Eloise brought those up too. She said he's been pushing for many things, in maybe a too-pushy way. Do you think he's the one who wanted the bookshop closed? And why would he?"

"No idea. He didn't seem pushy in the least at the dinner."

"He seemed the opposite of that. Tom, do you think it was all some setup? I mean, did Mary come to the shop and invite us to the dinner on purpose? Though I can't figure out why in the world she would do that."

"It's a possibility, but she couldn't manipulate the fact that you two look so much alike. That's just the way it is."

"I thought about that too."

"Delaney." Tom frowned. "I hate to even bring this up, but now maybe the vote regarding the bookshop will be delayed. There might be more time to figure things out."

"Well, I'm sorry to say that we all thought about that too. Before the bombing, Edwin had finally put in a call to the Lord Provost, but hadn't heard back. Who knows if he will, and we all feel bad enough about Henry that we feel guilty about worrying about the bookshop's fate, but we can't help it. We also feel like we should be talking to other councilors or something."

"That sounds like a big project."

"I know." I fell back into thought. "Maybe the fact that Mary and I look alike is totally random, just a bizarre coincidence."

Tom squinted at me. "Honestly, lass, I don't think so. I don't understand what's going on, but her timing of her first visit to the bookshop *is* curious. I'd like not to think so, but I can't help it."

"I love it when you talk all Scottish to me."

He smiled. "I said, 'lass.' I can do even better than that. Och, 'tis a bunchie of blashie we're speaking, perhaps."

"You just sounded so much like Elias."

Tom's smile turned back into a frown as he reached up and tucked my hair behind my ear. "You love this cottage, don't you?"

I blinked at the change of subject. "I do, but I will love the house too."

"Are you sure?"

"Yes. Why?"

"I see you looking around this place. We haven't left yet and you're already missing it."

"Tom, I will love wherever we are together."

Tom nodded. "Me too."

My phone buzzed in my pocket. I wrestled it free.

"Hey, Rosie, everything okay?"

"Aye," she said. "I just got a call from our new friend. She called my personal mobile. I was surprised."

"Who?"

"Mary Stewart. She wants to talk to you, Delaney. She said you're the only one who can understand what she's going through, that you're soul sisters of a sort. I said I would talk tae ye tomorrow, so ye dinnae need tae call her tonight. But here's her mobile. I gave her mine at dinner, but she said she neglected tae ask for yours."

At least there was a pen close by, but with no paper I wrote the number on my arm. "How was she?"

"Awful. A mess really. I tried tae console her, but I dinnae think I did much good. I feel bad for the wee lass, but I dinnae really know her, Delaney. Neither do ye. Don't feel obligated."

"I won't." I already did.

I disconnected the call and looked at the number on my arm.

"Want to call her tonight?" Tom asked, easily overhearing the call.

I punched in the number, but something stopped me from hitting Send.

"What?" Tom asked.

"I don't know. Her husband was killed and she wants to talk to someone she just met. I mean, I felt a connection too, but . . . something tells me not to call her just yet. Is that cruel?"

"No. Rosie was correct, you don't need to feel obligated. Listen to your gut," he said.

"I might call her tomorrow, but I'm not sure." I stopped looking at my arm and gave my attention to the cobalt eyes looking back at me. "Tonight is just for you and me."

He smiled and his eyes brightened. "Aye?"

"Oh, yes, aye."

TWELVE

By the time I headed into work the next day, I still hadn't called Mary, and someone was at the bookshop to further divert my attention. Considering she'd been wearing some of the crime-scene coveralls when I first saw her, it might have been surprising that I recognized her. But I did. Immediately.

She was tall, over six feet by a couple inches, and her eyes held the same scrutiny I'd noticed on the Royal Mile. In fact, when I first walked into the bookshop and saw her talking to Rosie, I had an urge to wave when she turned toward me, as though we'd shared more than brief eye contact.

"Delaney?" she said.

"Yes, you're with the police?" I said as I approached.

She hesitated a beat. "I am. Inspector Buchanan. You look so much like . . ."

"Mary Stewart. Yes, I know."

She frowned, for some reason not pleased with the resemblance. A scenario suddenly played through my mind. Was there video of someone somewhere doing something they shouldn't have been doing—like maybe planting a bomb? Did the person look like Mary and me, and was this going to be a problem? In fact, my mind had gone there a couple of times already. It was probably too paranoid a notion as well as part of the reason I hadn't called Mary back yet.

I continued, "I just met Mary a few days ago. It was a surprise for both of us."

Inspector Buchanan nodded and plunked her hands on her hips. "That was you I saw at the crime scene yesterday. I wondered when Mary said it hadn't been her and told me about the resemblance between the two of you. Why were you there?"

For a moment, I felt truly terrible. Maybe that's why Mary was trying to get ahold of me, to warn me the police might be coming to see me. I felt like a fool.

Inspector Buchanan hadn't even asked for a private place to talk. Behind the inspector's back, Rosie sent me some high eyebrows. Hector, not liking attitude thrown at any of his people, trotted around the desk and to me. He sat at my feet protectively and faced the inspector. We all looked down at him as he panted displeasingly at the tall woman. She shook her head once and then looked back at me.

"Well?" she said.

"I'm not exactly sure. The news about Henry was tough to take and I needed some air. I boarded the bus and I realized I needed to see where . . . where it happened. It was shocking that there weren't more injuries."

She blinked at me, once, twice, and then pursed her lips. "You just met Henry recently?"

"Three nights ago. He cooked us dinner." My voice cracked. Hector moved closer. I wanted to pick him up but that seemed too frivolous.

"I see. Can you please tell me about the dinner? Who was there? What occurred?"

"Excuse me," Rosie said. "Please, won't the two of ye take a seat in the back, or perhaps in one of the offices next door? Ye're sure tae scare away any potential customers."

Without a word, Inspector Buchanan glanced toward the table and then made her way to it. I picked up Hector and joined her, sitting down and ignoring her critical expression when she looked at the dog on my lap.

Rosie didn't offer to grab coffee or tea, which of course was Rosie code for "let's not keep her here too long."

"Your coworker," Inspector Buchanan nodded toward Rosie, who was now back at the front desk, "told me her version of the events at the dinner. I'd like to hear about it from your perspective."

I told her the details, but just their barest of bones. I didn't mention what'd I'd seen Mikey do, the expressions he'd shared with Henry and Dina. I would have told Inspector Winters, but I wasn't ready to trust Inspector Buchanan. I could see that she was suspicious of me too, but not enough to question me in any official capacity. For the time being at least.

"Who was the woman you were with at the scene yesterday?"

"Eloise. She's a doctor, but I'm afraid I never caught her last name. She was introduced to us only as Eloise."

"Introduced? At the dinner?"

"Yes."

Inspector Buchanan hadn't taken any notes, until that moment. She reached into her jacket pocket for a notebook and a pen. "Her name again?"

"Eloise is all I got."

She frowned deeply as if she was highly perturbed that I

didn't know more about the doctor. I held back the shrug that made its way to my shoulders. I didn't tell her I knew Eloise was Mary's doctor.

"But she was at the dinner?" Inspector Buchanan asked.

Hadn't I said that? "Yes. Along with her partner, Gretchen. As well as Mary's niece, Dina, and Dina's husband, Mikey."

"Right." She tapped her pencil on the paper. "What do you think of Mary's claim of reincarnation? Do you believe it?"

I wanted to ask her the relevance of such a question, and then I remembered my attorney. It hadn't occurred to me to tell the police I wouldn't talk to them without my attorney present. Inspector Buchanan had made it seem so casual that I'd done what all those people on TV do, just kept talking. As I watched them, I'd roll my eyes and exclaim that "that would never happen to me."

"I didn't *not* believe, but I wasn't convinced. Why?" I crossed my arms in front of myself. Hector whined.

"It's a curious thing, is all. A very curious thing. All right then. Well, your account of those attending the party is the same as your coworker's. I guess I just have one more thing." She looked over at Rosie who was looking at us. The inspector waved her to us.

Rosie frowned but came over to the table.

Inspector Buchanan seemed to like the audience. She gave a proper dramatic pause before she continued.

"At any time that evening, did Henry, the victim, mention that he was working to shut down this place? This bookshop was going to be closed down because it was something he set in motion?"

There it was. We'd all wondered, and it now seemed so devastatingly real. Nevertheless, I tried to keep a stiff upper lip.

"No," I said.

"No," Rosie said.

At least we both kept it simple.

"I see. I just wondered if that was something that came up during the dinner Henry cooked for you. That's all," Inspector Buchanan said.

I did not like her.

"It most certainly did not." Rosie stood up straight and held her chin defiantly.

"No, it didn't. Everyone was very friendly, welcoming," I said, sadness filling my chest. The question came to me again—had that entire dinner been some sort of setup for something? It wasn't clear what end result they were looking for, but Tom was correct, something wasn't right.

"Is that really the truth? Henry the councilor was trying to close the bookshop?" I asked.

"It seems he had proposed a vote, scheduled to take place next week, as to whether or not the council would agree to an inspector's findings that this building should be torn down, that it was beyond repair." Inspector Buchanan looked around with an odd twinkle in her eyes. Schadenfreude came to mind. Was she enjoying our misfortune?

"There's been no inspector to visit us," I said.

"No," Rosie added. "We've had no inspector."

Inspector Buchanan looked back and forth between us. She was either perplexed or thought we were lying, and was determined to figure out which it was.

"Well, that's certainly most interesting," the inspector said. "Are you sure?"

"Of course we're sure," Rosie said.

Hector decided Rosie might need him more so he hopped

off my lap and moved to sit at her feet. Inspector Buchanan rolled her eyes at the dog.

"Well, I'll have to look at that more closely," she said.

"In fact," I smiled, but it probably seemed faked and forced, "we would very much like it if someone would. If there hasn't been an inspection, there can't be a vote, right?"

"Well, I don't know about that. Signals have been crossed, that's apparent. I'll get to the bottom of it."

She stood and smoothed her slacks over her thighs, pulled once at the hem of her jacket. I realized she wasn't dressed in a uniform. I'd talked to her, done as she'd wanted me to do, and she didn't even look official. I was now one of those people on TV.

"Thank you for your time," she said. She looked around. "I heard this place was dangerous, not a safe place to be at all, that no repairs would be possible. You all might want to consider shutting it down anyway."

"Does it look dangerous?" I asked.

"No. It looks old though and that might be the same thing."

I stood. "You've seen the report?"

She didn't like my question, but she couldn't lie either. "Well, no, but I heard about it. I've spoken to some other council members."

"Please, Inspector Buchanan, if you see it, may we see it too?" I asked.

"I will follow protocol, whatever that might be. But you all should consider that you're in denial here."

I opened my mouth but she turned and marched away. Rosie put her hand on my arm and shook her head. I closed my mouth.

Inspector Buchanan didn't even look back as she opened the door and went through. She was gone, but she'd left a hell of a wake behind.

THIRTEEN

"Oh dear," Edwin said after Rosie and I gave him and Hamlet the news.

Rosie had sent them both a 999 text, not bothering to ask me to do the honors as she usually did when it came to mobile technology.

However, she'd looked at her phone seriously before she'd sent it.

"It's okay," I said. "It's a real emergency. At least we have more information."

She'd nodded and hit Send.

I was by far the most riled up of all of us. Rosie had been upset briefly but Edwin had remained cool. Hamlet was bothered by the police inspector's methods and wanted to tell her as much. I bit down on my anger when Edwin's demeanor wasn't as heated as I thought it should be.

I was ready for a fight. I didn't know who I was supposed to fight, but I wanted the rest of my coworkers to feel the same.

"What should we do?" I asked.

Edwin sat up straighter and nodded. He heard my desperation. "I haven't heard from the Lord Provost, but I know others
in his office. I will call them too, see if I can get more information. Surely, the vote will be postponed."

"Wait, can we go see the Lord Provost? Just stop by his
office? Maybe he'd see us." I shrugged.

"No, probably not." Edwin fell into thought and looked up
an instant later. "However, we *can* visit someone else, I think.
Someone who works for the city. Would you like to try?"

"Yes!" I said. Hell to the yes. "Let's go."

Edwin stood. "We can walk there."

"Oh, good. I'll grab the umbrellas."

The business licensing division for the city of Edinburgh was located on the Royal Mile, another bus ride or, as we'd chosen today, a quick walk past Tom's pub (we stuck our heads in and said
hello), up Victoria Street, and then not far down the Royal Mile,
the street that led to the sea, the street that had seen the terrible recent tragedy of Henry's murder as well as so many other
tragedies over the centuries. It was once the whole city, the place
where all of Edinburgh used to work and live back in the days
when people were far too crowded together and things like the
Black Plague could easily have its way with the population.

Today, clouds above threatened rain, but no raindrops fell.
I figured that was because I'd made sure we were well prepared
with the umbrellas. If I'd forgotten them, as I frequently did, it
would have surely rained. And that was an official observation.

Along the walk, we talked about Edwin's lady love and the
new menu she was incorporating into her restaurant. Until
he'd dated a restaurant owner, Edwin hadn't been interested in

food. Now it was one of his main topics of conversation. We'd probably had more conversations about spices and food preparation techniques than we'd had books over the last little while.

I was pleased to have something to talk about other than all the horrible things we'd talked about at the bookshop.

"Here we are," Edwin soon said.

The business licensing division was housed in another beautiful, old, historical building, on its bottom floor, adorned only with a calligraphed sign in the window announcing the office's hours. Edwin pulled the door open and waited as I went through.

The inside was contemporary. The office was just like any other government office I'd been inside in the States—gray and brown and generic. If it was a busy place, we managed to hit a lull in the traffic. Only one person stood on this side of the counter as three others looked up at us from behind it.

"Help you?" A young man said as he moved toward his side of the counter.

"Aye," Edwin said. "Is Lyle in?"

"Um, well, I'll have a look. May I tell him who's inquiring?"

"Edwin MacAlister."

"One moment."

I watched the man disappear through a doorway and down a hall. Like Mikey, he also reminded me of my friend at the museum, Joshua. Tall, thin, topped off with glasses with big, black frames. I sensed I needed to pay Joshua a visit.

"Lyle doesn't get much company?" I quietly asked Edwin. "That guy seemed surprised you asked for him."

"He likes to remain hidden. You'd be surprised by the level of vitriol some people can have regarding their business licenses."

I blinked at him. "No, Edwin, I don't think I would be."

Edwin's mouth made a straight line as he nodded. "Fair enough."

"Come through, Mr. MacAlister," the clerk said as he reappeared from the hallway.

Edwin and I looked at each other. *That was easy.*

We were led down the hallway to the last office on the left. I was always surprised when something in an Edinburgh building was so normal. Even now, after I'd been in the country long enough to see both spectacular architecture and boring, normal buildings, I pushed away some disappointment at the plain walls and common linoleum floor.

The clerk pushed open the door and then stood back out of our way.

"Edwin, what a lovely surprise!" The man, Lyle, I presumed, stood from behind the desk and extended his hand.

It wasn't a tiny office, but it wasn't roomy either. If he was the head of business licensing of the entire city, the position didn't come with a luxurious office.

"Lyle. Pleasure's all mine." They shook. "This is Delaney Nichols. She's a good friend and an employee at the bookshop. Delaney, this is Lyle Mercado."

Lyle wasn't as old or as distinguished at Edwin. Maybe in his sixties, he was rough around the edges, scruffy beard and wrinkled clothes, and above a friendly smile his eyes glinted with disapproval or discomfort. His accent was lighter than Edwin's, similar to Tom's, but, again, I knew I didn't hear them the same way anymore. Before long, I might actually speak some Scots.

"Nice to meet you, Delaney." We shook, and his tight smile melted as he looked at me. He withdrew his hand and looked away from my eyes and downward as his eyebrows came together. He recovered somewhat, but not all the way, giving me another quick smile.

"You too."

"Have a seat," he said. "Coffee machine's broken. I can't offer you anything at all. No, not true. I have gum in my desk." He pulled open the top drawer and rummaged around nervously. "Would you like some gum?"

"No, thank you," Edwin said.

I said the same, but then I looked over at Edwin. His demeanor had changed. He now looked at Lyle suspiciously.

"Lyle," Edwin said. "We've come to ask you a question and it might seem an odd one, but we've heard something recently and I knew the only way to get the answer was to come right to a source who might know."

Lyle sighed and sat back in his chair. "I've been expecting you."

"You have?"

"Of course. I . . . in fact, I should have come to talk to you myself. I just . . . well, I've been so busy. Anyway, I'm sorry for what has happened."

Edwin and I shared a look. Clearly, this wasn't going as Edwin might have expected. Me either, but I didn't know what I'd expected.

"Lyle," Edwin said. "I need you to tell me exactly what you're talking about. I'm not sure if it's the same thing we're here about, but I need you to be as forthcoming as you can be. All right?"

Lyle's eyes grew wide. In that instant, we could see his surprise too. We'd all come together with different levels of knowledge about something that was somehow connected. It was important that we all get up to the same speed as quickly as possible. Lyle clearly thought it unfortunate that he was going to have to be the one to do the work. But there was no getting out of it now. I sensed that if he tried to leave the room, Edwin would block all exits, if he got to them before I did.

Lyle sighed. "I'm talking about the revocation of the bookshop's business license, because of the failed building inspection, of course, Edwin. I'm so sorry for the turn of events."

Edwin stared at Lyle as he fell into concentrated thought. He spoke soon enough though.

"Lyle, until I received a phone call about a week ago, I had no idea there were potential problems with the bookshop's buildings. Can you please shed some light on what has happened?"

Lyle's face fell. "Oh dear, this is all so dicey."

"Nevertheless, I need you to tell me everything."

I didn't know what Edwin had on Lyle, but the man on the other side of the desk didn't fight. In fact, he seemed momentarily ashamed.

Lyle sighed. "We sent out formal notice in letter form, Edwin."

"No letter was received," Edwin said. "Did you ask for a signature or serve me legal papers?"

"Well, I thought we did."

No one was more vigilant than Rosie. She oversaw the bookshop's mail and was the one there, attending to customers, more than the rest of us. She opened and read everything, and then shredded whatever didn't need her or someone else's attention. If a notice had come by mail, Rosie would have sounded alarm bells. Those bells would have rung even louder if she'd been served legal papers.

"Things get lost in . . . oh, I don't know what might have

happened but bottom line, we've had to crack down on rules and regulations already in place, Edwin. The bookshop—the stairs you put in between the two buildings to connect them, to be specific—is not in code, or something like that. The business license is to be revoked. The shop will have to close as of the end of next month."

The words had come out in a jumble, but they were easy to understand, and, frankly, it was good to have a tiny bit of clarification. Okay, it was the spot in between the buildings that was the problem. Maybe we could still work with that.

"Lyle, I will simply fix whatever is out of code. I would have done so a long time ago if someone had just talked to me," Edwin said.

Edwin didn't say the words, "you fools" but they rang in my mind. I clamped my mouth closed.

And then Lyle shook his head. "No, Edwin, there's no fixing it. An inspector, apparently, deemed it too dangerous to try to fix."

"This is not good, Lyle."

"No, I suppose it isn't."

"I did receive approval to build the walkway, the stairs. I went through the proper channels, years ago when I first did the remodel."

"Aye?"

"Aye, I did. This was a long time ago, Lyle, but I remember the process we had to go though. We received the approval. I would never have taken on the project without approvals."

Lyle's eyes lit and he sat forward, placing his arms on the desk. "Do you still have the paperwork? Was there paperwork?"

"I believe there was, but I'm not sure where it would be now. I will find it. I will find it if that's what's needed."

"Good, well, that might help."

"Might?"

"It has been deemed that the safety of your two buildings has been compromised. Even if you received approval, that was a long time ago and the inspection showed issues. Times, expectations change."

"Have you seen the inspection?" I interrupted. "Can we see it."

"Oh. No, I haven't seen it and I don't have a copy, but the council has, or we wouldn't be at this point."

"Lyle, nothing has so much as settled with the structures in between the buildings," Edwin said. "I made sure it was built well, and built to last forever. However, we can do whatever we need to do to come back up to code, or appease the inspector. Whatever might be needed."

"It's too late, Edwin, the process has been set in motion. Your buildings are set to be torn down. If the vote goes through, there's no stopping it."

"What? That's unheard of. We value our old buildings. We keep them, take care of them. None of them gets torn down on purpose!" Edwin exclaimed.

Lyle lifted his hands. "And this is why I should have come to talk to you. I thought you were more in the loop."

"More in the loop? I should have been *the* loop. This is ridiculous, Lyle, and I think you know that."

I cleared my throat. The two men looked at me. "Henry Stewart. The man who was killed in the bombing two days ago. He was the one who set this in motion," I said. Lyle nodded. "He's been killed. I think that if for no other reason than respect, this should all be moved further down the council's calendar." It was maybe a heartless move, unsympathetic to

Henry's murder, but I had to try, and I hoped to diffuse Edwin's anger for a moment.

"I don't disagree with you, lass, but I'm not the one to decide that. That's for the council." Lyle paused as he looked at Edwin. "I'm so sorry for all of this, and I really should have come to talk to you. I apologize."

"There are no other meetings until next week?" Edwin said, anger still lining his words, but at least it wasn't quite as heated.

"Not that I'm aware of," Lyle said with a shrug.

Round and round we go, I thought.

It took a moment for us all to gather ourselves. The air was rife with anger and confusion. Almost in unison, we took deep, cleansing breaths.

Lyle was the first one to speak. He looked at me. "You look so much like her, you know. I was momentarily confused. Why would Edwin be walking into my office with Mary Stewart, the woman married to the man who wants, wanted, to tear down his bookshop? You are younger."

"We do look alike," I said. "How do you know her? Through knowing Henry?"

"Oh. Many people know Mary. She's vocal about her past lives." Lyle laughed.

"What does she know about the bookshop buildings being torn down?" I asked.

"I have no idea," Lyle said.

I would have bet Tom's wedding kilt that Lyle Mercado was lying. His face reddened ever so slightly, and he closed his mouth tightly, as if he wanted to keep truthful words locked inside.

Edwin and I didn't even try to hide our shared doubtful glances.

"How well did you know Henry?" Edwin asked.

Lyle paused, tapped his finger on the edge of his desk. "Henry and I got on all right. Until all of this occurred at least. I wasn't in agreement with the decisions being made. But you have to understand how these things work. Though I have power in my office, I can't make policies or laws."

"Lyle, what if I tore down and then rebuilt everything? I would do that if it came to it. I would hate every second of it, but I would do it."

"I'm sure, but . . . I just don't know, Edwin. The council is making the decisions here."

"Lyle," Edwin admonished. "This isn't making sense, and you know it. You also know that I have friends in high places. I will contact all of them and get to the bottom of this. It would behoove you to tell me what's really going on."

The more we learned, the less any of it made sense. Until something came to me, maybe the obvious thing.

"Lyle, someone wants that land. They want that space specifically," I said. "This is bigger than just some building codes, isn't it?"

"Not that I'm aware of, lass."

I thought as quickly as I could. "Does that spot have any sort of historic significance to Mary, Queen of Scots?"

"I guess I don't know," Lyle said.

"Nothing recorded," Edwin said.

"You think Henry might have been doing this for his wife?" Lyle said, sounding truly unsure.

"I think it's a possibility. Until we have an answer, it's a thought at least," I said.

Lyle looked at me a long moment. "I . . . I don't think Henry and Mary are like that."

"Like what?" Edwin said.

"I don't think they would ruin someone's livelihood, take someone's life's work just because Mary, Queen of Scots, happened to be at that location at one time. No, they'd be more inclined to get to know you first and then turn it into a party or something. Then try to get you to give them what they want."

Isn't that what had been set into motion?

I looked at Edwin. He thought the same thing. There had been a chance meeting, there had been a party. Maybe we hadn't made it far enough. Maybe getting what they wanted would have come next if Henry hadn't been killed.

But Edwin didn't want to point that out to Lyle. He changed the course of the conversation. "Did Henry have enemies that you know of, Lyle? Anyone who might want him killed?"

"Goodness, with all of this and his grand ideas, he might have had some disagreements," Lyle said. "I'm not aware of any enemies, but I really didn't know him *that* well." He looked at Edwin and then back at me and then back at Edwin. He cleared his throat. "This might sound terribly unfair, Edwin, but when I first heard about Henry, I thought that maybe you had something to do with his death . . . well, you have connections and all. I'm sorry, but it is what I considered."

"I'm sure the police will consider it too," Edwin said.

"For whatever it's worth, I'd be happy to vouch for you. We've had good tidings over the years."

"Well, if they speak with you, I wouldn't want anything more than the truth to be told. A killer needs to be found."

"There's nothing you can do to help fix this?" I said to Lyle.

"The best I can do is look into it and let you know." Lyle worked hard not to sound defeated.

"That would be appreciated," Edwin said.

Lyle nodded sadly. "All right. I'm sorry you didn't know more. Something's gone wrong here, and any part my office played in that is regrettable. I'm sorry about Henry. No matter that I might have disagreed with him regarding some things, he didn't deserve to be killed. It's a sad thing."

I looked at Lyle over the desk. I wasn't sure which side he was on.

We didn't learn much more from him. In fact, Edwin became so distracted by his own thoughts I decided he wasn't really listening anymore, and we just needed to leave.

Making excuses that we had to go, I led us out of the offices, but just as we stepped outside, I had to regroup again.

FOURTEEN

"Dina?" I said as I opened an umbrella.

Her head was down looking at some papers she was holding. The rain was light but she didn't have an umbrella and I could see water spots on the papers. She looked up and moved her hair off her forehead. "Oh . . . Delaney, hello."

Her eyes were rimmed in red and her nose was swollen.

"This is my boss, Edwin, we're both so sorry about your uncle."

"Thank you." She sniffed. "It's so terribly awful."

"Lass, deepest condolences," Edwin said with a polite nod of his head.

Dina wiped her hand under her nose and sniffed again. "And life goes on." She looked around, but I couldn't tell if she was looking for something specific or if she just needed a second. We waited patiently. "I forgot to pay my yearly fee. I'm late. Just got this late notice today." She waved the papers but I couldn't make out any specific writing. "I had no choice but to hurry down and take care of it." She looked at me. "But I can't stop crying. I'm . . ."

I reached out to put my hand on her arm, but she pulled it away. She sniffed again and then walked around us.

"Please don't mind me," she said over her shoulder. "I'm embarrassed, but I'm all right."

Edwin and I watched her hurry inside.

"Should I go after her?" I said.

"I don't know," Edwin said.

"Wait for me a second?" I said and handed Edwin the umbrella.

I hurried back inside, speed-walked down the hallway, and pulled open the door we'd gone through. The room was much fuller now, customers were filed into two crowded lines. I didn't see Dina, and there wasn't a way to ask anyone if they'd seen an upset woman. I left and looked around the hallway, spying the loo a few doors away. I went to turn the knob, but the door was locked. I lifted my hand to knock, but I hesitated. Maybe she did just need a moment. I wasn't even sure she was inside, but I thought she probably was.

I opened my mouth to say something but we didn't know each other well enough for me to find the right words. Finally, I just placed my hand on the door and sighed. I wanted to see her antique shop anyway. I would track her down later and see if there was anything I could do for her. Sometimes people just need to break down a little without being held responsible for it.

With one last look down the hallway, I finally rejoined Edwin outside.

"How'd it go?" He moved the brollie so it was over me more than him.

I shook my head. "Didn't see her. I think she went into the loo, locked the door."

"Understandable."

"She has an antique shop. We probably have a lot in common. I might go see her later."

"Aye?" he said. "Where's the shop?"

"Cowgate."

"I knew she looked familiar. She and I and her husband, I believe, had some dealings some years back. They are a lovely couple."

But I blinked at his tone. "It sounds like you aren't sure about something. The dealings or if they're a lovely couple?"

"No, I'm sure about both, I just can't remember what the ultimate result of our time together was. I sense there was some contention. I'll think about it."

"Okay. Let me know."

"I will. All right, let's go talk to Rosie, see if she's forgotten to give me any mail, or if, by chance, she has that construction paperwork from all those years ago. I need to be armed with as much as I can, and she'll be good at helping with that. Any luck with the Burgess Ticket?"

"None, but I haven't given it my all yet. I will. I see why it might be good to have."

"Ta, lass."

I remembered that I still hadn't called Mary. But now I wanted to talk to Rosie first. Despite the tragedy Mary was living, I still didn't want to believe I had somehow been set up for something. Just like Edwin, I wanted more information.

I hoped Rosie could offer some certainty, but I didn't count on it.

———

"No! We have never, ever received such a notice. I'm certain of it," Rosie exclaimed.

"I didn't think so, Rosie love," Edwin said.

We were all in the front of the shop, Rosie sitting behind her desk. I was pacing. Hamlet had already sent me a couple of frowns, probably wishing I would stop moving so much. I'd tried, I really had, but I couldn't stop.

I'd heard Edwin use the term of endearment for Rosie only one other time since I'd been in Scotland. She'd been upset about something then too, though I didn't remember what it had been.

"And I will find the paperwork for the approval of the construction," she continued. "I don't know where it is offhand. It was ages ago. But I never throw anything away."

"I know," Edwin said.

"This is ridiculous," she said. "They simply cannae have the power tae do such a thing."

"It *is* bizarre," Hamlet added. "There must be some sort of law that will protect our rights to do business here, particularly if the buildings are out of code and you agree to fix them. I really don't get it. I will see if we've missed something from a legal perspective."

"Something's going on," I said. "Something we can't understand because we don't have all the pieces. Things have been kept from us, purposefully. We'll figure it out."

Though I was having a hard time standing still, I'd calmed down a bit on the walk back to the bookshop. The buildings that housed both sides, the dark and the light, were still standing. And while they were still there, there was a chance we could find a way to save them. But we needed to hurry.

Hope *was* coming back little bit by little bit. We *would* figure this out.

"Aye, Hamlet, research the laws, but we need an attorney. A good one. A mean one," Rosie said. "Ruthless."

"Aye," Edwin said. "I think I have just the man in mind. Excuse me while I make a couple phone calls."

Edwin stood and took the stairs up and over to the dark side. I watched him, watched the floor he walked on, the walls he walked next to. I'd never once felt like anything was unstable. Nothing was uneven, everything was straight, level. Nothing was wrong with any of the structures' integrity.

After he went through the door, I turned to Hamlet. "While you're researching, is there any way for you to find out if this place, this location once had anything to do with Mary, Queen of Scots? Did she like the view of the castle from here? Did she have tea here? Did she sneeze in the vicinity? Something, anything."

"I see where ye're going," Rosie said. "Mary Stewart wanted this place for something and her husband was going to get it."

"I can try," Hamlet said, "but it's highly unlikely that anything would be noted that way. We don't know as much about our historical figures as we claim to. But I'll scour whatever I can find."

"Thanks." I fell into thought.

Rosie stood. She picked up Hector and joined me at the front of the shop, bringing my pacing to a stop. She handed Hector to me. I held him close.

"It's going tae be all right," she said. She wasn't usually the one doing the comforting, but she took on the role well.

"If this doesn't work, Rosie, I'm going to try to convince

Edwin to open up somewhere else," I said. I thought I heard Hector harrumph.

Rosie's eyebrows lifted. "Aye? Well, I dinnae want tae disappoint ye, but he's auld, set in his ways, and he loves this place. There's not another for him."

I thought about the bookshop in some shiny new location with pristine walls and floors. That would be awful. Not for a new bookshop, one that hadn't yet lived its life, but for this one, it would. The blood, the vital organs of The Cracked Spine were inside these lathe-and-plaster walls, these old shelves, that ladder. The marble floor was in terrible shape, but it was also one of the most beautiful floors I'd ever seen. Tears came to my eyes as I remembered the first time I walked into the shop and saw those floors, how scared I'd been, how, when I'd seen the ladder that rolled up and down the shelves, I'd so quickly felt at home. The light was bad, the furniture old and worn. It was the most perfect place ever.

"I guess you're right," I said to Rosie. "This is the only place the bookshop could ever be."

"Aye, lass. Aye."

I pulled out my cell phone. A resolve had come over me. I dialed Mary's number.

"Hello?" a voice said, but I didn't think it was Mary's.

"Yes, I'm returning Mary's call. Delaney Nichols from The Cracked Spine."

"Aye? It's Eloise, Delaney. Mary's resting but I'm happy to let her know you called."

Sometimes reaching out and taking someone's hand is the beginning of a journey.

The bookish voice didn't come from the book about Queen Elizabeth. It came from Hamlet's inspirational calendar. I looked at the back table and saw him there, peering at something on his laptop. His tear-away calendar was behind him. I must have read the words recently.

"Yes, thanks. Eloise . . ." I said.

"Aye?"

Maybe I did need to get going on the journey of knowing Eloise; she and I seemed to find each other easily. "Any chance you have time for dinner tonight?"

"Well, I suppose I do. I don't think Mary will be up to attending. Should I invite Gretchen?"

"Yes, please. I'll invite Tom."

We solidified plans and I told her I'd see her in a couple hours. I wondered if Mary would wake up and want to join us. I wasn't sure if that would be a good or a bad idea.

"That should be interesting," Rosie said when I hung up.

"Want to come?"

"I need tae search for those approval forms and the Burgess Ticket. Not this time, but I'll expect tae hear aboot it."

"Of course."

It wasn't long before Tom came through the door. He saw the expression on my face and stopped in the entryway.

"Uh-oh, what happened?" he asked.

"I'll tell you all about it on the way," I said as I tried to look less terrified. "We're going to dinner."

FIFTEEN

On the way, Tom had asked me why I'd wanted to ask Eloise and Gretchen out to dinner. I hadn't gone into detail about my bookish voices with him yet, so I didn't mention that a calendar had told me to. I'd shrugged and said it was just a feeling I'd had. He thought that was a good enough reason. However, it was then I decided we needed to have a conversation about the bookish voices. It wasn't technically a lie that I hadn't shared that quirky part of me, but quirky things were supposed to be shared with significant others. I wished I'd told him already.

We'd met at a pizza place right at the top of Victoria Street. When I first arrived in Scotland, I thought a pizza place didn't quite fit with my idea of Scottish food choices, but I'd come to accept that it was okay for restaurants in Scotland to prepare and serve international fare.

Though still tinged with grief, Eloise and Gretchen seemed happy to be joining us; happy to have a distraction maybe. We were all quickly comfortable with each other too, Eloise greeting me with a hug and a quick, "See, I told you, once you meet someone through Mary, you're friends for life."

Once the pizza had been served, I asked Gretchen, "Did you see Mary too? How's she doing?"

Gretchen said, "I'm not as close with those weirdos as Eloise is."

"Oh."

She chewed a bite of pizza and quickly stuffed it into her cheek. "I mean the past-life people. They are a strange group, and since Henry is—was—with Mary, they weren't my favorite people to hang out with. Eloise had to drag me to dinner the other night. But you were all fine."

"I've been Mary's doctor for years," Eloise said. "I was the very first person she told about her past lives, many years ago. It's okay for me to share; she tells people that all the time."

"I didn't know until much later, after they became friends and we started socializing together. I took an immediate disliking to Mary as she did to me. We've become friendlier over the years, but she and Eloise are much closer," Gretchen said.

"Would you still be friends if you weren't her doctor?" Tom asked Eloise.

"I think so, but we probably would never have established a relationship. Gretchen and I have been together thirty years. I met Mary about twenty years ago, in a clothing shop in Glasgow. She fainted, and told me she didn't have a doctor. I've been her physician ever since, and once she started talking about her past lives, she felt like she could trust me with whatever she wanted to say, get it all off her chest maybe. It was a burden she carried for years."

"Meeting Eloise opened the gates for her," Gretchen said with a hand flourish.

I wondered if Gretchen and Mary truly had become friendlier toward each other or if Gretchen just pretended.

"What has she told you about her lives?" I asked.

"Can't tell you any more than I have. Doctor-patient privilege and all," Eloise said.

"Of course," I said. "Were you Henry's doctor too?"

"No. In fact, I don't think Henry had been to a doctor in years, until recently. Mary mentioned that he'd gone to see someone about his knees but we never talked about it much."

"Tell me about your art studio," Tom asked Gretchen.

"I have a shop and a studio together." Gretchen smiled and then continued, "I sculpt animals, smaller than actual size."

"Where's your place?" Tom asked.

Gretchen sat back in her chair and wiped the corner of her mouth with a napkin. "I wondered when you'd ask that."

There was nothing light or fun in her tone. Almost in tandem, Tom and I cocked our heads as we looked at her.

"That's why you asked us to dinner, right?" Gretchen said.

"I don't understand," I said.

"Gretch, I don't think they know. I think they were just being sociable."

"Really," I said as Tom and I shared a glance, "we don't understand. Have we offended?"

Gretchen's expression softened. "Perhaps I'm being sensitive. Never mind."

Eloise gave one stress-lined laugh. "I think it's okay to tell them, hun. The police will clear you."

"I think so too, but I don't want anyone to accuse me of anything. . . ."

"Tom and I aren't quick to accuse," I said.

"All right." Gretchen sat forward, pushed her plate back, and put her arms on the table. "I think Henry was trying to shut down my shop, my whole studio."

"Let me guess. Was there an upcoming vote? An alleged bad report from an inspector?" I said, anxiety zipping through me. Is this why my intuition wanted me to make friends with these women?

Gretchen shook her head. "No, nothing like that. I received notice that I was to present something called a Burgess Ticket. . . ."

"Yes, the things that were once delivered in miniature coffin-like boxes?" I asked.

"That's right," Eloise said, but she didn't look at me. I wondered if she remembered our conversation on the bus about Henry angering people.

"Anyway, I don't have anything like that," Gretchen continued. "My studio and shop are in an old building that has been home to many different businesses over the years. There's no way to track down the original business owner, or maybe even what the original business was."

"There aren't city records?" I said.

"Not going back that far, not that I could find. The tickets go back to the *eighteenth* century. I guess some people kept them, but I didn't even know about them to inquire when I purchased the building. Since I don't have one, I have to spend a fortune to bring the building up to today's standards. Who's ever heard of such a thing? We are all about our old buildings, our history. Anyway, I think Henry was behind all of it."

"What are you going to do?" I asked.

"I don't know. I thought I would see if the council switches gears now that Henry is dead." Gretchen shrugged again. "I have an alibi though, I need to make that clear. I haven't talked to the police or anything, but I have an alibi for the morning that Henry was killed. I mean, I would never kill anyone anyway, but I was setting up a presentation at a local school when the car bomb exploded."

I wasn't sure that made much of an alibi. Where was she when the bomb was planted? Where were any of us? Supposedly all of us were home in our beds asleep, but I didn't know when the police thought the device had been put on the car. No one had questioned any of us at the bookshop; Gretchen either, it sounded like.

"Where's your studio and shop?" I asked.

"In Cowgate, right next to Dina's antique shop."

I slid a napkin over to her. "Write down the address? I want to come look closely at the building."

She looked at the napkin and back at me. "I don't understand."

I looked at Tom. He nodded. "Let me share with you our situation. Then you might understand."

I explained everything, giving them every detail I possibly could. Even if one of them had killed Henry, we were on the same team, of sorts. What had been Henry's motivation for wanting to close any business?

"That's terrible," Gretchen said when I finished. "That bookshop has been around forever. I've been in a few times over the years. Maybe the vote won't happen now. I'm sorry if that sounds unsympathetic."

It wasn't just Gretchen, we all felt guilty about looking at any bright side to Henry being gone.

"I think it's set in stone," I said.

"Go to the meeting, fight," Gretchen said.

"Oh, I will. We will," I said.

"Have you talked to Mikey about all of this?" Eloise asked.

"No," I said. "Why?"

"He's a councilor too," Eloise added. "That wasn't mentioned at dinner?"

"What?" I said. "I had no idea."

"Me either," Tom said.

"He's the one who told Gretchen and me that it was Henry who had started the whole mess with the Burgess Tickets," Eloise said.

"He probably knows about The Cracked Spine too," I said.

Eloise shrugged. "You'll have to ask him. I remember wondering why Henry didn't mention he was a councilor. He's usually . . . well, he usually liked people to know that about him. Mikey doesn't talk much no matter what, so I'm not surprised he didn't say anything."

"Do you think Mary knows about all of this?" I asked.

Eloise thought a long moment. "I really don't. She hasn't brought it up to me, and she tells me everything. Besides, she would have been angry with Henry for doing anything to jeopardize Gretchen's business. We were going to talk to Mary, Henry, and Mikey about it the night of the dinner, but then you all showed and it didn't feel right to bring it up, and then Henry was killed."

"Is that why there was a strain in the air when we came upstairs?" I asked.

"Probably," Eloise said.

I thought about telling them the state I'd seen Dina in earlier, but I didn't. It suddenly occurred to me, though, that she might have been at the licensing office because of something similar to what The Cracked Spine and Gretchen were going through. Was there more to her emotions than a late payment? What had those papers really been? Was she upset because of her uncle's murder or those papers, or both? Surely, Henry hadn't been trying to shut down his niece's business too?

It was tumultuous to have bad feelings for someone who had been killed, someone who had recently hosted a lovely dinner where you'd had a good time and enjoyed delicious food. But I was now more convinced that my meeting Mary and us being invited to their castle was some sort of setup. What I wasn't so sure of was if Mary was a willing participant in the setup, or a convenient pawn.

"Eloise, when you left Mary today, was she still resting?" I asked.

"She was. I left a note that you'd called though. She'll get back to you."

"I'm sure," I said. She'd called me first after all. However, I suddenly wished I hadn't stalled in calling her back. If not to tell me Inspector Buchanan was going to ask me some questions, what did she want?

The front of the restaurant was a long row of windows. That was one of the features I liked so much about the place, the people watching. I looked out through them now and saw the same sorts of people I always saw; tourists, locals (those who didn't look around with awe, but simply made their way along), and the random man in a kilt. There weren't enough kilt-wearing men in Scotland anymore.

It had rained recently, and things glimmered. The light from the old-fashioned streetlights sparkled everywhere, off the brick buildings, the cobblestone road, the old shopfronts.

This part of Edinburgh wasn't about modern and new, but old and traditional. However, this part of Edinburgh was also built right on top of another version, an older version. There were probably even Burgess Tickets buried somewhere under the surface.

Time marched on. Things changed.

Was it time for the bookshop to close?

No! I thought as my dinner partners laughed about something I hadn't paid attention to. My eyes landed on someone who was walking past the window, looking at a book they carried. I didn't know the stranger, but I couldn't help but wonder what he was reading, and if he'd maybe picked the book up from the greatest bookshop on the planet.

Oh, it couldn't close. It just couldn't.

I turned back to the pizza and our new friends, grateful that we stopped talking about all the sad things, and moved the conversation to happier things, things new friends typically discussed.

But even as we enjoyed dinner, time continued to march on all around us.

SIXTEEN

I checked my phone again as Joshua walked toward me. Mary hadn't called yet, but it was still early in the morning.

It was rare that Joshua and I didn't meet inside the museum, but he'd asked to meet outside it today. His long legs moved swiftly my direction and I smiled at the Gryffindor scarf around his neck. I hadn't thought about it before, but with his dark hair and black framed glasses, he was only a lightning bolt to the forehead away from looking like a tall version of the beloved Harry Potter. I was surprised I hadn't seen it before.

Joshua was surely magical, in that he knew so much about so many things. I enjoyed our sibling-like friendship, and I dreaded the day one of his PhDs would take him someplace other than the National Museum of Scotland only a few blocks from the bookshop. Mostly, I cherished his friendship, but I also liked his brain too. I had some questions for it today; stuff about Mary, Queen of Scots, of course, including the papers I'd read about, the ones Mary had written herself and had been found in a box in the basement of the museum.

The café's outside seating area was covered by a wide canopy, but if I aimed my face in the right direction, I could feel the warm sun peeking around some puffy clouds.

"Hello, my friend," Joshua said as he joined me at the table. "Where have you been? Oh, that's right, on a honeymoon. Was it lovely?"

Joshua hadn't been able to attend the small wedding.

"It was." I stood.

We hugged and then sat across from each other. The café was humming pleasantly with other customers, but not too many. We shared quick personal updates that were peppered with the sorts of things we always talked about—old things we'd read about that might have been discovered at archeological sites throughout the world as well as inquiries on each other's circle of people. Joshua and Rosie had struck up a fast friendship and I was surprised that she'd already told him about our dinner with Mary and Henry and their friends. I was glad they'd found a grandmother-grandson relationship with each other.

"She has quite the obsession," Joshua said, speaking about Mary Stewart after I told him (retold him from my perspective instead of Rosie's) about my time with the woman with the past lives and her murdered husband.

"Even Lyle, the business license guy mentioned it that way, an obsession. Do you think you've ever met her?" I asked.

"Not that I recall. No, in fact, I would have remembered her, particularly if she looks as much like you as you and Rosie say."

"We could be sisters."

"Not mother and daughter?"

"She's twenty years older, so it's feasible, but sisters seems more appropriate. So, what about the recent Mary, Queen of Scots' papers that have been found?" I asked.

Joshua smiled. "They are extraordinary. Well, they are both ordinary and extraordinary. Notes, journals, lists about some of the things she had to do as queen, things such as having taxes collected and such. But still, even ordinary things are interesting if you know they were written by Mary."

"What shape were they in when you found them?"

"Surprisingly good. They weren't bothered for centuries maybe. They aren't overly fragile, though we're treating them as if they are. Do you want me to give you a secret look one of these days?"

"Only if it won't get you in trouble." I really hoped it wouldn't get him in trouble.

"I'll let you know," he said. But then he fell into thought.

"What?" I asked a long moment later. "What's on your mind?"

"Mary was young when Queen Elizabeth had her executed. Only forty-four."

"Okay."

"Well, and don't share this opinion with others because some Scottish people won't like it. Admittedly, my opinion is also jaded by time and how things have changed over the centuries, but . . . on one hand, Mary was a brilliant queen and did more than most would have when being born into her circumstances and position. She was strong where others might have weakened. She never let go of the idea that she was the rightful queen of England, well, not publicly at least. But there was one area where she wasn't the brightest of bulbs. If Mary had just given up her Catholicism and even *pretended* to be Protestant earlier than it seemed she was going to attempt to do, I do think there was a chance her life might have been easier, probably longer."

"She might have become the rightful queen of England too?"

Joshua shook his head. "I don't know if it would have gone that far, but she *might* have lived longer, perhaps not have been imprisoned for so much of her life. Ultimately and 'officially,' Mary was put to death because she was accused of conspiring to assassinate Queen Elizabeth. The letters used as evidence were probably forged."

"Letters?"

"Yes, the Casket Letters, they are called, because they were discovered in a box that looked like a casket."

"Like the Burgess Tickets?" I said, guessing that Joshua would know what I was talking about.

"Ah, you know about the Burgess Tickets." He smiled. "No, the Freedom Caskets were smaller, I believe. Casket-like things just make everything more interesting maybe. Anyway, the eight letters and sonnets were allegedly written by Mary to her third husband, the Earl of Bothwell. It was thought that Bothwell was responsible for the murder of Mary's second husband, Darnley. In them, Mary commits treason toward Elizabeth as well as encourages Bothwell to hurry up and kill Darnley. To the end, Mary denied writing them."

"Where are the letters?"

"Copies are reproduced online and such, but the originals

are lost to time, I'm afraid, probably destroyed by someone who didn't want it proven that Mary didn't write them."

"Many people conspired against her?"

"Yes, including many that she trusted."

"That's too bad."

"Mary was fierce. I wouldn't have wanted her to be less fierce, just maybe more . . . self-preserving."

I nodded. "I get what you're saying. If the letters were forged, back then there was no reliable way to validate or in-validate them other than by sight. Handwriting analysis didn't exist, at least in its current form." I thought about when Rosie and I, on the internet via my cell phone, found an old letter Mary had written. She'd signed her name "Marie" and the M had been noticeable. It had taken us only seconds.

"Oh, I'm sure it was an awful time to live, but not as awful for royalty, even for a queen who had to be locked in a castle or two."

"Do you think she killed her second husband? Mary, Queen of Scots, I mean? Conspired to at least?" I said.

Joshua fell into thought again, but I didn't think it was because he was searching for an answer, I suspected it was because he had to organize all the facts in his mind about the subject matter. His mind overflowed with all manner of things.

"Lord Darnley, Henry, was not a good man, but no, I don't think she played any part in his murder. You do know she was also, for a time, queen consort of France, don't you?"

"When she was younger?"

"Yes. Her father was the king of Scotland, but he died of some such thing I'm sure we could take care of easily nowadays, and she ascended to the throne when she was only six days old. A deal was made that she would marry a future king of France, and she was sent off to the land of truffles and baguettes when she was five or so. Her mother stayed in Scotland and served as one of her regent rulers. One of her father's illegitimate sons later acted as regent for Mary's son too. Moray." He paused and I heard the ominous tone when he said the name. "But Moray wasn't on Mary's side. I do think he and his Protestant leanings caused problems and hastened Mary's execution. He might have even been somehow involved in the Casket Letters. Anyway, regarding France, she married the Dauphin of France, Francis, when they were young, fifteen and sixteen, I believe. He was small and appeared unhealthy next to her beauty, unusual height, and robust health, but from what I've read they got along splendidly, enjoyed each other's company. Nevertheless, just over a year and a half or so into the marriage, the Dauphin died of a middle ear infection that turned ugly, leaving Mary grief stricken. Nine months later, she returned to Scotland. She'd been in France since she was a child, keep that in mind. France was all about Catholicism, so Mary was too. She spoke French most of the time, but she could also speak English and Scots. I think what I'm trying to say is that she was groomed and manipulated, but no matter how smart she was, she was never given the tools to fight fairly, or make many of her own decisions early on."

I nodded. "But some thought she was the rightful heir to the throne of England? How would that have worked?"

Joshua sighed. "Okay. Henry VIII was such a force. A giant pain in the arse for many, but a strong, strong leader. You are probably aware he had many wives?"

"Of course."

"Very good. Mary Tudor—this is a whole different Mary than the Marys we've been talking about. Mary Tudor was the only child of Henry's first wife, Catherine of Aragon, to survive until adulthood, and was the queen of England for five years after her younger half *brother* died. She was all for Catholicism, and tried to reverse her father's reformations, which were definitely more Protestant." Joshua sighed. "Mary Tudor only reigned for five years, though, before she died. Who was to be the next ruler? Her only surviving sibling at the time was Elizabeth I, who was, indeed, the daughter of Henry VIII, but also of his second wife, Anne Boleyn; a marriage that was annulled—and that's the sticking point, right there. Here also was Mary Stuart—Mary, Queen of Scots—she was a surviving legitimate descendant of Henry *VII*, the first monarch of the House of Tudor. It seemed to some that Mary should have been the queen because she was a *legitimate* descendant."

"The 'legitimacy' was used, and then it became a battle of two religions?"

"Well, in a way, yes. The Catholics thought Mary should be the queen of England, the Protestants thought Elizabeth I was right where she should be, on the throne. Much blood was shed because of the differences."

"Elizabeth I lived and ruled a long time, right?"

"Oh, yes, and she was quite the queen too. It's hard to know if she ever regretted what she did to Mary, but if she believed Mary was out to kill her, she did what she thought she should."

"You don't believe it though, that Elizabeth really thought Mary wanted to kill her? I can hear it in your voice."

Joshua shook his head. "Impossible to know, but, no, I think it was all a setup, and I'm on Mary's side of that one."

"It was all so different then. Different things were important."

"Correct," Joshua said.

Last night, after Tom and I had gotten home from dinner, I

looked closely at some of the online pictures of the queen, and the similarity was undeniable. Weirdly, though, I saw it more with Mary than with me. Mary and I looked alike but I'd created some sort of distance between the queen and me.

"Do you know anything about a crown-shaped birthmark?" I asked.

"What?" Joshua laughed.

"Did Mary, Queen of Scots, have one?"

"Gosh, not that I'm aware of. That's a wonderful idea though, that all royalty be marked with a special birthmark. I've read such fictional stories before."

"I think Mary has too. She has one and thinks that's proof that she'd reincarnated."

Joshua half-smiled, half-rolled his eyes.

I continued, "I wonder what *would* prove it though. Is there something she could know that would prove she was once Mary, Queen of Scots?"

"That sounds like an impossible thing."

"I suppose so."

"You are disappointed."

"Well, it would be kind of awesome, wouldn't it? To have her here with us? Not that she'd get a second chance to rule England or anything, but having insight into those days would be kind of cool. She might have *memories,* but right now I don't feel like I can believe a word she says. If I could know . . ."

"Our time-travel games!"

Joshua and I often wished we could travel back in time, to all times, and just stay for a few minutes. Both of us were too happy with the technology of the present day to want to stay away for long.

"Yes, something like that," I said.

"How else can I help find the proof? Can I break in somewhere, spy on someone?" Joshua asked. "I'm always up for an adventure."

"No, I'll never ask you to do something like that again." I still felt guilty about asking his help for something sneaky I'd had up my sleeve a while back.

"That's a shame."

We finished breakfast and made a plan for me to come over and see one of the museum's newest displays, as well as hopefully a time when he could sneak me a look at the queen's handwritten notes.

We said goodbye and I watched him walk away toward the museum. He'd grown up so much in the last year. A sense of sisterly pride washed over me. I hadn't learned anything that might help me with Mary Stewart, but it didn't hurt to be armed with the information, just in case. Just in case of what, I wasn't sure, but still . . . besides, time with Joshua was always fun.

I checked my phone again. No calls at all. I took off for another museum, one I hadn't been to yet, but one I'd been wanting to see since close to the first moment I'd arrived in Scotland.

SEVENTEEN

The Writers' Museum was located off the Royal Mile on Lady Stair's Close, an alleyway named after another Elizabeth, the Lady of Stair, the widow of John Dalrymple, the first Earl of Stair. A museum dedicated to Scotland's literary heroes: Robert Burns, Sir Walter Scott, and Robert Lewis Stevenson, I knew it would be a wonderful place.

Also, maybe, for me a noisy place. I'd read lots of Burns, Scott, and Stevenson. Their words were in my head and might all want to talk at once.

And not just *inside* the museum, but the courtyard outside it as well. Of course, I'd heard about Makers' Court, the place with paving stones inscribed with literary quotes. I'd managed to get my voices under control in the bookshop, but I fully expected them to pipe up once I entered the courtyard.

But when I did enter it, all was quiet. At least the bookish voices were quiet. I could hear the faint noises of traffic, both from vehicles and pedestrians' voices on the Royal Mile, but I was able to read some of the quotes, unbothered.

Violet Jacob had said, *There's muckle lyin yont the Tay that Mair to me nor life.*

I shook my head at the Scots. I'd need Elias, Aggie, Rosie, or maybe Hamlet for that one.

But Robert Henryson had also been quoted in Scots. I could understand his better, *Blissed be the sempill lyfe withoutin dreid.*

"True that, Robert," I said aloud. "True that."

I read as I made my way to the front door, pleased I'd been able to keep my intuition at bay. It had been talking to me about things I thought were associated with queens, but maybe there was nothing here to learn. That might be disappointing, after all.

I pulled the door and went through.

Once inside I closed my eyes and stood still. I listened so hard I could feel the strain. There were no voices. Until there was one.

"May I help you?" it said.

My eyes sprung open. "Oh, hello, yes, I'm . . . do I need to purchase a ticket?"

The woman reminded me of the current Queen of England, Queen Elizabeth II. Topped off with perfectly styled gray hair and eyes that twinkled happily behind proper glasses.

"You look so much like the current queen," I said.

"I get that a lot, though she wouldnae be caught deed with my accent." The woman winked. "Laila Brisem." She extended her hand.

"Delaney Nichols."

"Welcome. Ye've come a long way."

"A year ago, I did. I've lived here since then."

"Aye? A transplant. Come along and have a look around.

Ye've picked a quiet time. No tickets. Donations are always welcome. See what we're worth, leave what ye'd like."

I did want to see the museum, but I had come to ask questions about Mary Stewart. I didn't see how I could jump right in though. I'd look for the right moment.

Unfortunately, I was left to tour on my own, Laila telling me she'd meet up with me in a wee bit. I fell into my museum meander, but kept telling myself to step it up, move a little faster today.

I came upon a hand-carved chess set. It was as I stood there looking at it that I thought I might have finally heard a bookish voice.

Checkmate!

Or maybe that was a ghost. Probably just my imagination, I decided as I looked around.

I continued my meander to Robert Burns's writing desk. I smiled as I took in its simplicity. A small desk with a green felt covered and angled lift top, there were no drawers or file cabinets, but only a place where Mr. Burns could place quill to parchment and create magnificent works of art.

I thought about my desk in the warehouse, having seen the likes of kings and queens. Oh, it was a beautiful piece of old furniture. Without warning, I became overwhelmed by the fortuitous adventures my life had seen over the last year. I sniffed and blinked away the flood of emotions. I hadn't had one of those moments for a long time, but evidently they would still happen every once and a while.

I moved along as my attention was drawn to the wall above the desk. Inside a gold-rimmed frame, I'd finally come upon my first real Burgess Ticket, and it had belonged to Robert Burns.

"I'll be," I said quietly as I leaned forward for a closer look.

"What do ye think?" Laila came up behind me.

"Hello. This is a Burgess Ticket?"

"Aye. Do ye ken what that is?"

"I think so. It's kind of like a business license."

"Och. In a way. At one time, they meant verra much to the holder. A considerable asset. It allowed merchants and craftsmen to work in a burgh—this one is from 1787, Dumfries—but it also gave the holder certain rights, including the title of freeman and allowing their children to be educated in the local school or academy. They were a verra big deal."

"I see," I said.

It was a certificate covered in difficult to decipher calligraphy. It could have been mistaken for any sort of certificate I'd ever seen.

Laila continued, "This was an honorary ticket, but later Mr. Burns did reside in Dumfries."

"So interesting." I turned my attention back to Laila.

"Aye."

"I love museums so much," I said. "I have a friend at the history museum. He and I spend hours looking at exhibits there together."

"I ken what ye mean."

Seemed like a good enough time for some small lies. "I was just there last week and was approached by a woman who works here, maybe volunteers. That's why I'm here today. She reminded me about this place. Anyway, she looks like me." I looked at Laila.

"Aye, I thought I saw the resemblance, but I wasnae sure what tae say. Ye've met our Mary then? Mary Stewart. Did ye ken she thinks she was once Mary, Queen of Scots?"

"I do. Is she here today?"

"No," Laila said sadly. "She's had a tragedy."

"Oh, I'm sorry."

Laila sized me up, but only for a few seconds. "Did ye hear about the car being blown tae smithereens?"

"I did."

"Terrifying."

"Yes."

"T'was her husband who was kil't. Henry."

"Oh, no!" I put my fingers to my mouth and was slightly ashamed by my act, but not enough to stop. "That's terrible. I'm so sorry. Did you know him?"

Laila nodded. "I met him a time or two."

"What was he like?" I asked sympathetically, still slightly ashamed of myself.

She shook her head. "I'm not sure I ken. We only had brief hellos. One time he smiled, the other time he'd come tae pick her up, I think he was impatient for Mary tae finish her day. He wanted tae go home."

"I see."

"I know he worked for the city of Edinburgh and I know he took his job verra seriously. Mary recently told me she was worrit about him, that he'd become . . . what was the word she used? 'Obsessed,' I think. Aye, he'd become obsessed with a task. She thought he was working too hard."

"What was it?" There was that word again, "*obsession*."

"I dinnae ken. I did try tae ask her, but she either ignored the question or didnae quite know what was happening. She was worrit though, I could tell. I wish I'd pushed more. Maybe that's the reason he was kil't. He was kil't, ye ken. The papers are saying it was murder."

"I'm sure the police will let us in on more as time goes on.

They'll figure it out," I said. "Also, Mary mentioned she'd gotten in some trouble here at the museum?"

That lie and question were based on a brief moment at the dinner party. Mary had mentioned that she had been welcomed back to the museum after Dina had seemed surprised that she'd been allowed to go back. The conversation had moved onto other things, but it was a moment that had stuck out to me then, and later too as I'd tried to contemplate what it had meant.

Laila's eyes opened wide. "Aye? She told ye that? I didnae think she'd tell a soul."

I'd been onto something, though I needed more. "She said it had all worked out, that she never really stole anything." That was the biggest lie of them all, but go big or go home.

"Och, not stole. No, she just shouldnae been exploring is all. She was looking in drawers and such." Laila looked at the desk next to us, but she didn't say anything about it being one of the pieces of furniture Mary had explored. "They're not to be touched. She was caught a few times, said she couldnae help herself, but *needed* tae ken what was inside them. We have given her no more chances. If she's caught again, we'll ask her tae leave permanently."

Well that had worked. "Oh, yes! That's right. She told me she was going to behave now."

Laila sent me a shameful bat of her eyes. "I called Mary and asked her not tae come in. I expressed my condolences, of course, but I told her not tae come in until things settle down or the killer is caught. Am I a terrible person? I just didn't know what tae do. Mary's such an odd creature, and Henry kil't—by a bomb! Gracious, I was worrit about the safety of everyone here. Is that reediculous?"

It was a little ridiculous, but I would never say that to her.

"Not at all. Safety first," I said.

"Aye. I suppose."

"Do you believe in reincarnation?" I asked.

She looked at me. "Sweet lass, I'm old enough tae believe in everything and nothing. You'll understand that when ye reach my age."

"Anything is possible?"

"*Everything* is possible, and nothing should surprise anyone, lass."

I nodded. "I think I understand."

More visitors came through the front door. Laila perked up and smiled to greet them. She turned back to me with another smile and told me she hoped to see me again someday soon.

I hadn't seen very much of the museum, not nearly enough in fact, but I told her goodbye and then left, happy to have seen the Burgess Ticket and the writing desk, and maybe heard someone playing chess. I left a sizable donation in the box before I walked out the door.

Why was Henry so *obsessed* with closing businesses? It all still seemed so random. None of the inscribed pavers were talking, even when I sent them my most stern look as I plopped my hands on my hips.

And then I had an idea. It came to me in a flash.

Sometimes, you just have to go back to the beginning.

I hurried back to where I'd come from.

Rosie and I helped three customers before we could talk. Over forty-five minutes, the weather outside the shop's windows went from cloudy to sunny to rainy. Customers liked it best when it was cloudy or rainy, and they would linger inside when storms hit. Usually, I enjoyed those who hung out with us. I liked learning their stories, where they'd come from, whatever their plans were. But today, I just wanted to talk to Rosie.

She sent me some side eyes and I noticed that my voice was clipped as I spoke to one of the customers. I cleared my throat and shaped up.

The customers didn't seem to notice and left on a happy note.

Once it was only Rosie, Hector, and me in the shop, Rosie said, "Did ye have something ye want tae discuss?"

"I do." I nodded toward the back table.

Rosie, holding Hector, followed me there. Once we sat, Hector squiggled from Rosie's lap and jumped into mine.

"What is it, lass?" Rosie asked.

"Two things. I never asked you again about the Mary, Queen of Scots' coins. Do you remember more?"

"I did check with Edwin but he's not sure what happened tae them, though he doesnae think they are in the warehouse. Do you think Henry or Mary heard about them and wanted them? Could that be what this is all aboot?"

"I have no idea but it's a possibility. Anything is. I'm just asking anything that comes to mind. Any idea what they might be worth?"

"Quite a bit, lass. Maybe priceless."

She hadn't said the word casually, but there was no infused awe either. Priceless items in the warehouse were not big surprises anymore. Although, there was something reckless about Edwin not knowing where they'd been put. Maybe he truly had forgotten, or he remembered but didn't want to share the details.

"I'll try to research them better," I said.

"What's the second thing?" Rosie asked.

"I know Edwin and the Lord Provost have clashed about some trees, but has he ever angered the council, or some of the members?"

"Oh, that's a fine question." She fell into thought again, her eyes coming out of focus as she looked toward the front window. "There *have* been moments over the years. Once, he singlehandedly rerouted a road."

"When?"

"Twenty years anon or so, I think,"

"Probably not that then. Anything else?"

"Aye, there was something . . . in Cowgate."

"Not far from here. Do you remember the details?"

"Zoning. Similar maybe tae what's going on now. There was a building. Someone wanted tae open a business there." Rosie tapped her lips with her fingers. "It wasnae all that long ago, but I cannae remember the details. I cannae even remember whose side Edwin fought for, but he went tae the meeting where there was a vote! Edwin's done this before." Rosie looked at me with surprised eyes. Then she sighed. "I suppose that doesnae mean anything at all though, does it?"

"Do you remember when?"

"Aboot ten years anon."

"Okay, well, that might be something. Rosie, any chance the business was either an art studio or an antique shop?"

"I simply dinnae ken, lass. I'm sorry." Rosie paused.

I grabbed a pen and piece of paper from Hamlet's stash in the drawer in the table. "Go on."

"There was also that time when one of the historical clocks stopped working. The council voted tae remove it and replace it. If I remember correctly, Edwin used his own money tae replace the antiquated parts inside the clock. Aye, that's exactly what happened. He had tae attend a council meeting on that one too, but he intervened before there was a vote."

"That seems like a good thing all the way around. No one would be upset. When?"

"That one was probably thirty years anon."

The floodgates had opened, and Rosie continued. Edwin had jumped in regarding the zoning for the zoo (I'd been and it's a wonderful zoo); some streetlight choices—older-looking was better in Old Town; castle hours—the Edinburgh castle wanted to be open longer hours, but the council fought against the plan. The castle won, with Edwin on their side.

There were many smaller things too. Book festival details that Edwin had been put in charge of; things like hosting an international author or perhaps introducing one. He'd worked with or argued with the council a number of times.

"My mind didnae even go tae all the other issues," Rosie said. "Edwin might have gotten off on a wrong foot with a number of the councilors."

"I don't know if any of it means anything or will give us any answers. It's more information though. I'll try to find and talk to some of them. Did you know Mikey is a councilor?"

"Mikey from dinner?"

"Yes. Neither he nor Henry mentioned their council positions that evening. I find that suspicious."

"Aye, I do too. Do ye think that any of this is tied to Henry's killer?"

"It's impossible to know at this point. I'm sad—and trying not to be too scared—about Henry's murder, but I don't want this bookshop shut down."

"Aye, but I *wouldnae* be surprised if the two answers are tied together."

"Why?"

Rosie shrugged and rubbed her arms. "I dinnae ken, lass. Just a feeling. Timing of everything meebe."

I looked at her. "Actually, I have one more thing to ask you about."

Rosie nodded and Hector panted along.

"Was what you said about the *Titanic* true or were you just playing along with Mary?"

"Oh, it was true, lass. I dinnae remember much of it anymore . . ."

I put my hand on her arm. "I'm sorry if my question bothered you."

"No, not at all. It's just. Well, I had a brief private conversation with our host, Mary, the other night too. A few years back, I wondered if there was any way for me tae recall any of those old memories. Back then, I found a place, no, it was a group, who gathered tae discuss their past lives. There was also hypnotism involved. When I went, I was gung-ho tae give it a try, but by the time I got there, I wasnae quite so interested. It was bothersome. I did observe a couple of times, but then moved on, not interested in remembering." Rosie blinked at me. "Mary is part of this group, she said. In fact, she said she was planning on attending this week, that it was royals' week and past royals are front and center, whatever that means."

"I'm sure she's decided not to go."

"I wouldnae be surprised if she does go. When she told me aboot it, she said they only do royals' week once a year and it's tae a full house. Everyone is interested in hearing some old royal blather."

Mary still hadn't returned my call. I was kicking myself for not calling her right back.

"When?" I said.

"Fridays. I guess that's tonight."

I pulled out my phone to search. "Do you remember what the group is called or where they meet?"

"Aye. At the Writers' Museum. It was called . . . Och, aye, Footsteps into the Past."

I was only surprised that it didn't have "ghost" in its title. I wasn't surprised that Mary volunteered at the place where the meetings occurred. "I was at that museum today, and met a woman named Laila. Do you know her?"

"No."

The information on my phone confirmed that the group did, indeed, meet tonight. "Should we go? We can leave if it's not interesting or if Mary isn't there."

Rosie laughed. "Ye'll not want tae leave, lass. Ye'll love every minute of it, unless it scares ye I suppose."

"Why would it scare me?"

"Well, if past lives are possible, then it stands to chance that all of us have lived them. If ye dinnae remember any, this sort of thing might cause ye tae remember. If I've learned anything at all, it's that not everyone wants tae remember."

I nodded, but I wasn't concerned.

"Delaney, I want tae make sure that ye ken that yer investigations, questions, just might lead you tae a killer," Rosie said.

"I'm aware," I said. "I'm not going to let The Cracked Spine close, Rosie. I'm just not. If it takes finding a killer, I'll be careful. I always am."

We frowned at each other. I *was* careful, but I heard what she wasn't saying aloud.

She nodded. "I'll go with ye then, but if it's bothersome, we have tae leave."

"Deal." I hugged her and kissed her cheek. And then scratched behind Hector's ears.

And they were only two of the reasons I didn't want the shop closed.

I looked out the window. "I need to run to Cowgate. That okay?"

"Aye. Call Edwin on the way, see if he remembers what trouble he ran into over there. Ask if he's found the coins."

"Will do."

"Dinnae forget a brollie," Rosie said.

"Right." I grabbed one from the collection on a front shelf and went back out into the rain.

EIGHTEEN

The art studio and the antique shop were, indeed, right next to each other. Two neighboring storefronts, different and yet similar in that they both gave off creative vibes. Gretchen's art studio was announced by a carved wood sign, simply stating Art Studio. Dina's awning was painted like a patchwork quilt behind letters that said Dina's Place, but both were welcoming.

I'd called Edwin on my way over, pulling him out of a meeting in Glasgow I didn't know he was attending. In an effort to make it a quick call, I said, "Edwin, three things. Do you remember what happened with the Mary, Queen of Scots' coins? How about something that happened in Cowgate, perhaps having to do with business zoning? What about any issues you might have had with Dina and Mikey Wooster?"

"I don't remember anything about zoning, lass, but the other two are one and same thing. Until you asked the question, I didn't remember."

"I don't understand."

"Some years back, I found Dina. She was young and had

just opened her shop. I thought I would see if she was interested in the coins. I like to meet up with new people, you know that. Anyway, I showed them to her and she wanted them, but she didn't have the money. She was upset that I wouldn't set up a payment plan for her. It's just not the way I work."

"What happened to the coins?"

Edwin laughed. "I saved them. I told her I would and she could find me when she had enough money. I think I remember where I put them now—they aren't in the bookshop, but I will track them down. I think they are in my house. This conversation has helped me remember."

"Did you give her a time limit?"

"I did not. But I never heard from her again. It wasn't contentious really, but she wasn't happy I wasn't willing to do business her way."

"Edwin, do you think there is a way that is tied to Henry wanting to shut down the bookshop?"

"Heavens, do I think Dina's uncle might have been offended enough by something that occurred years ago to shut down the bookshop? That would be quite the grudge."

"Some people hold them forever. Or maybe they just want the coins and this is, in their minds, a way to get them?"

"Lass, I simply don't know."

"I'm headed over there right now. If I don't make it back by dark, call the police," I said.

"Och, all right. Be careful, lass."

"Always."

I disconnected the call right after I disembarked the bus. For a long moment I stood across the street and watched the two buildings. No one went into or came out of the studio, but two customers entered and two others exited the antique shop.

I crossed the street and pulled on the door of the studio.

Soft background music played and pleasant floral scents filled the air.

"I'll be right there," Gretchen called from the back.

I zeroed in on a sculptured giraffe. Glazed to look like copper, it was an extraordinary work of art.

"Hello, Delaney," Gretchen said. "Good to see you again."

I'd decided that Gretchen just wasn't a smiler. She might seem unfriendly, but she really wasn't.

"Hi," I said.

"Here to have a look at the building?" she asked.

"Well, yes, I suppose so," I said. "And your sculptures too. They're extraordinary."

"Ta. Can I get you a cuppa or something?"

"No, thanks. I thought I'd stop by and see Dina too."

"Aye."

"Gretchen, may I ask you about Dina and Mikey?"

"What about them?"

"Do you really think Henry and Mikey are somehow involved in wanting a Burgess Ticket excuse to close your business, or do you think it's all something else? Do you think it's personal? Have you had any problems with them?" I cleared my throat. "That's a bunch of questions."

"I don't think I've had any problems with them," she said. "And I *have* wondered, but I can't think of a problem anywhere, other than I'm probably not being good at hiding how I feel about Mary. She's so strange. I don't know any of them all that well."

"Do you think Mary could have been involved in Henry's murder?"

She thought a moment. "No, I don't. They loved each other,

of course, but they were also a good partnership. Annoying with all that past-life stuff, but they were a team. I can't imagine either of them breaking it apart."

I nodded. "Okay, what about Eloise and Mary?"

"Have they had issues? Eloise not prescribing something Mary wanted so Henry sicced the Burgess Ticket police on me? Believe me, I've asked, and Eloise isn't aware of anything like that happening. I simply don't know. Look at this place though, Delaney, do you see any problems with it? Any reason I would have to reinforce the whole place? No, there isn't."

"It looks great to me. I don't know what's going on either and I'm no expert, but I can't see any reason you would have to do a thing here. Except keep sculpting." I smiled.

She didn't smile back, with her mouth at least. I thought I might have seen her eyes brighten some.

"Look around all you want," she said again. "I'll be in the back."

There wasn't much to look at regarding the building, but I did glance at corners, noting some cracks in the plaster walls, but thinking they were nothing dangerous. But again, I just didn't know what structurally unsound might look like, other than something obvious.

I loved every single one of Gretchen's sculptures and thought they would appeal to my new husband too. I wasn't in shopping mode, but I was genuine in telling her that Tom and I would come back in together soon. She walked back to the front to tell me it was good to see me as I left.

As I went into the antique shop, the two customers I'd observed walking in were leaving.

"Those desks! I can't believe how beautiful they are," one of them, with a distinctly American accent, said.

"I know," the other American said. "The shipping alone, let alone the cost of that one, would break the bank though."

"Yeah."

They nodded and smiled at me before they continued down the street.

The desk I'd most recently seen, Robert Burns's, was beautiful. I opened the door and looked forward to seeing something just as lovely.

"Welcome," Dina called from the back as the bell above the front door jingled. She looked up. "Oh." She cleared her throat. "Hello . . . Delaney."

She smoothed her jeans as she walked toward me. She kept her eyes down so I couldn't be sure how she felt about me being there, but it seemed she was working to normalize the tone of her voice. However, when she reached me and looked up, she smiled pleasantly as she extended her hand.

"I'm so sorry about my behavior at the business-licensing office. I'm still processing my uncle's murder, and that letter. I was distraught. I'm so sorry if I was rude."

"No, please, no need to even think twice about it. Did your license get fixed?"

"Oh, yes, it was easy in fact. I just had to pay a small late fee and I was good to go, back in business literally. I had infused it all with too much drama."

"That's great news! I really wanted to see your shop." I looked around. "It's extraordinary."

It was a more organized mess than the mess in the warehouse, but it still reminded me of the place where I did most of my work. Old things were everywhere—my eyes glanced over treasures such as swords, uniforms, dishes, and perfume bottles, but they landed on two desks next to each other in the middle and against a side wall.

Ornate, they reminded me of Marie Antoinette. So that we wouldn't linger on her uncle's murder, I pointed and said, "Those are French?"

"Aye. I mean *oui*." Dina smiled. "One of them is. Come look."

I followed her as we wove our way around some end tables and an old straight-back chair, more utilitarian than comfortable, a trunk covered in faded travel stickers, and a fireplace grate, *the soot well baked on,* I thought.

The shop assaulted my senses, in a good way. It was just the type of place I liked to explore, but that wasn't why I was there today.

The desks were more similar to my desk than Robert Burns's simple writing desk. These each had a couple of drawers, and, like mine, were too old to have been originally fitted with any sort of hanging-file mechanisms. Dina, trying hard not to sound like she was selling me, pointed out the finely carved markings and the dove-tailed joints. They were undoubtedly old and well preserved.

"The two customers who were in here just before you loved them both, but the shipping to the States would be a fortune," she said with a sigh.

"How long have you had them in the shop?"

"This one," she nodded, "for about three months, but this other one for about a year. It's expensive." She displayed the price tag.

"Ten thousand pounds?" I said with lifted eyebrows. "Yes, that's expensive."

Dina laughed. "Yes, it's rumored to have been in The Tower of London during Queen Elizabeth I's reign."

"Really? It's in great shape!"

"It's surprising how furniture can make it over the centuries, particularly if it's not exposed to the elements."

"Is there any way to authenticate it?" I asked.

"Well, the maker's mark burned into the back of the side panel of it fits." She pointed and I knelt to look at the mark, "As well as the structural style. I have the provenance papers, but they don't go back all the way. At some point, it became a 'good possibility.'"

The mark was a simple tree with the letter E underneath.

"E is for Elizabeth?" I said.

"No, I don't think so. I think that belonged to the person who made the desk. I'm not exactly sure."

Edwin had told me about my desk, but he had never shown me any papers. I suddenly had an urge to search for and research furniture maker's marks.

"Fascinating," I said as I stood straight again.

"I know. I love all this stuff. I love history, and I particularly love a good story." Dina smiled.

There was a chance she and I could be friends. We were alike in some obvious ways. But I had some questions for her, and even risking our potential friendship wasn't going to stop me from asking them.

"Dina," I began. "Do you remember meeting with Edwin MacAlister about some years back when you first opened your shop?"

"The name isn't familiar," she said a moment later as her eyebrows came together. She kept eye contact with me.

She seemed to be telling the truth, but I had a hard time

believing she neither remembered him nor his name being brought up at the dinner Mary and Henry had hosted. Still, I saw nothing that made me think she was lying. Her expression remained engaged and thoughtful.

"He owns the bookshop where I work."

She nodded. "Okay."

"Anyway, back then, he brought in some coins for you to consider buying. They were Mary, Queen of Scots' coins."

Her mouth made a quick O and her eyes opened wide. "Yes, now of course I remember him! Those coins, oh, how I wish I could have afforded them. I didn't put all of that together. He's the man who owns your bookshop?"

"Yes." I paused. I didn't ask her about why she didn't contact Edwin again about the coins. Maybe she still couldn't afford them. Instead, I said, "Yes, it's the same bookshop that Henry was trying to shut down when he was killed."

Her expression changed quickly. "What?"

I nodded. "It seems the council wants to close the bookshop, allegedly because it didn't pass some sort of structural inspection."

"I'm so sorry." Dina cleared her throat. "Can't Mr. Mac-Alister do what needs to be done to bring the building back up to code?"

"He would, if . . . do you have a minute? I'd like to tell you about all of it."

"Of course. Come sit back by the counter. Pick any chair and I'll gather us some tea."

She turned before I could protest the tea. I didn't want her to have time to get her story straight in her head, whatever that story might be. But I needed her. I needed her connections— her husband, a councilor, might be able to help. If they'd all been in this together, all been conspiring to shut the shop, then maybe I could get some answers as to why if I shared my side of the story.

Over tea, and around a few other customers who came in, I told her what had happened. She seemed truly interested and truly perplexed by the circumstances, saying more than once that there must be some sort of misunderstanding, that she and Mikey never really discussed that part of his life, so she hadn't heard anything about it.

"Of course, I will talk to Mikey," she finally said. "There has to be a way to fix this. It seems so very unfair."

"It does." A tiny bit of hope bubbled inside me. "Thank you. I would appreciate any help you could give."

Dina looked at me and nodded and then shook her head. "So very unfair."

The bell above the front door jingled and a large group of customers walked in. Dina had expected them.

"Oh, I'm so sorry, Delaney, I've a meeting—these are some costume people. I'll have to excuse myself."

"Thank you for your time." I stood.

"Don't worry, Delaney, I will get on this."

Dina walked me all the way to the door. Once there, I decided to ask her one more question.

"What does Mary think about you having one of her past-life-foe's desks?" I smiled.

But Dina didn't smile back. She glanced toward the customers—they weren't in hearing range—and said, "Delaney, Mary is sure the desk came from Elizabeth's time, and place. She told me she's sure it's real. She touched it and could sense Elizabeth's presence."

"Really?" My smile stiffened. That sort of prediction went beyond past life stuff, didn't it?

"Yes, really. She's more fascinated than bothered about it though."

I couldn't be sure if she almost rolled her eyes or not before she excused herself again to help the costume people.

I stood outside the shop and looked up at the awning. Dina had been friendly, offered to help. That bubble of hope grew a little bigger. I listened hard for a bookish voice to tell me things were going to be okay. None were talking. Maybe my intuition was off.

Or maybe I still didn't have quite enough information yet.

NINETEEN

"Even if she's here, I'm not sure we'll be able to see her," I said as I kept my arm threaded through Rosie's. It was too crowded to let her go.

The museum, including the courtyard we were currently walking through, was much busier than during my first visit. A lot of people were interested in past lives.

"Maybe not," Rosie said as she looked around at all the people. She didn't like crowds, but I didn't realize until this moment that they actually made her uncomfortable and anxious.

"Are you okay?" I veered us out of the flow of people and stopped walking. "We don't have to do this."

I'd wished I hadn't asked her to go with me from the moment she'd opened her door. Her expression had been drawn and distracted. If she had lived past lives, I sensed she'd said goodbye to them a long time ago. She wasn't interested in getting reacquainted with any of her old, possible selves. And, the crowd made it even less worth it.

Rosie took a deep breath and let it out. "No, lass, I'm fine. I'm sorry if I seem like I'm not. I'm fine. I'm not a fan of so many people, but I can get past that. I can't find that paper-work and that's on my mind. I ken I will find it though."

I frowned. "Why don't we go back home. I'll help you search."

"No, lass, I need tae get out a bit, and I need tae search for it by myself, later. I would worry someone else would miss it and I'd end up searching everything anyway. I'm truly fine."

Her eyes weren't saying the same thing.

"All right," I said. "We'll just swoop through. If I don't see Mary right off, we'll get out of here."

The museum was much different at night, as most places in Edinburgh were. Night brought out the ghosts, if you believed in that sort of thing. Again, I didn't not believe.

Laila was nowhere to be seen. And this crowd had no inter-est in any of the artifacts inside. They might have interest in the writers being honored by the museum, but only if they thought they might have once *been* one of them.

We merged back into the crowd and were herded inside, through the main lobby and then back to a room I hadn't noticed before. Set up as a meeting room, the building itself wasn't very big so the meeting space felt cramped. Chairs were set up in tight rows, but by the time we made it in, most of them were taken. I ushered Rosie to an empty seat on the end of a row and stood next to her.

"I can see better if I stand," I told her.

"Aye."

Only a few seconds later, the doors were shut. I scanned, but didn't see Mary anywhere. It didn't make sense that she had come to this event so soon after Henry's murder. I should have thought it through better, but I hadn't predicted it would be such a big event. In my mind, I'd seen a group, seated in a circle, sharing the stories of their lives. I'd wondered if maybe Mary would have received support from the circle.

Hello, my name is Mary, and I used to be Mary, Queen of Scots.

Hello, Mary.

I rolled my eyes at myself. This was nothing like that.

A woman appeared at the front of the room and the crowd quickly fell into a whispering hush.

"Hello, everyone," the woman said. "Welcome, welcome, welcome. Do we have a treat for you all tonight." She smiled and clasped her hands together, causing the crowd to cheer and applaud. I obligingly clapped too as I looked at Rosie. She smiled, but she still looked uncomfortable. I was going to reach for her arm and tell her we should just go when the woman continued. I'd wait for more applause or cheers before I snuck us out of there.

"My name is Tia Zevon, and I am thrilled to be your host for another night of royalty. I look forward to this every year. And, I know all of you do too. It's good to see that the crowd only continues to grow. We are closing the doors on this evening's attendance. If you aren't here yet, you won't be allowed to enter. You may leave at any time, of course, but doors are closed the other direction. No one else is coming in, even by royal order!" She smiled.

The crowd laughed and clapped again.

Well, *maybe* we'd leave in a bit.

"I know you all know our guest this evening. She's one of our regulars and she's always ready to share a story or two. However, tonight is the first time she has agreed to be hypnotized." Tia then took a step closer to the crowd and pulled a serious expression. "Ladies and gentlemen, our special guest is here this evening after an unthinkable tragedy has happened this week. We shan't discuss that tragedy, even if we've heard about it. All right?" She looked out expectantly, like a teacher laying down the law. The crowd murmured their okays. "Very good then. Our own Mary Stewart, our Mary, Queen of Scots, is here tonight. Is everyone ready?"

The cheers and hollers came again. This was more like a revival than a support group. I understood Rosie's discomfort. It felt like we were going to end the evening being asked to fork out $19.99 for something. *And that's not all!*

I wasn't leaving yet. I did, however, angle myself so that I was mostly hidden by two people standing in front of me. I could peer around them, but I didn't want Mary to see me in the crowd. Rosie was just part of the sea of people sitting. Mary wouldn't notice her.

"First, I'm going to introduce our hypnosis expert. Ladies and gentlemen, let's give a warm welcome to Mr. Lyle Mercado."

As the applause came again, I blinked and then moved back to a spot I could better see.

Lyle Mercado was the name of the man in charge of the business-license office for the city of Edinburgh. Beyond the fact that the man's jobs or hobbies or whatever they all were made a strange combination of ingredients, it was just plain weird that I'd recently met him too.

It was only a moment later that it was confirmed. Definitely the same man.

"What the hell?" I muttered quietly. Only Rosie looked at me. I bent over and whispered in her ear. "Do you know him?"

"No."

"Edwin took me to meet him. He's in charge of the city's business licenses."

"Aye?"

I nodded and stood up straight again. Rosie sat up straighter and removed any hesitation from her face, replacing it with determination and question. I liked those much better than the worry and discomfort that were there before. She was now in the game.

Lyle stood front and center, commanding the space better than he commanded his small office. Of course, Edwin wasn't with us, so maybe he wasn't as intimidated.

"Thank you, ladies and gentlemen. Thank you, Tia, for welcoming me. I'm so very excited to be a part of the festivities this year," Lyle said.

From the sidelines where she'd removed herself to, Tia nodded and then bowed slightly toward him, her hands in a prayer.

"Oh, boy," I said.

One of the women in front of me turned and sent me a frown. I smiled apologetically and she turned around again.

"Now, without further ado, let us welcome our very own queen, Mary Stewart, once and forever held in our hearts, Mary, Queen of Scots."

Mary approached from behind the trifold that had been set up to signify "backstage." She did, indeed, look as if she hadn't slept for a few days. And I was pretty sure she looked thinner, as if she hadn't eaten either. But she was a trooper, with a forced smile, excellent posture, and a good layer of makeup to attempt to hide dark circles under her eyes.

Or was she just trying to look like a trooper? I was feeling so many levels of untruth that I was suspicious of everything, every single action, almost every person in the room.

When the applause died down again, Lyle continued, "Many of us know our very own Mary Stewart, but for those who aren't aware, she is a reincarnated soul, having once been the martyred Mary, Queen of Scots."

Lyle paused momentarily to let the information soak in. There were a few ooohs and ahs, but no one yelled out in shock. This wasn't news.

"All right. Mary has agreed to allow me to hypnotize her for the crowd. She's susceptible, both she and I know, meaning that hypnotism works on her. She and I have had a few private sessions."

I inspected them both. Was there some other meaning behind "private sessions"? I didn't see any expression or shared glances that made me think there was. Was this Mary's next husband, the one who might be accused of killing Henry? Or was that just the past life? I gritted my teeth and watched closely.

Lyle continued, "Are we ready?"

The crowd was ready. Briefly, I thought that Lyle and I made eye contact. He hesitated, but not for long.

"Do you have any words for the audience before we get to work?" Lyle asked Mary.

She frowned and then shook her head.

Rosie and I looked at each other. She signaled at me. I leaned over so she could whisper in my ear.

"What in the name of Jesus, Mary, and Joseph is going on?" she asked.

"It looks like we're going to see some hypnotism."

"Lass, this isnae right. Her husband was just kil't. I dinnae ken if the police suspect her or not, but I sense that this is being staged for something other than the entertainment of this crowd. We're all being set up for something, maybe to sway some suspicion or something. I would bet Edwin's money on it."

"I think that's possible."

Rosie thought a moment and then reached into her purse. She kept her hand hidden inside. "I'm going tae record. I know they said no recordings allowed. I dinnae care. Someone needs a record of this."

"I agree. Good idea."

I wondered if she knew how to work the recording app on the phone, but she didn't fumble or seem confused.

I stood back up and watched her. She sent me a pursed lip, confident nod.

"The only person susceptible to my words will be Mary Stewart." Lyle took a step toward the audience, keeping his hands clutched together in front of himself.

He cut quite the figure. Had I just walked in tonight, I would never have guessed his day job was in government. With more casual, carefree clothes, his scruffy appearance had transformed into artistic.

But it wasn't just that Lyle seemed to be two different people. It was everything combined. There was a weird mix of things and people happening. I just had to figure out how the bookshop and Edwin fit into the mix.

Lyle stepped back again and turned to face Mary. A person appeared with a chair and Mary sat, her hands on her knees, her attention up on Lyle.

The words he used were things I'd heard before. You are tired. You are sleepy. You will do as I say. The power of suggestion seemed to work quickly, and within only a minute or so Mary's chin was down toward her chest and her eyes were closed.

"Are you Mary?" Lyle asked.

"I am," she mumbled.

You could feel the tension in the room as everyone worked

hard to keep quiet. Except for the woman on Rosie's other side. She leaned forward and looked at me.

"Are you two related?" she whispered as she nodded toward Mary.

"No," I said just as quietly.

"Gracious." The woman stared for another moment.

I pulled up the collar on my jacket a little higher and wished I'd worn a hat. Fortunately, Lyle garnered everyone's attention again.

"Mary, I would like for you to take some steps back in time. Are you willing to do that?" Lyle asked.

"Yes."

"Very good. Here we go. Let's go all the way back to when you were a child. What can you tell me about that?"

"I can see the wash," Mary said with a happy tone. "Momma put the wash out on the line. It's pretty in the breeze."

"Okay, let's go back even further if that's okay. Is that okay?"

"Yes."

"I'd like for you to go back to a time before you were born into this life you are living as Mary Stewart. I'd like for you to travel far, all the way back to when you were living in castles. Can you do that?"

"I think so."

"Let's travel together. Tell me what you see as you look backward. I am right here with you and you are safe. These are only memories we are looking at and nothing in them can hurt you."

"I understand."

"Tell me what you see as you venture through your memories."

"I see horses. There's a bridge. Birds, beautiful birds."

"Keep going. Just stop when you see castle walls, maybe walls you didn't want to be locked behind. You might have been there against your will, but you aren't to worry. Just go there today and we'll remember together. You are safe."

Mary nodded, her chin tapping her chest. "Oh! There, yes, there's a castle."

She lifted her head then, though her eyes remained closed. Inside the room, there were a few tiny gasps, but still no one else spoke.

"Are you inside the castle?"

"No, no, it's there in the distance. I see it though. It's so lovely." Mary's face fell. "Lovely from this view. I've run away, you see, and I know I can't stay away long. But the freedom! Oh, the fresh air. It smells so sweet. The sky is blue today. It's not so blue very often, but today it is."

Her voice was younger, even younger than mine, like it came from someone in her early twenties. As if reading my mind, Lyle asked, "How old are you, dear?"

"I'm twenty and one," Mary said, though she still seemed bothered.

"Mary, please remember that you are safe. These are only memories. All right?"

"Oh. Aye. All right."

"I need to ask, Mary, are you the queen of Scotland?"

"Aye, *certainment,*" she said after a brief pause, now using a French word and accent.

"Thank you for speaking with us, your highness."

"*Je suis heureux pour la distraction. L'homme m'a telle-ment dérange.*"

"*En Anglais, s'il vous plaît.*"

"I'm happy for the distraction. The man has so bothered me," she said as, with eyes still closed, she turned her face toward the audience.

"The man?"

"*Oui*, the man who was under my bed on St. Valentine's Day. I forgave him the trespass then, but no longer. He was there in my bedchamber tonight as I was readying for bed. I told the earl to use his dagger on the villain, but he didn't obey. I was so angry and upset that I ran away."

"Do you know the identity of the man in your room?"

"*Bien sûr*," she said. *Of course.* "The poet! He thought his way with words would woo me. His book of poetry would wind its way into my heart. He was mistaken! He shall be hung, if I have my way. And I am the queen, I will have my way. I'm *désolé* that my brother didn't do as I commanded. I shall have to deal with him too."

"Your brother?"

"The Earl of Moray, my bastard brother."

"Ah, aye, your closest advisor."

My eyebrows went up at the mention of the name, the same one Joshua had said in an ominous tone, the one who had potentially been involved in deceiving the queen.

"Well, yes, but I am angry, do not misunderstand," Mary said.

"I understand completely. Can you tell us the poet's name?"

"Pierre de Bocosel de Chastelard. His passion for me is untoward. I shall have him tried for treason in the morning. He will be found guilty."

"I have no doubt. Your highness, if you aren't in a hurry, may I ask you a question about something from a time ago?"

"If you must."

"I would like to ask you about your first husband."

"My first husband?"

"Aye. Your husband Francis. I want to know if you remember him."

"Oh, I loved him," she answered immediately. "No one thought I would. Everyone thought we wouldn't care for each other. We did. Perhaps we didn't have enough time to care for each other as we should have, as a husband and wife should have, but we got along so very well. I miss him. I miss my sweet friend."

"I'm sorry."

Mary nodded sadly. "I don't, however, miss his mother. I'm glad to be rid of her."

"The former queen of France, Catherine de' Medici?" Lyle looked out toward the audience.

"*Oui.*"

"The two of you didn't get along."

"*Mais, non,* but she wouldn't have been kind to anyone who married her son, the future king. Between you and me, she's quite the wicked woman."

"I see. I'm sorry you had to put up with her."

Mary waved away the concern.

I was suddenly struck by the way she held her body, even as she sat in the chair. There was an unmistakable nobility to her posture.

Or this was all a bunch of parlor tricks and I was falling for them.

"I have struggled, I must admit," Mary said. "I lived in France for so long. This new world, this place where I am queen was foreign to me. I have had to learn much."

Lyle paused as if in thought and then nodded. "Mary, can we go forward in time now, to when you are a little older?"

I was hoping we'd get to the part where the queen's second husband was murdered; perhaps that's where Lyle was directing her to go.

"*Oui . . . non!* I must take leave. The constable has arrived. I must see to it that the poet is locked away."

"Are you sure we can't just move past this?"

"*Non, non, non!* I must go! Please, I'm afraid!"

"All right. Mary, when I count down from three, you will wake up, refreshed and unconcerned about these memories. They all took place long ago, in the past. Three, two, one." Lyle snapped his fingers.

Mary's eyes popped open and she smiled at Lyle and then at the audience.

"How do you feel?" Lyle asked.

"Fine."

"Do you remember what we discussed?"

"I do. I knew about the poet, but I've never had those memories before. You didn't ask me about the weather on the castle grounds. I was quite chilled. You should have offered me a wrap."

Mary and Lyle laughed lightly. The crowd, having become captivated, followed along a few seconds later with some laughs of their own.

"I apologize," Lyle said.

One person in the audience began clapping enthusiastically, the rest of us followed behind. Except for Rosie. She didn't clap. She kept her doubtful gaze forward.

Amid the applause, Tia walked back onto the stage and whispered something into Lyle's ear. He pulled back and sent her some tight eyebrows before he turned to look at Mary again. I looked too. Mary didn't look well, at all. She was pale now, and her cheeks seemed to have become even more sunken.

Lyle turned back to the crowd as Tia went and stood by Mary.

"Ladies and gentlemen, that's all for this evening. I wish we'd been able explore further, but when it's time to go, it's simply time to go," Lyle said.

No one was happy to hear this news. I didn't know what everyone expected, but they all wanted more of something. Weren't there more royals in the audience? Maybe not.

"I have a question!" a voice rose above the discontent.

Lyle looked doubtful for a moment. He looked at Mary who nodded at him.

"All right," Lyle said.

A woman stood from the middle of the crowd. I put my hand up to my mouth to quiet the gasp that traveled up my throat. I knew her. One of Tom's former girlfriend's, she was a reporter with one of the alternative Edinburgh newspapers.

Rosie looked up at me. "Is that Brigid?"

"I think so," I said.

"Mary, I'd like to know if you have any memories of killing your husband, either back in the 1500s or the one who was killed earlier this week."

Mary sighed as she stood. She didn't wobble at all as she put her hand on Lyle's arm before he could voice a protest.

"I'm prepared to answer," Mary said. "In fact, I should have begun the evening with a statement. It's only fair that it's asked, and it's only right that I say what I need to say."

She looked at Lyle. He wasn't happy but he nodded her on.

Mary stepped forward, and I sensed this still might be part of the script, that Mary had either hoped someone would ask her about her husband or had told someone to. Maybe she'd planted Brigid in the audience. I wouldn't put such collusion past the pretty blond who used to date my husband.

"The history has been scandalized over time. Like any good story, we only want to hear the juicy bits," Mary began dramatically.

I couldn't take my eyes off her, so I didn't look at Rosie, but I sensed she rolled her eyes.

"I did not participate in either murder of either husband. If you look closely you will see that the queen's life was on course to improve. She was about to receive a new treaty from Elizabeth. Things were going well, and killing Darnley would only harm the friendlier path that was being forged. I didn't participate in any way in killing him. Unfortunately, my sister queen didn't believe me, of course."

Many years later, Mary was ultimately tried for treason and executed. Darnley's murder was the beginning of the end, even though the end came almost twenty years later, I thought. Inwardly I kicked myself for not yet taking the time to study the history better. I should have at least read more Wikipedia by now.

"And of course I had no reason at all to kill this Henry." Mary's voice caught as she put her fist to her chest and seemed to steel herself. "I loved him. I loved him ever so desperately. I will miss him forever."

My throat tightened as she spoke. I cleared it and stole a look toward Rosie. Even she looked less suspicious and more sympathetic.

"That is all I have to say." She paused, but only briefly. "No, no it isn't. I'm here tonight because doing this was a commitment I made and being here helps me too. Helps me think less about myself. And . . ." She first looked pointedly at Brigid before she scanned the rest of the audience. "Think about it, I am certain I have lived other lives. Many of you here feel the same, so you should understand that there might someday be another way to have Henry in my life. Or at least the light of the spirit he carried with him."

With that, Mary turned and disappeared behind the trifold divider. Lyle frowned a nod at the audience and then followed her.

I kept my eyes on Brigid. I wanted to talk to both Mary and Lyle, but Brigid even more so. "I'm going to try to catch her," I said to Rosie. "I'll meet you out front, next to the lamppost on the corner."

"Aye," Rosie said as she shooed me away.

It wasn't too difficult to watch Brigid's blond curls as they wove through the crowd and then out of the room.

"Brigid!" I said as I stepped outside and saw her walking hurriedly away.

She turned and spotted me. She tried not to look too put out, but her efforts were wasted. When I'd first come to know her, a part of me thought we might be friends if the circumstances had only been a little different.

"Hey," I said as I caught up to her. "How are you?"

"I am fine, and not surprised in the least to see you tonight. Are you and Mary Stewart related?"

"No, but the resemblance is uncanny, huh?" I said with a smile.

She didn't return the smile. "Yes, uncanny. So, I hear the deed is done. You married Tom."

"We got hitched, yes."

"Congratulations." She didn't sound like she meant it.

But I wasn't here to talk about that. "Thanks. Hey, I heard your question in there."

"Aye, that means you heard her answer too."

"I did, but I was wondering if there's more to it. Do you think she killed her husband?"

"Which one?"

"Fair question, I suppose. This one." I didn't much care about who killed Darnley, but I was going to research him at some point.

Brigid bit the inside of her cheek and fell into thought. "I really don't know. But someone killed him, and the spouse is usually suspected."

"So, that's all your question was based upon, the usual suspect? I was under the impression there was more."

"Sure, there's more. These past-lifers are a weird group and I wonder if some of them don't use their 'stories' to justify their actions of today. Mary, Queen of Scots, was ultimately beheaded because she was found guilty of treason, but suspicions about her involvement in his death stayed with her. Darnley was a complete louse by the way."

"The queen's husband was a bad guy?" I'd heard this from Joshua too.

"Sure. Opportunistic, mean, a narcissist who didn't like that Mary wouldn't crown him, even though she gave him equal power to reign in Scotland."

"What about the queen's lover? I heard he might have been the killer."

Brigid shook her head. "The queen claimed there was no other romance when Darnley was alive, though ultimately she did marry the suspect, Lord Bothwell. He was rotten too and probably did whatever he did at Queen Elizabeth's bidding. That's my interpretation."

"You think Mary should have been queen of England?"

"Yes. Elizabeth should never have ruled. Mary had the legitimate claim to the crown." Brigid took a deep breath. "Goodness, why anyone would let themselves get all worked up about something that happened four hundred years ago is ridiculous, but many of us do."

"Do you think that Henry's death has anything at all to do with Mary claiming to be a reincarnation of the queen? Do you suppose his job as a councilor to the Lord Provost might have had something to do with his murder?"

"I don't know. I haven't found anything substantial yet."

I did a quick, silent debate with myself. *Should I tell her?*

"What if I give you a lead?" I finally said.

"That would be quite rummy of you, Delaney, but why would you do that?"

"You'll understand once I tell you what it is. It's a bit self-serving, which might not be a surprise." She shook her head. I continued, "I'd like not to be named."

"An anonymous source?"

"Yes."

"I guess I can do that."

"Henry wanted some businesses to be shut down."

"What?" Even in the glow from the streetlights I could see Brigid's doubt.

"Yes. One of the businesses was The Cracked Spine."

Brigid looked at me a long moment and then laughed once. "I've heard about the Burgess Tickets, but I didn't pick up on using them to shut down any specific businesses. I sense you're telling me it might have been something deeper."

"I am. I think."

"So, you're telling me this why? You do realize that this makes you and everyone who works at The Cracked Spine possible suspects, right?"

"But I know we're all innocent."

"Hmm."

"Okay. Look, Brigid, I know what that looks and sounds like. You can either believe me or not. Even though I know that none of us at the shop killed Henry, the reason I'm telling you this is to give you another angle to explore. The Cracked Spine was not the only business on Henry's hoped-for chopping block. The Burgess Tickets were part of his plans, but there was more, even if I can't quite understand what all the more was."

"Ah, I now see the self-serving part."

I shrugged. "I'm being as up front with you as I can be."

"Aye."

"You can look into things better than I can, that's for sure."

"And you'd like me to let you know what I find."

"Actually, I'd like for you to also let the police know what you find."

"Well, it doesn't exactly work that way, but I hear what you're saying."

"If you found a killer, I'm sure you'd do the right thing." I wasn't. Not even close, but getting her on my side seemed like the way to go.

"Thanks for the info, Delaney. I'll be in touch."

Brigid turned and walked away, her curls bouncing haughtily. She turned around again. "It is definitely uncanny how much you look like her."

"I know," I said. I didn't want to tell her about my recent

meeting of Mary or the dinner party. It felt like too much information. The more I needed her, the more she might not want to
help. I was keeping it as simple as possible.

"Talk to you later, Mrs. Shannon," she said before she
turned one more time.

Very quietly, so she wouldn't hear, I said, "It's Delaney
Nichols, but that's okay."

She kept walking and I hurried back to Rosie.

TWENTY

I searched in vain for Mary and Lyle, but the crowd cleared quickly. Rosie waited for me right by the streetlight; there weren't many others around by the time I made it to her. We walked to a bus stop, boarded, and then walked slowly to her flat after we disembarked.

"Do we need to look more closely at the queen's life to understand this Mary? Do you think history is repeating?" I asked as we meandered under clear skies.

"It is all odd, and the explosion is certainly suspicious, but Mary Stewart isnae a real queen, even if she was one at one time," Rosie said.

"Do you think she was?"

Rosie laughed. "Lass, I have no idea."

"Do you think the queen killed her second husband?"

"The proper question is do I think she *conspired* tae have her husband kil't. No, lass, I dinnae think that at all, but I'm Scottish, aye. I think she was treated horribly by almost everyone, including her second and third husbands. If we're trying tae see if there are similarities, think about something else too.

We met Henry. He cooked us dinner. I thought he was a lovely man. Didnae you?"

"I did. Until I heard he wanted to shut down the bookshop."

"Aye," she said, doubt lining the word.

"What?"

"I would bet more of Edwin's money that the answer as to why he wanted the bookshop closed and why he was killed are one and the same."

"Why do you think that?"

"I'm not sure, except that it's all happened at the same time. Find the connection, or let the police find the connection, and we'll know all the answers."

"Sounds simple." I smiled.

"If it were easy, everyone would do it, not just a redheaded lass in a Scottish bookshop."

I laughed. "I sensed your doubt tonight. Was is all just a bunch of bunk to you?"

"No, not all of it." She sent me a half smile. "I do think there's something tae past lives, but I dinnae ken what exactly. Maybe our spirits do travel from body to body, or maybe our memories, our experiences are just too strong tae die. I think it's more something like that. My 'memories' of being aboard the *Titanic* might have just been someone else's that the universe didnae want tae die, so the memories were then passed along. There's much we dinnae ken."

"That's a lovely idea."

We'd arrived at the door to her building. "We need to somehow stop the bookshop from closing. That needs to be our goal. The other answers will come from that."

"Ye think ye will find the killer that way?"

"I hope the police find the killer. The sooner the better. I do think I'm going to go to Mary's house again. She hasn't returned my call, and I want to talk to her. Want to come with me in the morning to talk to her?"

"No, lass. I'm afraid I wouldnae do ye much good. I'm too focused on finding that paperwork. Take Elias or Tom."

"Will do."

Rosie laughed once. "I ken ye wonder where my anger is. It's here." She put her fist to her gut. "Just as strong as yers. Like a rock in my stomach. I can barely stand it. I just don't want Edwin tae see it. If the shop closes, it will be worse for him because of the rest of us than for him personally."

I nodded. I wasn't going to be able to hide anything, so I didn't make any promises to such.

Rosie stepped up onto a stair. "Ye'll be late coming in tomorrow then?"

"I think I will."

Rosie took another step, but then stopped and turned to look at me again. "Maybe Mary did kill her husband. She might be dangerous."

"I think I can talk Tom into joining me."

"Aye. G'night, lass. Sleep well."

"I'll walk you in."

"No, no. I'm fine. And I'm tired. I'll see you tomorrow."

I hooked my arm through hers. "I won't stay. I just want to say goodnight to Hector."

"Aye." She gave me a weary smile as she pulled my arm closer to her.

I made sure she got inside. Hector took care of her from there. My friend Rosie was sad, maybe a little scared, definitely angry. I hadn't realized how much until this evening. That almost upset me more than anything else. I should know how to read these things by now.

I left her flat and sent one more glance up to her front window.

"I'll fix this, Rosie," I said. Even though she hadn't heard, I felt a wave of guilt wash through me. What if I couldn't?

What if no one could?

TWENTY-ONE

"Hang on," I said as I put my hand on Tom's arm.

He stopped the car just short of turning up and onto the driveway.

"You're having second thoughts?" he asked.

"More like twentieth thoughts," I said. "I've been wrestling with this all night. We really shouldn't bother her. It's too soon. It's almost cruel."

Tom steered the car to the side of the street. He turned and looked at me.

"Delaney, you are not even close to cruel. I understand why you might not want to do this, but I think we should. I think it's the only way for you to get any peace. Perhaps she can't help. She might not know about Henry's desire to close the shop, but this is the best way to find out. Apologize and tell her you won't interrupt her day for long. If she breaks down, we'll apologize again and leave her be. It's okay to do this, it really is."

I'd tossed and turned all night and had been distracted over breakfast. Had I thrown Tom for his marriage's first loop? His support was wonderful, but were his encouraging words for my sanity or his, or both? And did it matter anyway? As we both navigated this new thing called marriage, hopefully I would handle his first bump as supportively as he'd handled mine.

"Thanks," I said, letting it soak in again how lucky I was. I took a deep breath. "Okay, I'm ready."

"Good." Tom smiled and put the car back into gear.

Knocking on the castle replica's door during the daytime was different than at night. Oddly, the structure seemed more fortress-like under the diffused light from the cloudy sky. At night, the scene was theatrical and appealing. During the day, it was cold and foreboding. Nevertheless, I knocked before Tom could, only to prove I was up for the task. He sent me a knowing nod and another smile.

The door opened slowly. I didn't think I'd had any expectation as to who might be on the other side, but I was surprised that Mary herself was the one to greet us.

"Oh. Hello," she said as she pulled the door even wider.

"Hi, Mary," I said. "We're so sorry to bother you during this time. We're sorry about Henry."

"Thank you," she said with a distinct question to her voice. "You returned my call. Thank you. I'm sorry I haven't gotten back to you again."

She looked much worse than she had the night before; more tired and even thinner. But she'd had to put on a show last night, entertain. I looked at Tom who nodded me on.

"Mary, do you have a few minutes? I know this is a bad time, but could we talk inside?"

"Aye. Come in."

She pulled the door and we followed her toward the large round table. There were no fresh flowers on it today. There were no flowers anywhere, which I thought was strange.

Usually death brought flowers. There were no chairs on this level, and she didn't invite us up to the next. Instead, she seemed uncomfortable and looked at us expectantly.

"Why did you call me?" I asked. "Can I help you with something?"

"I imagine I called you for the same reason you called me back."

When she didn't continue, I said, "You know where I work, of course."

She nodded.

"Did you ever talk with Henry about his plans for The Cracked Spine?"

She deflated and leaned against the table. "Aye, Delaney, I did, but not until after you all left that night. Henry was stunned that I had met my doppelgänger, surprised by where you worked. He had no idea that his wife's lookalike worked at the bookshop he was responsible for planning to shut down."

"Oh, Mary, why did he want the bookshop closed?" I said.

She shrugged. "From what I could understand, it wasn't something he wanted, but something that had to happen."

I blinked and frowned. "Did the fact that you and I look alike change anything?"

"Well, building codes and all . . ."

"There's nothing wrong with the structure of the buildings that house the bookshop and its offices!" My raised voice echoed up the entryway all the way to the upper floor and probably down to the gallows too, if there were any.

"Of course, there is," Mary said. "Henry said an inspection had taken place."

"There's been no inspection," I said, working hard not to clench either my jaw or my fists. "Before that, do you remember if the bookshop ever came up in conversation? There must have been another reason."

She'd blinked when I'd yelled, gotten flustered when I mentioned the lack of an inspection. Now she fell into weary thought. "I don't think so. I don't remember if it did. I had no idea. I know you might think there was some sort of setup going on that night, but there wasn't, I promise."

"Why did you choose to bring your books to my bookshop?" I said.

She looked at me. "Well. Someone might have mentioned the bookshop to me, but I'm not exactly sure who, except that I'm one hundred percent positive that it wasn't Henry. Delaney," she looked back and forth between Tom and me, "let me finish. After you left that night Henry told me about the council's plans and the inspection—okay, so that's what he told me, I can't prove one way or another whether an inspection happened—but, what I'm saying is that we talked about it. And I really do think he was going to try to call off the vote. He liked you and Rosie and Tom so much that he was going to make a case for giving your boss a chance to make structural changes."

"Really?"

"Yes," she said. "And then he was killed."

She looked at me. Accusation both dulled and lit her eyes.

"Mary, none of us killed Henry. We didn't know the details of the council's plans until after he was killed."

I didn't like her insinuations. Neither did Tom; he crossed his arms in front of himself.

"No, no, I believe that neither of you knew. But . . ." She stood straighter. "Edwin MacAlister knew. And from what Henry said, he wasn't happy at all, threatening to sue, get Henry removed from the council, offering bribery."

I stalled mentally. *This was new information, right?* Edwin hadn't admitted that he'd done any of that, just that he'd had a phone call, a recorded one at that. And, he was out of town, allegedly in Glasgow. I hadn't pressed, but I had wondered what in the heck he was doing in Glasgow while our entire world was falling apart. Had he purposefully not told us about his threats?

"Edwin didn't kill Henry either," I finally said.

"Are you sure about that?" she said.

"Yes. Completely."

"Well, whoever did kill Henry stopped him from attempting to stop the vote. There's nothing to be done now."

"Nothing? What about Mikey?" I asked.

She shook her head. "Mikey doesn't see any reason it should be stopped. He thinks Henry was being too emotional about wanting to change directions. Henry met you all at dinner and enjoyed your company. In Mikey's mind, that's not enough to invalidate a valid inspection."

"There wasn't an inspection," I repeated.

Mary shrugged, but not unsympathetically.

"Maybe Mikey killed Henry," I said. It was a cruel, low blow.

She frowned and crossed her arms in front of herself, matching Tom's pose. "I only spoke with him about all of this after Henry was killed. He didn't know Henry was going to try to stop the vote. I was trying to help you too. Ultimately, that's why I wanted to talk to you, to tell you that I was sorry, and Henry was sorry too. But there was nothing to be done to save the bookshop now. I wanted you to know Henry was sorry." Her voice cracked.

I blinked at her. Okay, so she hadn't been calling to warn me about Inspector Buchanan. I was so, so angry, so frustrated, but she was trying to do the right thing, at least in her mind. I couldn't muster up any kind words, but I did manage a nod.

"Mary," Tom jumped in. "Thank you for that. Please, if you can think of any other way for us to save the bookshop, stop the vote, let us know. We'd be forever in your debt. We *are* sorry for your loss."

"Yes, we are," I said. I wished I sounded as sincere as she and Tom had.

Mary nodded too.

I tried to calm my insides before I reached out and put my hand on her arm. "Mary, do the police have any idea who killed Henry?"

"No," she said, her voice tightening with emotion now. "And, just so you know, I haven't said one word about Edwin MacAlister to the police. You can show yourselves out."

She turned and hurried up the stairs as we blinked at her back.

"Thank you for your time," Tom called after her. "Again, we are sorry."

I had so much more I wanted to talk to her about, but we had been dismissed. I wanted to ask about her friendship with Lyle Mercado. I wanted to tell her I'd been there last night. But I wasn't ready to chase her through her own house. Tom and I left, closing the castle door quickly but softly behind us.

"I think we need to talk to Edwin," Tom said quietly as we made our way to his car.

"Couldn't agree more."

We made it back to the bookshop in record time.

TWENTY-TWO

"Inspector Buchanan," I said as I came though the bookshop's door. Tom had dropped me off. I hadn't noticed a police car out front. I couldn't help but steal a glance out the window to see if I'd missed it.

"I walked," she said. "I like to walk. It's good for the mind and body."

"Yes," I said.

From behind the inspector, Rosie sent me a smirk. No one else was in the bookshop and I sensed that the inspector knew exactly the expression on Rosie's face. Rosie normalized before she could be caught though.

"Do you usually arrive at work at this time of the morning?" Inspector Buchanan asked as she worried her thumb over a piece of paper she held.

I bit down on what I really wanted to say—that it was none of her business—and just said, "Can I help you with something?"

"I'm going to be your favorite person today," she said.

"You are?"

"I am. You have quite the reputation at the police station at the bottom of the Royal Mile."

"Okay," I said.

"They all seem to know you, and believe it or not, many of them like you."

"I'm happy to hear that."

"I couldn't reach Inspector Winters, but I had some good discussions with the other officers at the station. They assured me that Inspector Winters would do everything he could to help you keep your bookshop open, that it would be a terrible shame to see it closed."

"Yes, that's true." I hoped, at least. I moved closer to her as Hector trotted to my feet. I picked him up and scratched behind his ears.

"There *is* a vote set to take place that will determine the fate of your fair bookshop, though. On Monday," Inspector Buchanan said.

"We've figured that out."

"I thought you might have. I didn't know how much more you could figure out on your own though." She looked at the piece of paper. "I brought you a few names."

"Names?"

"Councilors who were particularly adamant about voting to close the bookshop. You see, people have to tell me things because I'm investigating a murder, and I have learned some things, perhaps a sort of map even—a map that includes these names."

I wasn't following completely but I nodded her forward.

"Here's what I know so far—well, what I can share with you. Henry made a few phone calls to some fellow councilors the night after your dinner with him. I am speculating that he wanted to try to cancel the vote to close this bookshop. How about that?"

"What makes you think that?"

"Mary. His wife told me that he talked about it that night. I'm putting two and two together. It's what I do."

Hearing it from her made it much more real than hearing it from Mary, but the news coming at me two times in the last hour lifted my hopes to a level I wasn't previously sure they could ever reach. Those hope bubbles floated in my mind again.

"That's wonderful!" I said.

"Ah, right, so it is. That doesn't mean the vote's been canceled. Others seem to still want the vote to happen, think it's the right thing to do, considering the inspection and all."

"There was no inspection," I said.

"Well, I'm still working on that, but the councilors believe there was one and that the bookshop failed it. Now, I need something from you before I can help you more."

My hopes were dashed a little but I said, "Okay."

Hector barked once.

"I need you to tell me where you were overnight, after the dinner."

I shouldn't talk to her about this without an attorney, but her blackmail was working. I wanted that list of names, even though I still wasn't quite sure what I would do with it. "Home, with my husband. Sleeping mostly. We didn't know about the bookshop issue and it had been an enjoyable dinner. I was tired. I slept well."

"They're newlyweds," Rosie said cheerfully.

I smiled at her.

"Can anyone besides your husband confirm that?"

"No . . . I mean, yes, my landlord, Elias, came over to give us some rolls that his wife, Aggie, had made. He wakes up early. He woke us up as he put them right outside our door. I went out and grabbed the rolls before he got back into his cottage. The rolls are the best when they're warm. I stuck my head out and thanked him. He could confirm, but that's the best I can do."

Inspector Buchanan stuck the piece of paper she held into her pocket and pulled out a notebook and pen. "Name?"

After I gave her Elias's and Aggie's names and numbers, she reached back into her pocket for the piece of paper and handed it to me. "Henry called these people. They were part of the committee spearheading the shutting down of the bookshop. He told them he wanted to talk to them about the vote, but he was killed before he could. Based upon what Mary has told me, I do believe he wanted to cancel the vote, though for the life of me I can't understand how you made such an impression on him that he would change his mind."

"I look like his wife?" I said.

"That you do. Anyway, for the record, I've vetted the people on the list. I am sure they weren't responsible for Henry's murder. I wouldn't send you to talk to possible killers."

"Do you have any idea who killed Henry?"

"I'm afraid I do," she said.

"Who?" I figured it wouldn't hurt to ask.

Inspector Buchanan just sent us a sad smile before she said goodbye, turned, and left the bookshop.

Rosie, Hector, and I blinked at the door as it shut after her.

"Do ye think she really kens the killer?" Rosie asked.

"I have no idea." I looked at Rosie. "Where's Edwin?"

"Och, he's still in Glasgow."

"What is he doing in Glasgow?"

"Yer guess is as good as mine."

My guess was that he was removing himself from easy police access, but I didn't say that out loud.

"Did Inspector Buchanan ask about him?"

"No."

"That's good."

"Why?"

"I'm not sure yet," I said. "But I'd like to talk to Edwin."

"Aye, so . . . who's on the list?" Rosie asked.

I unfolded and looked at the paper.

"Three women," I said. "Bella Montrose, Simone Lazar, and Monika Hidasi."

"I dinnae ken any of them."

"I have addresses. That's good."

"How did it go with Mary?"

"She claimed she was trying to call me to let me know that Henry was going to try to cancel the vote. After he met us that night and liked us so much and I looked so much like Mary, he was going to try to call it off. I think Henry ended up liking all of us, and that was enough."

"That's a good thing isnae it? And it confirms what Inspector Buchanan just said."

"But then he was killed, and now there's probably nothing we can do to stop the vote." I looked at the piece of paper. "Unless, I can convince other councilors, I guess."

"I think that's what Inspector Buchanan was thinking." Rosie sighed. "I havenae found the paperwork. I havenae found the Burgess Ticket, but now I truly believe everything will be fine."

"I don't know." I shook my head. "Rosie, is there any

chance Edwin has the current queen's number? I'm beginning to think a royal decree is our only hope."

Rosie smiled. "I dinnae think it would be easy, but if anyone can do it, ye can, lass."

I tried to call Edwin but he didn't answer. I wasn't surprised. I tapped my finger on my mouth as I paced the front of the store. Hector let me hold him and scratch his ears as Rosie helped some customers. Once it was just us in the shop again she reached for Hector.

I gave him up reluctantly and the crook of my arm felt much lonelier without him.

"Go talk tae those women, lass. Ye're of no use tae me here. Hector can only do so much. I'll tell Edwin tae ring ye the second I hear from him."

I could take a bus. In fact, I might even be able to walk to see them with little problem. But, I needed some extra input and I knew exactly whom I wanted to talk to. I called Elias.

"I can't figure out what's going on," I said to Elias.

"Aye," Elias said thoughtfully. "These women might help."

"I might need you the rest of the day."

"That's what I'm here for." Elias smiled as he kept his attention forward, out the windshield, toward the traffic.

"Not really, but I do appreciate it."

In fact, there were actual days that Elias operated his taxi like a real taxi; driving people places and taking fare for such trips. I liked to keep that in mind and not bother him too much. In the past I'd offered him money for his time and fuel, but he'd made it clear that I was never to do that again.

"There. There it is," I said. "Montrose Photography."

"Do you want me tae come in with ye?"

"Yes, please."

"Will do." Elias puffed slightly. Though I hadn't meant to assign him the role of my protector, he'd taken it on himself and seemed to like it. His wife, Aggie, had told me he enjoyed the role, giving him something to do other than help her clean the "guesthooses" and drive the taxicab. I wasn't afraid of Bella Montrose, Edinburgh City Councilor, but since I was pretty sure she wasn't a killer, it would be okay to bring him along. Neither of us would be in harm's way.

He parked the taxi not far from the front door. No one greeted us as we went inside, but I was immediately stopped short by the stunning photographs adorning the walls and filling the two tables at the front of the small space. A wall separated the gallery from what I guessed were offices behind it.

The room was a tourist's to-do list, or maybe a wish list. There were so many places to see, and if you couldn't see them in person, these stunning photographs were almost as much fun.

"How does the light do that?" I said as I looked at one of the pictures on the wall, a shot of the Edinburgh castle. I'd seen many pictures of the castle and I worked right below it, but I'd never seen it captured so beautifully. "Is that real or photoshopped?"

"I have no idea what ye're talking about, lass, but that's a beautiful picture, I agree."

As I heard a door open somewhere in the back, I tried to glance over the rest of the pictures.

"Hi, can I help you?" The woman approached. She was dressed in jeans and a white T-shirt, her long hair pulled back in a messy ponytail.

"Might you be Bella Montrose?" I said.

"Yes," she said suspiciously. I wondered if she rarely got customers or if she knew I was coming to talk to her.

"I'm Delaney Nichols. I work at The Cracked Spine. This is my friend, Elias."

"Ah, I thought someone from there might come see me."

"Yer pictures are stunning," Elias said as they shook hands.

"Thank you." The ghost of a smile pulled at her lips but only briefly.

"Ms. Montrose, we're sorry to bother you, but a police inspector told me I should talk to you about the vote to close the bookshop, that you are a councilor and that Henry talked to you the night before he was killed."

She sighed. "He did."

I hesitated. I wasn't exactly sure where to go from there. I jumped in. "I'm trying to figure out how the bookshop was originally targeted? I'm trying to understand because there's never been an inspection. Can you tell me how all this happened?"

Her eyes widened and she shook her head. "Delaney, I've seen the inspection."

"You have? Do you have a copy?"

"No, I don't. But I have seen it and it is valid."

"Is there any way to get a copy?"

"Not at the moment." She frowned. "Delaney, Henry called me the night before he was killed. He said he wanted to meet for breakfast and discuss the vote regarding The Cracked Spine. When the police were here earlier, they told me they think he wanted to cancel the vote. He didn't come out and say that to me, but I could tell he was . . . concerned about something."

"Meet for breakfast?" I said.

"Aye, he was killed on the way."

Gut punch. "I'm so sorry."

She cleared her throat. "Thank you. Yes, there was something else he wanted to tell us, something else he wanted us to know. That's why we were having breakfast."

I pulled out the note from my pocket and looked at it. "Were Simone Lazar and Monika Hidasi invited too?"

"Yes, we were part of the original committee. The four of us and Henry's nephew-in-law, Mikey Wooster. Simone, Monika, and I felt the explosion but none of us could have guessed that Henry was the victim. We called him once he was late and he didn't answer his mobile, but even then we still didn't suspect he'd been blown up in a car bomb!"

I swallowed but forged ahead, hoping I wasn't treading too insensitively. "Was Mikey also invited to the breakfast?"

"I don't know. He wasn't there, with the three of us as we waited."

He'd been at the dinner the night before. Maybe Henry had talked to him after Rosie, Tom, and I left.

I said, "Ms. Montrose, can you remember when The Cracked Spine first came up in council discussions?"

She nodded. "I've been thinking about it, and, yes, I think I do remember. It wasn't Henry who brought it up first at all."

"Who was it then?" I fully expected her to say that it was Mikey Wooster, though I wasn't exactly sure why. It just seemed like that answer would somehow fit.

"It was someone from outside the council. He came to a meeting and made a small presentation. It wasn't scheduled, but he showed up and was given the floor. He talked about the city's building issues and he wanted us to pay attention to the problems. He used The Cracked Spine as an example. I don't know how Henry took it all over and made it his, but shortly after that, closing The Cracked Spine as well as asking for old Burgess Tickets became council discussions."

"What was his name?"

"His name is Lyle Mercado. He's the head of the business-licensing division of the city."

"I know who he is," I said. "Can you tell me any more about that?"

"I wish I could," she said. "I'm afraid I wasn't paying close attention. I've heard strange things about him and I didn't like the man. I didn't think anyone was really listening to him. I apologize. It's my job to pay attention, but I didn't give him much credence. I didn't think anything would come of his visit, but Henry trudged forward."

"Strange things?" I said.

"Yes, he's one of those past-lives people. He's also an amateur hypnotist. He's a weird combination of things I don't believe in."

"Do you know who Mr. Mercado thought he once was?" I asked, wondering if he and Mary had spent a different time together. "In a past life?"

"I'm afraid I don't. I'm sorry."

"Do you know Henry's wife?"

"Of course, I do, and I think she's weird too, though I never would have said that to Henry."

"Did it ever seem that Henry and Mary had a bad marriage?"

"No, not at all. Henry didn't talk about his wife much but when he did, it was with only loving words. He was loyal to her, as far as I could tell. I told as much to the police."

"Who would want Henry dead?" Yes, I wanted to make sure the bookshop didn't close, but even in my one-track mind, finding Henry's killer did seem important.

"Not everyone liked him, but none of us are universally liked. We have opinions, we have city issues we all want to, need to, get taken care of."

"Would Lyle Mercado be upset that Henry wanted the vote canceled?"

"I don't have any idea. Delaney, I think you're thinking Henry was killed because of the bookshop issue, but there were other things he was working on too. The police know."

"The Burgess Tickets?"

"Yes, I admitted to the police that it seemed Henry was trying to keep the bookshop issue on the down low, but everyone had heard about the Burgess Tickets. In fact, none of us had heard from anyone from The Cracked Spine, as far as I know. At one point I was concerned that the vote would happen almost secretly—there are ways to hide things like that—but I didn't give it much thought. I'm busy, like everyone else. I'm sorry. But there are lots of things we work on, government salaries, budgets. I never saw or heard of anyone angry at Henry, but it's more than feasible that someone was angry enough to . . . well, unreasonably angry, I guess."

"Will the vote regarding the bookshop still take place?"

"I think so, but I will vote against closing the bookshop because I am guessing that's what Henry wanted. At least it should be postponed until we understand more. Simone and Monika probably will vote the same way, but I can't speak for the rest of the council. I will try to make the case that Henry had potentially changed his mind. But, you have to understand, we all saw the inspection report. There are dangers with your buildings."

"Thank you," I said. "We will fix whatever needs fixing. I promise."

"I'll make sure I let everyone know. No promises, Delaney, but I think it's only right to try to slow everything down until we understand what's going on."

More hope bubbles. I wanted to cry in relief. She was on our team. I didn't cry though; instead, I thanked her again. I almost pulled her into a hug, but fortunately I caught myself. She might have been okay with it, but I'm glad I held back.

Finally, we expressed our condolences again and left Bella Montrose and her extraordinary photographs.

"What do you think?" Elias said when he got into the taxi.

"I think she's wrong. I think Henry Stewart was killed because he changed his mind and didn't want the bookshop closed," I said.

"Really? That's not what I expected you tae say, not really what I expected would get your attention."

I nodded. I felt oddly sure about this, even if I didn't know why. "But we're missing the real reason behind closing the bookshop, Elias. There's something else there. I don't know how I'm going to figure it out, but I'm going to, and when I do, not only will we remain open for business, I'll find a killer too. I promise you."

"Aye. Lead the way."

TWENTY-THREE

I couldn't let go of what Bella had told us. With the new information, Lyle seemed much shiftier than I'd first thought, and much more involved than he'd appeared. I asked Elias to make our next stop the business-licensing office.

"Is Lyle Mercado available?" I asked one of the people behind the counter. I didn't remember this woman being there when Edwin and I had visited. She was the only one there today.

"Who's asking?" she said.

"Delaney and Elias. I work with Edwin MacAlister."

Elias puffed up next to me.

"One minute."

I noticed her name tag said Susan. Slowly, Susan made her way through the doorway that led to Lyle's office. Elias and I watched her and then shared a frown.

"Goodness, she's not happy tae be working today," he said.

There were no other customers in the office. It was Saturday and I'd been surprised to find the office open.

"She's not fond of the Saturday shift, I guess."

Susan reappeared quickly. "He's not here. Must have left."

"Are you sure?" I said.

"Aye," she said flatly.

"Okay. Thank you." I turned to leave but changed my mind. An image of Dina being upset came to me, and I remembered I hadn't seen where she'd gone before I tried to follow her inside. I'd thought the loo, but now that I suspected she somehow knew Lyle Mercado, I wondered. I turned around again.

"Susan, are business licenses public information? I mean, if I were to ask you if a certain business had a valid license, could you tell me yes or no and how long before it expires?"

"Aye, it's public information."

"How about a place called Art Studio in Cowgate?" I said.

"One minute." She moved to a computer and defied the earlier impression she'd made. Her fingers moved quickly over the keyboard. "Aye, it's got five months before it expires."

"How about Dina's Place? It's in Cowgate too."

She typed more. "Aye, it's not set to expire for eight months."

"Do you make note of when fees are paid late?"

She squinted. "I can see if there are late fees included, but I'm not sure that's public information."

"Okay, well, I guess I'd just like to know if there are late fees attached to Dina's Place, maybe if she paid her fees recently, if you can tell me."

"Um. Well." she looked at the screen and then back up at me. "No late fees. The last payment was received on time."

"Do you ever just not mark the fees, let customers not pay

them?" I smiled. "You know, if they promise to never, ever do it again."

"No, there's no system set up to remove them. It's all done on the computer. We can't override anything."

"I see. Thank you."

"You're welcome."

As Elias and I left, I explained how I'd seen Dina upset allegedly about being late with her payment.

"She was lying but I don't know why," I said.

"Maybe it's something as simple as she was embarrassed about being upset. Her uncle had just been killed."

"Maybe. Or she was coming to talk to Lyle Mercado."

"About what?"

"I'm not sure yet." Was I onto something, a connection? If I was, it was a vague notion that left me feeling more like I was missing something than that I was onto something. But I felt like I needed to keep searching for that missing part.

We got back into the taxi.

"Ready for our next stop?" I said.

"Aye."

Brigid McBride wasn't happy to see me, but that was okay.

"Hello," she said succinctly as Elias and I came through the front door of the small newspaper office.

Last time I had been there, the place had been buzzing with activity. Today, it was just Brigid and a man with thick glasses peering at a computer screen. I didn't think he noticed that Elias and I had come in.

"Hey, Brigid, you have some time?" I asked.

"You have something good for me?"

"I think I might."

Doubt wrinkled her pretty mouth and the pretty places next to her pretty eyes.

"It's good," Elias added his endorsement.

"Well, I'll be the judge of that. Come on back." She swooped her arm for us to follow.

And we did.

I told her everything I knew. I was pretty sure Edwin hadn't killed Henry; at least I really hoped he hadn't. I put it all out there, hoping her journalistic mind could bring it together and make some sense of it.

"Something's up," Brigid said when I finished.

"I know!" I said with happy exclamation. "There has to be, doesn't there?"

"I need more answers," she said.

"Me too! That's what I was hoping for."

"No, Delaney, I mean I need more answers before I consider whether or not it's something I want to continue to follow up on. It's all over the place. A car bomb—the murder of a man who wants to shut down the bookshop and then allegedly changes his mind after he meets you all. The man in charge of business licenses. They're tied together, aren't they? A woman who thinks she's the reincarnation of Mary, Queen of Scots, and you and she could be related. That's bizarre, by the way. If I were the police, I'd still be suspicious of everyone at the bookshop. Mostly Edwin and you. Edwin because he's Edwin and he's a suspicious man, and you because you look like the dead man's wife. Spitting image."

Well, that hadn't totally gone as I'd hoped. "None of us killed Henry, Brigid, but no matter what you say, I think you know that already."

"I know nothing of the sort. You're all a suspicious bunch."

"But we're not killers." I kept my face as neutral as possible. That might not be entirely true, but what had happened between a university-aged Edwin, his friends, and the love of his young life on a boat occurred a long time ago. And, it was probably justified. Nevertheless. "You know we aren't killers."

She did that thing with her mouth and eyes again. "I don't know how I can put together a story in enough time to help you with the vote, Delaney. There's a lot to look at here."

"I know. What I was hoping for was that, yes, you get the story. I think it will prove to be a good one. But, what I hope for today is that you give me your contact in the Lord Provost's office. Surely, there's someone there you talk to, the press person. That's how it works, right?"

"You told me all that so I'd tell you my contact?"

"Well . . ."

"That wouldn't do me much good in keeping that contact if I gave up her name all the time."

"I won't tell her you told me."

She looked at me.

"Promise I won't," I said. "I'm desperate here, Brigid. Please. You'll have a story, I'm sure. There's something, or a number of somethings fishy going on here. I bet the answers will converge and make one good story."

"It's not enough. I'm sorry."

I couldn't hand over my husband (and I wouldn't if I could), so I had nothing else. Or so I thought.

"How about," she leaned forward and put her arms on the table. "You do something else for me."

Elias shifted in his chair as I said, "What?"

"Let me interview Edwin about the warehouse. Let me take pictures."

The warehouse had officially been deemed not so much a secret anymore, but we still didn't advertise it. We hadn't released pictures to the public.

"Why?" I asked.

"Because everyone wants to see it, wants to know it's real."

"Edwin's stopped denying it's real," I said.

"But he hasn't let anyone in. I haven't seen any pictures yet."

"I'll talk to Edwin, and I'll make a strong case. Cross my heart." I did just that. "But I need your contact's name today. Please. Time is running out."

Brigid sat back in her chair. "Give Edwin a call."

I looked at Elias.

I said, "I'm not trying to be coy, Brigid, but I really think this is a conversation to have in person. I promise I will do that."

The weight of negotiation filled the air between us.

"All right. Aye, I'll do some of your legwork, Delaney. I look forward to hearing back from you. Today," Brigid said a long moment later.

I nodded. "Absolutely."

From her desk, Brigid found a piece of paper and a pen and scribbled a name, along with an address. She handed it to me. "If she's not at work in an office down the hall from the Lord Provost's, here's her assistant's mobile. I won't give you hers, but she usually works on the weekends, so does her assistant. I know time's tight or I wouldn't give you so much."

I looked at the paper briefly wondering if I might recognize the name, Grace Graham. Didn't ring a bell.

"Thank you, Brigid."

"You're welcome. Talk to Edwin. Call me today."

"Will do."

Brigid walked us to the door of the newspaper office and told us goodbye. I could tell she was anxious to get to work. She'd said there was too much information, but she smelled a story, and I knew she'd wrestle to get to it, no matter what she'd said. I hoped her enthusiasm would help her find something that might help keep the bookshop safe.

And find a killer too, of course.

TWENTY-FOUR

Elias and I tried to find Simone Lazar and Monika Hidasi, but they weren't in the places Inspector Buchanan had noted as their offices. Simone worked out of her home, and Monika had a coffee shop listed as her office space. I hoped they felt the same way Bella did about the vote, and I decided I'd try to reach them later. I wondered if I should just try to talk to all the councilors, but I didn't know how I could accomplish that with the short time left before the vote.

By the time we made it to the government office that housed the Lord Provost's office as well as Brigid's media relations contact, Grace Graham, the entire building was locked tight. I tried the mobile number, but the call went directly to voice mail. I couldn't help but wonder if Brigid had warned Grace I might try to find her.

"No matter, lass," Elias said. "May I suggest ye talk tae Edwin first? Ye are correct in that he kens so many people. Maybe he and Grace are acquainted. Start there. I ken ye've only a wee bit of time left, but let's not bother Ms. Graham on the weekend if we dinnae have tae."

I agreed. He was correct, and, besides, that earlier fluttering of hope I'd felt was becoming stronger. The truth would win out, I was sure.

I just hoped my version of the truth was the correct one.

Elias dropped me off at the bookshop, and I watched his cab until it turned the corner.

When I stepped inside the bookshop with my phone at the ready to call Edwin, I heard his voice. I raced around to the back table though not because of any promise I'd made to Brigid. Even though I'd told her I would try to get her an exclusive regarding the warehouse, I was going to work on a way to get out of that one. I would chalk up my breaking the promise to desperate times.

"You're here," I said.

"I am, lass. I'm sorry I didnae return yer calls immediately, but I was looking for someone and," he glanced at a man sitting across the table from him, "once I found him, we hurried back."

"I was just going tae ring you," Rosie said with a confident smile. She and Hamlet sat next to each other at the table too.

Edwin stood and said, "This is our attorney, Jack McGinnis. He's here to help us."

"So good to meet you," I effused as I walked to him and shook his hand after he stood too.

"Good to meet you, lass," he said, much less effusively, but friendly enough.

"Have a seat, Delaney. Jack was just telling us what we might be able to do legally to save the bookshop," Edwin said.

"Oh, I am ready to hear this. So ready."

Jack McGinnis looked like someone out of *The Sopranos*. His light Scottish accent was difficult to get used to mostly because I thought he should sound like someone from New Jersey or New York, someone who stereotypically kept brass knuckles in his pocket and liked pasta.

He was firm in the fact that there was no way the vote to close the bookshop was in the realm of legal. Unfortunately, illegal and unethical things happened all the time. He was there to make sure that, ultimately, the bookshop wouldn't have to close its doors, at least not forever.

"I don't think I can stop the vote," he said. "But we can make our case at the meeting, and I can demand to see all the documentation. After that, there are other measures we can take, but nothing works exactly like we'd all want it to. Nothing is going to happen quickly, and it might take some convincing, but I'm confident that it will work out."

"Unless, the vote fails?" I said. "Then we won't have to worry about it."

"There is that possibility," Jack said.

"Let's call all the councilors," I said. "Between all of us, we can get it done."

"I don't think that's reasonable, Delaney. It wouldn't be easy to acquire all the numbers," Edwin said. "We'll make our case at the meeting."

"Edwin, did you ever talk to Henry? Tell him or anyone you would sue to make sure the bookshop doesn't close? Did you threaten to sue? Were you angry with him?"

"I haven't spoken forcefully to anyone other than Lyle, and you were with me," Edwin said. "That's why I tracked down Jack in Glasgow, so I don't have to make such threats. He can take care of that for me."

Jack nodded.

"Really?"

The bell above the door jingled. Rosie stood and walked toward the front.

"Lass, hello," we heard her say.

I stood to see who'd come in and was shocked to see it was the person who I was just thinking about. Why had Mary told me that Edwin had threatened Henry? Perhaps the better question was why had Henry told her that? I hoped the even more correct question *wasn't* why was Edwin lying about making such threats.

Rosie escorted Mary Stewart toward us.

"Oh. Hello. I'm sorry to interrupt," Mary said.

"Hello, Mary," I said.

"Edwin, Jack, this is one of our new friends, Mary Stewart. Mary, this is Edwin, Jack, and Hamlet," Rosie said. "What can we do for ye, lass?"

Mary frowned as she surveyed us. I didn't know if she'd come in just to see Rosie or me, but now she had us all.

"Lass, we're sorry for your loss," Edwin said.

Mary nodded.

"Wow," Hamlet said, "I heard about the resemblance, but it's . . ."

"Unbelievable," Jack said as he looked back and forth between Mary and me.

"Truly," Hamlet added. "Deepest condolences, Ms. Stewart."

"Thank you," Mary said with a sad smile. She gathered herself and continued, "I feel like now might be a bad time, but I have some important information to share. I might be able to help."

"We're listening," I said. "It's not a bad time, Mary."

"I . . . remembered something. I searched and found . . . I'm a wee bit afraid, though. It might be, I don't know. It might cause more trouble."

"Did you talk to the police about it?" Edwin asked as Jack continued to look curiously back and forth between Mary and me.

"No," she said. "I . . . feel responsible. May I explain from the beginning?"

"Aye," Edwin said. "One moment." He hurried to the door, locked it, and turned the sign to Closed.

As we all sat around the table, Edwin made it clear to Mary that Jack McGinnis was our attorney, that he was there specifically to help them fight the council, keep the bookshop open. No one tried to hide anything.

"I'm not going to ask him to leave," Edwin said.

Mary nodded. "I don't care. It's fine." She pursed her lips a moment. "I think this all began about two years ago. Henry and I were on holiday in France." She frowned at Jack as he, unashamedly, took notes. She didn't ask him to stop. "You all probably know that the queen spent much of her youth in France." We nodded. "On my holiday with Henry, we were enjoying Paris when a docent, a gentleman, in one of the museums there started talking to us. I'm afraid I don't remember his name—maybe Jean or Jacque, I'm not sure. He was just as intrigued by Mary, Queen of Scots, as I am. Though I didn't let him know about my past life as the queen, he mentioned that he thought I looked like her, and he wanted to tell us something when we said we were from Edinburgh." Mary looked at Edwin so pointedly that it was briefly uncomfortable. "And then he brought up the name of this bookshop. I just remembered this afternoon. Delaney must have jogged my memory. I don't think the man said your name, Edwin MacAlister; I would have remembered sooner if he had. But he mentioned The Cracked Spine, I'm sure of it."

She stopped talking and fell into thought.

"In what context was the bookshop brought up?" Edwin asked.

She looked at him again. "In his story, he said that the owner of this bookshop had some important documents, some so rare they might actually change the world."

"We have some rare documents, aye. Was he more specific?" Edwin said.

"He said that in your records, somewhere in your files, you have some notes, handwritten by Elizabeth I herself, regarding a letter aboot a sort of truce between her and Mary."

"Mary, Queen of Scots?" Jack asked, but I thought it was just for extra clarification. We all knew who she was talking about.

"Aye," she said.

Jack nodded.

"That's exactly what we were told," Mary continued. "I rang the museum just before I came over today and, based on my description of him, that man is no longer there. They couldn't or wouldn't give me a forwarding number or address, but I know it happened. I know what he said."

"Mary, you just remembered this?" I said. "Forgive me, but it was about the queen. I would think you would never forget anything said about her."

"Why? Because I should remember knowing everything about her, because I *was* her?"

"No," I said. "Because you *truly believe* you were her, I would guess you would remember everything that you learned about her. You would be interested in everything."

Mary laughed once. "Delaney, people tell me things about the queen every single day. I don't remember most. I don't pay attention most of the time, because I can sense what's real and what isn't. I know that sounds strange, but believe me—believe *in* me or not—for whatever reason, what that man said didn't stay with me. Maybe it didn't ring true at the time. Maybe it was more about Elizabeth than Mary. I don't know, but I finally did remember the conversation. Today."

"Fair enough," I said. "What else did he say?"

"The gentleman at the museum said that Elizabeth wrote down some thoughts right before Lord Darnley, Mary's husband, was killed. Her notes were being used as she drafted a letter to Mary. The man in the French museum said that Elizabeth had been considering ways to make the relationship between her and Mary—England and Scotland—better. This notion is backed up some by history, but not the notes or letter specifically. When Darnley was killed, the letter was either destroyed, hidden, or stolen. The docent speculated that perhaps, Moray, Mary's half brother, had taken the letter, maybe to use against someone at some point. Maybe he just didn't want it to come to light. Who knows what Moray was up to, but he certainly betrayed Mary."

Moray again, I thought. "Why did the docent think this letter existed? What proof did he have?"

Mary shook her head. "That's why I tried to find him today. I don't think Henry and I asked him for more details. I can't remember if we were interrupted, if we'd had too much wine, or if we thought the docent was a wee bit off in his head. I think I forgot about it all quickly. Until today."

"I'm not aware of anything of the sort," Edwin said. "Existing here in the bookshop or anywhere else for that matter."

Rosie, Hamlet, and I said we hadn't seen anything that might be a letter written by Elizabeth I. We all would have noticed something that significant.

"Mary, the likelihood that those documents, if they existed at all, could stand the test of time is . . . almost impossible," I said.

"Not necessarily," Mary said. "At dinner, you yourself mentioned Mary's recently discovered notes. The ones found in a box in the basement of the museum. It's very possible for documents to stand the test of time."

I nodded. "True."

"Edwin, what if you *do* have the letter or the notes? And," Mary paused and seemed to steel herself, "what if Henry *didn't* forget? I've forgotten much from that holiday, but I also remember this: I told him, in jest I thought, that we should buy the bookshop and all its contents. We shouldn't tell the owner—I didn't know your name at the time—what we'd learned but that we should just buy everything. We have plenty of money. I was just being silly. I was not serious. We were just having a good time."

"Oh, no," I said aloud.

Everyone looked at me.

"Edwin, you've said that you would give the shop to Rosie or Hamlet or even me, or you'd just shut it down, before you ever took a dime for it," I said.

"Aye."

"Did Henry approach you to purchase the shop?" I asked.

"I have no recollection of any such thing, but many people have approached me to buy the shop over the years."

"If he did approach you and you told him no, then closing the shop could have been Henry's revenge," I said. I looked at Mary. "Edwin says he never spoke with Henry about the vote, a bad inspection, about suing. Edwin just received a recorded call."

"That is the absolute truth," Edwin said.

"If Henry made that up, who knows what else he fabricated," I said.

"Delaney," Mary said. "Henry is the one who was killed."

"I'm sorry," I said to Mary. I looked at Edwin. "We need to search the shop again. If those papers are here, we need to find them."

Everyone agreed.

Edwin turned to Mary. "I know this was hard, this is a difficult time, but thank you. We will search and we'll let you know."

"I really hope . . ." Her eyes filled with tears but she blinked fast and furious. "That it will all be okay. I'm . . ."

"What?" I said.

"I'm trying understand what Henry was up to, what he was thinking, and what he did shortly before he died. I know that keeping the bookshop open is your priority, but I'd like his killer brought to justice, even if I'm afraid he was in the middle of doing something less than noble. I will tell the police all of this. I will tell the council. I will do what I can."

Rosie stood. "Lass, can we get ye a cuppa or some coffee? Perhaps a glass of water?"

"No, thank you. I've got to go. I need to talk to someone else today."

I couldn't help myself. "Who?"

Mary blinked at me. "Oh. Well, Henry's brother. I believe they spoke the day before Henry was killed. They shared secrets with each other, sometimes."

I didn't even for one second consider that I might be stepping over some line, butting into something that wasn't my business. I stood. "Want some company?"

TWENTY-FIVE

At first, Mary wasn't sure what to make of my offer. No one was. I sensed everyone's surprise or maybe it was embarrassment, but I didn't care. I didn't know what else I wanted from Mary, but I knew I wanted something. I wasn't ready to tell her goodbye for the day.

However, I thought she was somehow relieved to have someone with her. Henry's brother worked evenings at the castle on the hill. I'd been prepared to call Elias for a ride to wherever we needed to go, but it turned out we were only a short walk away. As we made our way, passing Tom's pub without stopping, I told Mary I'd seen the hypnotism.

"You were there?" she said, genuinely surprised.

"I was. It was interesting. Do you remember being . . . under?"

"I do. I remember it all."

"Are you and Lyle Mercado friends?" I asked.

"Oh, yes, Lyle and I have known each other for years. He remembers his past lives too."

"Who was he?"

"No one famous."

"No one associated with the queen?"

"No, I don't believe so."

"Mary, do you know he was the one who first planted the seed for not only closing the bookshop but the resurgence of the Burgess Tickets."

"I don't think so," Mary said.

"That's what Bella Montrose told me. Do you know her?"

"Of course I do."

"Would Henry and Lyle have been in on this together?" I asked again.

Mary sighed. "No, Delaney, but I could see Lyle doing Henry's bidding. Lyle is enamored with us, Henry and me. Lyle and I met through the past-lives group, but when we all became friends, it was clear that Lyle thought Henry and I were something special. It's a terribly vain thing to say, but it's the truth. If Henry didn't want to present a new idea that he wasn't sure he should present, Lyle would jump aboard and do it for him."

"Does he have any sort of romantic feelings for you?"

"No," she said after a long pause. "I'm sure of that."

No matter, I hoped the police were taking a good look at Lyle Mercado. Maybe I'd mentioned his name to Inspector Buchanan.

"You know, I blame Mary of Guise for the whole mess," Mary said.

"Hold on—who is Mary of Guise? And why do you blame her?" I said as we came upon the castle courtyard, thankfully stopping so I could catch my breath.

"There were a lot of other reasons, but she was Mary Stuart's mother. Mary of Guise ruled as regent for her infant daughter. And then she died when Mary was eighteen, still in France about to move to Scotland. Died!—right when Mary needed her the most. Mary never saw her mother again after she was sent to France as a child. Mary might have been able to fight those against her better if her mother hadn't left her. Her mother was trying to forge a better relationship with Elizabeth. She might have accomplished it and helped her daughter. But death was only a half a breath away back in 1560, one tiny scratch gone wrong."

"Did Mary of Guise die of an infection?"

"There was speculation she was poisoned, but it was never proved. The official cause was dropsy."

"Dropsy?"

"Too much fluid under the skin, around the organs."

"Tragic."

"The queen's life was one tragedy after another."

"No kidding," I said.

Mary's energetic march up to the castle had tired my calves. I was used to walking around the city, but whatever was fueling her energy felt more like a jog than a walk.

"Mary was young," I added. "She might not have had the sophistication to deal with Elizabeth."

"Exactly."

"How did their meetings go?"

Mary eyebrows came together. "Delaney, they never met, face-to-face."

"What?"

"No, never."

"I had no idea."

Mary turned and faced me. She reached up and held onto my arms. The moment was over the top, uncomfortable, though I didn't pull away.

"However, I have a distinct feeling that Elizabeth felt that we—she and Mary—would be queens *together*. I'm so sure of those words, that sentiment, but I can't understand why."

I swallowed hard. "Do you have a distinct memory of that? You can be straight with me. I won't tell either way. I'll be straight with you, I don't think the birthmark is much proof, though I'm not saying I disbelieve you."

"But you don't *believe* me?"

"Something like that."

She took her hands off my arms but still faced me. "Delaney, when I was four years old, I found some wild violets and brought a bouquet of them into my house. I told my mother I wanted to make some jelly or marmalade with them. She laughed and said that wasn't how those things were made."

"Seems reasonable."

"But at one time, it was exactly how marmalade was made—with the powder of violets into boiling quinces and sugar. To this day I remember being upset with my mother that she wouldn't let me into the kitchen. It was later when I started studying the queen that I learned that was one of her favorite pastimes. She liked to spend her time in the kitchen making cotignac, which is a marmalade-like creation made with the powder of violets. How else would a four-year-old know such a thing if she hadn't lived a past life doing it?"

"Maybe someone read it to you in a child's book."

"I don't think so, and I challenge anyone to find such a book. I've lost many of the memories, but they used to come at me all the time. Visions, colors, fabrics, smells, people's faces. When I was twelve, still before I started studying the queen, I started embroidery—and it not only was a passion, I was immediately good at it. Guess who else was?"

"The queen."

"Exactly. I'm not pulling anyone's leg. I'm not making anything up. I was Mary, Queen of Scots."

A tiny ray of sunshine peaked out from behind the clouds and seemed to illuminate Mary, and then it was gone, behind a cloud again. But, for that instant, I thought I was seeing a queen. I knew it could just be all the talk, and I knew she could still be making everything up. But, there's something different about a queen, and I thought I might have glimpsed that difference. Briefly.

I was still looking at her, processing her words when she emphatically added, "And guess what I was obsessed about embroidering? Just guess."

"I have no idea."

"Cats! That was one of Mary's first embroideries. Will you believe me now?"

"I don't think you're lying," I said, though I wasn't exactly sure. "But I don't want to lie to you either and tell you that I do believe you. I'm pretty open to anything, but this is a big leap to make. And I always feel like there's usually a believable explanation for everything, Mary. For now, I'm willing to just continue on not disbelieving. Is that okay?"

She looked at me with the same study I had made of her. "It's uncanny how we look alike."

"Yes, it is," I agreed. "But it's not because we're twins."

I hoped that made the point I was trying so hard not to offensively make.

She smiled a moment later and laughed once. "Fair enough. All right, come along. I need to see if Henry was at the castle the day before his death."

"Why?" I hurried to follow her resumed pace.

"He told his brother everything he couldn't tell me. They were close, and when he felt like he couldn't talk to me about something, he would talk to Clayton. He would always come up to the castle, where they were surrounded by mostly tourists, by people who probably wouldn't know he was a councilor. I always joked about Henry plotting battles at this castle just like was done in the olden days." A ghost of a smile rode over her mouth and then disappeared. "Maybe Henry said something to Clayton the day or days before he was killed that will help find the killer."

"Will he be here? I mean, he might be home, in mourning."

"No," she shook her head, "he'll be here. He'll mourn in his way, but it will include a stiff Scottish upper lip and a notion that he can't miss work for anything but his own death. Henry was the same way."

"Did you tell the police about Henry and Clayton's relationship?"

"Of course, but that woman who is heading up the investigation is not interested in what I have to say. She thinks I'm nutty in the head."

"I sensed she was a good officer though, thorough. Maybe she'll do okay."

She sent me another look. "I don't know, Delaney, the police didn't much like Henry either."

"Why?"

"They pay attention to which of the councilors vote to decrease things like police salaries and such."

"Oh dear. Did something like that just go through?'

"No, not recently, but Henry voted against an increase a while back. Though he only voted against it because he thought they should get more. He had to explain himself several times. People were angry."

"Angry enough to kill?"

"I don't know."

We reached the lines of tourists and Mary led us around, taking us directly to the ticket booth. We were none too popular for it, but once at the counter, Mary just waved at the woman in the booth.

"Och, Mary, what a surprise! So sorry about Henry, love."

"Ta," Mary said. "We're going in, Janice."

"Aye. G'on," Janice said before she signaled for the next person in line to step up to the window.

With swift feet I followed Mary as I sent a frown of apology back to the people in the line.

"It'll do you no good," Mary said. "We have business to do and we have to get on with it. We don't have time to wait in any lines."

"Okay," I said. "Do you have special privileges?"

"I do," she said.

She was behaving more like the Mary I'd first met. She'd struck me as confident and bossy then, and now too. In between, though, I'd seen sad, apologetic, and unsure.

However, she cleared her throat as if she'd heard herself. "It's not what you think. I have volunteered at all the museums. I love them, but you could probably already imagine that. Anyway, they all know me and they have all given me the freedom to come and go as I please."

A privilege fit for a queen.

"That's wonderful. I love museums too."

"I'm not surprised." She paused. "Do you think it's possible that Edwin has Elizabeth's notes?"

"I have no idea," I said, "but it's doubtful."

"Why is it doubtful?"

"It's hard to imagine that something like that would be overlooked."

"But it's possible?"

"Sure. I guess."

"Do you think you could take an extra look?"

"Absolutely. We all will."

"Thanks."

We'd crossed the courtyard and went through the wide entry doors.

"Mary!" A man in costume said as he walked toward us. "Hello!"

Mary hugged him. "Sammy."

I thought I saw tears in his eyes when he pulled back, "I heard about Henry. Everyone's heard about Henry. Do the police know what happened yet?"

"Not yet, I'm afraid."

"I'm so sorry, lass."

"Thank you, Sammy." She looked toward me the same time Sammy did.

"Is this . . . you don't have a sister or a daughter, do you?" Sammy said.

"I don't. This is a friend who happens to look like me."

"I'd say. Were ye the queen too?" he asked me sincerely.

"I don't think so," I said as we shook hands.

For a few beats, Sammy looked back and forth between the two of us. "Goodness."

"Yes," Mary said. "Sammy, is Clayton here?"

Sammy took two more quick looks back and forth and said, "Aye, I believe he is."

"Can we go on back?"

"Aye, certainly. He's going tae be as surprised as I am. Maybe more."

Mary nodded and they hugged quickly again before we turned and started walking deeper into the castle.

I'd been through it a time or two—maybe six or seven—over the last year. There was much to see, though I wasn't surprised when Mary led us in the direction of the Royal Apartments, which had at one time been home to the queen, and her husband—the one who was blown to smithereens, in fact.

"You do know that the queen gave birth to her only child here," she said to me over her shoulder.

"I didn't know that," I said.

"Bastard, he turned out to be. Well, not in the official definition. No, he was an arse to his mother," she said. "However, later, after the queen was cruelly beheaded, it must be pointed out that King James I turned out to be a pretty good king."

"How was he an ass?"

Mary slowed her footsteps as we entered the Laich Hall with its dark gold embossed wood paneling and magnificent fireplace. "Mary was not in control of her own life, even as she was queen. When Mary gave birth to James, who would be the heir to the British throne, both Mary and the baby had to be protected. They were separated. But it was toward the end of Mary's life, when she was close to execution that her son wouldn't come see her, wouldn't help make a case to save his mother."

"The end of her life was pretty terrible."

"You mean her assassination disguised as an execution?"

"Yes, I suppose."

"She was betrayed by everyone, her son included. Well, her servants were still on her side, her four Marys, all of her ladies were named Mary, did you know?"

"I think I heard that."

Mary stopped suddenly and looked at the walls. I knew that look—something deep that searched for clues to everything that had happened here. I'd had many of those moments in Scotland.

"Can you feel them?" she asked.

"Feel what?" I asked.

"The ghosts of the past."

I didn't feel them, though that didn't make the castle less impressive or less interesting to me. However, it was at that moment that I became one hundred percent certain that if I'd ever lived a past life, it hadn't been lived in this castle. I knew it, bone deep. Which made me wonder if Mary knew she *had,* bone deep.

No bookish voices were talking either.

"I feel the history," I said. "I don't feel the ghosts, I'm afraid. I have felt them at other times though, so I get what you're saying. That sensation is strong, isn't it?"

"Do you think everyone feels such things?"

"Oh, no," I said with a laugh.

She blinked at me. "See, it was destined that we were to meet."

I laughed again. "Maybe. But even though Edinburgh is a big city, we were either bound to run into each other someday, or someone would meet us both and let us know about the other."

She nodded, but then turned and resumed walking. We made our way through to the great hall. The only great hall I'd seen that compared in any way was Hogwarts. I'd seen a few castles while in Scotland, but this one was done up in its finest.

"Mary was crowned when she was nine months old," Mary said. "It was the solemnest of all events or ceremonies. And here," she stopped next to a display case, "the scepter, the crown, and the sword. They were carried behind her. We are not in a position to understand how important these were, but they were mightily important. Look at them. Do they look real to you?"

They were impressive, but . . . "They look like something that might be found in a costume shop."

"See," she said, "sometimes it's difficult to find the real stuff. Those notes could be in Edwin's things, right under your noses, looking like something from a costume shop, some forgeries, some scribbles."

"Point taken."

"Mary?" Another costumed gentleman came into the room.

"Clayton," Mary said.

This greeting was somewhat icier than Sammy's.

"I'm sorry about Henry," he said stiffly.

"Condolences to you too," Mary said.

They looked at each other for a long, silent moment. I sensed they were both sad, but trying hard not to be. The family dynamics were strained—Mary and Clayton didn't like each other, but that was psychology for another day.

"This is my friend, Delaney," Mary said.

Surprisingly, Clayton only shook my hand and said it was good to meet me. Either he didn't notice my resemblance to his sister-in-law or it didn't matter to him.

"Do you have time to steal away to a private room for a moment?" Mary asked.

"Right this way." Clayton turned and we followed him.

I was disappointed that the private room was nothing special, just something that had been walled off—not a secret castle cubbie or passageway, just a small, modern semiprivate space.

We sat in boring twenty-first-century office chairs around an even more boring small twentieth-century coffee table.

Briefly, I wondered if I could manage to get my phone out to record the conversation, but I dismissed the idea quickly enough. It wasn't a task I could handle subtly, and I didn't even know what was going to be discussed.

"How may I be of service?" Clayton asked Mary.

"Clayton, I need to know if Henry was here the day or few days before he was killed. I need to also know if he spoke to you, what you spoke about."

"Why? Are you investigating his murder?"

"The police are doing what they do, Clayton, but I need some peace and the only way I'm going to get that is to try to understand what my husband was up to. He talked to you about many things. He told you things he didn't tell me and I have a theory. I just need to know if my theory is correct."

Clayton frowned and nodded slowly.

"Henry *was* here the day before he was killed," Clayton said. "He came specifically to talk to me. He was upset about something he'd set into place."

"What?" Mary and I asked together.

"I'm not sure exactly," Clayton said.

Mary put her hand over his. "This is so very important, Clayton. Please tell me what you know."

Clayton sighed. "He was going to get you something, though he wouldn't tell me exactly what it was. He came to me upset that he'd set something in motion with the council that wasn't going to be reversible. It was going to cause harm to some people who probably didn't deserve it, people you'd recently met. He needed to work it out in his head, but he'd done it for you."

"What time was this?" Mary asked.

Clayton thought a moment. "I think it was around two in

the afternoon. I'd already had lunch, but that's as close as I can get."

"That's close enough," Mary said as she deflated.

"What?" I said.

"It was as I was finishing lunch that I rang him. I told him I'd found the most charming of bookshops and that someone there looked so much like me, he was going to be thrown for a loop. I told him the bookshop was called The Cracked Spine, and I'd invited you all over for dinner that night."

"That one call made him feel guilty?" I said.

"I can see that. He asked me if I liked the shop. He asked me about you, the woman who looked so much like me. And, he said something to the effect that it was some sort of sign or something. I asked him to clarify, but he just laughed off the statement and said he had to go. I wouldn't be surprised if he'd already been feeing badly about what he'd done, guilty, and that call with me was the tipping point."

I turned to Clayton, "What did you say to him?"

"All I said was that whatever he'd set into motion, if it wasn't already done, then he should be able to stop it."

"How did he react?" Mary asked.

"He said it was going to be dangerous to stop it, that he could be in trouble."

"Why dangerous?" Mary asked. I really wished I'd turned on the recorder app.

Clayton frowned and shook his head. "He said that 'they' were going to be upset. I asked if he meant you, but he said you had no idea what he'd been doing."

"Did you talk to the police?" I interrupted.

"No, what was I to say?"

"That he knew he might be in danger," I said.

"But that's all I knew. He didn't give me any further details."

"So when he began to change his mind about what he'd done, someone killed him?" I said.

"It seems that way," Mary said.

"Who in the world would that be?" I said.

"That's what the police need to figure out," Mary said.

Clayton sat forward and put his elbows on the table. "Mary, you need to tell me what's going on. I will go talk to the police if I feel I need to, but I need some missing puzzle pieces here."

In a scattered way, with my intermittent input, we told Clayton what had been going on.

By the end of the conversation, it didn't take much coaxing to get Clayton to say he would call the police.

Mary didn't walk with me back to the bookshop. She said goodbye as she hailed a taxi. She said she was going home, that it had been a tiring day, but that she hoped everyone at the bookshop would search for the notes and the letter.

"Do you really think they exist?" I asked her as she got into the cab.

She hesitated and looked at me a long moment. "I don't know if they're in the bookshop, Delaney, but, aye, I think they exist. A big part of me hopes so."

I didn't tell her as much, but it crossed my mind that maybe we'd find the Burgess Ticket, the old construction approvals, and the letter all together. It was just some more hope bubbling up.

If I were something that needed to hide inside the bookshop, where would I hide?

I have no idea, I thought as I watched the taxi drive away.

TWENTY-SIX

"What are you doing?" Tom asked in the dark. It was the middle of the night, and he hadn't been home from the pub long before I was up again, getting dressed.

"I can't sleep," I said quietly, even though there was no one else in our cottage.

"Where are you going?"

"I'm going into the bookshop. I need to search some more."

I'd stopped by the pub on the way back from the castle and updated Tom. Back at the bookshop, we all took on the search, except Jack. He'd left by the time I made it back. But our search had been interrupted by a tour group of twenty that had been caught out in the rain. We'd invited them inside until the storm passed. They'd been there a couple hours, ultimately buying many more books than they probably wanted. We'd left at five for the day, saying we'd resume searching again the next day. It was the next day, though earlier than the others had in mind.

"I'll come with you," Tom said as he swung his legs off the bed.

"No, you need sleep."

"I won't sleep now anyway. It's all right. It's my day off. I'll catch some rest later."

I hadn't meant for him to go, but it would be much better having him along.

I loved Edinburgh, during the daytime and at night. At night, particularly after it had rained though, when puddles glimmered and streetlights and dimmed shop lights shone differently. There was a sense of magic in the air, that sense of history that the older Scottish men in my life: Edwin, Elias, and Tom's father, Artair, held onto with a fierce stubbornness. They weren't stuck in the past, but they carried it with them, always. I understood them more at night.

Tom drove us through town and toward Grassmarket. The rain had only recently stopped, and steam came up from gutters as people moved along the streets. Like so many bigger cities, Edinburgh didn't really sleep, but it rested well. Still, night people, tourists, artists, and restless residents could always find something to do, and something to eat.

Plenty of takeaway restaurants stayed open. A couple of theaters played movies all night long, usually older American films. I'd even come upon one that hosted Rocky Horror interactive shows.

Early on in my time here, I'd spent a few nights making my way through the streets and back to the bookshop in order to work on a project that wouldn't let me rest.

The warehouse was mine now, no doubt. Mine slightly more than Edwin's. I thought he wanted it that way, but sometimes I wasn't sure. Sometimes I saw that look in his eyes, the one that glances back at the way things used to be. He never kept his gaze there long. He was also a firm believer in life going on.

"Delaney, after talking to Clayton, do you still want to talk to Grace Graham?" Tom asked as we made our way.

"First thing, when the sun comes up, I'm going to try to reach her," I said.

"Not confident that there's enough to cancel or postpone the vote yet?"

"Oh, no, not yet. I'm not going to stop until we know for sure."

"Did Mary think even for a minute that Clayton might be responsible for Henry's murder?" Tom asked.

"I don't think so. I admit it crossed my mind, but only because I'm suspicious of everyone. I'm still wondering about Mary," I said.

"An interesting couple. Interesting lives, a tragic death," Tom said.

"Do . . . did you like them?" I hadn't asked him that yet.

"Yes, particularly Henry, until I heard he wanted to shut down the bookshop."

Tom pulled to a stop in front of said bookshop. Over the last year, I'd come upon people and packages that had led to other surprises. Now, I took a good look at the shop and its surroundings before entering.

"All clear?" Tom asked me.

"Looks good."

It was unusually warm outside as we sidestepped the puddles along the cobblestone walkway. After I unlocked the door and we were inside, I relocked it behind us. All the while, Tom watched me and we nodded at each other, confirming we both saw the lock go into place.

Using the light on my phone, we made our way over to the dark side and down the stairs. It was colder on the dark side but not unbearable.

I turned the oversize blue skeleton key in the lock three times to the left before we pushed through the big red door, shutting and locking it behind us.

I flipped on the overhead fluorescents and Tom and I shared another nod and a smile. We were there, the place that even more than the city, more than McKenna's cottage, I'd lived in since moving to Scotland. More than Tom's blue house by the sea, this place was my home. Wherever Tom lived was my true home now, but if he wasn't part of the equation, this warehouse, this space was where my soul truly danced.

"Where do we begin?" Tom asked.

Tonight, the moon shone through one of the high windows, and I took in the rare sight. It would move behind a cloud or away from my view soon, but for an instant, it was lovely. Shelves lined the walls—and they were all packed with things, a wide variety. Need a Fabergé egg? Hang on, there was one here not long ago. How about some things that came from ancient Egyptian tombs? Right over there. Books filled some shelves but there were fewer books than one might think would be in storage in a bookshop. Mostly, the shelves overflowed with Edwin's collections, and the things he'd hired me to organize. I would never be done, there was no end to the project. For someone who liked to tick things off on their to-do list, it would be a surprise to most that I was thrilled I had a job I would never finish. But when it's the best job in the entire universe, who would want it to be over?

"There's a file cabinet under the bottom shelf on that wall. There are hundreds of documents inside it. I looked through it briefly twice today, but another pair of eyes wouldn't hurt."

"All right." Tom pushed up his sleeves.

The wood file cabinet wasn't valuable, but it was old, having seen its better days about a hundred scratches and dings ago. As I'd done earlier, we unwedged it from next to the wall.

I pulled open the top drawer. "There's so much in here. Lots of interesting notes, a couple of maps that would get my attention if I wasn't looking for something else, but I saw no letter that might have come from Elizabeth I, no notes hinting at a letter, no Burgess Tickets, and no construction paperwork."

We peered in at the packed drawer.

"No place to begin but the beginning." Tom reached into the drawer and carefully lifted out the top bits and pieces and carried them to the worktable.

I moved to the tapestries I'd been looking at a few days earlier. They were the real reason I couldn't sleep. I'd forgotten that I'd discovered what I thought was Queen Elizabeth's crest on one of them. I'd looked many places earlier today, but I hadn't taken a closer look at the tapestries. I didn't know what I might find, but it had suddenly seemed important that I investigate.

I lifted one over to my desk.

"You're more comfortable working on the desk than you used to be," Tom said.

The best we could date it was back to the seventeenth century. Edwin had said it had once resided in the castle I'd visited with Mary earlier today, maybe right next to the royal scepter and crown. At least, that's what I liked to think.

"I still cover it with paper, but I'm not as intimidated by it. Did I tell you about the desks at Dina's antique shop?"

"No."

I shared the details and added, "Edwin thinks this one is even more valuable. Yeah, I'm not *as* intimidated, but I'm aware."

"You're looking at a tapestry?" Tom asked.

I'd found a magnifying glass and held it over a corner. "Yes, I think Elizabeth I's crest is embroidered on it."

"You think it came from her time?"

"Possibly. I didn't double-check these earlier today."

"Are you looking for a hidden pocket or something?"

"I'm not really sure."

"Well, I have just come upon a receipt for some internal organs."

"I think I saw that receipt."

"It looks as if Edwin purchased a sarcophagus back in nineteen seventy-eight. The internal organs are listed as a separate line item."

"I've heard the stories about the sarcophagus. As you might imagine, it was quite a thing back then. Rosie wasn't happy because Edwin wanted to keep it in the front part of the shop."

"What?"

"I know. And she won. It was gotten rid of shortly thereafter."

I put on some gloves and ran my fingers along the tapestry. I *was* looking for a pocket or some place where the alleged notes or letter might be hidden. But I found nothing. I put that tapestry back and gathered another one; this one was a cat. I was reminded of Mary's comments about the queen enjoying tapestry and a cat being one of her first subjects. I hesitated. This wouldn't be Mary's tapestry, would it?

"What?" Tom said.

"I'm not sure." I slipped off the gloves and opened my laptop. "I need to look up something."

It didn't take long. In fact, it only took a few minutes, but that might have been because I knew my way around the internet.

I found exactly what I was looking for. Yes, Mary, Queen of

Scots, did like to embroider. It was easy to find a picture of a cat she had, indeed, created.

I sat back in my chair.

Tom joined me, crouching to see what I was looking at. "What's going on?"

"This was easy to find," I said.

Tom inspected the screen. "A wee cat?"

"A cat that Mary, Queen of Scots, embroidered. It's not the same one I have here."

"Aye?"

"I wonder if it's all this easy to find though. I mean, what if Mary, the one we know, is making it all up? I've thought it was a possibility this whole time, but what would that mean? That she's a liar or something more nefarious?"

"Or simply something else," Tom said. "Some people are compelled to lie, make up stories for attention. Sometimes it's not ill intended."

"You know those dreams where you're chasing something that just keeps getting farther away?" I said.

"Aye."

"That's what this feels like."

Tom stood and then leaned on the corner of the desk. "It's going to be fine, love, I know it. The truth is coming out little by little."

"I'm holding you to that."

"I would expect nothing less. It's going to be fine."

We continued searching but didn't find one note from Elizabeth I. We didn't even find anything that mentioned her. After we finished with the warehouse, we moved over to the other side to search Hamlet's files. We found nothing there either.

The sun had started to rise, but we'd kept working until we

heard the key in the front door and the bell jingle as someone came in.

"Hello?" Rosie called.

"It's me and Tom," I said back.

"What's going on?" Rosie asked as she joined us.

I told Rosie what we'd been up to.

"I havenae found the construction paperwork, and I'm sick aboot it. But, there's good news!"

I really wanted some good news.

"Jack says he can find the inspection paperwork if it exists. He said it had to be filed with the city and even if someone destroyed copies of it, he can track it down. Somehow, some way," Rosie said.

"When?"

"Soon, I hope."

"Oh, that *is* good news," I said, feeling another bubble of hope.

And then I started feeling guilty. If the bookshop hadn't been on the chopping block, I thought I would have thrown myself into trying to figure out who killed Henry. If he hadn't been the one to want the bookshop closed, he might have been a good friend. He *had* been delightful at dinner. We'd all liked all of them, and it had seemed mutual.

"Delaney?" Rosie asked.

I hadn't been listening to my bookish voices. I'd been listening to the sound of my priorities shifting, perhaps toward the direction they should have already settled. It was a deafening noise.

"Who killed Henry?" I said aloud.

"I dinnae ken, lass," Rosie said.

"Well, we need to figure it out," I said.

No one argued.

TWENTY-SEVEN

The answer wasn't going to be found in the next few minutes. In a brief moment of discomfort—that shouldn't have been because we were all grown-ups, for goodness' sake—Brigid walked into the bookshop just as Tom was leaving.

I sensed we all wanted to get past the fact that she was upset about Tom breaking up with her. It had been a long time ago, but some snark filled the air for a moment or two.

"Brigid," Tom said as he left. "Nice to see you."

She nodded and they did a quick awkward dance as he walked out and she moved in toward me.

"Delaney," she said.

"Hey, Brigid," I said.

"I wondered. Have you had a chance to talk to the person I told you about? Grace?"

"Not yet. I tried, but the offices were closed yesterday. I was going to track her down this morning."

Brigid smiled. "Good. Do you have time to come with me right now then?"

"Where?"

"A press conference. Grace will be there." Brigid smiled.

"On a Sunday?"

"The news doesn't take weekends off, Delaney."

Spoken like a true journalist.

"Okay," I said. "Do you think we can talk to her?"

"Maybe." Brigid shrugged.

I told Rosie what we were doing, and Hector gave us a bark of encouragement.

"Be careful, lass," Rosie said to me.

"We're not going anywhere dangerous," Brigid said. "It's a public place with many other reporters. It will be fine. But we have to get going."

I'd stashed my bag under the back table, and I went to retrieve it. Brigid, ever observant, stretched her neck to see if she was missing something in the corner.

"What do you have out?" she asked as she hurried next to me. Some of the documents that we'd found in our search were still spread out over the table. "Look at these. What are you doing with them?"

"Just organizing," I said.

"So interesting." She couldn't pull her eyes away, even though she'd just said we needed to get going.

"There are a million stories here," I said, giving her a little something. I picked up a letter kept inside a clear folder. "Here, here's a letter that talks specifically about William Wallace. The writer of the letter knew him, apparently."

"Really?" she said as she looked closer.

"Indeed."

"What's it say?"

The writing was next to impossible to decipher, but Hamlet

had done the work. Underneath the protected document was his modern version, his translation. In fact, there were three copies.

"Here." I gave her a copy. "Take this with you."

"Thank you." She blinked at me.

I still didn't think she and I would be friends, but we might get past the snarky moments. And, I wasn't going to talk to Edwin about an interview. Maybe the William Wallace letter would later help to diffuse some of her future anger.

She folded the piece of paper and put it in her bag. I sent Rosie a reassuring nod as we headed toward the door.

"Want to pop in for a quick one at Tom's pub?" Brigid asked.

"Only if you do," I said. "He's not going in today, and I'm just along for the ride."

She sent me a frown and then shook her head. "I was kidding. You know, I keep thinking he's going to show his true colors and you're going to end up terribly disappointed."

And the hopes for diffusing her anger were gone, just like that. "I know you do."

"I'm really beginning to wonder if I'm wrong. I might need to just accept that he didn't care for me enough."

Good feelings coming back. Brigid and my relationship was going to be rough, no matter what.

She glanced at me and laughed once. "I won't deny that I'm jealous, but not because it's Tom. I'm long over him. I guess I just admire you."

"For keeping a man around. That's not very feminist of you."

"No, that's not it. I admire your sense of self, your ability to see what's there even if everyone else is telling you differently."

"I think I've misrepresented myself to you. I have plenty of self-doubt, thank you very much." I paused. "But when you know, you know. I had no doubt about Tom. And, I'm glad to hear you're over him, because I admire you too. You're a very good journalist, an exceptional writer."

"You've been reading my stories?"

"I have, and they're very good."

"Prove it."

Boy, she was going to be a needy friend, but good feelings were still overriding the bad ones. I proceeded to list a few of the stories she'd covered in the last couple of months. I had been following her stuff. And she was good.

"I'm honored," she said.

I shrugged. "Like I said, you're very good."

"All right, that's enough of our mutual admiration society. It's time to get down to business. We are attending a press conference about Henry. Sort of."

"What's going on? Has someone been arrested for his murder?"

"I don't think so. The Lord Provost didn't express any condolences. Some folks thought that was wrong, tacky, and maybe even suspicious. The press conference should rectify the problem. That's why it's on a Sunday. They couldn't wait a day more."

"Maybe the police have someone though. I hope so."

"That would be good," Brigid said doubtfully.

I looked at her. "What?"

"I don't think the police have the killer yet. I would know."

"How?"

"You'll see. Come on."

We came upon Princes Street Gardens. A far corner I'd not visited yet. The garden was at the bottom of the other side of the castle than where the bookshop was located, and was once the place where the citizens of Edinburgh tossed their waste. And threw in accused witches, of course. If the accused drowned she was deemed not to be a witch. But if she didn't, she was pulled from the waste and marched to another, different horrific death, some taking place over in Grassmarket. It was a brutal history in more ways than that one, but I was particularly and morbidly fascinated by the witchcraft angles.

We were at least on time for the press conference, but if we'd wanted to be up front we should have been there earlier. Still, the weather was cooperating—some clouds but no rain. Yet.

We took up a spot at the back of the crowd.

"There are so many people here. On a Sunday," I said quietly.

There were probably about fifty people in attendance. A small area had been cordoned off for the press conference. At one end a podium with a microphone was up on a small riser and stood alone and unattended.

Brigid only gave me half her attention. She was stretching her neck, standing on her tiptoes, trying to see a way up closer. I looked too but there were no open routes.

"There she is," Brigid said.

"Grace Graham?" I asked.

"The one and only."

A woman appeared on the riser and made her way to the podium. The air about her was no-nonsense. She wore her clothes like a uniform and her hair like a bulletproof helmet. If she wore makeup, it wasn't visible from where we stood. She sent the crowd an impatient frown. I was immediately intimidated by her.

"Come on," Brigid said as she took my arm and pulled me with her.

I sent strained smiles and "excuse me's" as we made our

way. Brigid stopped in a small pocket close to the front, only two people back from the rail.

Brigid made eye contact with Grace, and I thought I saw them send each other a small nod, but it could have been my imagination.

"Thank you all for coming out today." Grace seemed solemn. "This will be quick. It has been brought to the Lord Provost's attention that his office has been remiss in expressing condolences for the friends and loved ones of our dear Henry Stewart. I shall read a statement directly from the Lord Provost." She looked down at the podium. "'We apologize sincerely for our oversight regarding esteemed councilor Henry Stewart. We, like so many of you, were shocked by the tragedy and haven't been able to get our heads around our loss. We should have said something sooner. We apologize and do, indeed, send our deepest condolences.'" Grace looked up. "That's it, ladies and gentlemen. Other than, thank you so much for giving me some of your Sunday."

A murmur spread through the crowd. Everyone wanted more, and hands shot up. Brigid's included.

Grace said, "I'm not here today to answer questions, but I'll take a couple. Yes, Mason," she nodded at a man in a blue shirt, "what's your question?"

"Are the police still sticking to their story that Stewart was the only person targeted in the bombing?"

"Yes," Grace said. She hesitated briefly "We have been assured that there is no further imminent threat to our city or to the citizens of Edinburgh."

"Grace, what evidence do the police have regarding Mr. Stewart's killer?" a woman in a green jacket asked without waiting to be called upon.

The press conference was exactly what Brigid thought it was going to be. So many people had attended because so little information had been released. Everyone was curious, everyone wanted answers.

"The police haven't shared with us any evidence they've discovered, but I know they are working diligently to find the killer." Grace leaned closer to the microphone. "Thank you all for coming out."

Just as Grace began to turn to leave, Brigid yelled, "Grace, Grace!"

Grace heard her, sent her a frown, but then faced forward again. "Yes, Brigid."

"What had Henry Stewart been working on right before he was killed?" Brigid asked.

A rumble went through the crowd.

"I don't know exactly," Grace said.

"I'd really like to get your statement on that, Ms. Graham," Brigid said.

"I just gave you the statement I came here to share today." She looked away from Brigid and back out at the crowd. "Thank you all."

This time Grace turned and walked away, ignoring any further questions.

"Don't worry," Brigid said to me. "She'll want to talk to me in person now. That's what we want, right?"

"Okay, whatever you say," I said.

Considering how Brigid had interrupted Grace's departure and the tone with which she had answered Brigid's question, I couldn't see how there was any way at all that Grace Graham would want to talk to either of us. Ever probably.

TWENTY-EIGHT

I was wrong, but I'd been tricked. Grace not only wanted to talk to Brigid, but she welcomed us, opening the door wide and signaling us in before she marched to her desk.

"She's my aunt," Brigid said quietly and with a satisfied smile as we made our way into a lovely office, much bigger than Lyle Mercado's, and furnished with modern lines and splashes of chrome.

"That's how you knew so much about the press conference," I said.

"Aye," Brigid said. "And that's why she's talking to us personally."

"Aye," Grace said as we came to two chairs and she turned to face us. "Brigid and I have been discussing many things lately. You must be Delaney." She extended her hand over the desk.

We shook. "I am. It's nice to meet you."

"Have a seat," Grace said. "I would have told you I was her aunt if you'd found me."

"I'm sorry," I said as I sat, but it was only in answer to her accusing tone. "I tried to call once, but I was worried about bothering you."

Grace laughed without humor. "If only my niece felt the same."

Brigid smiled again. "Thanks for seeing us, Auntie."

"I'm not sure I had much choice, but I'm happy you're both here." Grace leaned back in her chair and looked at me. "I've been researching everything Brigid told me. My first question is—is it true that none of you at the bookshop are aware of any inspection?"

"That's absolutely correct," I said.

"I've spoken with the Lord Provost, Delaney, and he is convinced the inspection is valid. I looked up the inspector. His name is Dwayne Stover. Do you know him?"

"I don't think so." The name didn't sound familiar at all. "It's not valid though!"

"However." Grace held up her hand. "The Lord Provost is going to make sure. He's contacting the inspector, Dwayne, himself and said he will investigate. He won't stop the vote because that would go against protocol, but he will make sure the council is fully informed."

"Well. That's good," I said, filing the inspector's name away in my mind.

"Yes, that's good," Grace said. "But, understand, if the buildings are dangerous, they'll have to come down."

I swallowed hard. "They aren't dangerous, I'm sure."

"Let's hope not," Grace said.

"Is the Lord Provost going to investigate Henry's actions?" Brigid said. "Aunt Grace, he was up to so many things, the Burgess Tickets, the bookshop. Maybe there were other things going on."

"Ah, now that would make a good story, wouldn't it? More secret stuff that government officials were trying to get done secretly and got Henry killed."

"Aye, that would be great."

"Brigid, the Lord Provost has looked, is looking, and will look at everything." Her eyebrows came together. "And I'm afraid this part is off the record, but perhaps some things *have* slipped through the cracks, but I promise you, many people are on the case now. The police are investigating, and we have many internal investigations going on too."

"Any idea who killed Henry?" Brigid asked.

Grace looked at me. "She's asked me every day. I still have the same answer. No, I don't have any idea."

"Okay, off the record still, who do you *think* killed Henry?" Brigid asked.

Grace sighed. "If I'd had my own children, maybe I wouldn't be wrapped around my niece's finger. Henry *was* respected, but he was sometimes a difficult man, may he rest in peace. He would become impassioned about something none of the rest of the council could rouse up any interest in. He was famous amongst council members for it. He would campaign, he would ask others to plant seeds of ideas because he knew people sometimes tired of hearing from him. But, I don't know of anyone who disliked him so much they would kill him."

"They would just vote against him?" Brigid said.

"Aye. Or just not listen to him." Grace looked at me again. "Are you aware that his nephew-in-law, Mikey Wooster, is also a council member? He was a part of the committee working on the things Henry had set in motion."

"Yes, I met Mikey," I said. "I talked to his wife recently. She didn't know anything about Mikey's actions on the committee, said she was going to talk to him, but I haven't double-checked to see what has happened."

Grace pursed her lips tightly as she inspected Brigid and me. "All right. Brigid, this is still off the record, but you might be able to use it for some background, okay?"

"Absolutely," Brigid said.

"I don't know the details, but Henry and Mikey argued the day before Henry was killed. Loudly. A couple of the councilors witnessed the argument."

"Who?" Brigid asked.

"We are still off the record."

"Aye," Brigid said.

I wondered why Grace shared information so easily with Brigid, even off the record. Was it because they were family, or did Grace have other motivations? Did she use Brigid to put information out to the public to help the Lord Provost behind the scenes?

"They were also on Henry's committee. Their names are Monika Hidasi and Simone Lazar."

I'd found Bella Montrose, but not Monika or Simone. They were the three names Inspector Buchanan had given me, the councilors she'd spoken to. She'd thought I might be able to convince them to at least postpone the vote. I wasn't going to tell Brigid and Grace about Inspector Buchanan's note. Brigid wrote down the names, but didn't ask more questions about them.

I sat forward on the chair. "Ms. Graham, if there really is a failed inspection, the results just can't be accurate. The building is sound, I'm sure." I hoped. "Could we hire an independent party to evaluate the building? Would that help?"

"I don't know. I can suggest that as an idea."

"I will do all the legwork, Ms. Graham," I said. "I'll take any direction you might give me."

"I hear you. Let me see what I can do."

"Thank you."

Grace nodded. "You are welcome. Now, I have other work to do. If the two of you will excuse me."

Brigid and I stood and moved toward the door, but Brigid stopped. "You'll be there for dinner this weekend, Auntie?"

"I wouldn't miss it." Grace smiled.

"Thank you," I said again.

"I'll be in touch," Grace said to me.

"Well, we know something more," Brigid said as we left the building and started walking back up the Royal Mile. "Let's track down Mikey Wooster."

"Because he argued with Henry? What about Monika and Simone? Or the inspector, Dwayne Stover?"

"Let's start with Mikey. Grace said that Monika and Simone didn't hear the exact words of the argument. Maybe later for Dwayne. Let's go directly to the source, see if the argument might have led to a murder."

"Okay." I shrugged.

"Delaney, there's a big story here, I can smell it."

"What if it turns out to be boring and something from a simple clerical error?" I said as we turned a corner I didn't remember exploring yet.

"It won't. There was murder. There's something big going on here."

"What if we find a killer?" I asked, thinking that perhaps that should have been an obvious concern.

"Isn't that the goal? I mean other than keeping the bookshop open," Brigid said with a smile. "Come on, I know where we can probably find Wooster, and it's a public place."

TWENTY-NINE

"Why do you think he's here?" I asked as we stood outside the restaurant.

"I looked him up already. When I heard he was married to Mary's niece, I thought he might be someone I should talk to. He eats here all the time, particularly on the weekends."

"Impressive," I said.

Tom had taken me to Makers Gourmet Mash Bar once before. It was a lively place with a variety of delicious food. Some American, some Scottish. Haggis, which was, of course, distinctly Scottish, was a big part of the menu and something I was sure I would never acquire a taste for, even when its reputation was talked about as lovingly as Makers' was.

The name of the restaurant jarred a memory loose. Or maybe it was the talk about Mikey and his wife in conjunction with the name of the restaurant that had done it.

After visiting Dina at her antique shop, I'd been gung-ho to check the maker's mark on my desk, but I'd forgotten to do so. Even when Tom and I had spent the night searching through files and noting that I was now more comfortable working on the valuable antique, I hadn't checked the mark. I still needed to do that, and I mentally filed the task away for later.

The restaurant was packed. *At least Mikey might not spot us right away,* I thought as we went through the door. Of course, we couldn't find him easily either.

"Let me know if you see him," Brigid said. "I'll either get him outside to talk to us or you can."

I stepped around her and to the side of two men blocking the way. I scanned the room and thought I saw Mikey in the back. It looked as if he was talking to someone, but I couldn't see the other person.

"He's in the back," I said to Brigid. I pulled her closer and pointed.

As we watched him, he leaned forward on the table, placing his arms on it. We could see him grasp other hands. We could see all four hands, but nothing else of the other person.

"Who is he with?" Brigid asked.

"We'll have to get closer. I can't tell."

It wasn't easy. First of all, we had to explain to the greeter that we were just there to meet someone. That didn't go over well with the other people waiting to be seated; they weren't happy to have anyone go around them. Brigid made no apologies, but I did. A few.

She led the way through the maze of tables, but a group of customers was suddenly leaving. We all dodged and darted and danced around each other, and Mikey Wooster was out of our sight for a long few moments.

And then, when we were only a couple of tables away, another customer stood up quickly from his chair. He and I collided.

"I'm so sorry," he said as he took my arms in his hands.

"No problem," I said.

But he'd inadvertently turned me a little so I was now facing the front of the restaurant more than the direction I'd intended to go. I still couldn't see Mikey, but I caught sight of a flash of red hair. Lots of people had red hair, in Scotland and everywhere else for that matter, but that flash I'd seen reminded me so much of me that I was at least ninety percent certain I'd seen Mary leaving the restaurant. I knew her hair because it was so much like mine. I blinked and did a double-take toward the front door. But the flash of familiarity was now gone, either out through the door or behind the waiting customers.

I'd thought Brigid's idea to find Mikey was potentially a waste of time. So what that he'd argued with a fellow councilor who happened to be his wife's uncle. Councilors argued, but Mikey wouldn't have done anything to hurt Henry. I still didn't want to think so, and even if him having lunch with his wife's aunt wasn't weird, there was something about the holding hands that struck me funny. Well, not funny so much as curious.

Was I working way too hard to try to find Mary, Queen of Scots' third husband, the one she allegedly had an affair with, the one who probably killed her second husband?

Eureka!

A bookish voice suddenly spoke up in my mind. It was Archimedes, talking about the amount of gold in a crown. He probably hadn't said the word, but many gave him credit for it. It all suddenly seemed so fitting.

"Damn," I said to the bookish voice. "Damn," I said to the whole entire mess.

"Are you okay?" the man said again.

I focused on him and smiled. "Fine, thanks."

He let go of my arms and turned to leave. I sent one more

glance toward the front of the restaurant, but whoever I'd seen was gone now.

"Excuse me," a server said as I continued to stand in the way.

I turned and made my way back to the table, where I joined Brigid and a clearly irritated Mikey. Whoever he'd been holding hands with was gone.

"Nice to see you again, Mikey," I said as I sat down.

"Likewise," Mikey said, his voice clipped.

I gestured toward Brigid. "This is my friend, Brigid."

"Yes, she introduced herself. Hello," Mikey said. "I'm afraid I was just leaving, but feel free to take the table."

As Mikey stood, I put my hand on his arm. "I swear I just saw Mary Stewart walk out of here. Was she here with you?"

"What? No."

He was a terrible liar, but more than being offended that he was lying, I wondered why he would do so. Why did it matter if he and his wife's aunt were having lunch? Unless that handhold did mean more than what should be between the two of them.

I wished my mind hadn't gone there, but it had.

"Okay," I said. "Mikey, I need to talk to you about something. Can you please stay a few minutes longer?"

He made a big display of looking at the expensive watch on his wrist. "I can't. I've got a meeting."

"We'll walk you out," Brigid said.

We were going to follow him no matter what he said, no matter how fast he hurried away. The crowd wasn't so bothersome when it was slowing him down too.

"Are you the councilor who originally wanted the bookshop closed?" I asked when we made it outside.

"Excuse me?" he said as he took quick, long steps toward a car.

"Did you argue with Henry the day before he was killed? Was it something about the bookshop?" I asked.

"What? No!" he said again.

"Okay, what about something else?" I said. Brigid looked at me with wide-eyed approval. She wanted me to keep talking. I didn't even know that what I was about to say was something I'd been thinking about, maybe processing. It was a shot in the dark, but I felt compelled to try. "You had a building inspector deem it unsafe, didn't you?"

He shrugged far too casually. "I would never ask an inspector to falsify documents."

"It's not unsafe," I said as I grabbed his arm, far too forcefully.

He stopped walking, frowned at my hand on his arm, and then pulled it gently away. "Ms. Nichols, I'm not sure what you are trying to say, but you'd better be careful."

"Just tell me why you wanted the bookshop closed? Or why Henry did. What do you want?"

"I don't want any business closed, but things have to be done correctly. There are rules to follow."

"Did Henry want the bookshop closed? Was he trying to get something for Mary?" I couldn't give up.

"Henry was also about doing things correctly. Nothing done has been done inappropriately."

I squinted and tried to think. "I know you from somewhere, I'm sure I do. It was in the rain. Where was it?" I'd all but forgotten that when I'd met him, I'd found him familiar, but as I looked into those blue eyes now, I remembered. Where had we met? "Did you come into the bookshop during a storm? Wait it out inside?"

"I have no idea what you're talking about."

"We have the name of the inspector," Brigid cut in. "We've already got an appointment with him."

Concern, maybe even fear, flitted briefly over his features. "Not that it would matter, but I don't believe you. Inspectors' names aren't shared with the public."

"I'm a reporter," Brigid said as she crossed her arms in front of herself. She didn't mention her aunt's name, but she did say, "Dwayne Stover."

He blinked again in surprise, but quickly regained his composure. "I wish you the best of luck, but I assure you—again—that everything has been done appropriately and within the letter of the law. And everything is set in motion. The vote is scheduled and cannot be unscheduled. Now, if you'll excuse me."

Mikey opened his car door and got inside. He shut the door too gently, trying to prove he wasn't ruffled by our questions, I thought.

"He's such a liar," Brigid said.

"About what?" I said. "Which part?"

"I wish I knew, but I just know he's not being truthful about *something*."

"But everything *is* set in motion," I said.

"The vote will not pass, Delaney. Grace will spread the word and it won't pass. I'll help. I'll write an article for tomorrow."

"The day of the vote."

"It's better than the day after."

I watched as Brigid stared toward where Mikey's car had turned.

"What are you thinking about?" I said.

She ignored the question. "Why did you ask if he was having lunch with Mary?"

"I thought I saw red hair that looked like mine."

"I didn't see that. I wish I had. Come on, let's go find Dwayne Stover."

"Do you really know where he is?"

"I have no idea, but I have people who can find anyone." She pulled out her phone. "I suspect Mikey will ring him and let him know we're coming. We need to move quickly."

"Let's go."

Dwayne Stover's office was hidden behind another building. In fact, we had to venture down a close to find the door. Painted on its front was simply: Dwayne Stover, City Building Inspector.

There were no windows, and neither of us was surprised that the door was locked. We knocked a few times, but also weren't surprised we didn't get an answer.

"Do you think he's out inspecting?" I said. "On a Sunday?"

"Anything is possible, but I'm more inclined to believe that Mikey Wooster told him not to be here when we got here. Damn, I shouldn't have played that card, but I couldn't stop myself. Mikey Wooster is an arrogant twit."

"It's okay, we'll track Dwayne down at some point. You have people."

"Sure." Brigid didn't sound as confident as I would have liked.

We called the number we found for his business, but no answer there either. The atmosphere in the close was a stark contrast with our moods. A park bench and some planter box trees made it a comfortable retreat. We knocked on the two other doors—one belonging to an artist, one a potter with some beautiful work we spied through the window, and the last one an accountant. None of them knew Dwayne well, but they saw him every now and then. He was described as a typical older guy with no distinguishing features.

"What about Monika and Simone? There are others we could try to talk to," I said.

Brigid looked at her phone. "I've got to head back to the newspaper office and get that article written. I'll keep working on this. I'll call you if I come up with anything else. I'd like to talk to Dwayne before the vote. I'll keep trying to find him. If he tells me more about why the bookshop's buildings aren't safe, I'll ring you right away. Maybe I'll send him over to you. You all should know—it's your right to know."

"We should have a copy of the inspection."

"Aye," she said doubtfully.

"What?"

"It's all so cagey," she said. "None of this is making sense. At first I thought you might just be using me to try to hide problems the bookshop was having, but I'm beginning to think you all were set up. I just wish I knew why."

"I do too."

We said goodbye and I watched her walk down the Royal Mile. I had a dinner date scheduled with Tom, but I was going to be late. I texted him that I was taking a quick detour first.

I couldn't stop thinking about the red hair I'd seen at the restaurant. I couldn't let go of the sense that Mikey was lying. *But about which part?* Mary had behaved like we might be friends. I'd gone along with her to talk to Clayton. Now, I needed something from her.

Tom texted back that he'd see me soon, and that I should be careful.

Always, I replied.

THIRTY

"That's her hoose?" Elias asked as the cab moved slowly up the driveway.

"Yes, it's something else, isn't it?"

"Aye."

Immediately after I'd texted Tom, I called Elias. He was close to dropping off a paying customer but could come get me after that. I only waited ten minutes, and when he arrived, I asked if he was up to being the Watson to my Sherlock again. He was willing and drove us to Mary's castle, parking the taxi in the same spot Tom had.

"Ye're not going into that hoose by yerself. I'm going with ye. That place is terreffeen," he said.

"Terrifying?"

"Aye."

With him by my side and as he puffed up some, I knocked and was surprised again when Mary opened the door. I wasn't sure who I kept expecting, but it seemed so ordinary that the person who lived in a castle be the one to answer the door. Didn't they have knights in shining armor for those sorts of things?

The first thing I noticed was that her red hair was pulled up into a ponytail. The second thing I noticed was that her eyes were rimmed in red. She'd been crying, though that was to be expected. I got no sense that she was being medicated, that Eloise had been here again today.

"Delaney," she said. "Hello?"

"Mary, this is my friend, Elias. Do you have a minute?"

Mary smiled tightly and nodded at Elias. "It's been a rough day, Delaney . . . but, sure, come in."

"Thanks," I said as Elias sent me some raised eyebrows before we followed her inside.

"What's going on?" Mary asked after she closed the door.

"I'm sorry it's been a rough day," I said.

She nodded impatiently. I needed to ask her what I'd come to ask her.

"Mary, did you have lunch today at Makers Gourmet Mash Bar?"

It was such a brief flash of surprise that I might not have caught it if I hadn't been looking so closely at her eyes.

"I did. Were you there?" she said.

"I was. I tried to say hello, but you seemed in a hurry to leave."

Ignoring my questioning tone, she said, "I had lunch with my niece's husband. Mikey—oh, you know him."

"I do. You seemed upset," I said. It was a guess. I hadn't seen her face.

"No, not at all. I just had another appointment I had to get to. I *was* in a hurry." She looked at her fingernails, and I wondered if she was pondering if she could say she'd had her nails done. "Just another appointment." She stopped looking at her nails and sent me a strained frown.

I put my hand on her arm, suddenly feeling more sympathy

for her than I'd expected to feel. "Mary, do you think Mikey had anything to do with Henry's murder?"

She blinked hard and fast, but didn't protest, didn't make a move to kick us out of there. "I don't think so."

"But ye dinnae ken for sure?" Elias said.

She shook her head and then looked me in the eye. "He said he didn't. I asked. I came out and asked him."

"Why? Why did you ask him?" I said.

"I'm just trying to figure it all out," she said. "Delaney, do you remember the night of the dinner?"

"Of course."

"I saw something between Henry and Mikey. There was some animosity."

"I think I saw that too."

I sensed Elias unpuffing a little with Mary's vulnerability. He was such a softy.

She looked at me. "I told you that Henry and I discussed the bookshop later that night, but I'm sure I sensed there was a problem between Mikey and Henry. Dina went home first, by herself. Mikey stayed and talked to Henry a while. I'm trying to put things together, and I wondered if maybe Henry told Mikey he was going to try to either cancel or postpone the vote about the bookshop and if that upset Mikey."

"Enough to kill?" I said.

"Enough to kill, aye, or enough to do something to get Henry killed. I don't know, but I just wanted some answers."

"What did Mikey say?"

"That he and Henry didn't discuss anything about the bookshop, that they spoke about all manner of council business that night except the bookshop."

"You don't believe him?"

"I don't know what to believe. Henry was so upset about what he'd done to get the bookshop shut down that I can't imagine him talking about anything else that night, and that contention I thought I sensed . . ."

"Did Mikey tell you any specifics about their conversation?"

"Mikey told me he would never do anything to hurt Henry. He couldn't understand why I would even ask him such things. That's all he would really say. I pressed him about the bookshop, the Burgess Tickets, anything I could think of, but he avoided answering specifically. He just kept saying he would never hurt Henry. Delaney, I'd insisted on meeting in a public place because it was that much of a concern, but maybe I'm not thinking clearly. He *sounded* sincere."

"But you still don't believe him, do you?" I said.

She shook her head slowly. "I wish I did."

"Did they have any problems in the past?" I said.

"No, and Delaney, I knew my husband. He could barely brush his teeth that night for thinking about the bookshop. I'm sure that if they had a disagreement, it must have been about the bookshop."

"Closing it or keeping it open?" I asked.

"I can't be sure, but Henry was bent on making sure he fixed what he'd set in motion, that it would stay open."

"Why would Mikey want to close the bookshop?" I said, but I had my own answer. The Mary, Queen of Scots' coins, even if parts of that idea weren't clear. I didn't say that aloud.

"I can't think of any reason at all," Mary said. "I didn't even ask him that. There didn't seem to be any point."

"Did you tell the police about your suspicions, lass?" Elias said.

Tears came to her eyes. "No, they'd probably think I'm crazier than they already do. Besides, he's my niece's husband."

"Are ye worriet aboot yer or yer niece's safety? If so, aye, ring the police immediately," Elias said.

"I rang the Lord Provost, left him a message that I needed to talk to him about what Henry had been working on. I will tell him he can't let a vote happen."

"I think the Lord Provost will be hearing that from a few people, but thank you."

Mary nodded and looked down, keeping her eyes away from my almost-matching ones.

"Do you want to come with us? Do you feel unsafe?" I asked. "You can stay with me if you'd like."

"That's lovely, Delaney, but no, I'm fine here. I can still talk to Henry here. Ta, though."

It was difficult to leave her in such a state, but she made it clear she wanted to be alone. I hadn't asked about anything lascivious between her and Mikey, but my mind had changed from that being a possibility. I hoped I wasn't letting my sympathy change my instincts or suspicions.

Mary walked us to the door. I heard locks being set, the noise sounding so much more modern than a castle's locks should sound.

As we got into the cab, Elias looked at me and said, "I hope it wasnae her. I hope she didnae kill Henry."

"Me too, but I didn't get a sense of that. Did you?"

"I dinnae ken what I got a sense of, but I dinnae trust her, or her niece's husband. Probably not her niece either if I think aboot it, and I've never even met her."

"I know. What a mess, huh?"

"Aye. Home?"

"Actually, back to the bookshop, if you don't mind."

"Not a t'all."

THIRTY-ONE

"She's sad, mourning," Tom said as he reached over to my paper boat for one of the chips I hadn't eaten. "She should probably let the police know about Mikey though, even if it leads to nothing."

We were at our favorite takeaway; a small shop in Grassmarket close to both our places of work.

"I agree," I said. "I know you didn't notice the same things I thought I saw that night, but what were your thoughts about Mikey and Dina?"

"Mikey was quiet, Dina was lovely. That's about all I got."

"Mikey didn't seem familiar to you?"

"Not even a little bit."

"I recognize him from somewhere, and the fuzzy memory has a yellow raincoat attached to it."

"It rains a lot here."

"Why can't I place him?"

"The councilors are in the news sometimes, maybe you saw his picture."

"Maybe."

We were sitting on stools at the small counter along the front window. It was rare that we managed to get a spot inside—simply because there were only three seats in the place. Sometimes we moved back outside to enjoy our fish and chips, sometimes we would walk around Grassmarket. Sometimes we'd take the food back to the pub. But atop a stool this evening, I enjoyed the break from the rest of the world. However, I could still see the bookshop at the end of the market, still open though Rosie and Hector would close in a few minutes. I tried to imagine something else in that spot. A convenience store, a souvenir shop, maybe even another takeaway. Tears came to my eyes, but I blinked them away. I didn't have time to cry. I truly believed things were going to be okay, but until the vote was either canceled or over, I didn't want to let down my guard.

"Lass," Tom said as he wiped his fingers on the paper napkin. "It's going tae be all right."

"I really do think so too, but I'm not ready to relax."

Tom's eyebrows came together. "What has Inspector Winters said?"

"He's on holiday. I called but didn't leave a message. I couldn't bring myself to bother him."

Tom sat up a little straighter. "I think you'd better bother him. Put in a call. Either he'll take it or he won't. I think he can help sew up the last pieces of this puzzle of the vote. Just in case you need someone else on your side."

I nodded and felt no need to argue. It suddenly seemed just fine to interrupt his vacation. "Makes sense."

I pulled out my phone.

Rosie and Hector didn't close on time because a storm hit. It was fierce and Rosie didn't want to get drenched on her way to the bus. Her staying open worked out just fine though. Edwin, Hamlet, Tom, and I joined them and sat around the table in the back as we told Inspector Winters everything.

He *had* been on holiday, but he'd been home for a full two hours when I called. He'd said he was surprised he hadn't heard from me earlier and that he and his family had very much enjoyed Ireland. His wife (I'd yet to meet her) had inquired a couple of times if I'd rung him.

As I'd tried to explain all the circumstances over the phone, he said, "Lass, I'll meet you at the bookshop. This is too much to digest on the phone and I've a wee'un who wants my attention. I'll be there shortly."

I'd never met his family, but I thought he probably made a great father. He did as he said and met us all at the bookshop. He hadn't shaved for a week and the beard slimmed his round face, reminding me of an artist's beard, though somewhat shorter. I knew it would be gone when he had to resume being a police inspector. But between the beard and his casual clothing, Rosie told him she might not have recognized him and he might want to consider some undercover work at some point.

I thought it curious that he didn't acknowledge the comment. Rosie and I shared a look. Maybe he'd already done undercover work.

"Have you received notices of the shop closing? There's due process," Inspector Winters asked Edwin. "Even beyond an inspection report, there are other procedures too."

"Not one word," Edwin said. "It makes no sense."

Inspector Winters looked at his notebook on the table in

front of him and then up at me. "You say the building inspector's name is Dwayne Stover?"

"Yes."

Back to Edwin. "Did you try to talk to the Lord Provost?"

"I did, left messages, but he's not returned my calls."

Back to me. "And you've spoken with his media relations person. Grace Graham?"

"Yes."

"I know her. She's good at what she does, but I'm not sure what power she holds," Inspector Winters said.

"She works directly with the Lord Provost?" I asked.

"Aye, but not in a policy advisor capacity, not really. She's his communications director. I'll figure it out."

"Do you know if the police have found anything pointing to Henry Stewart's killer?" I asked.

"I'll have to check, lass. Until you called, I had only heard a little about Henry. I didn't know the bookshop was somehow a part of it." He sent me a surprisingly friendly smile. "It looks like I'm going to have to stop taking vacations."

"I'm sorry to bother you," I said.

"Not at all. If the vote had taken place while I was gone, I would have been disappointed. I'm glad you rang."

You could feel the sense of relief fill the room. Yes, the vote was only one day away, but Inspector Winters was on the job. Everything was going to be fine.

The bell above the door jingled, but before anyone could move quickly enough to greet whoever was coming in, he hurried around to us, his bright yellow raincoat dripping all over the floor.

"Jack!" Edwin said as he stood. "Thank you for taking my late call, I'd like you to meet—"

"No time for that, Edwin, no time," Jack McGinnis said. "I'm afraid we've got a problem, a big one."

And just like that the sense of relief was washed clean away.

THIRTY-TWO

Jack McGinnis had been working hard. He'd pushed his way into every government official's home that he could find. He'd talked to councilors. He'd even managed to talk to the Minister for Local Government, Housing and Planning—a position I hadn't even been made aware of yet.

"There's no stopping the vote," Jack said. "There's no delaying it, but it's probably going to be okay."

"How can that be?" I said.

"Rules, regulations, procedures," Jack said. "It can't be taken off the docket."

"But there was no inspection!" I said.

That's when Jack reached into his back pocket. He'd rolled up some stapled pages so casually, as if they didn't mean the end of the world as we all knew it.

He placed the papers on the table, smoothing them even as the corners still battled back. "That's actually the bad news, and why it's only *probably* going to be okay."

Yes, the inspection was real, official, there was no doubt about it. We read it together and then we all took our turns inspecting it. And then, one by one, we marched up the stairs on this side of the shop, crouched at the top to look at the space where the wall had once been cut, a long time ago, to make way for the connection to the neighboring building. There was absolutely no sense that the connection was going to fail. Nothing was sinking, nothing crumbling. I even jumped up and down on it. It didn't move.

However, there was a crack in the plaster. One, tiny, five-inch-long crack—that, by the way, seemed to get longer every time I looked at it.

The failure of the building was based upon this crack. There was a picture and everything! Someone had come in and done an inspection, even taken this picture, and no one had noticed.

Or maybe remembered.

"Edwin, I'm sure this didnae happen," Rosie said several times, becoming less emphatic and more distraught each time she said it.

There came a point when we transitioned from being worried about the building to worrying about Rosie, mostly when Hector, atop her lap, barked at us to get our priorities straight.

"Rosie, it's going to be fine," Edwin said. "This isn't your fault, love."

She held her fist to her chin and nodded sadly. I'd never known her to have any sort of memory problems. In fact, she was the one who seemed to remember everything.

We'd all come back to the table and I grabbed the report. I'd memorized the part that Jack had highlighted, the part that had been stamped with a big red "fail" over it. There were other pages too, all with small print; legal stuff that reinforced the validity of this inspection.

Until the very last page, at the bottom. Because there was so much black print on the page, I hadn't noticed the small, hand-written note, also in black.

"Hey," I said aloud. "What's this?"

Everyone looked at me.

"What?" Jack asked.

"There's a handwritten note. The writing is so small, it al-most just looks like a continuation of the typed print on the page."

Either not noticing or not caring that it was rude, Jack grabbed the inspection from my hands. I had to restrain myself from grabbing it back.

"This is a copy. They wouldn't give me the original, of course. Damn, I need a magnifying glass," Jack said.

Hamlet reached to a drawer against the wall. He had a few magnifying glasses.

"Ta," Jack said as he grabbed a glass from Hamlet.

Hamlet and I shared a shrug. At least Jack had said thanks to him.

"Huh."

"For heavens' sake, Jack, what?" Edwin said.

"It says, and I quote: 'The young woman tending the shop wouldn't let me go to the other side. She looks so much like Mary. I'll have to come back.'"

We all exclaimed something along the lines of "What?"

I grabbed the report and glass from Jack.

"I was here when the inspector came by?" I said as I repeat-edly read the small print. "I . . . I don't remember it at all. No! I would remember it. I wouldn't have allowed it."

"No, I don't think you would have," Edwin said.

"No," Hamlet said.

"I think there's something more important here," Tom

added. "Whoever came into the bookshop and allegedly conducted the inspection knew Mary Stewart, well enough to just say 'Mary.' "

"And they thought it was important to communicate the fact that Delaney looked like her," Hamlet added.

"Unbelievable," I said.

"Well," Edwin said as he looked at Jack. "I don't understand everything going on here, but I think this was just a note to someone, and the inspector was an imposter, just someone who wanted to see the other side of this bookshop." He looked at the inspection. "And somehow had access to official paperwork."

"The warehouse is not a secret anymore, Edwin. If someone asks about it, we tell them. But not many people ask. I remember each and every one . . ."

Jack had taken off the raincoat and placed it over the back of a chair. He lifted it from the chair, noticing it was still wet, and moved it over to a small table we weren't using. He sat down in the chair and looked at me intently.

"What, Delaney?" Rosie prompted.

No bookish voices had been talking, but pictures of memories had suddenly started flooding my mind.

Hector, again sensing who needed him the most, hopped onto my lap.

"Oh, no," I said a moment later. The memories weren't fuzzy this time. "About three months ago, there was a man dressed in a bright yellow raincoat, just like the one Jack wore tonight. It was just me and Hector that day, and it wasn't raining. At first the man kept his gaze averted when I tried to talk to him. I just let him look around, tried not to bother him—and he definitely seemed bothered. He seemed to need to move closer to the shelves to read the books' spines, he hummed to himself. I thought about offering him one of the magnifying glasses. I thought briefly about seeing if Hamlet was on his way in, but then I decided that the man wasn't dangerous. Just odd. He climbed the stairs to look at the books up there. I let him be, but then he got quiet. I came around and didn't see him. I wondered if he'd left and I didn't notice. I just asked if he was okay. He popped upright, as if he'd been sitting in the corner—or now I think taking pictures probably—and he said he was fine. He asked if there were books on the other side of the door up there. I told him there weren't. He asked what was there. I said there were just offices." I looked at Edwin. "He didn't ask specifically about the warehouse or I would have told him. I don't just offer it up, I wouldn't have given him a tour, but I would have told him."

"Makes sense," Edwin said. "What happened next?"

"He left."

"What was the inspector's name?" Hamlet asked Jack.

"No, no it doesn't matter. Or maybe it matters, but . . ." I said. "The man who was here was Mikey Wooster. I have no doubt. He had dirt smudged on his face, but those eyes. I saw them and I remembered thinking how lovely they were. I remember him so clearly now. I don't understand the act he was putting on, but there must be a reason he took the picture and forged the inspection. Was it just because I wouldn't tell him what was on the other side?"

"No," Tom said. "If he'd come in as Mikey Wooster, you would have given him more information, more details, as you would to any councilor who asked you questions. He wanted the bookshop, or to harm it in some way. I have no doubt."

"The coins?" I said. "Did he want to try to find the Mary, Queen of Scots' coins Edwin wouldn't sell to Dina ten years ago?"

"Oh, lass," Edwin said. "I found them. They were at my house, but I didn't think they had anything at all to do with what we're going through. No idea at all. I didn't even think to let you know I found them. I'm sorry."

"Why would ye?" Rosie said.

"You thought he looked familiar from the moment you met him," Tom said.

"Hang on," Inspector Winters said. "We need to get Inspector Buchanan here too."

We watched as he moved to the front of the bookshop to make a call.

"If Mikey was posing as an inspector, this will of course change everything," Jack said. "But an investigation will have to happen. The vote can't be stopped, but we will ultimately win, no matter the tally."

"I've something I need to attend to," Edwin said, surprising us all.

"What?" Rosie asked.

"What are you up to, Edwin?" Jack asked. "You can't leave until Buchanan gets here."

"I've an idea," he said. "I'll be in my office on the other side."

"Edwin?" Rosie said. "What's going on?"

Edwin stepped to Rosie. He took her hand and held it. "It's going to be fine, love, but I've an idea. I think I know how to seal the deal, if that's the proper expression."

"All right. Let me know." Tears came to Rosie's eyes.

Hector jumped off my lap and back to Rosie.

"It's going to be fine," Edwin said as he hurried over to the dark side.

The rest of us looked at each other for a long moment. Hector couldn't decide whose lap needed him the most.

THIRTY-THREE

It was a very late night. I hadn't slept much the last few days, but I was so revved with adrenaline, I didn't notice. Well, not much.

Inspector Buchanan showed up and we rehashed everything. Unfortunately, there was no proof that the inspector had been Mikey Wooster. There were no pictures of the man in the raincoat who had come in, just my word to go on. At least Inspector Buchanan had found Mr. Stover earlier that day. He was, indeed, an older man with no distinguishing features. From his front porch as he peered out his front door, she'd asked him if he had inspected The Cracked Spine. She shared with us how the conversation had gone:

"Is my name on the paperwork? Then, aye, I did the deed. You can't expect me to remember every detail of every building I inspect, including the names of the businesses inside."

"Any chance you could check your records?" Inspector Buchanan had asked him. *"Did you keep a copy of the paperwork?"*

"No, there is no chance I will check my paperwork. Not

today. If my name's on it, then it was me. I'm not going into my office on a weekend. Not without a warrant of some sort. Next time I'm there, I'll look."

"Any chance your name could be forged?"

"Who in the name of the queen herself would do that?"

Who indeed?

Mikey Wooster, I thought.

Now that there might be more to go on, Inspector Buchanan could be more forceful in requesting a copy of Dwayne Stover's records, but that wasn't a huge priority.

Once all the information was shared, the police inspectors quit caring about the bookshop. They wanted to catch a killer, and they were trying to figure out if there was any evidence that Mikey had killed Henry. Did the murder have something to do with the coins? Were the coins as valuable as Edwin had thought? He assured the police they were. He told them he would gather them if they wanted. He wanted me to see them too. I wasn't prepared to figure out their value, but a look wouldn't hurt. However, the police weren't ready to see the coins, wanted them to stay safe for the time being.

When Edwin had rejoined us, he'd had a mischievous sparkle to his eyes, but he wouldn't tell us what he'd been up to. He assured the police his activities in no way interfered with the police's murder investigation.

At around two in the morning, I spied a van pulling up to a newspaper machine halfway up Grassmarket. I knew it was Brigid's paper being delivered; that was the machine where I'd picked up other copies of her articles, though never so soon after they'd been delivered.

The rain had stopped, and I excused myself to go get a paper. Tom came with me.

"Brigid said she was going to write an article. She didn't have any of the new information we've discovered tonight. I need to see what she wrote," I said.

"Aye?"

I laughed once. It was the middle of the night and the air smelled like rain. For the first time ever, I didn't see any other people in Grassmarket. Of all the magic I'd felt over the last year, this moment with Tom, the relief I felt over the answers we seemed to have, the concern over the continuing questions, might have been one of the most magical. I was either under Edinburgh's or Tom's spell. Maybe both. Even the doubt I heard in his tone couldn't ruin the sensations I felt, the electric giddiness.

"I think it will be a good article," I said.

"I hope so."

It was.

It was also on the front page, headlined with: "The Fate of a Beloved Bookshop Hangs in the Balance. Vote Today."

Brigid turned the facts as she knew them into a favorable article for the bookshop. She used the space to further condemn the council and some of their secretive ways. But I only skimmed that part, glad that, bottom line, she made it clear that it seemed the bookshop had been wrongly put on a potential chopping block, and the council should consider taking a step back until the facts were given another look.

The other interesting part was about Henry Stewart and his murder. A killer was still on the loose, but it seemed obvious to "this reporter" that Mr. Stewart was killed because of something nefarious he'd been involved in via his councilor capacity. It only made sense, after all. Get to work, police.

"Oh dear," Edwin said when we all finished the article.

"What?" I said. "It's great."

"It is, but I might have put something in motion that will prove to be an overkill, in the grandest of ways."

"To save the bookshop? I'm all about overkill until the vote is over, killed," I said with a weary smile.

"Aye," he said doubtfully.

Inspectors Buchanan and Winters discussed the best way to approach Mikey Wooster. Buchanan wanted to knock on his door right then and ask him a few questions. Winters suggested that she wait until the vote, not because Mikey's vote was important, but because all the councilors would be together for the vote. Maybe there was a way to gather some strong evidence against Mikey. Or not, if he was innocent.

No one thought he was innocent though. But it would take evidence for an arrest.

With only a few hours of night left, we all went home, with the plan to meet again at the vote. None of us were going to miss it.

I looked at myself in the mirror and sighed. Oh, boy, did I look tired, but today just had to go well.

"You look perfect," Tom said. "Beautiful, aye, but also fierce, like you won't put up with any crap anyone wants to try to give you."

I'd pulled my hair back, though there were some frizzy fly-aways. I wore a white shirt and a black skirt and black pumps. It wasn't a fancy outfit, but it was fancier than I usually sported. In fact, other than our wedding day, I couldn't remember the last time I'd given much thought to my clothes. I hadn't worn heels even that day.

"Thank you, sir, and you look . . . well, Tom, if you don't know what I think about how you look then I need to work on my communication skills. Also, keep an eye out for me falling down. I'm not sure I've retained any muscle memory regarding how to wear these shoes."

He laughed and pulled me in for a hug. It would have been wonderful to stay that way for the rest of the day, but we had a vote to attend.

The City Chambers building of Edinburgh looked just like a building one would expect in this beautiful old city. A cobblestoned courtyard decorated with flowerpots and the statue of a man and a horse greeted us as we walked under a stone arch. The U-shaped building extended up three floors. The old brown stones of the building were blackened around the edges. The only splashes of color came from flags and some circular crests attached to the turrets right outside the courtyard. I scanned the crests, looking for the one I'd recently become acquainted with: Elizabeth I's, but it wasn't there. Of course, it wasn't. This was Scotland, not England. I shook my head at myself and wished I'd looked up Mary, Queen of Scots' crest.

I'd walked past the chambers many times, but I'd never seen such a crowd as was gathering today. And, I'd never seen so many kilts.

"Is this normal?" I asked Tom about the crowd.

"I don't know. Maybe Brigid's article got some attention."

"Lass," a voice said behind me.

"Rosie! We would have come to get you," I said as I saw her walking toward us. When we'd left her last night, she wasn't going to attend, but sleep in.

"Look what I found!" She waved some papers.

"The construction approvals?" I said.

"Aye." She smiled. "Guess where they were?"

"I have no idea."

"I'd slipped them inside a book. The first book that Edwin gave me, poems by Robert Burns. Last night, just as I was aboot tae fall asleep, I remembered putting them in the book. Edwin had told me how important they were, how he was so excited about receiving approval. I slipped them in the book I cherished, the first book he gave me. I should have remembered sooner."

"That's perfect," I said as I pulled her into a hug.

"I dinnae even think we'll need them, but I'm ready if we do."

"Aye," Tom said with a smile.

"Hamlet will be here too. I called him an hour ago. I saw Inspector Winters already. He's over by the front of the courtyard."

"That's good news," I said. "What about Edwin?"

"I dinnae ken, lass. He's not answering his mobile. But he'll be here."

"He's not answering?"

"No, I've been trying tae ring him all morning."

"He'll be here," Tom said. "Come on, let's go find some seats."

"Rosie!"

We turned to see Jack hurrying toward us. "Good morning, everyone." Once he made it to us, he wiped his forehead with a handkerchief and continued, "Has anyone talked to Edwin? I've been trying to reach him since last night."

A thread of concern tightened my stomach. Had something happened to him? What had he been up to the night before that might lead to overkill in the grandest of ways? Why wasn't he answering his phone?

"Should I run by his house?" I asked.

"No, no. He's up tae something is all. He'll be here," Rosie said unsurely.

I blinked at her.

"Edwin is always up tae something. Come on," she said.

We walked toward the building, toward a door decorated with a sign above that said: City Chambers.

"Here we go," I muttered as we went inside.

There were sixty-three councilors, the council having added six to the count during the 2017 election. Each councilor represented a different part of the city designated as a ward. Council members worked together but they were also broken out into committees to work on specific issues.

The Council Chamber hall oozed history. Historical king and queen scenes were painted on the wood paneled walls. Diffused light set a respectful tone as it came through the domed stained-glass ceiling. The roomed buzzed and hummed with the growing crowd. As we found some seats along the perimeter, I realized that though many of the people in the room were councilors, many weren't. And many observers held Brigid's newspaper. She had hit a nerve.

Just as I sat down in a cushioned chair, I noticed Mary. She walked in, her arm looped through Lyle Mercado's. I locked gazes with them both. Mary sent me a weak smile and wave as Lyle frowned and nodded. Oh dear, he wasn't playing the part of the third husband, was he? I shook my head. No, enough of that. They were friends, and maybe Mary just wanted someone there with her.

Hamlet slid into an empty seat behind me and touched my shoulder. "Where's Edwin?"

"Hello! No one knows," I said quietly.

"Okay."

"All right," Jack said. "Technically we must get permission to speak a week or so before the meeting, but I managed to get ahold of someone last night who said we could have the floor for a few minutes. But I really, really hope Edwin joins us. It will all mean so much more coming from him. And, from what I'm seeing, the public is going to want to have their say too. Your friend's article might have done some good."

Tom and I shared a knowing smile. Brigid wasn't necessarily a friend, but maybe she would be.

"We *all* hope Edwin shows up," I said.

"Did you see the bust?" Hamlet asked me.

"What?" I turned to look at him.

He pointed. I would have known her even if there hadn't been a small metal tag on the base. Mary, Queen of Scots.

"Wow," Hamlet said. "You do look like her."

I did. Or at least I sort of looked like the bust. It was made of white porcelain, so the hair wasn't red, but there was a similarity to our chins and our cheekbones as well as the set of our eyes. The red hair might have sealed the deal. A morbid thought regarding Mary's beheading crossed my mind.

I still hadn't taken the time to do any extra research, but I knew that one of the biggest surprises the queen had sprung on the people who witnessed her execution was the fact that she wore a wig. Yes, she'd had red hair, but at some point, probably during the time of her last castle imprisonment, it thinned, fell out probably. She'd only been forty-four when she'd been beheaded, but her final imprisonment had been more seriously imposed than the others. She'd been confined inside. A woman who'd loved to ride horses, she'd been trim and healthy most of her life, able to exercise even during other imprisonments. But being stuck inside with no exercise, no fresh air, had taken its toll. She'd gained weight, her legs becoming so puffy that she struggled to walk to her own execution.

I had no thought that I'd lived a past life, the queen's included, but my heart suddenly went out to her. For whatever reason, I suddenly sensed that on some strange level, I finally understood her. She'd only wanted what she deemed best. She was a kind ruler, at least from everything I knew. She'd had her beliefs and she'd been born into circumstances that she wasn't able to become victorious over. She'd become a victim of her circumstances.

"I do look like her. Sort of," I said.

But I wasn't her. Never had been, I was sure.

As I turned to face front again, my eyes landed on Dina Wooster. She was walking purposefully toward someone. I craned my neck to watch as she handed a piece of paper to someone. Mikey. If Inspector Buchanan had visited Mikey in the middle of the night, no arrest had occurred. He looked at the note his wife had given him and then directly at me. Dina seemed irritated that he'd been so obvious, but after she rolled her eyes at him, she turned and made her way back to another chair on the perimeter. She wasn't sitting close to Mary and Lyle. She didn't smile at me. In fact, there was nothing friendly in her glance.

Hadn't she said she was bothered by what the council had done regarding the bookshop? Hadn't she said she was going to talk to Mikey? I saw no reason for her to be bothered to see me.

Maybe I hadn't read her expression correctly. Or, maybe she'd known what her husband was up to all along.

Something about that idea niggled at me. What had Dina known? Had she even tried to do anything about it?

"The gang's all here," Hamlet said quietly, pulling me out of my thoughts about Dina.

"Everyone but Edwin," Tom said just as quietly.

"And Inspector Buchanan, but we just might not be able to see her," I said.

"Aye," Tom agreed.

Someone pounded a gavel somewhere but just as I tried to figure out where it was coming from, sirens interrupted the proceedings. The buzz of noise in the room ramped up as we all noticed the siren noises coming closer.

"What's happening?" Rosie asked.

"I don't know."

More noises came from outside the chambers. We were all looking toward the door we'd come through as a slew of men paraded in. Dressed in black suits, they moved purposefully and then seemed to make some sort of planned formation.

"MI6?" Tom said.

"Really?" I said. I craned my neck even more.

"Ladies and gentlemen, excuse me," a voice said through the sound system. "Please, may I have your attention."

The room fell into a hushed silence and I saw the podium where the voice had come from. Grace Graham stood at the microphone. Brigid was behind her a bit. Brigid's eyes caught mine and she smiled and nodded. Then she winked.

What the hell did that mean?

"Thank you," Grace said. "Thank you. Well, it seems we have a very special guest today. It's a surprise and a wee bit unreal, but I assure you, it's very real. We are breaking protocol, but I think you'll all understand why. Without further ado, ladies and gentlemen, please may I present Her Royal Highness, Her Majesty, the Queen of England."

Gasps and murmurs filled the chamber as we looked toward the door again. A moment later, along with none other than Edwin MacAlister following behind her, the Queen of England walked into the chamber. Everyone stood then and bows and curtsies moved like a wave as the Queen made her way to the podium.

"You have got to be kidding me," I said as I laughed. I didn't realize I was crying too until Tom wiped a tear from my cheek.

"It's going to be okay," he said.

"That's the freaking Queen of England," I said, almost too loudly.

"Aye," Tom said with a crooked smile.

She was adorable, just like she was on TV. She wore a yellow suit and carried a piece of paper and an off-white purse. I wondered for a moment if, perhaps, she was an actress playing the part. But she wasn't; she was the real Queen.

With Edwin still in tow, she made her way to the podium and tapped on the microphone.

"Hello," she said with a smile. "Thank you for giving me a few moments. I'll be brief. The Cracked Spine is one of Scotland's, of Britain's beloved bookshops, and Britains don't take any bookshop lightly. We cherish them, one and all. But this one might be a little more special than some. This is a place I have visited myself, a place where I met Rosie, a lovely woman who knew exactly what book would be fit for a queen."

I smiled at Rosie as she wiped a tear away as well. She'd never told me she helped the Queen shop for a book.

"If there are any sort of safety concerns regarding the buildings the bookshop is housed in, Mr. Edwin MacAlister will take care of the problems." She waved the piece of paper she'd brought with her. "In case it is necessary, I have The Cracked

Spine's Burgess Ticket here with me. It seems Mr. MacAlister still holds every right afforded him by this ticket, which includes operating the business of selling books. Surely, the council sees that today is not a good day to vote to close the shop. Perhaps more inspections need to take place before such drastic measures are taken. Please consider the circumstances. Thank you all for your time."

By the end of the lovely speech, even Jack McGinnis had to sniff and wipe away a stray tear.

"That did not just happen," I said.

"Aye, it did," Tom said. "Only Edwin."

"Where did he find the Burgess Ticket?" Rosie asked me.

"Somewhere on the dark side last night, I suppose," I said. Where would it have been?

Without further ado, the MI6 men led the Queen out of the building. Once she was gone and after a stunned silence filled the air for a few minutes, cheers broke out and soon cries of "Vote! Vote! Vote!" rang through the hall.

THIRTY-FOUR

"Ladies and gentlemen," another voice came from the podium. I didn't know the woman speaking and pounding the gavel. "I'm going to call for the vote. Item number 425, regarding The Cracked Spine. Shall the failed building inspection be considered appropriate to invalidate the business license? Those in favor, say aye."

Not one "aye." Not even from Mikey Wooster. I craned my neck again to try to watch him, but I couldn't see him. Nevertheless, not one "aye" broke the silence.

"Those against, nay," the woman on the podium said.

"Nay!" rang through the chamber.

And then more cheers.

"The nays have it!"

"It's over," Rosie said. "It's over."

I felt the same relief as I hugged her, but it wasn't over, not for Mary. A killer still needed to be found.

"Come on, let's go find Edwin," I said when we disengaged.

Edwin wasn't far away, just outside the chambers, in the court-yard and waiting for the rest of us.

"Overkill?" he said to me as we approached him.

"Maybe a little." I laughed. "But it was the best overkill ever. Where was the Burgess Ticket?"

"In the box with the coins," Edwin said. "I have no recollection of keeping them together, but I must have. When I went to gather the coins this morning, I looked through the box. And, there it was. Finding it this morning seemed fortuitous. The Queen was lovely to do the favor she did. The ticket was the icing on the cake, I suppose."

Tom, Rosie, Hamlet, and Jack and I gathered around him.

"How do you know her?" I said.

"She's stopped by the bookshop a few times, but it's not me she knows. It's Rosie." Edwin pulled Rosie close as he put his arm around her. "Rosie has helped her find some of the best books. Rosie's skills and ways with people brought the Queen. It wasn't me, truly it wasn't."

"Och, on with ye then." Rosie waved away the compliment.

"Rosie found the construction papers too," I said.

"Aye?" Edwin said. "Everything's been found then! That's lovely."

But everything hadn't been found, I thought as I saw Mary and Lyle walking toward us. No, there was still something missing.

"Hello," Mary said to us all. "I'm shocked by the Queen's visit, but I'm thrilled the bookshop was saved. I apologize for whatever Henry did, and whoever he recruited to help him do it. Please accept our apologies." She looked toward Lyle who nodded.

"Aye. Me too," Lyle said.

"Lyle, did you present the idea of closing down the bookshop to the council?" I asked.

"Aye, I'm afraid I was requested to do so and I did. I'm so sorry."

"Henry requested you do it?" I said.

Lyle blinked at me. "No, Mikey Wooster asked me."

"What?" Mary said.

"Aye. You thought it was Henry?" he said. "No, Henry led the way later because he was the senior member of the council, but all of this was set in motion by Mikey. Henry was helping him."

"Helping him do what?" Mary said.

"He wanted the bookshop," I said as I looked at Lyle.

"I don't know. I was never told why, I was just asked to be a part of setting things in motion," Lyle said.

"Did Dina come talk to you right after Edwin and I did, in your office?" I asked.

"Oh, aye, I was told she stopped by, but I'd left by then. I was upset by the conversation with you and Edwin. Later, I tried to ring her, but she didn't return my call. My staff told me she demanded to see for herself that my office was empty, so they showed her."

"Why would they do that? Why did you set things in motion?" Mary said.

"Because Mikey is married to Dina, your niece, Mary. I'd do anything for your family, you know that. My staff knows that."

I pulled out my phone and called Inspector Winters.

"Delaney? I'm in the chambers. Where are you?" Inspector Winter said.

"In the courtyard. Where's Inspector Buchanan?"

"Talking to Mikey Wooster, I think."

"Hang on a second," I said as I pulled the phone away and held it so he could hear.

I looked around the courtyard. The crowd was dispersing. If the council was voting on anything else, we hadn't stayed to see it. Neither had the wonderful people who it seemed had come out to support the bookshop.

"Mary, you were in trouble for looking inside drawers and such at the museum. That's why they asked you to leave, right?" I said.

"Well, I suppose," she said, embarrassed.

"I'm sorry. I don't mean to make you uncomfortable, but I need to know something, and this is more important than anything else because it's about Henry's murder. I need you to be one hundred percent honest with me."

"Okay."

"The letter, Queen Elizabeth I's letter that talked about a truce with Mary, Queen of Scots."

"Aye," she said. Her cheeks reddened. I knew the look. My cheeks reddened the same way.

"You came into the bookshop to tell us you just remembered the trip to Paris, the alleged letter, but, and tell me the truth, you didn't just remember it that day, did you? You and Henry talked about it after the dinner party, didn't you? You told other people about that time in Paris too. Of course you did. A letter like that would be too important to Mary, Queen of Scots, and extremely valuable. Dina and Mikey knew."

"Delaney," she said.

"Didn't they!"

She blinked at me. "She's my niece."

"She might have killed your husband."

"No, I can't believe that." Tears started to fall down Mary's cheeks. "Mikey said she didn't, that he must have been killed for something else. No!"

"You were looking in drawers because Dina asked you to. You were searching desks and drawers for some sign of that letter. Dina had desks in her shop—she'd bought them because she thought it was a possibility that the letter was inside them? You were all searching, weren't you?"

After a long pause, Mary nodded once.

"When did you think the letter might be in The Cracked Spine?" I asked.

"A few months ago." Mary deflated. "The first time we met the docent in Paris about five years ago, he told us about the alleged letter being stolen by the queen's bastard brother, Moray, and then hidden inside a desk in a castle. He didn't know which castle. We found him again a few months ago, and he said he had it on good authority that Edwin MacAlister at The Cracked Spine had the letter."

"And you don't think Mikey or Dina killed Henry?" Tom said to her.

"Henry was going to come forward with everything, wasn't he?" Jack asked.

"I don't. I . . . I didn't want the bookshop closed. Henry didn't either. I didn't know . . . I tried to help."

I put the phone back up to my ear. "Did you get all that?"

"I did," Inspector Winters said. "I'll find Buchanan."

"I have an idea," I said.

"I'm listening," Inspector Winters said.

I stepped away from the group and told him my idea.

THIRTY-FIVE

Edwin relocked the bookshop's front door after we'd all entered.

"Follow me, everyone," I said.

Edwin, Rosie, Hamlet, Tom, Mary, Lyle, Inspectors Buchanan and Winters, and Mikey and Dina Wooster were all there. Jack had headed back to Glasgow. It was going to be very crowded, but we'd make it work.

The inspectors had been put on alert. Mikey, Dina, Mary, and Lyle were being watched closely. In fact, Inspector Winters hadn't liked my idea, but I thought it was probably the only way to find the killer. My plan was to push the suspects to the brink of their obsession, and hope the killer would crack.

It might not have been the best, but it was all I had.

I led the way over to the dark side. I was the pied piper of a sort. We snaked over the stairs and then down the dark hallway on the other side. I put the key into the door and turned three times to the left.

"What in the world?" Inspector Buchanan said as she followed me directly inside.

"I'll explain it to you later," I said as I started removing things from the desk, including the paper I'd spread over the top of it. "Come in, everyone. Edwin, help me."

He made his way around everyone else to join me. The space was too small for three people, let alone eleven, but we crowded in.

"First of all, is there a maker's mark anywhere on this desk?" I asked Edwin.

"Aye, I've seen one," he said as he walked to one side and crouched. "Right here."

I crouched too. A tree with an E underneath. It looked just like the mark on one of the desks at Dina's.

I looked at her as she put her hand to her mouth.

I looked back at Edwin. "Do you know where any secret compartment might be?"

"False drawers? Backs? I don't know," Edwin said. "Let's look."

There were five drawers on the desk. Once by one, Edwin and I pulled them out and looked at each one closely. Then we passed them around for everyone else to look at too. Inspector Winters and I shared a glance as we both noticed that our suspect guests were particularly focused on the task, but I went back to the desk with Edwin.

There were no false fronts, no false backs, nothing that seemed like a secret hidey-hole.

"May I see the maker's mark?" Dina asked.

"Sure," I said as I moved to the side.

Inspector Buchanan stayed right next to her as she inspected. Dina looked at the mark and nodded at Mikey.

"This is the desk you wanted?" I said to Dina. "You and

Mikey were willing to ruin the bookshop just so you could have it."

"They didn't know what else to do," Mary said. "They tried to figure out a way to break in. They knew they couldn't just talk to Edwin. They didn't know what to do."

"Mary," Mikey said.

"Don't . . ," she said to him. "Henry changed his mind. He knew better."

Mikey shook his head, but no one admitted to murder. Yet.

We continued searching but to no avail. A thread of disappointment mixed with panic inside my gut. My plan was falling apart.

But someone else didn't think so.

You're too focused on where you've been to pay attention to where you're going.

I laughed. It was Mary. But not any of the Marys we'd become acquainted with lately. It was Mary Poppins. Close enough.

"What?" Tom said.

"We've got to turn it over! I mean, we need to be really, really careful, but we have to turn it upside down. See it from another angle."

Three people had to leave the room—Rosie, Hamlet, and Lyle—to open the space enough to turn the desk as gently as we needed to turn it. Tom, Edwin, and I managed it quickly though and the three who'd left returned.

At first glance, there was nothing unusual about the bottom of the desk. It looked like the bottom of any desk, except maybe this one was made with real wood. Hamlet started knocking on the bottom—the areas where there were drawer spaces on the other side as well as the area where there was just desk.

And suddenly, something sounded different.

"Wait! What was that?" I asked.

Hamlet knocked again. "Aye, it sounds as if there's something missing there."

I tried to look at the piece he was knocking on from different angles. "Do we have to cut it open to get inside?"

"We can't do that," Inspector Winters said. "It's too valuable."

"I'll do it," Edwin said. "I'll need a knife or something."

A second later, I handed him a letter open, one with a pearl handle that I'd found on a shelf.

Edwin placed the blade of the letter opener into a seam.

He looked up at the rest of us. "Here we go."

He pried the wood—once, twice, and then three times. And on the third and most exuberant try, it sprang free. Well, a piece of it came off easily, hopefully intact, but none of us double-checked right away.

We were too interested in what was there. There was a secret space where secret things not only could be hidden, but had been.

Parchment with writing.

"Nobody touch it," I said as I reached for some gloves.

Maybe it should have fallen apart, crumbled to dust. But it didn't, it hadn't. With tweezers and my gloved hands, I pulled out a single sheet of parchment and took it to the worktable, where I unfolded it and we all stared.

The parchment might have stayed together, but the ink had faded. There was still some of it there, but it was difficult to read. I would need to use a special light as well as take other precautions to save it, but for now, we all looked closely at the final few words that had been written on the page and were still legible.

We shall be queens together. Elizabeth.

Mary cried out once and then turned to Mikey. "Did you kill Henry for this?"

"No!"

"He did!" Dina said. "He killed Henry for this letter, this bookshop. Our future."

"I didn't!" Mikey exclaimed as both he and Dina were being handcuffed by the inspectors.

"It wasn't ever about the coins, was it?" I asked.

Mikey and Dina wouldn't look at me.

"I can't believe this!" Mary said.

But I wasn't sure what she couldn't believe. Was she overcome by the letter, surprised about the coins, did she still think Mikey killed Henry?

Both inspectors were informing their suspects that they were being arrested for the murder of Henry Stewart.

I looked at Mikey. "The thing is, if you'd just talked to Edwin, he would have worked with you in searching for this. You killed Henry and you didn't have to."

Mikey looked at me with a long, evil glare. He finally said, "I didn't kill Henry."

"Yes, you did!" Dina exclaimed.

"No, I didn't." He looked at his wife. "You did, and I have the proof."

Dina's glare at her husband was even more evil than Mikey's. We all waited, hoping one of them would say more, keep spilling the beans. Even the inspectors seemed to pause a beat. The suspects had been read their rights. Was there more they wanted to share?

But there wasn't. Mikey stopped talking and Dina stopped speaking real words; strange mewling sounds came around some tears, but no more words came.

The inspectors, with Rosie leading the way, took the suspects away.

My plan had worked. I wasn't sure how it was going to play out, but I knew that if we'd found a letter, the strange obsessions these people had would take over, and the killer would somehow be uncovered. I was glad it had worked. At least we knew the killer was one of the Woosters. I had faith the police would sort it out from there.

I was really glad that Mary wasn't a killer. I liked her. Lyle wasn't a killer either. I couldn't envision him and Mary becoming a couple, but who knew. Hamlet escorted them out of the bookshop, and soon it was only Tom, Edwin, and me.

As Tom and Edwin looked at the letter and pondered its validity, I became lost in something else. I didn't know yet if the note had anything to do with Mary, Queen of Scots. I might never know because I might not be able to save the letter completely. But I knew one thing without a doubt—the woman I'd recently met, the one who'd just left with Hamlet, the one who claimed she was once a martyred queen of Scotland, had spoken the same words I'd just read to me as she and I had visited the Edinburgh Castle.

We shall be queens together.

Maybe that was proof enough.

THIRTY-SIX

I held the paper on my lap and read aloud to Tom:

Edinburgh resident Dina Wooster has been arrested for the murder of her uncle, Henry Stewart. A city councilman, Stewart had been working with his niece and her husband, fellow councilman Mikey Wooster, attempting to steal a priceless letter hidden inside a desk at a Grassmarket bookshop, The Cracked Spine. When their efforts to take the letter were unsuccessful, they planned to use government procedures to shut down the bookshop so they might attempt to take possession of its full inventory. Their plan went awry when Mr. Stewart told his niece that he was not going to follow through with their nefarious activities. In a fit of rage, Ms. Wooster attached an explosive device to Mr. Stewart's automobile, using instructions on the internet to build the bomb. He was killed in the explosion; there were no other casualties. Ms. Wooster had hoped to prevent Mr. Stewart from reversing the decision to vote on the bookshop's demise. As it happened, the bookshop was saved by none other than the Queen of England herself.

Full story to be printed in this weekend's special edition, "When Queens Collide," by Brigid McBride.

"She's a good writer," I said. "I can't wait to read this weekend's version."

Tom sat next to me on the couch and kept a doubtful expression on his face. "She's not bad."

I laughed. "I'm not that insecure. You may fully admit that she's good at her job."

Tom smiled. "So, what now, my bride? Now that you've solved another murder."

"It just all came together."

Tom laughed. "Aye, with your help."

"Well . . ."

"That was one of the craziest things I've ever seen. I'm sad about the murder, but you are one adventure after another, Delaney."

"I still can't believe it." I laughed. "The real Queen!"

"Aye." Tom shook his head. "How about the other queen? Do you think you and Mary will be friends?"

"Well, we've been invited to another dinner. Eloise and Gretchen are hosting. Along with voting in favor of keeping the bookshop open, the council is no longer pushing for the revival of the Burgess Tickets. Gretchen is relieved and thankful. It's a celebratory dinner, but also something to honor Henry. Mary should be there too. Tomorrow night? Are you available?"

"I am."

"There will be more details in the article, but Brigid told me that Dina decided to use an explosive because that's how Mary, Queen of Scots' second husband was killed. She thought it would throw the police off track, make them think Mary was having an affair. No one would guess that Dina Wooster would attach an explosive to a car. Bridgid also learned that Dina had forgotten about the coins until I mentioned them. They weren't nearly as important as the letter."

"She's wicked."

"And we fell for it a little. I mean, the affair idea seemed feasible to me, until it didn't. Inspector Buchanan said she never considered it, but maybe she's just saying that."

Mikey had done a good job preserving evidence. He thought his wife would try to throw him under the bus if it came down to it. Dina's fingerprints were on the bomb-making materials still at their house. Her fingerprints only. When he told the police what he'd saved, Dina cracked and said she should have killed him too.

Tom said, "Mikey got lucky."

"I think he was trying to protect her but, in the end, he just couldn't any longer. He was smart to save the evidence, but he should have spoken up sooner. He's in some trouble."

"Any word on the letter?" Tom asked.

Reluctantly, and after the Scottish authorities had become involved, I had to hand over the letter.

It was going to be a *very* big deal. And I had an in with the person who would be in charge of transcribing and preserving it. Joshua had been chosen to do the job. He'd already told me I'd get to be the first one to read his transcription. I couldn't wait. I'd take Mary with me, but I hadn't told her that yet.

"Joshua will let me know the second it's ready. Maybe the second before." I smiled.

Tom's phone rang and I watched as he seemed pleased by what the caller was telling him.

"Aye, that's wonderful. All right. We'll be there." He disconnected the call.

"What?" I asked.

"The house is ready, love. The electrical is fixed. It's ready to move into. What about you? I don't want to rush you, but are you ready?"

I looked around my wonderful cottage and at my wonderful husband. Elias, Aggie, and I were going to be friends, family, forever. But it was time. There was a blue cottage by the sea waiting for Tom and me and our life together.

"I'm so ready," I said.

It was time for our next chapter.

ACKNOWLEDGMENTS

As always, thank you to my agent Jessica Faust, editor Hannah Braaten, assistant editor Nettie Finn, and everyone at Minotaur. It's so cool that you all aren't tired of me yet. An extra shout-out to cover designer, Mary Ann Lasher. I love this cover so much! Thank you. As I was finishing up this book, a box of letters written by Mary, Queen of Scots, was found in a museum storage facility in Scotland. Since Mary plays a role in this story, I couldn't help but feel the timing was somehow fortuitous. I love it when stuff like that happens. If you're interested in reading the real letters, the Smithsonian Mag online has a great article on it.

As far as I know, the Robert Burns's Burgess Ticket is real, but not housed in the Writers' Museum. It would be a good place to put it though.

Mary, Queen of Scots, is a completely fascinating historical figure. I loved researching her life. In fact, I ended up reading much more about her than I would ever use in this book. If you have interest in knowing more about the martyred queen, I fully recommend you begin with *Queen of Scots: The True*

Life of Mary Stuart, by John Guy. It was captivating, and is on my reread list.

Any mistakes regarding Edinburgh government are not only mine, but purposeful for the benefit of the story. Apologies.

Thanks always to Charlie and Tyler. Love you both so much.

Read on for a look ahead to
DEADLY EDITIONS –

the next installment in the Scottish
Bookshop mystery series,

coming soon in hardcover
from Paige Shelton and Minotaur Books!

The bell above the bookshop's front door jingled. I scooted my chair and stood from where I'd been working at the back table and peered around the dividing half wall. I saw Rosie at her desk. She'd been so quiet that I wasn't sure, but there she was, standing to help the customer who had entered. I could get back to my project. However, when I caught sight of who'd come in, I paused again, curious enough to join Rosie and Hector—the cutest dog in the world—up front.

A young man had come through the door. He stomped snow from his boots and swiped some off the top of his pillbox-like cap before standing at attention. "Ms. Delaney Nichols, please," he said.

"Can I help ye?" Rosie asked as I made my way to the front.

Suited in black from head to toe and wearing that unexpected cap, the young man squinted at her. "Are you Ms. Nichols?"

"I'm Delaney," I said as I put my hand on Rosie's arm. He seemed harmless enough.

"Aye?" He smiled. "I have a note for you."

He and I met halfway, and he handed me the folded note.

"Thank you," I said automatically.

The messenger nodded, smiled again, and then left as if in a big hurry to get out of there. I blinked at his exit, shared some raised eyebrows with Rosie, and then read the note aloud:

Ms. Delaney Nichols,

Your presence is requested this afternoon at two o'clock at Deacon Brodie's Tavern to discuss Ms. Shelagh O'Conner's vast collection of rare and valuable books. Please don't be tardy.

Sincerely and with gratitude,

Ms. O'Conner's representative, Mr. Louis Chantrell.

"Well, isn't that strange?" I said. "What about the collection would we be discussing?"

"Aye." Rosie moved closer to me and peered down at the note.

"Do you think it's . . . for real? Maybe the books are for sale?" I asked.

"I dinnae ken."

I laughed once and glanced at the time. It was slightly after noon. "Do you think I should just go and find out?"

Hector, a miniature Yorkie who lived with Rosie but took care of us all, trotted to my feet and put his paws on my boot. I lifted him to the crook of my arm.

"Do ye ken who she is?" Rosie asked.

"I do, but only because of an article I read recently. It was about her and her books, not to mention her mansion and all her money. Brigid wrote it."

"Aye. I ken who she is and I read that too."

"You're reading Brigid's articles now?" I said with a small smile.

Rosie's mouth quirked. "Sometimes."

"She's really good, huh?"

"Not as good as you."

"I'm not a journalist."

"Och, that's not what I meant."

I laughed. "Well, thank you, but she *is* a fine journalist."

Rosie, my grandmotherly coworker, was protective of me and my recent marriage to Tom Shannon, handsome pub owner—who had also, at one time, been boyfriend to Brigid McBride, pretty blonde newspaper journalist. Brigid and I had become friends, sort of, but that hadn't stopped her from barely reining in snarky comments regarding Tom's previous commitment issues. To his credit he was ashamed of his behavior regarding their breakup, and he'd apologized to Brigid. She wasn't ready to let it go.

Rosie was the most loyal person I'd ever known, and she would always have a suspicious side-eye for Brigid. That was okay.

"Anyway," Rosie continued, "what do ye think? Are ye intrigued by the inveet?"

I looked at the note and then out the front window. I hadn't paid attention to where the messenger had gone. Grassmarket Square's first-of-the-season snowfall had turned the world into a winter wonderland.

"I wish I could ask someone more questions first. Maybe I could find"—I looked at the note—"Louis Chantrell."

Rosie shrugged. "I doubt it. It all seems purposefully mysterious and delivered with little time tae spare."

Briefly, I listened for a bookish voice. My intuition sometimes spoke to me, lent some guidance, using the voices of characters from books I'd read. But all was silent; there wasn't even enough information for my intuition to have an opinion.

"Yes, mysterious. Weird," I said.

"A wee bit. Are ye going?"

"I'm interested in any book collection, of course, but something about it feels manipulative."

"Aye, it does, but if ye want tae go, I dinnae think there'd be any harm done."

"It *is* a public place."

"Aye," she said with a distinctly doubtful tone.

"What?" I prodded, wondering what was bothering her.

Rosie looked at me a long moment. "I think ye should go, but I think ye should call Edwin first. Not because ye need permission from him but because he's met Shelagh a few times I think, and he can give you some insight as tae her personality." She nodded toward the note. "I doubt you'll be able to reach Mr. Chantrell."

"Good plan." I glanced at the time again. "Have you ever met Shelagh O'Conner?"

"Aye, a long time ago, she came into the shop. She didnae stay long but searched for some books. When she didnae find what she was looking for, she left and never came back in, as far as I ken."

"How does she know me?" I asked.

"Ye've been here a while. Ye have a reputation."

"Really? Well, I hope it's a good one."

"I believe it is." Rosie smiled, but only briefly. "Except with the local police—they might be a wee bit worrit about ye."

Inspector Winters, local police inspector and friend, had an esteemed place on my phone's favorite-numbers list, but it wasn't necessarily because *I'd* been in trouble. I'd just found myself in places where a variety of troubles had occurred, and

I'd helped a little to clean up the messes. Inspector Winters and I got along just fine.

Still holding Hector, I made my way to the table in the back.

My younger coworker, Hamlet, usually worked in this space, but he wasn't in yet. I'd been the first one to the bookshop today and had been briefly worried that Rosie hadn't arrived before me as she usually did—it was cold and wintry out there—so I'd stayed on this side of the shop instead of moving to the other side, where my desk was located. By the time Rosie came in, fifteen minutes later, I was enjoying the snowy view and my cozy comfort too much to move.

The Cracked Spine, the Edinburgh bookshop that had called to me from over the sea—*Leave your safe Kansas world and come live an adventure*—was made of two separate buildings that had, many years earlier, been remodeled and connected by a short hallway up a flight of stairs on each side. I'd named the two sides the light side and the dark side, but simply because the light just wasn't quite as good over there—until you went inside my workspace, the warehouse, at the very back of the building. The warehouse was behind a locked door and topped off by a line of windows that, even when it was cloudy outside, let through plenty of natural light. With the help of a bright desk lamp or two, it was easy for me to work, day and night.

The small bookshop's light side, the side where the customers came in to browse and buy, had been homey today . . . well, once I'd turned up the old radiator. Even if I hadn't wanted to wait for Rosie, I might have stayed. The falling snow out the front windows made a beautiful backdrop for the pedestrian traffic moving through Grassmarket Square. I'd seen it snow in

Edinburgh the year before, but it was always hard to resist a season's first fall.

The book-filled old wooden shelves were in decent shape, and anything newer would have seemed misplaced atop the scuffed marble floor. The shelves were more organized than I'd imagined I could make them. But I had worked hard, and my system was pretty good. My current project was to create a master list of the location of each and every book, not just the sections they were shelved in. It was a huge process, but I was ready to tackle it, and I'd been jotting down some spreadsheet ideas when the messenger came in.

Rosie had an office on the dark side too, but mostly she sat at her desk on this side. She preferred talking to customers, welcoming them in with her innate warmth. I'd recently learned that she'd even sold a book to the queen a few years back. Yes, *that* queen.

Though Edwin MacAlister owned The Cracked Spine, and it seemed almost everyone knew who he was, it was Rosie who brought people back in time and time again.

I would be honored if my reputation at the bookshop were anywhere near hers, but I knew it wasn't. As I thought about the note, I decided that it must have been Edwin who'd told someone—Mr. Chantrell or Ms. O'Conner—that I was the person to work with if a large book collection were being discussed, perhaps put up for sale.

I was thrilled that Edwin trusted me with such tasks and not surprised that he might have forgotten to mention this one. Lately he'd been stepping away more and more from the bookshop. In his mid-seventies, he'd found a new romance with an Irishwoman who owned and operated a local restaurant. When he wasn't there, they were together somewhere else, enjoying everything from mundane everyday tasks to traveling the world. They'd recently returned from Australia.

It's why he'd hired me—so he could work as minimally as possible and have more fun in his older years. I was happy to accommodate, and his lady love had been a perfectly timed surprise.

Settling Hector on my lap, I grabbed my phone and rang Edwin.

"Lass, hello, how are you this beautiful snowy morning?" he answered.

"I'm well. You sound cheery."

"It's a lovely wintry day."

I smiled. "Yes, it is. Are you heading into the shop this morning?"

"I can if you need me."

"No, no, it's all right." I unfolded the note again. "A messenger just stopped by the shop and delivered a letter, but I'm wondering if you might know about it."

"Tell me more."

"It's from a representative of Shelagh O'Conner. It's signed by a man named Louis Chantrell. They've asked me to meet them this afternoon at Deacon Brodie's pub to discuss Shelagh's book collection."

"Aye? Of course, I know Shelagh some, and her love of books is legendary, but I don't know Mr. Chantrell. The invitation is completely fascinating."

"I thought so too, but I wondered if they'd heard about me because of you."

"No, not at all. Are you going to go?"

"Do you think I should?"

"Seems safe enough. Aye. If her collection is being put up

for sale, I would most definitely be interested in it. No budget. Pay what you think they're worth."

I laughed. "I have the best job ever."

"No, lass. *I* do."

I laughed again. "All right. I'll keep you up to date."

"Have fun." Edwin disconnected the call before I could ask another question. I was going to do as Rosie'd suggested and inquire about Shelagh's personality, but I put the phone down and looked at Hector. "I think I remember reading that there was something unusual about her collection. Do you suppose Hamlet still has a copy of that paper?"

Hector panted up at me as Rosie came around the corner. "What did Edwin say?"

"That I could buy the books no matter the budget. That sounds extreme, Rosie, but I appreciate the leeway. I didn't get a chance to ask about Shelagh's personality, but Edwin said he's aware of her love of books. He didn't even hesitate."

I turned in the chair and reached for the stack of newspapers Hamlet kept on top of a file cabinet. Brigid worked for one of Edinburgh's alternative papers, the *Renegade Scot*. Despite the fate of many of them, this one was defying all odds and doing very well, much of the credit belonging to Brigid herself. She could be highly irritating, but she was quite good at getting and writing a story, and that skill brought in lots of paying advertisers.

I found the edition from a couple weeks earlier and spread it open on the table. Hector stood up and put his front paws on the table so he could better read too. Rosie sat in a chair across from us.

"Here it is, the article about Shelagh O'Conner," I said. I read aloud, relearning that Ms. O'Conner was fond of all literature but most particularly anything written by Scottish native Robert Louis Stevenson. And though Ms. O'Conner enjoyed books like Stevenson's *Treasure Island* and others, it was his *Strange Case of Dr. Jekyll and Mr. Hyde* that she loved the most.

Ms. O'Conner had multiple shelves filled with copies of the short horror novel from the late 1800s, many of her copies considered priceless.

I looked at Rosie. "Is that what you meant about her personality?"

Rosie had fallen into thought. I didn't want to interrupt, but she was silent a long time.

"Oh, lass, it's a wee bit more than that. Ye might not want tae go after all," she finally said.

"Why?"

"Maybe Brigid simply isnae auld enough tae ken some things, things that happened a long time ago. It wasnae in the article, and I didnae even think aboot it until right this minute. Michty me."

Hamlet usually translated the Scots that my older friends spoke, but he wasn't here. "Michty me?"

Rosie looked at me. "It means I'm *surprised*. I should have remembered something sooner."

"Remembered what?"

"There's a story from back in the 1960s, I believe, back when Ms. O'Conner herself was caught imitating a beggar on the street; just like in that book, she dressed as a Mr. Hyde. She was even suspected of murder but was never officially arrested. I wish I could remember all the details."

"What? Really?" I looked at the article and then back at Rosie. "How does Brigid not know something so juicy?"

Rosie shrugged. "Maybe she's not as good as ye think."

Hector barked. I closed the paper.

"What else do you remember?" I asked.

"It was strange. Shelagh was strange. Oh, it's been such a long time, and she was young enough tae do strange things without being held too accountable, I suppose. When she was released, it all blew over. At least that's what I remember. Once that happened, the story disappeared. It was much more interesting to think that a young, rich woman who had everything was misbehaving, committing *murder,* rather than just dressing up and playing a part, roaming the streets."

"Did they catch the killer? Who was killed?"

"I cannae remember, Delaney. I'm sorry, but it's been a long time, and we all came tae know Shelagh as a lovely, philanthropic woman who gives when it's most needed. She's very charitable."

This new information solidified my plans. "I'm going to that meeting. Want to come with me? Hamlet will be here soon, so he can watch the shop."

"No, lass, ye go and report back." She squinted. "It occurs to me, though, that ye might not know something else ye should. Deacon Brodie's Tavern—it's said that *Dr. Jekyll and Mr. Hyde* was at least partially inspired by the real Master Brodie."

"Who was Master Brodie?"

"A man who built cabinets, for Mr. Stevenson's family and others. He led a double life and stole from his clients. He went sae far as tae have duplicate house keys made so he could later sneak back in where he'd worked tae take the valuables."

"What happened to him?"

"He was hanged before he was an old man. A big crowd showed up to watch his execution, his posture proud and his clothing regal. He was quite the character. We learned about him in school. Now, that part I remember."

"Goodness," I said as the bell above the front door jingled again. Hector seemed to shrug as Rosie stood to greet whoever had come in.

I was still lost in the stories of Deacon Brodie, Dr. Jekyll, and Mr. Hyde—as well as Shelagh's strange behavior and the murder that Brigid McBride, fierce reporter, had forgotten to add to her story. What was going on here? Two o'clock couldn't come fast enough.

STAR TREK
DEEP SPACE NINE®

WHAT YOU LEAVE BEHIND

A Novel by Diane Carey
Based on the Episode
Written by Ira Stephen Behr &
Hans Beimler

POCKET BOOKS

New York   London   Toronto   Sydney   Tokyo   Singapore

An *Original* Publication of POCKET BOOKS

POCKET BOOKS, a division of Simon & Schuster Inc.
1230 Avenue of the Americas, New York, NY 10020

A VIACOM COMPANY

STAR TREK is a Registered Trademark of
Paramount Pictures.

This book is published by Pocket Books, a division of
Simon & Schuster Inc., under exclusive license from
Paramount Pictures.

ISBN: 0-671 03476-6

First Pocket Books printing June 1999

10 9 8 7 6 5 4 3 2 1

POCKET and colophon are registered trademarks of
Simon & Schuster Inc.

Printed in the U.S.A.

CHAPTER
1

"Doctor Bashir. The time is oh-five-hundred."

At least he wasn't alone.

"Right. . . ." Oh, how he hated the garlicky voice of that computer in the morning.

The light hurt his eyes.

"Julian . . . we have to get up."

A much nicer voice. Julian Bashir shifted his arm to cuddle mode as Ezri Dax maneuvered herself closer. "Are you sure?" he asked.

"It's a big day," she told him. There was a faint dose of fearful anticipation in her voice. A week ago, he wouldn't have noticed it, but things changed here every day lately.

"It was a big night," he countered. "It cleared up a lot of questions."

She turned her pixie-like face up to him. A childlike

1

face, framed in boyish short-clipped black hair, a permanent flicker of uncertainty always passing through it.

"Such as?" she asked.

He brushed his hand along the trail of melanin spots on the side of her face, the subtle markings that identified her as one of the most elegantly unique creatures of the known galaxy. "How far those spots go down, for one thing."

She smiled, but not without a sparkle of embarrassment. "I suppose you're going to want to tell Miles."

"Why would I do that?"

"Because you tell him everything?"

Without saying that today they'd all have other things on their minds, Bashir pushed away the rush of possible answers—she was right, he did tell Miles O'Brien everything—and how did she know that about the two men already? She was wrong, and he knew when things between a man and a woman, or a man and a Trill, or a somebody and a somebody else were better kept private.

Rather than blurting what he was thinking—*my God, you're so young!*—he admitted, "True, but this time, I'll make an exception."

"Good," Ezri murmured. She didn't believe him, he was sure of that. "Now, we really should get up. We don't want the *Defiant* leaving without us."

"You know," Bashir mentioned, "I've never gone into battle with someone I've slept with."

She smiled. "There's a first time for everything."

Not making any move to get up, Bashir added, "Now that we're finally together, it'd be a shame if anything happened to one of us."

Another twist came into her expression, and she didn't say any more, but Bashir picked up her thoughts as if he had suddenly become clairvoyant. She had been so lonely, so unsure of herself since having seven lifetimes of memories thrust upon her from another person, and another and another . . . her own identity had abruptly been put on hold, and she was now responsible for a cache of thoughts and knowledge that she hadn't absorbed. Not all Trill prepared all their lives to have a squirmy receptacle thrust into their bodies and then take over their existence. She was, as far as anyone knew, the only Trill never to be prepared for joining. That made her very special.

Bashir tried to empathize, but how could he? He was one man, inside one body, with one lifetime to worry about. Yet he admired and pitied Ezri Dax in the same moment, and he questioned his own reasons for wanting the comfort of her touch in these troubled times in deep space.

"Let's make a pact," she said. "We both come home alive."

A handshake—simple, but potent.

He took the hand. "You've got yourself a deal."

She smiled. "I'm going to hold you to that."

No, no, this wouldn't do. He leaned toward her, and she met his kiss thankfully, with welcome in her eyes. But then it was over, and before anything else could set in they had rolled out of bed on opposite sides and might as well have landed at opposite ends of a football field.

Ezri drew her uniform on very quickly, as if the blankets had been her protector and now she couldn't be unprotected. And Bashir, ridiculously, had yanked on his trousers quite faster than usual—now how was that a way for a grown man and physician to behave? As if he were dressing in front of a . . . all right, she was *very* young, never mind that she was three hundred years old.

The medical wonder of Trilldom struck him again—certainly this girl was no three hundred years old, yet the eight accumulated lifetimes and those of eight hosts all stored within her unprepared mind reached back all those centuries, racking her with confusions he could only guess toward. Sixteen lives bottled up inside that girl over there, who yet was pitiful in her isolation.

As were they all, upon this turning wonder. As were they all. . . .

"Miles! You're late! You have to report in fifteen minutes."

"Coming, dear."

Oh, yes, the joy and fulfillment of having his family with him finally! If only there weren't a war. Every beginning of watch was like this now—the laughter of his children, the humming of his wife, the clatter of family life—and he knew too well how quickly that paradise could crash and burn. He'd seen it before, the war coming out of nowhere to *Deep Space Nine* and rushing the station with all the complex agonies and strife caught up in those three little letters . . . w, a, r. . . .

Thank the Lord the baby couldn't spell yet. But Molly could, and she understood.

That caused pain to Miles O'Brien, as he stepped from his bedroom, pretending there was no care in the universe that could shatter him today. It was only for the children. He couldn't fool Keiko.

"Now, remember," he told his wife as she turned to him while feeding the baby, "Kirayoshi has his checkup tomorrow morning at oh-nine-hundred."

She nodded, and he felt silly for having pretended she didn't remember. By reminding her, he was also putting a spotlight on the fact that he wouldn't be here tomorrow. He was leaving, and asking her to go on with family life as if nothing were wrong, nothing were happening.

"I've already confirmed the appointment with Nurse Bandee," she said courageously. "One more bite. . . ."

"And try to get some rest," O'Brien pressed on, "and don't stay up too late writing that paper on whatever those trees are called—"

"They're called Arfillian blossoms and they're not trees, they're shrubs."

He sighed. "All right . . . anyway, be sure to get some sleep and . . . oh, yeah, and—"

"Miles," Keiko scolded gently, "stop worrying. We're going to be fine."

Fine, she said so easily. Back here on the station, trying to play house on the edge of a war zone, living in a pretty little cottage made of alien metal, just barely managing to keep out the inhospitableness of space with bulkheads that could be so easily ruptured by enemy fire. Just a few light-years from the front—was this a place to raise a family? He had thought being together would make up for all the risks, for the tortures of knowing where he would be for the coming days.

He'd been wrong.

"I know," he said anyway, and leaned over for a kiss.

"Just you be careful," Keiko told him.

"I always am—Molly, don't touch that!"

His daughter recalled her hand just before it would've violated the sacred space around the model he and Bashir had so lovingly built. Then she realized her hand had come away with one of the miniature US Army soldiers. Quickly she reassigned the soldier within the Alamo walls.

Only as his little girl's ivory hand dipped over the adobe stone partition did O'Brien realize how very large the model had grown. Now taking up a significant portion of the room, the Alamo seemed very real and consequential to him, its soldiers like shipmates. He and Julian had committed many hours to this historical problem of siege and conflict, supply and isolation. One needn't be a scholar to see the symbolism, and how close he felt to those trapped men and women, struggling to hold out against impossible odds—

"I let you play with my toys," Molly complained.

"It's not a toy," he insisted. "It's a model."

Keiko's doll-like eyes teased him as she continued feeding the baby. "Then maybe it belongs in a museum."

O'Brien glanced at her, suddenly embarrassed that the Alamo had sucked away such a large portion of their living quarters. Did seem to have taken over, didn't it?

"I suppose I could give it to Julian. . . ."

"Sounds good to me," Keiko instantly said. "Speaking of Julian, have you told him about Starfleet's offer yet?"

"I haven't had time," he stalled.

Molly wedged her way between them. "I knew it!"

O'Brien looked down. "What's that supposed to mean?"

"We're not going back to Earth," his daughter told him bluntly, "that's what it means."

"Of course we are," O'Brien said to her. "Daddy's going to teach at the Academy . . . as soon as the war's over."

Molly's big brown eyes batted at him. "Then why haven't you told Julian?"

As O'Brien groaned, Keiko smiled. "Out of the mouths of babes."

Guilt grazed O'Brien's sense of honor and duty. "I'll tell him . . . when I think he's ready to hear it." To get himself out of this, he ducked down to kiss Kirayoshi's plump little face. "I love you. Be a good boy, now. And you," he said, turning again to Molly, "listen to Mommy while I'm gone."

"I *always* listen to Mommy."

As his daughter pranced away, Miles O'Brien found his wife in his arms, a rather more poignant gesture than his little girl's farewell. He felt ghastly about Molly's not knowing where he was going today, that this wasn't an ordinary patrol or your average mission away from the station. Was she old enough to know the truth about where he was going? Should he pay her the respect of telling her? What did the men tell their daughters as they left for Normandy Beach? Protect them with soft deceptions, or give them the honor of knowing what their fathers were setting off to do? Tell them it was nothing, or that it was more important than anything ever before?

Should he spare the little girl, or should he think of the woman she would be someday, a woman who deserved to be proud, to remember a significant and poetic moment of farewell with her father, who might never return?

Why wasn't he wise enough to know what to do?

Keiko held him tightly, not in a kind of goodbye, but in a kind of sorrowful pledge. Every parting was the last, just in case, and every kiss a promise.

"Just you be careful," she murmured.

"I always am."

He always said that, or something like that. An extra squeeze—the sure sign that he could no longer fool her or assure her away from the cold bitter truths of Starfleet service in these dangerous days. She knew too well how quickly, how permanently, things could change on, and around, and because of . . . *Deep Space Nine.*

"How's that?"

"It's doing wonders for my head. Except it's my stomach that's bothering me."

"Well, if it helps, morning sickness usually ends after the first trimester."

"That's three months! I don't think I'm going to make it!"

"You'll make it."

That's an order.

Oh, better not add that part. Still, it so often did the trick—once a commander, always a commander. Don't say it, don't say it. . . .

Orders came much better from his low-pitched and

decidedly unfeminine voice. How could he rumble out a comfort without sounding like a foghorn in the distance? He could no more make her feel better than create wind in space.

Always a commander, but it had been twenty-odd years since Benjamin Sisko had last become a father. Twenty very odd years, one might say. Tending a deep space station in upheaval, in a war zone, with cloaked enemies spinning around at arm's length was nothing to tending a woman in the first grip of motherhood. He'd completely forgotten the whole idea, having had absolutely no plan of getting himself into this all over again.

Still, he found himself working too hard to press down a grin. Couldn't let Kasidy think he was laughing at her discomfort. For her, this feeling represented no real live baby, not yet anyway, for she had never experienced the wonder of new life in her arms. For Kasidy Yates, this was little more than a recollection of spacesickness, so long ago conquered. For Ben Sisko, though, it was a tiny beacon of hope and joy in a very bleak void. He longed for the cry of his child, the wonderment in tiny searching eyes, and as any soldier understands, something more in his life to fight for instead of fight against.

She lay her head on his shoulder. "Promise me something, Ben," she moaned. "Promise you'll come back to us."

"I promise."

Yet they both knew the power of that promise wasn't in his control.

Suddenly her eyes shot wide, her face flushed, and

she bolted to her feet, rushing for the head like a phaser shot. The door panel slid open, barely fast enough, then hissed shut behind her in time to spare Sisko the joyous sounds of impending motherhood.

"I don't believe it. . . ." she said slowly.

"I said I promise," he insisted.

"It's not that—"

He wanted to help her, to change things on her behalf—but he'd learned long ago he couldn't take a hit for anyone in his crew, and there were certainly things he couldn't do for the woman he loved. Men since time immemorial had been unable to do much, no matter what technology they concocted for the advancement of life's qualities.

Oh, well. . . .

The main door chime spared his having to go over there and mutter comforting sounds into the bulkhead.

"Come in," he called.

The door opened and his first claim to empathy wraithed in, yawning and rubbing his eyes.

"Glad I caught you." Jake Sisko bumbled to the replicator, apparently thinking about coffee, then changed his mind and didn't order anything. "I figured I'd walk you to the *Defiant*."

Sisko stood up. "I'd like that."

"How's Kas?"

Through the bulkhead she answered for herself with a trumpeting moan.

"That answer your question?" Sisko said as the head panel opened again and the light of his life staggered back to the couch.

"Reports of my death," Kasidy complained, "have been greatly exaggerated. But not by much."

Jake frowned. "Isn't there something you can take to make you feel better?"

Sisko shook his head and waved a quick hand, not wanting that subject opened up again. He'd been bitten often enough on that suggestion. "She doesn't believe in taking medication unless it's absolutely necessary."

When Kasidy groaned again, Jake shook his head. "Sounds necessary to me. . . ."

"If you're going to go," Kasidy snarled, "then go. Waiting for you to leave only makes me feel worse."

Sisko moved to gaze down at her, determined by proximity if nothing else to show her that he was trying to be supportive. "You're sure I can't get you anything?"

But she was gone again—back to the head. Zoom. Hiss. Clack. Heave.

Despite his amusement, Sisko's pride as he turned to his son got the better of him, and he grinned. "I think she's sure."

"Times like this," Jake commented, "make me glad I'm a man."

"Me too," Sisko admitted as they went out the door side by side. "Damn it, now I feel guilty about it. Well, I suppose that Mother Nature in her wisdom put the better individuals in charge of . . . of . . ."

"The hard part?" Jake leered sidelong at him. "Are you saying men are wimps?"

"No, but I do feel bad lately."

"About what?"

"Well . . . about getting a good night's sleep, for one thing."

"Why should that make you feel bad?"

"First of all, because it's hard for Kasidy to get one. She keeps tossing and turning. And that excuse for a goodbye . . . she was doing everything she could to avoid a real goodbye. She thinks they're bad luck."

"She told you that?"

"Not in so many—"

"And what else?" Jake interrupted. "What've you got to feel guilty about? You're in charge of a primary outpost in the middle of a center of action. Most military men would grovel to get a position like yours! All the news networks are constantly buzzing about activity at and around *Deep Space Nine!* The comings and goings, the ships in and out, the changes of control over areas of space around here—Dad, WTYX on Devona Four actually has a DS9 update twice a day!"

"Hm. There's not that much news coming out of here, I hope," Sisko drawled. "After all, we do have our strategic and tactical secrets to keep. There's a limit to the 'people's right to know.' "

"*I* don't think so," Jake countered. "Freedom of the press is—"

"Not going to be the first topic of this day, of all days, thank you very much. I already tell you too much, if you get my meaning."

"And I've put my position as the commander's son before the people's right to know. I understand the importance of secrecy too, you know." Jake shrugged.

"It's still no reason to feel guilty. Getting a good night's sleep, I mean."

"That's not really it," Sisko admitted. "The station's on constant alert status, permanent yellow alert, every Starfleet crewman required to be ready to report to battle stations in three minutes or less, and every one of us, including the illustrious commander, required to get rest on pain of siccing Dr. Bashir on you with a sedative. Did I give that order? What was I thinking?"

"You were thinking," Jake said instantly, "that everyone in uniform on this station is just like you—wanting to stand three watches in a row because you can't get work off your mind and you know the Dominion or the Jem'Hadar or the Cardassians or somebody's going to come out of the darkness at us at any given time. And you also know that the longer the quiet, the louder the attack. You know they're not just sitting out there quietly contemplating the stars. They're building up for assault."

Sisko drilled him with a glare. "Who told you that?"

"Nobody. I just know how you think."

"Hm . . . that's what I get for being such an open and forthcoming fellow."

"Oh, brother."

"Got myself into this," Sisko miserated. "Now even I can't come back to my office after my watch without breaking my own order and setting a bad example. And even today, of all days, I have to keep up a sense of order and not come out of that door one minute early. I've been up for two hours."

"When everything breaks loose," Jake said, "you'll be glad your crew is rested."

"I know, I know. But weeks of making every morning seem normal—it takes its own kind of toll. I see it in their faces. He nodded as two young officers passed by, offering their commander a curt good-morning. "They're not fooled by the illusion of normalcy. It's like we're all lying to each other a little more every day, Jake. They know this can't go on, but no one knows when it'll break. The tension's growing. I know how to fight a battle . . . but there's nothing I can do to hurry an incoming tidal wave that I really hope never gets here. Here we are in the middle of a war, suffering from actually not having enough to do, hour by hour. It's like the Alamo, waiting to be attacked, unable to prepare any more, and knowing it's coming."

"The Alamo," Jake droned. "You've been listening to Miles and Julian, haven't you?"

Sisko gazed down the long curve of the Promenade, and noticed that the clutter of activity wasn't as noisy as usual. "The irony of their little project hasn't been lost on me, let's just admit."

"It's only their way of . . ."

"Coping, I know. That's what I mean. They can't do any more to get ready for what we have to face, and we have no idea when we'll have to face the next wave. A war of intrigue is a lot harder to fight than a war of battles. Unfortunately, we've settled into the intrigue stage. There are fewer casualties, but the price is still high. We're being eaten by millimeters instead of in gulps. Look at them, Jake . . . trying to live their lives as if nothing's wrong. As if sector-wide communications blackouts happen every day."

"They're brave," his son attempted as they passed the shops, rounding the bend toward Quark's bar.

"They're lying to themselves," Sisko reminded. "And to each other. There's nothing normal here, certainly not today. They can't even write home to their relatives about it. We're under a general alert—no private communiques, no advances to the news service, and not even a DS9 update. Not today, and maybe never again."

He stopped walking, and took his son's arm. "I don't want you to see me off. I want to say goodbye right here."

Jake seemed briefly insulted, then instantly knew better. "Why?"

Sisko paused. "Finally the Cardassians and the Jem'Hadar are going to have to face all of us—together—rather than just the Klingons in a single growly line. This is the kind of thing that makes history, Jake. I'd rather you remember me here, the way we lived together. Just in case history gets a little too personal."

"Dad . . ."

Determined to keep this on a higher plane, Sisko reached for his son's hand and clasped it firmly, but not tightly. "Take care of my family and my station. I'll be back if I'm lucky, but dying doesn't mean you lost. Understand? Don't follow me."

"You're up early today."

As Quark plunked a drink in front of him, Worf pretended it was an ordinary morning. The only other customer in the pub besides himself was Morn, over there in his giant slug mode, sitting alone as always, his big shapeless paw around a mug of klapri drippings.

Here at the bar, Worf stewed over his drink, but said only, "I am always up early."

In his periphery he saw Quark lean closer, pretending he could keep a secret. "It's a good day to die," the Ferengi barkeep whispered.

Worf felt fury burn in his eyes. "Every day is a good day to die."

"But some days are better," Quark baited, "than others. Like today, for instance. The day the Federation-Klingon-Romulan Alliance launches its invasion of Cardassia. The final push in the long struggle to rid the Alpha Quadrant of the Dominion . . . and save my bar in the process."

Though he fought to mask his anger, Worf knew his withholding was in itself a giveaway.

But how could the Ferengi know?

"Who told you that?" he demanded.

Quark nodded toward the mulchy figure of Morn. "He did."

"Morn? And how does he know?"

"He's friends with Admiral Ross. Or maybe Sisko told him while they were having dinner. I don't know how he knows! He just *knows*."

Worf slugged his drink. "I have to go."

Without another glance at the clever and annoying Quark, Worf wheeled full about and beat it for the door. The gulp of bloodwine had galvanized him for what was to come, on this very important day they were all trying so hard to make appear ordinary. Yet his stomach rebelled as he headed for the airlock.

He was grateful for solitude, but in this proximity—a space station that seemed large upon approach and quickly showed itself for the small town it was—soon caved to Odo's appearance.

The shapeshifter floated into being at Worf's side before the Klingon had even noticed someone was walking with him.

"Mind if I walk with you, Commander?" Odo asked, as if reading his thoughts.

"Not at all," Worf accepted. "Captain Sisko informed me you were joining us on our mission." He paused, then offered a morsel of empathy. "I hope that when we reach Cardassia we find Colonel Kira alive and well."

"So do I, Commander," the shapeshifter said with unmasked fear. "So do I. Everyone's taking the blackout with great courage," he added. "I find it disconcerting— the waves are full of normal chatter, but it's all a lie."

"It is a tactical disguise. We have filled our communications channels with recordings. The enemy would notice a total blackout. Our assault would sacrifice its surprise, Constable."

"Yes, but it's surreal to monitor the channels and hear people talking whom I perfectly well know aren't even on the station, and others whom I know are boarding ships to join the Allied Fleet. As the security officer, I still have to listen. It's like . . . hearing ghosts."

Worf winced, then hoped the constable was not watching at that instant. Ghosts haunted his every moment, the dead of his past constantly with him. His father, his shipmates, his fellow warriors, his wife—ghosts all.

Today they would create many more.

The two men fell to silence. It was a relief. Worf found himself instinctively leading the way, with Odo a step behind him, as they came through the airlock and boarded the muscular deep-space endurance battleship that had been the other half of their existence for so long.

The *Defiant*. Latest descendant of a line of proud fighting ships of the same name, leading back into the past of Starfleet, and even farther back to the planetary service from which Starfleet had grown. Not so graceful as a heavy cruiser nor so crude as a fighter, this new *Defiant*, like those before her, was something in the middle—built exclusively for the hard punches of close combat, without labs or comforts. The essence of minimalism and survival, she had more weaponry ordnance than any other provision, even more than food and engine power. She knew her purpose. Today she would fly her finest.

Ben Sisko stood on the upper level, surveying his bridge thoughtfully, absorbing the newness of this ship, the updates and fresh technology that his tough old ship hadn't possessed. It was time to put some scratches in her hull. Finally, the allied powers would make a singular strike!

Months of preparation, secret coordinations, meetings, councils of war, spies, trickery, subterfuge—finally! An assault fleet was moving laterally across *Deep*

Space Nine, gathering strength as it flowed, plucking grains of sand which it would soon fling at the enemy. Even now, before they'd left the docking pylon, *Defiant*'s forward screen bristled with a thousand ships passing by in loose coordination—Federation starships, Klingon cruisers, Romulan war wings, combat support tenders and picket ships, supply freighters and medical packets—vessels from all over the plagued quadrant swarmed together before him. A grain of sand is nothing, but together they make a mighty stone. But beneath his pride in this moment, Sisko feared where the crack might appear.

Oh, well, that was the adventure, wasn't it?

Silently he counted the crew. Worf, O'Brien, Bashir, Ezri Dax, all at their posts. Nog at the helm, Odo standing beside the command chair. They were pretending to be powering up the ship, but it was already powered up. They were waiting for him, really.

"All right, people," he began. All eyes turned to him. "What do you say we end this war?"

O'Brien couldn't quite muster a smile. "Sounds good to me."

"To me too. I have something very important for you to keep in mind for the time to come. We've been out here at *Deep Space Nine* for many years, usually on our own, depending only on each other and no one else. We've become a family, and I appreciate that very much. Today something different is happening. We aren't on our own anymore. We aren't the spearhead of the final frontier. Today we have to do something even more important—we have to remember what it means to be part of a fleet, one of many. The goal isn't to be heroes today. The goal is to be one strong muscle in a much bigger body. We have to work together with a lot of strangers to take back our quadrant. That's not easy for people who've had to be pioneers as long as we have. We're used to defending our own fort, all by ourselves. Today, that kind of spirit will not only get us killed but might ruin a good effort. I'm counting on all of you to have the humility and courage to let others be the heroes for a change. We all think we have that in us, but when the moment comes, it's hard to do. I know you're all grownup enough to understand what I'm saying. Today, I want to be proud of you for something that might not make headlines. I promise you, though . . . it'll matter."

For a moment his words had no effect. Then he started to notice a subtle change. Worf's posture eased a little. Odo gazed at him more kindly. Bashir was smiling. O'Brien closed his eyes briefly. Nog seemed less afraid. Ezri's eyes shined with embarrassing affection, as if he'd given them a charm they could put in their pockets. Yes, they understood.

He drew a sustaining breath and stepped down to the command deck. Odo offered a nod of encouragement. Sisko almost paused, but managed not to. He couldn't absorb—never had—the idea that by looking at Odo's homogeneous face he was actually looking at the very face of the Dominion, the eyes of his enemy.

Without breaking stride he slid into his chair and swiveled to face the forward screen.

"Docking clamps released," Nog reported, without waiting for an order.

"Ensign," Sisko began, "I believe you know the way to Cardassia."

The young Ferengi gingerly touched his helm. "If I get lost, I'll just follow the ship in front of me."

With a hum of confidence, the *Defiant* smoothly swam out toward the crowded spacelane. There she fell into formation with the largest combined invasion fleet ever amassed in the Alpha Quadrant.

And out there, far before them, the enemy would soon awaken.

CHAPTER
2

"She's got a concussion. Look at that head wound."

"Can't you bind it up and save her?"

"She could be bleeding in the brain, Damar. We've got to get out. Ten minutes in the infirmary and she'll be fine."

"I'm glad you have the problem solved. Colonel! Don't go to sleep. You may not wake up. Do you understand?"

Colonel Kira Nerys of the Bajoran Military Guard moaned and forced her eyes open. Her head swam and pounded from inside her skull. The side of her neck was wet.

"Am I bleeding?" she asked. "Because . . . it's getting on my clothes. Garak, make me some new clothes."

"Kira, can you see me?"

She blinked again, and saw—surprisingly clearly—

the goofy face of Garak bending over her. Those wide buggy eyes, that funny flat mouth, and all that Cardassian gray snakeskin, like bathroom tiles. Yup, that was Garak.

"I see you fine," she complained. "Where are we?"

"We're trapped." The other Cardassian—why was she lying around with so many Cardassians?—was dirty and covered with soot as he climbed a tallus of broken bricks and shattered wood and metal support bars. "The whole building has come down on us. We miscalculated the explosion."

"I didn't miscalculate anything," Garak protested as he put a pad of wet cloth to the side of Kira's head. "My fuses were perfect. It was your calculation of the escape route that failed us. We should've gone out from the north entrance, as I first suggested."

"If you don't come over here and help me lift these blocks, the south entrance will be your tomb."

"You better go help him," Kira told Garak. "I'll be right over there in a minute, as soon as I sew my feet back on."

"That's right, Kira," Garak told her soothingly. "You rest right here on this plank. Keep sewing your feet and don't go to sleep. I'll help our illustrious leader dig us out of the hole he's gotten us into."

Kira let her shoulders sink back against the slab of wood they had laid her on. This was a nasty place, some kind of basement room. They'd fallen right through the ceiling when the bomb went off. It was a good bomb, big enough to take out half a city block. Another ten minutes and BOOM. . . .

Or had it already gone off?

"Oh, sure," she said. "I remember the sound. Three buildings fell at the same time, and four more in a row afterward. We're in the fourth one, isn't that right?"

Across the room, Garak and Damar hefted the two-foot-long blocks of conglomerate and metal bars one at a time—it took both of them to lift a single block, and there were hundreds of blocks collapsed in the corridor . . . that *was* a corridor, wasn't it? Oh, yes, there was the lintel. Neither of them responded to her question. Oh, they were busy.

"That's all right," she said. "You're busy. Just keep working. I'll sit here and paint a phaser."

That was all they needed to get out—one phaser. No hand weapons, though. The Breen patrols would pick them up on scanners. Seemed so silly. Why couldn't she just go out and talk to the Breen and tell them that she and her team of conspirators and saboteurs had work to do and couldn't be bothered going to the brig and facing a firing squad. They'd understand.

"She's going to die like this," Garak said, straining as he pitched one of the blocks sideways. It splashed to the floor with a dull clunk. "She deserves better."

"Everyone deserves better. Quit complaining. An invasion tomorrow, and we end up in a stone box underground."

"I thought you said *quit* complaining."

"You quit. I'll say what I please."

Damar was on top of the pile of bricks, up by the lintel, trying to stick his arm through to open air. Kira watched him for a few moments, fascinated by the action of his belt as it rode on his hips, and the way his boots scratched at the uneven mess he was standing on.

What a funny thing. Here they were, Garak of the Obsidian Order and Damar of the Cardassian Military, two important natives of this condemnable planet who had both turned against their planet and its allies—and they were dying like squirrels underground while the big invasion prepared itself light-years away, unable to get through ten feet of rocks.

Hah.

Kira laughed out loud, then winced when her head started hurting again. She should get up and go help them move the rocks so they could all get out of here and go invade something. She felt like taking over a province or subduing a fleet.

Of course, standing up would help.

Nope, couldn't do that. No feet.

Garak was coming toward her now. Wow, were his hands huge! They were two feet long! He could smother her with those!

"Your hands are big," she commented as he probed her head.

"Just lie still," Garak told her. "You've got a cracked skull. If you move, you'll cause more bleeding. I have nothing with which to cauterize the wound. We should start bringing medikits with us on these raids."

"You always were pampered," Damar said, without turning for a caustic glance. "You enjoy comfort too much, Garak. It makes you weak. The Obsidian Order was perfect for you. Sneaking and hiding, never confronting your enemy except to lurk behind him and find some way to bring him down before he even knew you were there. Even here, in the midst of a resistance squadron, you want your tea and biscuits every day."

"The Obsidian order, my primate friend, was the elite of the Cardassian intelligence network, feared and respected across the entire Alpha Quadrant, *unlike,* I should mention, the rest of Cardassia's authorities."

Garak's musical tone betrayed an irritation that Kira recognized. Was he frightened? She couldn't tell that much, but something was bothering him.

"Yes," Damar droned, "and if you don't elite yourself over here and lift some stones, you're going to be respected very deeply. Ten meters deeply, I estimate."

With a bitter glare, Garak said, "I'm tending to the Colonel's injuries. I have to lift this board. Prop her up."

"Why are you bothering to do that? We have to dig ourselves out of here."

"Damar, that would be futile. Look at the size of those blocks. If we are still and patient, I'm sure that soon other members of the resistance will be along to dig us out. They've got scanners. They'll be able to find our life-signs and get us out of here."

"It wouldn't be wise to wait, Garak."

"Why not?"

"Primarily because the room is filling with water. Obviously the blast broke an alluvial line under the buildings."

Garak turned and gawked down at the floor.

Water? Oh, yes. Kira let her hand slip from her side, and it fell into icy liquid swirling just below the thing she was lying on. That felt good. She liked cold water. Bracing!

"Maybe we can swim out," she said. "We can build a raft and float out. I can knit some oars. Give me a couple of minutes. You want yours pink or brown?"

"If we don't escape, Garak," Damar said sharply, "then you would be better doing the merciful thing."

Turning away from Kira, Garak glared fiercely. "Are you serious? What are you suggesting?"

"I'm suggesting you stop tending her and let her slip into a coma, rather than tend her until she's conscious just so she can be aware that we're about to drown or have the rest of this building fall in upon us."

"She can hear you, fool!"

"She's unconscious, Garak. Look at her. Her eyes are glazed over."

"At least they're open. I'll take care of her. She isn't your concern."

"Get back here and help me! If we're going to get out, you've got to lift some of these blocks."

"Very well, but if you mention—what you just said again, I'll—"

"Yes, I'm sure you'll throttle me with a crumpet. Get over here."

Kira listened with amusement at their argument. They thought she was dead, and really she was just lying here painting and knitting and sewing her feet on.

"Oh, look," she said. "A rat."

They didn't pay any attention. Over there, climbing out of a metal pipe, was a little northern provincial redrat. The redrat bobbed its pointy head up and down, surveying the rising water that was draining into their cavity. As it paused at the mouth of its little pipe, more water began to flow out of the pipe, preventing the rat from going back up the way it had come. Desperate and confused, it clawed around the mouth of the pipe, trying to climb the metal, but there was no way to do it. Frantic, the rat scratched furiously, then fell two feet to a jagged ledge of broken rock. From there, it scurried down a single metal rod, then jumped onto the end of the wooden slab upon which Kira lay, near her knee.

"It's going to bite me," she mentioned.

Garak ignored her. He was back over there, accepting chunks of conglomerate from Damar and pitching them aside.

"Have you noticed that wherever you go in the whole galaxy, no matter what kind of planet you're on," she muttered, "there are some kind of rodents? You're everywhere. I mean, some of you have different colors or extra feet, or hair that looks more like feathers, but you're all rodents. There's got to be something evolutionarily inevitable about rodents. There's not that much difference. Look at you, for instance. You're bright red, and you've got the prettiest blue eyes. Blue? Look at me! . . . I'm right, they're blue. And you don't have a tail. All the other rats I've seen have tails. There must be some predator on Cardassia that catches prey by the tail, so you evolved away your tail and that way it's harder to catch you. That makes sense, doesn't it?"

The rat raised its snout and sniffed around, standing up on its little feet and grasping with its tiny pink hands at Kira's kneecap while it had a look around. As the water rose beside her, Kira watched the redrat waddle up along her thigh to her resting hand. It sniffed her hand.

"Don't bite me," she told it. "I don't want to knock you into the water. Truce, all right?"

The rat didn't bite her. Instead it climbed onto her hand and moved hesitantly up her arm to sit just south of her elbow. It looked around again, sniffing furiously, hearing the rush of incoming water. The water was up around Kira's ankles now, making its way toward her knees.

"Here," she said. "Stay where you are."

Summoning all her strength, concentrating hard, she flexed the fingers of her right hand. Her thumb had no feeling, but her wrist moved. Closing one eye with determination, she raised her entire right arm as if it were already floating. The rat rose too, as Kira lifted her arm. Up, up, finally to a shelf of broken wood that looked as if it might have been a piece of furniture an hour ago.

"There you go," she huffed, weakened by the effort. "Go on, get off."

The rat made a single little jump, and landed on the jut of wood.

Kira's arm slumped back to her side, falling partly over her body. "Better now?"

"Thank you," the rat said. "What are you doing here?"

"We planted a bomb to harass a clutch of Breen patrols. We blew up their barracks. We got caught in our own explosion through. Miscalculated."

"The fuse or the escape route?" it asked.

"Oh, well, that's what those two were arguing about,"

Kira explained. "They're blaming each other for getting caught down here."

"Do they argue much?"

"All the time. Just like they're doing now. Listen."

Kira gestured with her limp hand at Garak and Damar, who were now calf-deep in water even though they were standing on the slanted side of the collapsed pile of building conglomerate.

"All the potential glory of an empire, and this is what it comes to," Garak was complaining. "Subservient to the prancing Founders and the insipid Vorta, and now we're even lower than the Breen."

"Look who's talking," Damar snarled back. "The Obsidian Order got thrown out because you spent so much time sneaking about, preparing for a conquest while never launching one, stabbing everyone in the back, trying to gain advantage, avoiding what you were preparing for. Eventually you ended up even stabbing each other in the back. While Cardassia was involved in stealth and suspicion, sneaking around, trying to be clever, trying to gain influence and loyalty, and gaining strength, the Klingons and Romulans and Federation were gaining territory. When you were finally ready, we were already surrounded. So much for the wonders of stealth."

"We survived," Garak argued, heaving another stone from the pile. "We prospered, our children were healthy—we were gaining power. Have you ever played that human game chess? Sometimes you can look at the board and still not really see who's winning. But you wouldn't understand that, Damar. You just count pieces."

"How have we done under your way? Strutting and blustering—even when you can take an enemy by stealth, you announce to him you're going to do it, and then you have to either completely expend yourself winning, or you lose. If it weren't for the Klingons, you'd be the biggest fools in the galaxy!"

Damar smashed a stone hard into the water with a terrific splash that lanced them all with sharp cold droplets. "At least the galaxy knew we existed! We didn't plan and plan and think and hide. We had a chance to win! We came closer than ever before! Yes, when you do something you have the chance to lose, but we won! Cardassia was in its heyday under us!"

"But you didn't win! You got kicked out of Bajor," Garak told him. "If the Dominion hadn't come in and saved you, you would've been pushed back here to the home planet and locked in your rooms. And even the Dominion is only using Cardassia—"

"Look out!"

A deafening rumble tore through their basement room. Garak pulled Damar down from the sheet of tallus. Together they splashed into the rising water. Less than a second later, the whole wall of tallus erupted, pushed outward as if swelling, then crumbled and collapsed into a somewhat flatter heap of wreckage. Where the wall of blocks had been was now an obstacle of solid iron in a tangle of pipes.

"What is that!" Garak sputtered, coming up in an oily slick on the water.

"It's a furnace boiler," Damar bitterly said. "We must've loosened the floor under it."

He swam to the enormous mass of iron and pressed against it with both hand. It budged not a centimeter.

"That's the end of it. We can't possibly move this. We're finished unless they find us in the next few minutes."

"Yes, well, if I were in a better mood I'd wring your neck before the water drowns you." Garak paddled over to Kira's plank, but there was nothing he could do for her. The water now lapped at her pelvis and she could feel the chill up her spine.

"They don't like each other," the rat observed, "do they?"

"Oh, there's a certain commonality," Kira explained. "They're not all that different. Garak was on the political outside and Damar was on the political inside. If you ask me, under neither of them has Cardassia done particularly well." She paused, and looked up at Garak as he plucked at the padding he'd placed on the side of her head. "It's funny . . . what he said. If Martok and Worf were here, those words would be stuffed right back down Garak's throat."

"About the Klingons?"

As Garak and Damar split to opposite sides of the wreckage, seeking an alternative way out of their underground coffin, Kira raised herself to a sitting position with tremendous effort. This way she could read a long stick that looked like it might've been a chair leg. Now, if she lay back again, she could use her right hand—her left wouldn't move at all—to raise the chair leg onto the crashed furniture where the rat was struggling along, flanked by lapping water.

"There. Climb a little higher," she offered.

The rat thanked her again, turned its back, and scurried up the chair leg to the top of a cabinet. Its ruby red back glinted in the single electrical light that still worked.

A light? Until now, she hadn't paid any attention to the fact that she could still see down here. She hoped the light stayed on. Suddenly the idea of darkness frightened her. She shivered.

"It's getting cold," she mentioned. "Don't come down here again or you'll get wet."

"It's nice of you to worry about me. That Cardassian seems to be worried about you."

"Well," Kira murmured, "I have to admit we've become friends over the years. Didn't start out that way."

"Is something wrong, Kira?" Garak slipped back into the water from where he'd been inspecting the upper wall. "Did you say something?"

"She's been muttering all along," Damar said from the other side. "She's delirious."

"I'm not delirious," Kira told him. "I'm talking to the rat, not to you. You see," she went on, "I wanted nothing more than to kill them both for a while there. Look at us now. Working together to try to get out of here before the rest of the block comes down on us."

"Which one of them do you like better?"

Kira laughed. Only a rat would think like that.

"Well," she began, "from my point of view, they're both wrong. Look at Garak. He's spent years on *Deep Space Nine* and he's gotten to like the people there, but he still doesn't realize that if he gains, someone else doesn't necessarily lose. When something good is created, everyone gains! That's why the Federation, without blustering, without threats, without conquering, just keeps moving along and getting bigger and better—and people want to join it."

"Is that who you are? Federation?"

"I'm Bajoran. I'm just trapped here. Temporarily. And don't forget it's just temporary. I'm sure not staying on this Cardassian rock any longer than I absolutely have to. Sooner or later somebody'll break through and get us all off. Until then, we're working to break the Dominion's hold on Cardassia. The Federation'll be here eventually. That's how it works."

"Not by conquest?"

"Not unless it's really provoked. It moves inexorably along and along, not forcing anybody to come in, and it just works better. If you push and take and just be a bully, eventually somebody's going to stand up to you, you're going to run into somebody bigger—or three people who are collectively bigger. The Klingons, Cardassians, Romulans, Breen—even the Dominion—they spend all their time trying to figure out the best way to bully. That's the only difference between Garak's way and Damar's. Should they bully by walking right up to someone and trying to hit him, or by sneaking up and punching him in the back? Eventually, neither way gets the best results. The Klingons figured that out, y'know, now that I think about it. They still strut around, and they like their facade of bullying, but they know that all those years of galactic snarling just brought them to poverty. Now they go along with the Federation. It's about time. I wonder what's taking the cook so long?"

She lay back again, exhausted. The air was stuffy and dusty, in spite of the water gushing in. Crumbs of broken rock, insulation, brick, and wood layered her clothing and made her mouth dry.

She wanted to drink some of the water crawling up her legs, but her hands wouldn't form into a cup.

The rat climbed higher on the crushed furniture, ran to the edge to look over at the rising water, then sniffed around the perimeter. "I smell fresh air."

Kira raised her aching head again. "What?"

"There's air coming through this hole," the rat said. "I don't think the building is completely collapsed."

"If it's not, maybe there's another way out!" Kira pushed herself up on an elbow.

"Kira, don't move!" Garak called. "If you fall off that board, you'll drown."

"The rat found some fresh air. Garak, come over here! Damar!"

"What does she want, Garak?" Damar appeared around a slanted piece of ceiling material, swimming up to the shoulders.

"Something about fresh air," the other Cardassian told him, and also paddled closer.

"I don't blame her. It smells like dead gutfish in this sewer."

"I wish it were a sewer," Garak commented. "Then perhaps there would be a way out."

"There is!" Kira insisted. "Look! The rat's climbing through an opening up in that corner. Look. Well, look!"

"She's pointing up there."

Garak moved to Kira's side and squinted into the corner where the rat had disappeared through a ragged hole near the ceiling.

"Damar, I see some light!" he exclaimed.

"Stay with her. I'll go."

As Kira sank back against Garak and he pulled her higher on the plank, they watched Damar pick his way up the strewn wreckage to the corner and peer into the nearly hidden hole. Drawing a breath through his nostrils, he proclaimed, *"That* is open air!"

"Can you see anything?" Garak called.

"I see light . . . I can see part of the street! There must be a room that hasn't collapsed, and an outside wall that fell away! Hurry! Bring those steel bars and help me tear away this wall material!"

"There's a hammer over there!"

Vigorously now, Garak splashed around Kira to the place he had seen a hammer, which would until now have been useless to them. He also gathered several reinforcement rods, then carefully made his way up the pile of furniture and crushed building wreckage to where Damar was already pulling at the wallboard.

"Stay awake, Colonel," he called back to Kira. "We'll have you out of here in a matter of minutes!"

Damar put his powerful shoulders into using a steel rod as a crowbar, causing part of the wall to rip like paper. The wall protested, making a terrible squawk, and for a moment Kira thought her friend the rat might have been stabbed.

"Don't hurt him!" she called. "After all, he's the one who found the fresh air."

"Relax, Kira," Garak insisted. "We'll have you in the infirmary in no time. Our unit medic will cure you in a flash. By tonight you'll be back to your old vigorous self, with a phaser in your hand and a gleam in your eye."

"And you will be back in your nanny's arms," Damar commented, "sipping tea and having your feet massaged."

Garak's eyes gleamed. "Is that an offer I can count on? I never knew you could be so accommodating!"

"At least we'll be free in time for the regional resistance meeting tonight," Damar said, typically already thinking of what had to happen next. "We've got to convince them of our plan. If I have anything to do with it, we will wrest our planet from the fools who would collaborate with the Dominion."

"If I recall correctly, not too long ago that was you doing the collaborating. Now look at you—you're a Cardassian legend. The great Damar, who the Jem'Hadar thought they had killed, but who rose again out of the ashes of shame to destroy so many of the enemy and fire an entire rebellion on his home planet! You're a born rebel, Damar. You just don't know which side to be on at any given moment."

"Look who's talking," Damar grumbled back.

Kira smiled. They didn't really hate each other. Necessity had made them compatriots. Now they both knew what they wanted—the Dominion's paws off their home planet.

Could be worse. She'd fought for the same thing. Except that her fight had been against the Cardassians.

Now she was fighting with them.

What a silly universe. Painted feet, talking rats, and Bajorans fighting alongside Cardassians. What unexpected leap would happen next?

Who said wars had to be bad? Look how much good this one had brought. She'd make friends of enemies. She was part of a whole planet's finding out what it meant to have to fight for its identity.

"After all," she said, "that's all I wanted to teach the Cardassians all along. Maybe this time they'll learn."

"Hold on, Colonel," Garak called as he and Damar tore the wall apart.

More and more outside air piled in through the hole they were making.

Of course, the water was up to her neck now. Whose bright idea was it to take a bath at a time like this?

"There aren't even any bubbles. Garak, why didn't you bring me bubbles?"

"Coming, I'm coming. Clear this away, Damar. You know your way around garbage, don't you?"

"After long association with you, yes."

Garak climbed back down in time to clasp Kira under the arms and haul her up out of the water. "You've lost weight," he commented. "I'll have to make you a whole new wardrobe."

"That's all right, Garak, perfectly all right," she said, grinning as he hoisted her out of the cold wet basement. "I made six new suits while I was waiting for you. And some boots for my rat.

CHAPTER
3

If a planet could be beautiful, Cardassia Prime surely must be a jewel in the random night. Like a giant crystal ball, the planet seemed constantly to glitter in its subdued sun. Though he had been programmed with all necessary historical texts and the poetry that described them, Weyoun found himself still baffled by the romance with which many of the curious creatures in this quadrant seemed to speak of their homes. Yet he had come over the many weeks to see some of the attraction of Cardassia against the night.

The Dominion Briefing Room, set well below the equator of the planet he was here to defend, had many pictures of the planet from surveillance satellites and outposts on the moons. Weyoun broke from his communion with these monitors and went back to the one that counted. With enjoyable hatred he glared at the incoming swarm.

"Founder, the Federation invasion fleet has left *Deep Space Nine*. They'll reach the Cardassian border in twelve hours."

Seated at a desk near him, the glorious Founder was difficult to look at in these advanced stages of her disease. Her skin, once smooth as bisque soup, was now cracked and desiccated. She had no power to mask the advancement of the plague which was upon her and her people. The sight made Weyoun feel ill himself, though he fought to keep from glancing at her, to keep the disgust and horror from his voice. He knew her intelligence had not suffered—she would read his glance with all the cunning she had ever possessed.

Yet also it was a relief not to glance that way in order to avoid looking at the Breen general. Thot Pran was a sickening clod who was better ignored. The Breen were servicers, nothing more. Weyoun would tolerate them for now.

"Good," the Founder quietly said. She had trouble forming words through her scabby lips, but turned to the Breen and added, "Our brave Jem'Hadar soldiers have a motto . . . 'Victory is life.' "

The Breen answered her in his unintelligible static. His voice was nothing more than a crackle of electrical noise to Weyoun, but the Founder understood what was being said.

"I'm glad you're familiar with it," she said. "For today, those words have meaning for us all. I have no doubt," she went on, speaking very slowly, and with trouble, "that the outcome of this battle will determine the outcome of the war. Either we destroy the Federation invasion force, or they destroy us. There are no other options."

Weyoun overheard without looking, knowing he was not being spoken to, and yearned to rush to her, to extol the wonders of the Founders, the glory of the Dominion, to declare that nothing so petty could pull it down. As he clamped his lips tight, he listened to the static of the Breen general speaking in his barbaric manner.

"Fight well today," the Founder told her minion, "and Romulus will be yours to do with as you please."

How petty! Weyoun tightened his fists in disgust. To have to bribe the fools! To have to give them a planet just so they would defend the Dominion! Pathetic!

The Breen was buzzing again. He had better be groveling!

"Yes, yes," the Founder said now. "And Earth too. I assure you, the pleasure is all mine."

Apparently satisfied, if such a clod could be measured by body language, the Breen offered one more burst of sizzle, then went to a monitor and began clicking and snapping his troops into formation—at least that was what Weyoun assumed was going on.

Bribes! Giving away huge portions of their conquests to buffoons! Weyoun bottled his rage. He had no right to interrupt, yet a certain quiver of insult boiled up inside him.

His hands trembled. He pressed his lips tight. He glared at the screen in inconsolable fury.

"Is something bothering you?"

The Founder was looking at him again.

With monumental control Weyoun kept the contempt out of his voice.

"Apparently," he said tightly, "I was under the mistaken impression that all Federation territories would fall under my jurisdiction . . . including Earth."

The Founder lowered her voice. "And so they shall."

He looked at her. "But you just promised the Breen. . . ."

Was she smiling beneath the scales of disease?

"I'd *promise* the Breen the entire Alpha Quadrant," she told him quietly, "if I thought it would help win this war."

How fluidly she conjured the future! What a wonder she was! To think of so many things at once, to understand so much, to know when integrity served and when it stalled—

He bowed before her. "The Founder is wise in all things," he murmured.

He was about to say something else, to elaborate on his opinion about this turn, but was cut off when Legate Broca came into the briefing room without even chiming the door notice.

"Founder," he began rudely, "I've heard a disturbing rumor about the traitor Damar."

The Founder did not look at him. "What about him?"

"He may be alive."

Now she turned to Broca. "Is this possible?"

"I don't see how," Weyoun attempted. "We destroyed his ship, his rebel base—"

"But his body was never found."

"They say he's here," Broca insisted, "on Cardassia Prime. Here in the capital, no less. . . ."

Weyoun stiffened. Would she be angry? What action would she want him to take? The detested traitor Damar—Weyoun could think of many fates he would inflict upon a Cardassian who had turned on the wondrous Dominion, which had once again raised the Cardassians to power in the quadrant. How could he turn on the saviors of his people?

The Founder showed no outer emotion at this news. She seemed, for a moment, not to have heard Broca at all. Then she gave him a beautiful gift, charging him with authority that would resonate far.

"Look into this matter," she said.

Broca nodded.

Weyoun narrowed his eyes. "If Damar is alive—"

Broca snapped him a bitter glare. "He won't be for long."

"I smell smoke. Musky . . . thin. A cookfire."

"The Jem'Hadar don't cook. They don't eat either."

"Shh."

"It could be Cardassian, but it doesn't smell familiar."

"Don't obsess, Garak. You're letting hunger get the best of you. Keep quiet. For a spy, you make a terrible sneak. Follow me."

The alley was dank and slippery with lichen embedded between the bricks in the broken floor. They had been hurrying through these back alleys for hours, hugging walls, avoiding the main streets, climbing over walls, through ducts, and under piping. This was a slow way to traverse a whole city, but the only way to avoid patrols. Garak was clumsy, too long separated from soldiering. He had forgotten how to be stealthy. Now they had to move into the main streets, for their maze of back alleys had come to a dead end.

As they rounded a cold-molded building and moved out of the protection of the alley, their good fortune instantly dissolved in a disruptor strike against the building that nearly took both their heads off.

"Halt!"

A Jem'Hadar voice. Familiar enough, by now.

And a light—a spotlight, struck the wall, bouncing to brighten this whole side of the street.

Two Jem'Hadar soldiers blocked their path, if the light were not creating illusions. Yes, two, with one holding a palm beacon.

"Step forward. Slowly."

"At last!" Garak tentatively moved toward the two palefaced demons. "Some friendly faces! We're new to the city and I'm afraid we've gotten lost—"

"Quiet!" the soldier on the left ordered.

Both soldiers stepped closer now, closing the distance between them.

The one who had spoken came farther forward by one step, and spoke again, but not to Garak.

"You are Legate Damar."

Damar clamped his mouth shut, knowing his wide eyes had already given too much away. For what could he say?

Garak flopped his arms and shook his head and laughed. "You see? I *told* you you looked like him!" To the Jem'Hadar he attempted, "this isn't the first time my cousin has been mistaken for that traitor—"

"He is Damar," the unswayed Jem'Hadar insisted. "He will be taken to Dominion Headquarters. You," it said then, looking at Garak, "will die here."

Fear crossed Garak's face as he apparently realized there was no way out of this. Damar's mind ran with possibilities, though each one fell short. The Jem'Hadar's weapon snapped up to Garak's frightened eyes. The final seconds pulsed.

A crackle of animate noise burst through the street. Breen!

Over there—the Jem'Hadar turned his light down the street. A Breen soldier stood at the other end of the alley from which Damar and Garak had just come. Had they been followed the whole time?

It came forward now, chittering its staticky voice. If Damar were any judge, it had just repeated itself. Perhaps it wanted one of Garak's arms to chew on. How could any of them possibly know?

"I do not understand you," the Jem'Hadar called. "There must be a malfunction in your communication device."

In answer, the Breen soldier halted, squared both legs, raised his weapon and quickly fired it. Damar threw himself to one side, driving Garak out of the line of fire. They reeled briefly in the blast wash, but they had not been in the line of fire at all! The two Jem'Hadar had been struck instead—dead, both of them! What a wonderful sight!

"Actually," the Breen soldier said in perfect English, "I don't speak Breen."

It pulled off its helmet. But how could it breathe?

Ah—there was the answer. Kira's short red hair ruffled in the fallen light, which still shined at a funny angle on the bricks. Her bright brown eyes were lit with irony and superiority. She knew she'd done well to anticipate this, and she was happy to lord it over them.

Actually, Damar was pleased—even for a moment—to have been proven imprudent. In that one instant, Kira had shown herself as the experience-hardened guerrilla fighter whose youth had been forged in the oven of resistance. Though it had been his own people—an empire he had once served—that had driven her and all her Bajoran people down for so very long, Damar found himself feeling respect for her quickness and foresight. He determined to learn from this, to be better next time—and every time after that.

With a gush of relief, Garak blurted, "I hope you don't consider me ungrateful, but what are you doing here!"

"Watching your backs," Kira told them, with something less than affection.

She looked healthy enough, but they all knew she was still recuperating from her head wound down in that collapsed building. For hours they had made her rest, but as soon as the medic announced that her subdural injury had been healed she had insisted upon getting up and going back to their collective job as terrorists. Now she had saved their lives.

"I thought we agreed," Damar said, turning to her, "it would be safer if you stayed off the streets and out of sight."

"That's what the helmet's for," she told him. "You

should be wearing one too. Every Jem'Hadar and Breen soldier on Cardassia is looking for you."

"If I'm going to lead this revolt," Damar protested, "I can't do it hiding in a cellar. I had to attend tonight's gathering."

"It was a great success," Garak lauded, still breathing a little too rapidly from his near encounter with unfriendly fire.

Kira gestured them off the street. "You can tell me the details later." Kira put her helmet back on, gingerly because there was still some swelling on the side of her head. "If anyone asks, you're my prisoners."

Damar bristled, but Garak clasped him by both arms and pushed him forward. "We're honored," the other Cardassian said, and they were off.

They made their way this time not through the alleys of Cardassia's capital city, but down the main streets, at gunpoint, courtesy of the clever Bajoran woman who had gained their respect over the years. Her versatility was to be lauded. Her bravery was a given. But bravery is expected of soldiers and Damar gave her no extra credit for that. He both admired and was jealous of her ability to foresee intrigue. He must learn to do that, so as never to be humiliated again. Perhaps carrying weapons would have been wiser, even with the chance of their being detected by energy scanners. He must learn better to judge risks against each other, or find ways, as the colonel had, to use the negatives of his situation in his favor. Pretending to be Breen had never occurred to him, yet now it seemed so simple. . . .

They hurried back to their secret cellar without further

incident, other than one quick pass beside the Cardassian patrols, who failed to notice them in the darkness. They saw no other Jem'Hadar, no other Breen. Not surprising, given how many troopers had been sent to space duty. The planetary divisions were sparse now, and that was a good thing.

Once safe—relatively—in their hideout, Colonel Kira shed her Breen uniform and helmet as if they were infected. Despite their service, she hated them. Kira hid her feelings poorly. That which represented her enemy was also her enemy. Irrational. Damar decided to also learn from that.

"Well?" she asked abruptly. "What happened at the resistance meeting? We have to make a plan, know what to do."

They sat together around a small crude table. Garak was fairly bursting to tell it, so Damar motioned for him to speak.

"The vote was unanimous," Garak bubbled. "Everyone agreed that the work disruptions would begin tomorrow morning!"

Damar paused as Mila, Garak's old family friend and the only Cardassian woman here, came down the steps with a tray of food. "Power, transportation, and communications facilities all over Cardassia will be sabotaged."

"The Dominion fleet," Garak barreled on, "will be cut off from all ground support."

"That way," Kira appreciated, "they'll have to face the Federation alliance invasion force on their own."

Damar nodded. "And once the Dominion is crushed—"

"Cardassia will be free again." Mila spoke firmly,

interrupting the men with a confidence she had rarely shown. Hope shined in her silvery face as she gazed down at Garak. "Elim, I have to admit than when you were a little boy, I was worried about you. Always getting into trouble . . . quiet, secretive, so full of deceit. Little did I know you would turn such distasteful characteristics into virtues. More tea?"

"You're too kind." Garak smiled up at her.

Damar leaned toward him. "She's right, you know."

"About me?" Garak asked.

"About Cardassia. We will be free again. we will rid ourselves of the Dominion once and for all."

Never again, he held back from saying, would they allow themselves to be turned into stooges of another power. No, he couldn't say that aloud! There was too much bitterness. It hurt too much to think how the Dominion had embraced the Cardassians, then shunted them lower than the Jem'Hadar, then lower than the Vorta, and now once again even lower than the Breen. A proud nation could only stand so much, no matter how much was promised. Some victories were simply not worth the price paid.

He turned to Kira before those unfortunate words came out.

"How ironic," Garak added, "that the famous Bajoran of *Deep Space Nine* should come to Cardassia's aid."

Damar nearly struck him for his foolishness in reminding her of what she was doing, and for whom she was doing it, the strange bedfellows created by conquest and necessity. Here he was fighting against the official Cardassian allies, and she, a Bajoran, was in her way fighting for the salvation of the Cardassian nation which had so long tormented her and her people. Oh, irony and its many winds.

Though a flint of insult sprang in her eyes, Kira smiled. "Tonight is going to be a long night. A lot can go wrong."

"Nothing will go wrong," Damar told her. "too much is at stake."

No one responded to that. It fell with a clunk to the stone floor, and he was sure it echoed.

"Have you assigned duties for the assault team?" Kira asked. Her question was firmly pointed—if he hadn't, he should have, and if he didn't, she would.

"We have a schematic of the city," he responded. "I'll lay it in a grid pattern and assign one commando to each grid. Whatever target facilities fall within a certain grid will determine how many resisters are assigned to each commando."

"I can lay the grid," Garak volunteered.

Kira added, "I can brief the teams."

Damar agreed, then asked, "Do you have any information about when the invasion fleet will arrive?"

She sighed. "Well, it's hard to keep a thousand ships a secret, but the allied force has done a fair job of distracting and confusing the Dominion spies—and ours right along with them. We know the fleet is coming soon, but if it were me I wouldn't pull the squadrons together until they all rendezvoused at *Deep Space Nine*. Until then, no one would be sure how many ships were involved."

"You saw how empty the streets are," Damar pointed out. "Significant portions of the planetary forces have been depleted. That means the Jem'Hadar and Breen are being put back in space. That is why we must act tomorrow, while facility guards are at a minimum."

"Two fronts, gentlemen," Kira said. "The fleet in space, and us down here. Both had better succeed, or everything will collapse faster than you can say 'labor camp.' "

Damar stood up, signaling that the talk was over and the action must begin. "Either way, by noon tomorrow our resistance movement will either be famous or we will all be dead. I'm looking forward to it."

Through black open space, the massive Federation-Klingon-Romulan offensive fleet moved like a great shoal of herring seeking a spawning ground. They were many, but with a single purpose. When a thousand ships come together, the logistics of not knocking into one another becomes a moment by moment obsession for a thousand captains, a thousand engineering chiefs, and a thousand helmsmen. Space, normally wide enough for galaxies to pass through each other without collision, suddenly becomes very crowded and limited indeed.

They knew they couldn't hide anymore, and therefore speed and organization became the primary factors. Who would be the vanguard? Who would flank? How much strength would be committed to a first wave and how much held in reserve? Commodores from each allied division powwowed through the night, causing reports and rumors to chitter constantly despite the reduction of general communication.

And each ship had its private problems. Systems were

imperfect in general—on a ship, it's never a matter of whether something will break down, but *when* it will. Mechanics had no loyalties, no stamina in adversity, no idea that today was of particular importance. If the last molecule cracked, something would break and would have to be fixed.

Between the captain's chair and the helm on board the new *Defiant,* Ben Sisko was listening to something that only long experience allowed him to perceive.

"You hear that, Chief?"

At his engineering console, O'Brien frowned. "Sounds like the Doppler compensators are out of phase."

Sisko looked at Nog. "How's she handling, ensign?"

"She's not quite as smooth as the old *Defiant,* sir," the young Ferengi said. "Feels a bit sluggish."

"Chief?"

"I'm on it," O'Brien said, annoyed. "O'Brien to engineering. Recalibrate the inertial dampers and check the plasma flow regulators while you're at it."

"Right away, Chief."

Sisko understood how the senior engineer felt. The ship might or might not be a good ship—they didn't know yet. She hadn't even had time for a shakedown cruise at high warp, or a sustained cruise at impulse to weed out her problems. There had throughout history been beautiful ships, powerful ships, bigger-than-ever-before ships that had proven very quickly that they weren't among the "good ships." Some had been lucky enough to survive the discovery of their inner weaknesses. Others fell apart, sank, failed, or couldn't stand up to trouble on their first or second voyage. Until a ship was tried by real use, there was no way to know how well all the engineered parts would actually work together—no matter how tight, no matter how exactly manufactured—no way but work to find the flaws. Time was the only saturation treatment for a ship. Sail out, see how she stresses, see what breaks and replace it, see what bends and strengthen it . . . only time and trouble could hammer a new ship into a good ship. *Defiant* hadn't yet been given that time.

He tried not to resent the new ship, even as he wished for the security and familiarity of the old ship. The old *Defiant* had hammered through every test. They'd repaired her themselves, with their own hands, not having to take anybody else's word that fixes had been done and done well. They knew her weaknesses and could circumvent them. They knew her strengths and could use them. Going into an invasion scheme with a brand new untried ship—it demanded a trust he just couldn't give yet.

At the engineering console, Miles O'Brien grumbled at the acknowledgement from engineering. His mood could stand improvement. Beside him, passively watching the fleet on the main screen, Julian Bashir just had to be sitting right here on this side of the bridge—why couldn't he be down in sickbay treating a hangnail or something?

"You'd think someone would've come up with a better inertial control system," O'Brien grumbled. "Just because a man has plans to return to Earth and teach at a nice quiet academy doesn't mean he's not . . . oh, the devil with it . . . what idiot changed the color code on this panel?"

Bashir finally turned and asked, "What's that you're saying, Miles?"

"I said, could you please wipe that grin off your face? You're not the first person to ever fall in love, you know."

The grin fell away. "I thought you'd be happy for me."

"I *am* happy for you. O'Brien to engineering. Try realigning the induction coils."

"Aligning the induction coils now."

"You do that . . . look, Julian . . ." He forced himself to swivel halfway around. "There's something I have to talk to you about. . . ."

Bashir gently bridged, "You're getting pressure from Keiko, aren't you?"

"How'd you know!"

"It's a big decision. I'm surprised it didn't come up sooner."

Sunken partially by relief and partially because he'd been so easy to read, O'Brien felt his shoulders sag. "Actually, we've been talking about it for quite a while."

"Well, you can stop talking about it," the doctor offered. "You can put the model of the Alamo into my quarters."

"Oh . . . model . . ."

At the helm, Nog turned toward port. "I could still use a little more equalization on the torque buffers."

O'Brien flinched. "Oh—right. I'll try to compensate with the impulse response filters."

"That way," Bashir accommodated, "your quarters

won't be so cluttered, and you can still use it whenever you want."

He worked a moment or two, forcing himself to concentrate. There had to be equalization, or Nog wouldn't be able to hold the ship laterally in this crowd. Usually it didn't matter so much, when all of space was there for moving around in, but in the middle of a fleet—

"I wasn't talking about the Alamo model," he suddenly said. "Besides, it's too big for your quarters."

"You let me worry about that," Bashir offered. "So, what did you want to talk to me about?"

Ouch—he knew there was something else going on. O'Brien surveyed his own reaction to moving to Earth, leaving his long-time post, and recalled that when he'd first worked with Bashir he hadn't really liked him much. Strange how completely things could change over the years. He'd never expected to find so much in common with the young doctor, never mind ultimately building models together and playing out historical problems of battle—and really liking it.

"It's nothing that can't wait," he finally lied. "Is that any better, Nog?"

"Torque buffers are stable," Nog said from the helm.

Bashir nodded in silent agreement. He knew he was being put off, and it worried him. Why wouldn't Miles tell him what was the problem? He watched as his friend disappeared into the aft lift and was swallowed by the ship. Why did happiness and problems have to balance each other? Why couldn't everything just go well for once?

He swiveled around forward again, and as he did that

his eyes fell upon Ezri, sitting at her station beside Worf. The two of them were as different as feathers from stone, yet it disturbed him to see them together. They were speaking to each other now. If he watched, he might be able to know what they were saying. They were keeping their voices down—quite a trick for Worf.

No, he shouldn't watch. He really shouldn't.

"The color coding on the weapons display panel is different from that on our *Defiant*."

Worf's chunky declaration was a poor effort to avoid the problem between them. Ezri watched his face, and she knew he was aware of her, very much too aware. She remembered how his eyes changed when they kissed. So many lives were roaming within her mind, but the one she could focus most easily on was the one that made the two of them most uncomfortable. The most recent life . . . his dead wife.

Yes, Jadzia was dead. There was undeniable finality even for a Trill, though the essence lived on in the next host. The Dax symbiont within Ezri was a stranger in many ways, having invaded a girl who had never prepared for symbiosis. That was strange for him, too. All the other hosts had been ready, even eager. Ezri continued to struggle, her mind cluttered and disorganized. Controlling the impulses of the Dax's former lives, and all the memories, was like trying to conduct an orchestra when she had no idea how to hold the baton.

"You sure you're not angry?" she urged, insisting that the panel's color code would not be the subject.

"About the weapons display?" Worf toyed.

She tipped her head. "About Julian."

Worf's face hardened visibly. "Why should I be angry? I've been asking you to tell the doctor how you feel about him for the past month."

"Well, now that he knows how I feel—"

"I am happy for *you*."

In a mountainous kind of way.

She smiled. "That's a relief."

"But I am going to kill *him*."

Ezri tilted forward a little, trying to read his eyes, and rewarded him with half a giggle.

His eyes bothered her.

"You're kidding, right?" she asked.

Worf made a grumble in the bottom of his throat. "And Jadzia complained I had no sense of humor."

On the main deck, Captain Sisko listened in frustration to the imbalances of his new ship and also noticed the sad imbalance among his crew. He heard the rumblings of Worf and the musical lilt of Ezri behind him, though he consciously refused to pay attention to what was obviously a private conversation. He missed Jadzia almost as much as he had missed Curzon Dax before her. Yes, it was a little prejudicial, but Jadzia hadn't really been able to take Curzon's place. She'd become a special friend in her own right. Now, Ezri was doing her best to take Jadzia's place, and she couldn't. Not for Sisko, and certainly not for Worf. No essence of memory could replace a living, breathing person, and no other person could slip into a haven of special affection. That was asking and expecting too much.

Both men were dealing with the handicap of not being

Trill themselves. Both Sisko and Worf were single individuals, living out their lives as one and only one. He knew in his mind that all the Dax's and hosts were in there somewhere, and yet his heart wanted to grieve. He could only imagine what Worf must be feeling behind that armored personality.

Beside him, Odo gazed up at the tactical station where Worf and Ezri were talking. Sisko watched him without really looking. Another cracked soul.

"I wish she was here, constable," he offered. Odd—he actually meant two different women with that "she."

Odo averted his gaze from up there, a little self-conscious now. "Actually, captain, I wasn't thinking about Kira just then."

He paused, and Sisko had the sense not to pointedly ask what he meant. If Odo wanted to talk—

"For years now," the shapeshifter began tentatively, "I've been ashamed of my fellow Changelings . . . knowing about the races they've enslaved . . . the atrocities they've committed . . . but now, knowing that it was Section Thirty-One—that it was a band of rogue Federation citizens who'd infected my people with the Changeling disease . . . an act of genocide as cold and calculated as anything the Dominion ever did—"

"You can't help but feel some sympathy for your people," Sisko completed.

Odo nodded. "It makes a difficult situation even more complicated. This war, Captain . . . it has to end."

"One way or another," Sisko agreed. "It will, and soon. Wars always—Odo? Odo? Is something wrong? You look—"

Why was Odo's heart beating so loudly? Why had a spotlight come on at the bridge ceiling? Sisko flinched and squinted into the light. He wanted to turn and order the light off. Malfunction, obviously. O'Brien? What's going on?

"*My . . . son.*"

The heartbeat grew louder. He could feel it physically now. Was it his own? Odo had no heart. . . .

Before him a physical form began to take shape. A building. Pillars. A shrine. A Bajoran shrine. Instinctively he recognized it, though the lines were muddled by brightness.

And another form. A pillar changing shape, moving toward him.

"Mother?" he began.

What a bizarre thing. His natural mother, not the mother he knew in childhood, but the one who had abandoned him to grow up human, to think he was normal, ordinary, fit to face the challenges of humanity. The Prophets were calling to him through this woman of nonessence, this ethereal being who had ceded him to his place so long ago, forcing him to live two lives now.

"Why have you brought me here?" he demanded.

"*This is the last time I will ever speak to you like this,*" the Prophet said in her musical voice. "*The Emissary's task is nearing completion.*"

What was that supposed to mean? Was he out of a spiritual job? Day after day, he'd managed to put aside his mystical assignment and do the duty he preferred—and now, right in the middle of trouble, this.

"You mean the war is coming to an end?" he asked.

"You have walked the path the Prophets have laid out for you, Benjamin. Do not falter now."

"I don't intend to."

"Know this, my son. Your journey's end lies not before you, but behind you."

Oh, fine. Sisko felt a very tangible groan rumble through his chest despite the dreamy circumstance. Why must highly advanced superbeings always speak in vague riddles? Why did they have to be the wind? Just once couldn't they say, "Go over to this specific place and kick the behind off this specific person and come home and have a brew?"

"Captain? Captain?"

"I hate poetry," he muttered. "I'm a Starfleet officer. Why can't you just give me a direct order? And I refuse to look backward. The future isn't set or I wouldn't bother to get up in the morning. Do you hear me?"

His prophet-mother lowered her hands, and the light went away. The bridge filtered back to solidity before him.

"Captain, are you all right?"

Odo was watching him, his plastic face tight with concern.

Sisko thought about explaining, describing the vision forced upon him by his mystical connection. He thought about voicing the frustration of living two lives—one as a Starfleet captain with a real ship and solid crew to handle, the other as a mysterious floaty being from the Wormhole Collection, without awareness of concrete purpose. He'd come to realize that he didn't like talk of destiny. He had defied prophesy before and was ready to do it again. He'd rather have free choice and make the honest wrong one.

"The Prophets just came to me in a vision," he said bluntly, hoping it didn't sound as silly in the receiving as it did in the saying.

Odo seemed cautious. "I take it they weren't bringing good news."

"I'm not sure," Sisko muttered. "I suppose only time will tell."

"Hello, Adami."

Dukat didn't wait for the Kai to turn at his greeting before walking right in on her. In fact, Kai Winn didn't even look up from her reading of the Kosst Amojan. So she knew it was Dukat intruding upon her and was determined to let him know she was unimpressed. Ah, well.

"You're back," was her manner of greeting.

He wanted her to look up. He wanted her to see him as a Bajoran, a surgically altered Cardassian quite insisting upon looking like one of the native people on this planet. His clothing was ragged, caked with dust from the streets of Bajor. Somehow he was proud of that, proud that he had survived being the lowest of the low, the condemned, the downcast, and had yet somehow kept his identity through the great wringer of adversity. All his years as a Cardassian officer, eventually as high commander, leader of planets, and leader of fleets; through all the dozen changes of circumstance in the struggles between the Federation, the Alpha Quadrant Empires, the Dominion, and the Cardassians, through the many shifts of power—somehow this latest incarnation satisfied him most of all, for it proved he could go low and still return.

Would she speak to him? Was she still sufficiently insulted by the Prophets' choice of Sisko as their Emissary instead of her, or had she repented in the time Dukat had been banished to the streets?

He wanted to know, but he stayed back, on the opposite side of the room, near the door. He would never again go near that forbidden book. His eyes still stung with its vengeful magic.

"Is that all you have to say to me?" he asked eventually.

Kai Winn dawdled over her book, then finally looked up. "I see the Pah-wraiths have restored your sight."

A warning triggered in Dukat's head. Blindness had given him insights he never expected. He needed the Kai's good graces. Resentment must be controlled. If she still resented the Prophets, if she would still help him free the anti-Prophet Pah-wraiths, then Sisko and the Prophets could be overthrown with a power that matched their own.

He hid his anger behind a smile. "The Pah-wraiths have forgiven my trespasses. They have accepted that my attempt to read the Kosst Amojan was a desperate mistake. I hope you can find it in your heart to do the same."

The Kai leaned back in her chair and eyed him coldly. "Forgive you? I don't forgive Cardassian war criminals."

Dukat remained silent. Might as well take whatever she had to say. Hereafter they would both know the wound had been purged, that she had said what needed to be said.

"All you've ever done," she continued after a moment,

"is lie to me. Pretending to be a poor farmer from Bajor when in actuality you're a Cardassian war criminal. To think I took Gul Dukat to my bed, one of the most hated men in Bajoran history—"

"I wasn't lying when I offered you my heart," he claimed bluntly.

"Of course not!" her scorn painted the room. "Well, you'll be happy to know that I have completed my study of the text of the Kosst Amojan. Its secrets are now my secrets."

That didn't sound very hopeful, did it? It meant she had more power than he could have, and influence with the Pah-wraiths, which he had failed to acquire. She was the Kai, the religious leader of Bajor, and the Pah-wraiths had let her read their book without blinding her, while the Prophets had never even let her have a single vision and had chosen an offworlder as their representative.

He would have to find a way to make her work with him, and definitely not against him. She had banished him, blinded, to the streets, and now he had returned. Checking his own bitterness might be the best path.

"You've learned how to release the Pah-wraiths?" he asked, unable to hide his real thoughts or his admiration for her obvious spiritual stature, which had been ignored by the Prophets.

"I have," she claimed proudly.

"Then why haven't you gone to the Fire Caves and freed them?"

Offering only a beguiling smile, Kai Winn leered at him. "I was waiting for you."

Relief poured through Dukat. "Then you *have* forgiven me!"

"I need your help, Dukat." She rose from her chair, crossed the rug that separated them, and finally stood before him. "It's as simple as that."

He turned his hands up. "All you have to do is ask."

He reached for her hand—amazingly, she gave it. So she was still angry with the Prophets, or perhaps beyond anger and well into bitterness.

"Together," he said, "we will free the Pah-wraiths so that they can tear down the Celestial Temple and destroy the Prophets."

"And their Emissary as well."

Dukat tucked his chin. "No. Benjamin Sisko will be dealt with by me, and me alone."

"Assuming he survives the invasion of Cardassia," the Kai observed cryptically.

"He'll survive," Dukat grumbled. "But I promise you, he'll wish he hadn't."

CHAPTER
4

Bad hand. Figured.

"Do you have any threes?"

Quark surveyed his cards again, but they hadn't changed. He kept them close to his face, as if the computer in the holosuite didn't perfectly well know what cards he was holding.

"Go fish." The computer-generated lounge lizard of the hololounge eyed him from his seat across the table.

Annoyed, Quark sighed and dumped his cards on the table. This just wasn't working.

"Don't tell me you're quitting," Vic Fontaine challenged.

"It's just not my game," Quark complained.

"Want to try pinochle again?"

Quark shook his head. If the computer couldn't cough up something more interesting than these games, how could he possibly offer something new to his customers in his real bar, down the real stairs, with the real money?

"How about rummy?" Vic offered. "Or gin rummy? Five-card stud? Canasta?"

Quark kept shaking his head. There just wasn't enough zap in any of those to distract the denizens of *Deep Space Nine* from what was going on way off in space. Not enough to get them to come in and start spending, anyway.

"How about some Tongo?" he countered snidely.

Vic eyed him. "Did they play Tongo in Las Vegas in 1962?"

A smart-ass computer. Great. "How could they?" he bothered to answer. "It's a Ferengi game."

He thought about shutting down the program, but for some odd reason he liked Vic's company. Wasn't that pathetic?

"Right," Vic said. "Which is why my holographic program can't create it."

"I know, I know, this place is period-specific . . . but for a hologram, you're not very accommodating."

Ich—he'd been trying to be friendly with non-Ferengis for way too long. He was starting to be like them. He'd be humiliated to admit it to a fellow Ferengi, that the people around here—even the holopeople—were more like friends than customers. A moment of sadness and worry pushed in on his fantasy. He *did* want them all to come back safely—even if it didn't make him a bit richer.

What if they lost? What if the Federation fleet were defeated and the Cardassians reclaimed *Deep Space*

Nine? He didn't like that idea at all, and—shamefully—it had nothing to do with the change of business. The Cardassians had been a lot easier to snooker than the humans and Bajorans, but he still didn't want them back.

"Is that why you came by?" Vic asked. "To insult me?"

"I stopped by because I had nothing else to do," Quark admitted. "My bar hasn't had half a dozen customers all day. Seems like everyone's off fighting this stupid war."

"It's not easy to stay behind, is it?" Vic asked. "Knowing your friends are out there risking their lives?"

How could a computer-generation possibly see through him like that! Had the hardware grown intuition?

He shrugged. "They think they have it tough. They should try living my life for a day. The hospitality industry isn't for the faint-hearted."

Vic nodded. "A bartender's life is a lonely one."

"That's right. But few people understand that. They think it's one big happy party. They forget that the person giving the party never has any fun. He's busy making sure everyone else is having fun. All I do, all day long, is give, give, give—"

"Bartending is a very noble profession," Vic agreed. "And you do it well. Under some very difficult circumstances, I might add. You should be proud."

"You think so?"

"I know so, pallie."

Quark sighed, then muttered, "I just hope Nog and the rest of those heroic idiots come back in one piece. . . .

Just then, the girl called Ginger snaked up to Vic dressed for a night of questionable morality and purred, "Vic, sweetie, are you ready? Jimmy and Petey are about to go on."

Vic got to his feet and let Ginger slip under his arm. "Sorry, pallie," he said to Quark, "gotta run. Durante and Lawford are at the Sands. Can't miss that."

"I thought you said a bartender's life was a lonely one," Quark challenged.

"It is—but I'm not a bartender."

So much for a friendly ear. Quark watched as the hologuy and gal slithered away into their own world.

"Go fish," he grumbled.

This must be the computer's way of telling him he had to live a real life, deal with the lack of personnel on the station, and accept where they had gone. Strange how lifelike the holoprograms could be, how feeling and understanding, even to the point of forcing him to think about reality in the midst of fantasy. He'd tried to escape his real situation by coming to a fake bar at a fake time, and it hadn't worked.

Of course it hadn't. The station knew it was on alert, and it knew perfectly well why. Could a machine programmed to connect reactions and responses to appropriate information—could it comprehend fear? Anticipation? Could it sense that things were not normal today? Would a station on yellow alert warn a hologuy and a hologal not to get too involved?

"Yes, it could," Quark muttered. "Why not? It's the age of miracles, isn't it? The time of the Prophets? The eon of starships and like wonders? All right, then, you win. Hear me? I've had my hand slapped. Back to reality. Program off."

The Fire Caves were well-named: hot and moist, walls dripping with condensate, shots of steam spurting from cracks in the rocky floor. The climb up to them was no easy jog either, yet somehow Dukat felt more invigorated than exhausted.

Behind him, however, he knew Kai Winn was suffering from the excessive heat—which did not bother him much, as he was Cardassian under the skin. His heavy backpack, filled with artifacts and ceremonial relics, was a good burden. Because he would not touch the Kosst Amojan, though, Kai Winn was charged with carrying the heavy book all the way by herself. She sank against another stone outcropping, looking as if she were about to melt.

Dukat paused. "Is it really necessary to rest every few minutes?"

She heaved a series of breaths, obviously troubled by the altitude as well as the heat. "I don't need . . . you . . . to wait for me. . . . Go on ahead . . . wander around aimlessly in these caves for . . . the rest of your miserable life."

Ah—pushed the wrong buttons that time.

He settled back on a rock that almost provided a seat. "I'm in no hurry."

Around them, the caves seethed and dripped, creating for themselves a mystical voice that had over the ages gained a reputation. The caves sang, some said. They cried, said others. They cursed, wept, or whispered. The caves were sorrow, some villagers thought, or threat, thought others. There were mystical injunctions against trespassing, or compelling charges to come here—perhaps to die as a sacrifice to the Pah-wraiths, spirits who claimed to be the true Prophets of Bajor. Some thought that the caves were the throat of hell.

Amazing.

"You know, during the Occupation my people found the Bajorans' fear of these caves amusing. Yet somehow none of us ever found the time to visit them. And now, here I am. Ironic, isn't it?"

"I don't care," Winn heaved.

Dukat looked at her. "Excuse me?"

"I'm sure you have many interesting anecdotes about the Occupation," she dismissed, "but I have no desire to hear them."

"I meant no disrespect, Adami—"

"And stop calling me 'Adami.' That privilege is no longer yours."

Temper boiled in Dukat's chest. Though he might appear Bajoran, he was Cardassian to the core and this was a severe lowering of himself, to coddle a Bajoran woman, to be forced to show her respect he was disinclined to give, to bend to her wishes, and now to be denied the right to call her by her primary name.

He held his rage.

"I see," he allowed. "Then how should I—?"

Though he had some ideas about what to call her instead, Kai Winn said, "From now on, you will address me as 'Eminence.' Is that clear?"

Some day . . . some day. . . .

Dukat gritted his teeth. "Perfectly," he said. "Your Eminence."

How far must they go? How deeply into these caves, how far into the belly of the planet would they have to trek before they could find the prison of the Pah-wraiths and use the power of the book to free them?

Nothing ever came easy, it seemed. Once he had been stripped of all past glories, he had been given another chance to defeat the Federation and the Prophets and everything that had worked to humiliate him in his life. Now he would make yet another pact with power in order to rise up again, yet it seemed he would have to travel into the pit before he could free that power.

Very well. He would no longer be driven down. The time of reckoning was here. If he had to walk through the molten core of Bajor in his bare feet, he would succeed.

"I see your point, general, but for two millennia the Jem'Hadar have always been the Dominion's first line of defense. It would damage their morale to take a back seat to the Breen."

The Founder shuddered against her illness, hoping the Breen general would not see her weakness. She was, in fact, not sure exactly what the Breen were able to see through their life-sustaining helmets. Perhaps his frosted face-shield blurred the crackling scabs of her face and hands. Perhaps he saw her only as a blur of humanoid form, but did not realize she was stuck holding that form, without the strength to revert to her natural shape. The sickness had made her a solid.

His static-voice erupted in a tone she had come to recognize as anger, impatience. She listened to his argument—that the Jem'Hadar had served for two millennia without managing to carry the Dominion to preeminence. Only since the Breen forces had become aligned with the Dominion had victory been within grasp.

True enough; it was certainly possible that the Jem'Hadar had outlived their collective purpose. Still, how would it appear to give in totally so soon?

A compromise might serve, and she would not have to give all her advantages away at once.

"Very well," she told him. "In the spirit of our new alliance, I will inform the Jem'Hadar that the Breen forces will be positioned alongside them on the front lines."

He chittered again, not entirely satisfied, but at least put off for now.

The Founder pressed painfully out of her chair. Her skin cracked and withered as she moved. She could barely hold the human form and had to pause to gather strength—or more accurately, to fend off weakness—before leading the general to one of the access monitors.

"I'm glad that pleases you," she told him, even though that hadn't been exactly what he'd said.

They turned their attention to the strategic layout, where Weyoun was studying the distribution of ships. "I fear," he said, "our lines are spread too thin, especially here at the center."

The Founder painfully rose from her chair and struggled to the monitor. "Do you agree?" she asked the Breen general.

He scrambled that he did agree, and thus the Founder told Weyoun, "Notify the Jem'Hadar. Order them to reinforce the center of our lines. The Federation fleet usually begins their assault by sending the smaller attack fighters to create distractions and weaken the—"

As she touched the controls, the picture on the screen suddenly flickered and went black. In the room, the lights dimmed, wobbled, dimmed still more and did not come back to brightness. The computer screen flashed once, then died.

"Now what?" she complained.

Seconds crawled by. What was happening? She hated lack of control. Surprises were almost always bad.

As she was about to call for Weyoun, the lights burped back to life. The monitor also regained a picture, but it was only a screen pattern. Connection with the strategic mainframe had been disrupted.

Before the Founder could curse the darkness, the door opened and the newly appointed liaison from the Cardassian force, Legate Broca, rushed in.

"Founder! I'm relieved to see you're all right."

She turned on him, bothered that he should use the term "all right" when she was so obviously ill and could no longer disguise the dessicating malady that was slowly debilitating her.

"What caused the power outage?" she demanded.

"Sabotage," Broca dutifully told her, without frilling up the bad news. "Almost every Dominion installation on Cardassia Prime has suffered some form of damage!"

"Damar!" the Founder gritted. "I thought you said you had eliminated his rebel forces."

"We captured some of the terrorists, but—"

"But what?"

"These acts of terrorism," Weyoun attempted, "they weren't carried out by a small group of disgruntled Cardassian soldiers. The culprits were ordinary citizens."

The announcement embarrassed Broca, she could clearly see—in fact, he was completely ashamed.

And rightly so. Why hadn't he seen this coming? She had charged him with keeping order on the planet.

She raised her hand, much faster than she expected herself capable of, and clasped him by the throat. "Are you telling me the Cardassian people are rising up against us?"

Broca choked, but did not fight her. "I'm sure . . . it's only . . . a small number of malcontents. . . ."

"We have no way of knowing that, do we?"

It was an enraging revelation. People who had been controlled, finding a way to rise up? Average citizens with no military support? Rise against the greatness of the Dominion? The Cardassians? The Jem'Hadar? Even the Breen?

The Founder cast a glance at the Breen general, and briefly entertained the idea of blaming him for not seeing this coming and assigning troopers to stop it. She could use that to deny him superiority over the Jem'Hadar and force him to struggle harder on the Dominion's behalf. . . . Ultimately, though, she decided to keep using Weyoun, for he was the one with a stake in control on Bajor. She would wait for another time, when upsetting the balance would serve even better.

"Founder," Weyoun began, "may I make a suggestion?"

Still strangling the Legate, the Founder said, "I'm sure Broca is most interested in what you have to say."

The Vorta attaché nodded elegantly and let an extra second or two pass before saying, "If the Cardassian people are responsible for these acts of terrorism . . . if they've allowed Damar and his fanatics to turn them against us, then it's the people who should be punished."

"What do you say to that?" she asked Broca.

Only his lips moved. "Severely punished. . . ."

Nearly exhausted herself, she dropped him abruptly. "I'm glad we're all in agreement."

All the lights had been cut off. Any buildings without emergency backup generators were still shut down and even some of those generators had been damaged. The whole capital city was in blackout, as well as almost every industrial center planetwide. Wonderful. . . .

Unfortunately, that also meant there was no power in the resistance's cellar headquarters.

Damar reviewed with satisfaction the success of a very long night's coordinated efforts. He had to give Kira and her rebels credit. They had done everything he had told them to, and with great deliberation and purpose. He had laid out every industrial and tactical center on the planet, and through clever coded messages they had organized themselves and carried out the night's assault. If the invasion fleet failed, it would not be because the planet was in too good order and provided too solid a support for the Cardassian fleet. A planet in turmoil could do no fleet any favors, and that was all he meant for Cardassia to offer. No longer after this week would Cardassia be minion to the arrogant Founders. Lower than the Jem'Hadar, lower than the Breen—finally Cardassia would be driven as low as any civilization could go, and would have nowhere to travel but up again, up to greatness and power and dominance in an Alpha Quadrant free of the interloping shapeshifters.

If only they could see. . . .

He peered through the darkness to the circuit box, where Garak was fussing at the junction, trying to trim off enough power to give them a monitor, even just one. The only source of light was a single struggling lightstick near Garak, not enough to prevent Garak from making some sort of mistake and getting his fingers zapped by a rogue arc.

Frustrated, Garak muttered, "I could use some more light over here. . . ."

Hardly more than a silhouette as she stood guard near the doorway, Kira accommodated, "Mila's looking for some upstairs—here she comes."

"Twenty-four minutes," Damar finalized.

Kira congratulated him with a "Not bad."

"If the Dominion hasn't been able to restore the power in the capital," Garak observed, "then the entire planet must be in chaos."

"Let's hope so," Damar said.

The old woman Mila appeared down the stairs with two more lightsticks.

"I'm afraid I could only find two lightsticks," she apologized. "I know there are others in the house somewhere."

"Stop dawdling," Garak snapped, waving a hand, "and bring them over to me!"

The old Cardassian woman did as instructed. "Ah, how well I remember that tone of voice . . . it reminds me of the demanding and inconsiderate little boy you used to be."

On his side of the cellar, Damar chuckled. Only a Cardassian woman could look back with reverie on a nasty child.

Garak gazed up at her. "I haven't changed much, have I?" he asked.

"Enough reminiscing," Damar chastised. "We have to get the power back up. I need to know how much damage we have caused the Dominion."

"If this part of the city is any indication," Mila commented, "I'd say a lot."

Damar squinted at the padd. "I'd love to see the look on Weyoun's face right now."

"Let's not fool ourselves, Damar," Kira cautioned. "At best, we've won a skirmish. We have to hit them again—harder this time."

"That won't be easy," Garak said. "They'll have tightened their security."

"It doesn't matter. We can't lose our momentum."

Damar offered her a smile. "The commander is right. We can't rest until we've rid ourselves of the Dominion once and for all. And when we do, we'll have you to thank. This rebellion would've died in infancy if not for you."

"How ironic," Garak added, "that Cardassia's savior should be a former Bajoran terrorist."

"Don't canonize me just yet," Kira demurred.

All at once, the lights came back on. So their work had come and gone now.

"Twenty-six and a half minutes," Damar concluded. "Let's see what the Dominion has to say for itself."

As he went to the monitor and tried to get it back online, Garak added, "One thing's for sure—we've inconvenienced millions of Cardassian citizens."

Kira moved impatiently toward him. "Don't you think it's a small price to pay if it helps to bring down the Dominion?"

Garak opened his mouth to shoot back a remark, but his own success cut him off as the power was suddenly restored, at least to this one room. The stairway remained dark, and there was no light shining from upstairs. That could be for the good.

"I always said you were a smart boy," Mila lauded.

Ignoring their self-congratulating, Damar was concentrating on getting the monitor to operate. Finally it did, flickering to life just as Weyoun appeared on the screen, the hated face of that obsequious clown on the planetwide address system, cooing his pompous opinion around the world.

"Citizens of Cardassia . . . I speak to you tonight with a heavy heart. This latest wave of vandalism directed against your Dominion allies must stop."

"I wouldn't count on it," Garak muttered.

"The Dominion views these acts of vandalism as nothing less than a cruel betrayal by a once-valued ally. Let me assure you, we know that these disgraceful acts of sabotage were carried out by a mere handful of disgruntled extremists who alone are to blame for this treachery. . . ."

"That's us," Kira muttered, "disgruntled to the core."

"And extreme," Garak tacked on.

Damar waved a hand. "Quiet."

"But these radicals," the picture of Weyoun continued, his violet eyes, bitter and concerned, set in a face abnormally pale even for a Vorta, "must come to realize that their disobedience will not be tolerated . . . that you, the Cardassian people, must suffer the consequences of their cowardly actions."

"Uh-oh," Kira breathed.

Damar couldn't remain quiet this time. "I don't like the sound of that. . . ."

"That's why," the monitor continued, 'a few moments ago, Dominion troops reduced Lakarian City to ashes. There were no survivors . . . two million men, women, and children . . . gone in a matter of seconds.''

Mila sank into the nearest chair. Disturbing, since at her age it was she who had seen more atrocity and barbarism than the rest of them put together. Kira folded her arms in visible anguish. Even Garak had no words to ease the astonishment.

Damar was also appalled, the more so because he thought he should have seen this coming. Still, the Vorta had been cunning before, while not openly brutal.

Weyoun had stopped talking for a few long painful seconds, as if allowing the news to sink in all over the planet. What were the other millions of Cardassians thinking, hoping, feeling, wishing? For the deaths of the Vorta? The Dominion? Or the deaths of the rebels?

"Appalling, isn't it?" he cooed. "Life is so precious . . . and now all that's left of those vibrant, precious people are cinders in the dust. And that's just the beginning."

"Damar," Garak began.

"Quiet!" Damar shot back.

"From now on," Weyoun said, "for each act of sabotage committed against the Dominion, another Cardassian city will be destroyed."

In each mind throughout the cellar, perhaps throughout the planet, each man and woman calculated how many acts of sabotage must go by before there was nothing left of Cardassia. Hardly anyone lived in the countryside . . . everyone else lived in a city. It was a planet of cities. There was nowhere else to hide, no way to live without the comforting infrastructure of civilization. Even their farmed foodstuffs were imported.

Such a system had laid itself bare for slaughter. Weyoun had apparently found that out—Cardassians were creatures of modern times, and could easily be herded to the butcher's block.

No one else had ever figured that out before. In all of Cardassia's conquests, never before had the battle come to their planet itself.

"I implore you," the false sympathy of Weyoun continued, "not to let that happen. Let us look beyond the mistakes of the past and return to the spirit of friendship and cooperation that existed between the Dominion and Cardassia. Together we can accomplish what we set out to do—defeat our common enemies . . . the Federation, the Klingons, the Romulans, and all others who stand against us. Thank you."

The screen went blank.

No one spoke. Only the sound of Mila's soft weeping disturbed the blanket of horror.

"I knew there'd be reprisals," Kira struggled, "but I didn't think they'd go this far. . . ."

Damar swung away from the monitor as if dismissing it and Weyoun with it. "Do they really think this is going to stop us?" he threatened.

"Doesn't it?" Garak challenged. "How many cities can we afford to lose?"

"We can't afford to lose any," Damar told him, "but we have to be willing to lose them all. We *must* be free! Even if it costs us everything."

Would they accept his charge? Were they as committed as he was to throwing off the yoke of the Dominion?

He looked at Garak, then Kira. Oddly, the one who gave him support was the one he didn't address.

Mila. The old Cardassian woman who seemed the weakest among them, reduced to bringing tea and lightsticks, now turned her tear-streaked face up to him. She was no longer crying, though. She had passed through that, and now drove them on to something far more moving.

"We must be free," she said.

Damar gazed at her in gratitude, the first gaze of credibility he had ever offered her. She deserved recognition for her bravery, for being willing to stand behind his rash words, indeed words that might result in the utter eradication of their race.

Seeing what was happening, and that there was no going back, Kira unfolded her arms and straightened her shoulders. "Then we have to hit them again. Right away. They won't be expecting that."

Shoring up his own posture, Damar took a single step to the center of the cellar. "I should've killed that Vorta jackal when I had the chance."

"You might get another chance," Kira told him. "We have to attack Dominion Headquarters."

Garak stepped into Damar's periphery. "Chop off a snake's head and its body dies."

"Damar," Kira said, stepping closer, "for the past two years you practically lived in that building—"

"If you're asking me whether I know a way to get us inside, the answer is no," he told her irascibly. "Not without valid security protocols."

"Then we'll have to force our way in. Garak, we'll need some kind of explosive device."

"I'll get right on it."

Mila stood up slowly. "What you're proposing . . . is suicide!"

"Mila," Garak snapped, "if you don't have anything positive to say—"

The old woman looked at him with an expression that caused even the gregarious Garak to fall silent with respect. She had been through more in her life than the three of them could claim in their combined lives. Something changed for her in that moment, and for them because of her expression.

Though her words were simple and pedestrian, her meaning was profound.

"I'll prepare you some food. No one should die on an empty stomach."

CHAPTER
5

Ben Sisko felt his pride buffeted by what he saw on the new battleship's wide forward screen.

Yes, the combined allied fleet must be an impressive sight—he could only see part of it from the port- and starboard-side auxiliary monitors—but what was coming at them out of the night was even more formidable in its ruthlessness.

Before them the combined forces of the angry, insulted Dominion, Breen, and Cardassian fleets were arrayed, fully armed, shielded, and ready for this last great battle with the civilizations they had decided to conquer.

While Starfleet, the Klingons, and the Romulans were defending their very homes and had much to lose, the Dominion armada had nothing here to protect and could afford to be bold. Sisko would be lying to himself if he hadn't admitted to a cold ball in the pit of his stomach at the sight of the enemy armada. It was downright intimidating to see them coming.

Emissary or not, Prophet's son or not, commander and captain or not, Sisko was stricken with an all-too-human instinctive shudder at the sight of Romulan warbirds and Cardassian battleships left over from the days when the Romulans were enemies. Those ships carried with them echoes of two brutal civilizations that had variously targeted human beings and Earth as their ultimate enemy in both spirit and cause. In the past, Starfleet had been forced to fight for the life of the Federation against both those mighty organizations, and more lately against the Dominion and those pesky, purposeful Jem'Hadar who did the Founders' bidding. How many more times in history would the Federation have to come up against determined conquerors? And could they prevail one more time? This was an old song, and no one yet knew the last verse.

"Sir?"

Ezri shook him out of his doomful thoughts.

He looked toward her, but couldn't summon a simple response.

"Admiral Ross would like to speak to you," she said.

Well, he had to find his voice for that, didn't he?

"Onscreen," he managed.

The forward viewscreen changed away from the ominous view of the distant and closing enemy armada to the somehow less heartening vision of Admiral Ross on the bridge of his flagship, the *Starship Farragut*.

"I'd say we have our work cut out for us, Captain," he simply said.

No point being formal or particularly mystical—everybody could see the armada by now.

"Looks that way," Sisko bluntly said.

Ross offered a nonregulation shrug. "Good luck."

That was it? Just good luck?

Sisko suddenly empathized with the admiral—what else could he say? A rousing speech of hope and glory, or just a simple exhortation, like Nelson before Trafalgar . . . we expect every man to do his duty . . .

"Sir," Ezri interrupted. "Chancellor Martok is requesting a three-way communication with you and Admiral Ross."

Why not? Barring any more bright telegrams from his mother, how many more surprises could happen with the enemy in sight?

Should ask Ross, though, just to be polite.

"Admiral?" he offered.

Ross paused, then said, "Put him through."

The screen split into two halves, one with Ross, the other with the famous and deserving Klingon warrior Martok who had been so true a friend to Sisko for . . . was it almost a year?

"Gentlemen!" Martok looked invigorated as he raised both arms in greeting. "A glorious victory lies before us!"

"I trust those are prophetic words, Chancellor." Admiral Ross said, not seeming to want to commit just yet.

"They are." Martok apparently read the subdued admiral's tone correctly, and lowered his own voice. "I haven't forgotten the promise I made to both of you."

Sisko smiled. "That the three of us would share a bottle of bloodwine on Cardassia Prime."

"A bottle! I brought a barrel of 2309! There is no finer vintage!"

Ross nodded resignedly, obviously not in the spirit of this at all. "Then I'll meet you both on Cardassia."

"Let us see who gets there first!" Martok raised a fist, and instantly cut off his transmission.

Without ceremony, Ross cut his own off, and once again Sisko was alone with his own ship and crew. He had to admit admiration for Martok's old-fashioned Klingon spirit, for which the battle gave as much satisfaction as the victory, if any. The mere act of fighting held its own kind of honor. He understood that, in its ancient Viking way, but today he also clearly saw the results of failure lurking in their dim future. They wouldn't get a second chance against a force as determined and providential as the Dominion. Perhaps it was all the years of close proximity to Odo, discovering and later depending upon the shapeshifter's strong personal resolve, his versatility, and the depth of his conviction. To come up against a whole race of such mystical beings—so physically advanced, so intelligent, and yet determined . . . this was a frightening thing. The Founders were advanced in many ways, yes, but their backward sense of superiority and lack of respect for other life forms made them very dangerous indeed.

At the helm, Nog broke the silence. "The chancellor makes it sound like an easy victory."

Maybe the ensign wanted somebody to agree with Martok. Sisko couldn't offer him that.

"He knows it won't be," he said instead. This was it. He struck the comm unit on the arm of his command chair, broadcasting his voice directly to every deck. "Sisko to all hands. Prepare to engage the enemy."

The Federation fleet was made up of six squadrons of Starfleet vessels, each led by two heavy cruiser starships, vanguarded by four assault ships and twenty fighters, and rearguarded by two destroyers charged not to let the enemy get past them. Sisko remembered picket duty—it was critical and frustrating to lag behind, to be the last line of defense, waiting to swat down any enemy ships that punched through the primary line. Here there were no home planets to defend, but the destroyers were charged with making sure that any Cardassian, Breen, or Jem'Hadar ships that ruptured the Allied lines couldn't turn around and attack unsuspecting ships who might be engaged to forward and not expect attacks from the rear.

Starfleet flanked the main body of the Allied fleet to portside. On the starboard were the Klingon heavy cruisers and their support wings. In the middle, making up the biggest portion, were the Romulan warwings, motherships, and a phalanx of birds-of-prey in front. Over the past ten years or so, the Romulans had been at war least of any of the three civilizations, and simply had more ships in better condition than either the Federation or the Klingons. Sisko might have been bothered by the primary position of the Romulans, except that it was his own idea to put them there. He'd suggested this formation to Ross when they'd first discussed the idea of a mass assault. Unlike the Klingons, who could be rash, the Romulans were unflappable, fearless, calm, and calculating. They would make a very firm trunk for the Allied tree. Bristling with a hedgehog of Klingon fighters along the whole vanguard of all three battalions, the Allied fleet was as well organized and positioned as Sisko could ever have hoped.

Soon, he knew, the beautiful formation would smash headlong into the ovoid cluster of enemy ships, make its best first assault, then dissolve into a hundred individual dogfights. At that moment, the glorious painting of martial wonder would turn bloody.

He was ready. They all were. In fact, they were impatient to get going, to lance the wound that had so long festered.

"There go the Klingon advance fighters!" O'Brien gasped.

On the forward screen they watched as the prickly Klingon line suddenly surged forward, gaining speed in a shocking rush, firing as they went, not waiting to be fired upon.

In the distance, the egg-shaped enemy formation spread apart suddenly as if to engulf the approaching fighters. A fireworks of ice-green bulbs of light erupted across open space, as Klingon streaks of yellow disuptor fire encountered Jem'Hadar shields. Then the Jem'Hadar returned fire and advanced to meet the fighters.

"Hold formation," Sisko ordered, sensing the rush of adrenaline getting the better of his crew. "Let them come to us."

To their starboard, the *Farragut* and *Nelson* surged forward suddenly, and before them the line of Starfleet fighters broke formation, parted like a melon cut with a knife, and peeled off in two different directions.

"When we engage," Sisko began evenly, "I want to concentrate on one enemy ship at a time. That's going to be hard. They'll be all around us. Unless we're being fired upon, don't respond to any passes. Keep your eyes on the one ship we target and stay on its tail. Understood?"

"Understood," Nog answered, echoed by Ezri and Worf behind him.

"They'll be expecting us to try fighting whatever comes within a certain radius of us," O'Brien commented.

"That's my point," Sisko told him. "They'll be caught off guard if we act as mechanically as they will. The Jem'Hadar, the Breen—they haven't got much in common, but one thing's for sure—and that's their collective lack of imagination. They've no doubt been told to expect surprises. It'll confound them completely if we don't give them what they expect. So let's be as tenacious as pitbulls and see how far we get. One ship at a time—that's the trick."

"No glory," Bashir commented with a noble smile.

"No heroes," Odo agreed.

Sisko nodded. "Shields up. Red alert. Battle stations."

Ezri's voice quivered just a little on the PA. *"Battle stations. All hands to battle stations. General quarters, all hands. Full red alert."*

They'd been wondering when he was going to order that. He had deliberately held off until the last sensible second, so they wouldn't be poised for so long that the rush wore off. He needed that rush right now, not an hour ago.

The turbolift hissed open and spilled six more crewmen onto the bridge, backup and support teams for engineering, sensory, and tactical stations. These were the men who would've taken O'Brien's, Ezri's and Worf's posts on a watch rotation. Now it was all hands on deck. Everybody had plenty to do. Every monitor now had a crewman manning it, spreading the duty out and letting each of them concentrate on specific readouts and breakdowns.

On the screen, the enemy formation continued to break up in an organized fashion, typical of programmed soldiers all taking orders from a few key braincores. That could work in the Allies' favor—they weren't really fighting dozens of smart, quick-thinking captains; instead, they were fighting only a handful of masterminds, perhaps Vorta, or even a Founder or two. That was the problem with central control—no variety. Sisko saw it immediately in the way all the enemy lines of ships moved in the same order, on both sides and the top and bottom of the egg-shaped assault formation.

The Allied fleet, though, was made up of a thousand time-tried captains, each clever in his way, each with different tactics and different experience. Every Jem'Hadar or Breen ship would find itself facing a completely unique set of talents. They wouldn't be able to distill what happened, then carry that experience to the next ship and the next: what worked once wouldn't necessarily work twice.

"Put some distance laterally between us and the starships," he ordered.

"Aye, sir," Nog nervously responded.

The *Defiant* hummed purposefully about them, and pressed off to port. Before them now were at least two dozen Breen fighters on full-impulse approach. The distance was closing fast.

"Pick one, Mr. Worf," Sisko offered, "and fire when ready. Ensign, plot an intercept course, then be prepared to bear off on a pursuit vector."

"I'm ready," the helmsman claimed with false boldness.

Sisko didn't say anything. Once they were actually shooting, actually chasing, something else would replace the fear he heard in Nog's voice.

Despite his preparation, mentally and physically, Sisko flinched a little when he felt the energy of phaser fire blast through the coils and into open space from the *Defiant*. Their first shot in this ship—would she stand up to the pressure?

In the herd of rushing Jem'Hadar and Breen fighters, one Jem'Hadar ship heaved and crumpled into a ball of yellow fire.

"Good girl," he murmured. "Excellent shot, Mr. Worf, pick another one—"

"Incoming!" someone shouted, and the ship rocked up on her starboard edge.

Emergency klaxons erupted. Hull breach!

"Plug it up, Chief," Sisko said, charging O'Brien with making sure himself that their first hit wasn't their last.

"Aye, sir!" O'Brien dodged for the forward lockdown, shoving an ensign out of the way.

"Pursuit, Ensign. Don't let him get away with it."

"Pursuing, sir!"

The ship surged mightily, still possessing all her power despite the hull hit. There wasn't a sense of sluggishness now, that was for sure!

Nog spun them off in pursuit of a Breen fighter, and off the two ships went into space in a furious dance, as if held together by a string.

"I'll say one thing for the Breen," Nog said through gritted fangs, "they know how to pilot a ship."

"So do you, Ensign," Sisko told him. "Stay with him."

"I'm trying, but he's slippery!"

"Mr. Worf?"

"Unable to lock target," Worf reported, frustration showing in his tone.

Suddenly, as the Breen ship ducked abruptly below the screen's line of view, the *Defiant* jolted twice, hard, and the bridge filled with bitter smoke. One of the ensigns at the engineering deck went down in a cloud.

"We have two Jem'Hadar ships coming in behind us," Odo reported over the whine of the vents, "bearing one-three-six mark four!"

"Evasive action, pattern Delta," Sisko order, breaking his own advice to ignoring whatever came around behind them. One, yes. Two, no.

"Hang on!" Nog leaned into his helm.

"Worf, get one of those bastards!" Sisko called.

"Targeting," Worf answered, and instantly opened fire, laying down a scatter pattern that smeared one of the Jem'Hadar and skinned the other.

They watched as one of the enemy ships spun hideously, then blew itself to bits, spraying debris and energy wash over them and over the wobbling

Jem'Hadar ship that had veered off in hopes of staying alive long enough to repair its damage.

"Well done, Ensign," Sisko offered.

"I lost the Breen ship we were after," Nog howled.

"I wouldn't be too worried about it. There are plenty of others to choose from. Pick another one and advance. Damage control, to the bridge. Engineering, what's the status down there? Report to Chief O'Brien. Worf, let's have tactical display on both beams. Nog, full about. The battle's back there!"

"I don't care how many of their installations you target. You have to strike at their headquarters, or they won't be crippled enough for it to have any real effect."

Kira huddled over their one monitor and made her comments as if speaking directly to the little map of Cardassia City that showed on the flickering screen.

Damar appreciated her boldness as he scanned the map from her side. Now that they had decided what to do, they were severely stalled over just how to do it.

"That would be suicide," he eventually concluded. "Besides, without the security protocols, we'll never penetrate the outer defense perimeter.

"Damar," Kira protested, "you must have some knowledge about their security protocols—something you haven't thought of."

"It's not complicated enough to have forgotten much. I assure you, my personal codes are no longer valid."

She sighed. "There has to be another way in. A back door, some weakness in their security system that you noticed. . . ."

Think, she added without actually saying it.

Damar sifted through his years coming and going freely at Dominion Headquarters, a trusted aide de camp. He had never had to think about sneaking in or out or breaking in. In fact, he had never had to break in or out of anything. He'd pursued criminals in his time, recaptured others who'd done the breaking, but he had always arrived after the Cardassians already held a particular facility.

Now he had to learn to think differently—as Kira's firelike eyes were now charging him. Over there, Garak was watching him with his wide-eyed glare also, expecting him to fail the task.

Think . . . what were the headquarters' priorities? How would they change if there were a battle in space to pulling away the warders who normally stood watch around the perimeter? How would the troops inside be reassigned to make the most of their depleted numbers, if there were trouble on the planet and insufficient forces remained inside headquarters? What would *he* do if he were in charge? What entrances would he assume the citizenry might target, and which would he assume they knew nothing about? And which of those lesser temptations might go unprotected? Something a civilian would never think of?

"As I recall," he began tentatively, "there is a rear cargo door that wasn't heavily guarded. . . ."

Kira instantly turned to Garak, who was saying, "We'll need some kind of explosive device. I'll get right on it."

Before he could stand, Mila reached past him to his

plate of half-eaten rations. "Elim, I remember when you used to love my cooking."

"I still do," Garak placated.

"You have a strange way of showing it. You've hardly touched your meal. No wonder you don't look well."

"Of course I don't look well! I've been living in a cellar!"

Mila picked up Damar's empty plate. "So has Legate Damar."

"What about him?" Garak snapped.

"He finished everything on his plate, and it shows. Which explains why he's fine handsome figure of a man."

"I'm not sure I follow you."

"I do," Kira said with a catty smile. "Mila, I believe you're falling in love."

Mila actually blushed, her gray faced turning a distinct purple. "I'm old enough to be his mother."

"Nonsense," Damar spoke up.

Mila smiled at him, charmed by his favor. "He's such a politician!"

Damar started to say something more, but the warning light from the upstairs alley entrance clicked on. It was Mila's house—for anyone else to answer the door would be to give themselves away.

"Who could that be?" Garak explored.

Mila held up a hand. "I'll find out."

She trundled up the stairs and disappeared around the bend of the landing.

"One of our informants, maybe?" Kira wondered. "They're all waiting for orders. We've put them on alert."

"And I contacted all my former shipmates," Damar said. "The ones I trust, in any—"

"You did what?" Kira rounded on him. "Did you tell them where we are? What we're planning?"

"I told you, they were men I *trust*," he insisted, angry that she would challenge him and yet not particularly surprised that she had. "We cannot possibly act alone, with only a few clusters of civilians moving with us, Colonel. We must have military backing if we are ultimately to succeed."

Kira's ink-dot eyes flared. "I think you overestimate your friends, Damar."

"That is my decision. I am Cardassian," he told her with sudden pride. "We understand conquest, and whatever you think about us, we understand struggle too. We never engaged in wholesale slaughter like the Dominion did today."

Kira raised a warning hand. "This is a bad subject."

"Yes, let's change it," Garak quickly agreed. "I'd rather worry about the actions we have to take tonight. I hope our regional operatives all have the nerve to go through with our plan, even if it means sacrificing another city."

Damar drew a breath and slowly let it out. "I know it's a grim plan, but we cannot allow ourselves to fall back because of a threat from Weyoun."

"It's hardly an idle threat," Garak pointed out. "Weyoun is not one to play games, despite the sickening sauce of his manner. After all, he did wipe out a whole city of innocent civilians just to teach us a lesson. I have no doubt he'll do it again."

Damar ignored him and went to the foot of the stairs. "What's taking her so long?"

Garak peered up the stairs. "I'm not sure. . . ."

At the top of the stairs another door opened. Light flooded the stairwell—outdoor light!

Kira drew her sidearm. Some instinct had triggered her reaction. Damar pulled Garak back a step.

"Mila!"

Garak's shriek was bloodcurdling. For an instant Damar almost scolded him for bellowing needlessly. Then, he saw the need.

Mila's lifeless body came rolling down the stairs like some kind of hideous sponge falling off a ledge.

"Mila!" Garak shouted again, and plunged for the body of his old nanny.

Kira bolted, "Garak, look out!"

As Garak reached Mila's body, a small metal device came looping down the steps.

"Concussion grenade!" Damar shouted, and dove for cover.

Kira grasped for Garak. That was the last thing Damar saw, as a flash of detonation engulfed the small quarters, punching them all backward in a blur of energy.

Flat on his back in a place that had no cover to duck for, Damar tried to roll over, but his paralyzed limbs mocked him. Even his eyes lay open, unable to blink. Kira was moving a few steps from him, her clawed hand crawling for her weapon, which lay somewhere over there . . . when a booted foot kicked away the weapon.

Motion flurried through the room. Kira seemed to float up into the middle of the air, then collapse into a chair.

Now Garak was floating by.

A bulging white face appeared in Damar's vision, blocking everything else. Jem'Hadar!

Damar tried to raise his arms, and there was some groggy movement, but his body was still stunned and not under control. He was dragged to his feet, moved across the room to Kira and Garak, and deposited with them, as they too began to shake away the daze of the stun.

Captured!

CHAPTER
6

"I congratulate you, Thot Pran. The Breen's worthiness in battle proves itself once again."

The Founder looked with appreciation at the successful measures being taken in space, as broadcast to them by their forces now challenging the Allied invasion fleet.

"Founder," Weyoun said from the other side of the monitor system, "more good news. Our troops have captured the traitor Damar."

"Excellent!"

"That's not all. Colonel Kira and Garak have been apprehended with him."

"Even better."

"Shall I have them brought here?"

She considered that, lingering briefly over the possibility of witnessing their execution herself and how much satisfaction that would provide. Also, though, it provided a chance for escape.

"What for?" she told him. "Have them executed immediately."

Weyoun turned away. "With pleasure."

When she was sure he could no longer see her face, the Founder indulged in a rarity. She smiled.

Dead. They were finished. The whole resistance was finished. The regional operatives would hold back their action until Damar gave the signal, and he was suddenly in no position to do so.

Two Cardassian guards loomed over Kira. Two Jem'Hadar kept watch on Garak and Damar.

That made some sense, Damar realized. They weren't allowing Cardassians to watch other Cardassians. Sentiment might overtake someone. He had to give the Jem'Hadar more credit than he ever had before. They were beginning, in their programmed and limited way, to understand the nature of emotional beings. They had no intuition, but they had learned to anticipate the behavior of their enemies. He would have to remember this.

If he had a future from which to gaze back.

He noted Garak glancing at him, wondering if he had a plan to get them out of this. But Damar had no answer for him. He had genuinely thought their presence hadn't been detected. Apparently he would never get the chance to become an even better rebel leader than he had managed so far.

The Jem'Hadar First was over there talking into his

comm device and getting orders from his commander. Now he broke off, and came to face the three captives.

"On your feet," he snapped.

"Why?" Kira defied. She didn't get up.

The First nodded to his men, who reached down, clasped Kira by the collar and dragged her to her feet. Damar almost lashed out, but he had no chance against the armed guards. A moment, and he and Garak were also both against the wall at Kira's side.

"We prefer our prisoners to be standing when they die," the First announced, as if the Jem'Hadar had any traditions at all.

Damar glanced at the other two prisoners. They both looked at him, and each knew they had no way out of this.

Garak cleared his throat. "Does anyone have any final words?" he asked ridiculously.

Damar glared at the Jem'Hadar. "We may die, but Cardassia will—"

"Enough!" the First barked. "Final words are not permitted."

Garak sighed. "How disappointing."

The First stepped back. "Ready weapons!"

Kira raised her chin, staring death in the face.

Admiring her, Damar did the same. Even Garak was willing to stand death down without a whimper, and Damar had to give him respect for that.

Damar felt his eyes tighten. He refused to close them. He waited for the blast, calculating absurdly in his mind how quickly the body would seize up from an energy overload, what his muscles would do, how long his brain would sizzle, how much it might hurt to die this way. Perhaps the worst thing was seeing it coming, having to stand here and wait for it without being able to fight. He should lunge—at least die in a scuffle—

The blast brightened the cellar room in mockery of the pathetic lightsticks Mila had so dutifully provided. Damar held his breath. It took longer than he had expected.

Was this some kind of freezing ray? Why wasn't he falling down? Or dissolving?

Before him, the two Jem'Hadar soldiers seized and fell. The First swung around and aimed his weapon at the two Cardassian guards he had himself brought in, fired and killed one of them. The other Cardassian, though, fired his own weapon, and the Jem'Hadar First buckled, rolled away, and lay dying seconds later on the cold stone floor.

"That's for Lakarian City," the remaining Cardassian growled. Kicking aside one of the Jem'Hadar at his feet, the Cardassian stepped over the body and came to Damar.

"Legate Damar, I am Ekoor. I pledge my life to free Cardassia from the Dominion!"

Giddy with pleasure at this turn, Damar clapped the newcomer on his shoulder and cried, "Welcome, Ekoor! Tell me—how many are with you?"

"Dozens," Ekoor claimed instantly. "And hundreds more moment by moment. Weyoun's announcement enraged Cardassians to wake up from our slumber."

"Finally!" Garak gushed.

"Your resistance has shamed many of us," Ekoor went

on, rewarding Kira with a nod that seemed to indicate that he also understood who she was.

"Our armada has gone off to stand by the Dominion in the fight against the Allied fleet," Ekoor said, "but we're getting contacts now from many ship commanders. Weyoun—"

"Don't tell me that fool broadcast his threat to the ships!" Kira burst out.

Ekoor nodded vigorously. "He did!"

"He doesn't understand Cardassians at all," Damar announced with contempt. "We will only collaborate so far. We will not be threatened."

"Sounds familiar," Kira grumbled.

Damar grasped Ekoor's arm. "What are the commanders saying? Our ships—what are they saying!"

"Whatever they're saying," Kira interrupted, "we've got to get a message through to Starfleet and tell them about it. Ekoor, where's the nearest planet-to-space communications system?"

"I know where it is," Damar said. "Follow me."

The edge of an abyss. Beyond, the abyss stretched nearly beyond sight, and at that point a sheer red wall rose. Dukat surveyed the surreal environment, its steaming gushers and unseen source of light despite the depths, and contemplated the alienness of Bajor.

"This is it, isn't it?" he asked.

Nearly exhausted, Kai Winn paused to rest. "We've reached the end of one journey and stand ready to begin another."

Yes, well, that was an answer to a simple question.

Dukat moved to the edge of the abyss and peered down into the spiraling canyon. Trite though it sounded in his mind, the pit really did look bottomless.

"What's the matter, Dukat?" Winn pestered. "You look disappointed."

"I know this sounds naive," he allowed, "but I was expecting to see fire. After all, they are called the Fire Caves."

"And with good reason." She gathered her robes, knelt to the gnarly rocks, and put the Kosst Amojan down before her. Reverently she opened the enormous book, selected a particular passage, and closed her eyes.

She began to chant.

LANO KA'LA BO'SHAR LANU NO'VALA
PAHROM GARANA MOKAO BA'JAH
KO'SE NUSSO MA'KORA KAJANI . . .
LANO KA'LA KOSST AMOJAN!

Dukat frowned. He didn't undertand the words, and he wondered for a moment if she was leading him on.

That thought dissolved when the Fire Caves's gaping abyss erupted into wall after wall of flames. Every tier was now burning as if giant curtains had been soaked in oil.

Such a sight! Breathless, Dukat absorbed the magnificence of mysticism and pondered the unrevealed science that made all this a wonder and a mystery. He felt as if the fires had come for him alone, to make him believe. The Pah-wraiths were sending him a message of victory. They would come if he freed them, they would go before him and knock down the Prophets and Sisko and the Federation and all its allies. The Cardassian Empire would gain its old greatness in the Alpha Quadrant. The name of Dukat would once again carry influence, instill fear, deserve respect.

This time, though, it would all be different. He would have his own respect, for a change.

Kai Winn opened her eyes. "Is that better?"

Derelict and wounded ships trailed sickeningly across the black skies all around. Some limped by, still firing, streaming leakage and flowing energy like life's blood. Others speared through the damaged lines, scattering formations that struggled to recongeal. Two hours into the battle, and no side showed signs of retreat. Now the fighting at these speeds and with these maneuvers became far more dangerous, adding the very good chance of slamming headlong into a ship that no longer had the power to move out of the way.

Sisko snapped orders every few seconds, pausing in between to assess the ever-changing situation outside. He was trying to be Nog's eyes and ears, for no one person could do it all. Nog had a very good ability to concentrate, but he had tunnel vision, and frequently concentrated too hard on one enemy while another slipped up behind him.

They were all working together, all watching, patching, fighting in their own way. Bashir hovered over a wounded man on the lower deck, the sixth emergency on the bridge alone, while funneling orders down to triage nurses on the lower decks.

"Captain," Ezri called over the clatter and noise, "I have Admiral Ross."

"Onscreen."

The Admiral's crackled figure appeared on the forward screen. Sisko couldn't tell if it was *Defiant*'s damage or *Farragut*'s that was causing the disruption, though it didn't matter.

"The Romulan flagship *D'ridthau* has been destroyed," Ross said without formality. "Their entire line is collapsing"

"We'll try to help," Sisko offered.

"With what? Ben, we're losing too many ships! We've got to find a way to turn the Dominion's flank."

"It's too well protected," Sisko assessed, knowing he could see the flank better from his position than Ross possibly could. "But their lines are spread pretty thin in the middle," he offered as an alternative.

The *Defiant* took another hard hit, which luckily didn't cut off the communication.

"You stick with the Romulans," Ross told him. "Martok and I will hammer away at their center."

"On my way." He turned to Ezri. "Have attack fighters six-four and six-five follow us."

"Aye, sir."

"Jem'Hadar ship off the port bow!" Nog shouted as the ship took another rocking hit.

Sisko scanned the readouts on the starboard side from his place midships. They couldn't plug any holes unless they could get out of here alive.

"Shields are down to sixty percent," Worf reported.

Sisko almost said something about the shields, but

O'Brien would be on it without prodding, and sixty percent was still a lot of deflecting power.

A second direct hit nearly threw them to their knees. Sisko clung to the helm, adding up numbers.

"Another Jem'Hadar!" Nog announced uselessly.

O'Brien climbed up from the lower trunks. "Diverting auxiliary power to port shield vectors!"

"Dax, we need some support from our fighters," Sisko requested, far more calmly than he felt.

"Breen ship attacking off the starboard stern," Nog reported, seeming to lose the will to shout anymore.

Just as well.

"Sir," Ezri turned, "most of our attack fighters are either destroyed or under attack themselves."

Sisko acknowledged with a dismissing nod, then turned to the helm. "You're going to have to get us out of here, Ensign."

"I'm trying, sir."

Odo appeared out of a cloud of rank smoke from the ops console. "Sir, there's a squadron of Romulan warbirds decloaking ahead, bearing one-seven-four mark one-three-nine."

Ah, the cavalry.

"Make a beeline for them," he ordered.

"On the way!" Nog said with a new cheer in his voice. "I just hope we get there in one piece."

Around them dozens of Jem'Hadar ships and Breen fighters closed on *Defiant*. Sisko knew he'd been suckered—his reputation had preceded him. It would be a victory for them to take down the bulldog of *Deep Space Nine*, to destroy yet a second *Defiant*, and perhaps kill the crew that had stood them off for so long, sometimes single-handedly. He knew now that the holes had been punched in the Romulan lines to bait help from Starfleet, and he had attempted to answer that call. They knew he would.

Did they know how hard he would fight? He hoped so. Bring 'em on!

"Open fire," he called. "Shoot at anything that gets in range. Never mind the shields. Everyone concentrate on firepower, understand?"

"Aye, sir!" Worf eagerly answered.

"Understood!" O'Brien said, and they went to work.

Shot after shot rolled from the *Defiant*, blasting herself a path in the cluttered pool of space. Several ships tried to get out of their way, which felt good, but three persistent enemy vessels dogged them mercilessly—two Breen, one Jem'Hadar. As they beat off two of them, one Breen ship gunned its power and came around underneath *Defiant*. Sisko saw it on one of the monitors, but there was nothing to be done with all working weapons and all sensors engaged on the two that had them by the tail.

He was knocked breathless by an abrupt surge of the whole ship a full length sideways. As he grasped the command chair and tried to recover, half the engineering console blew out toward him. Only a quickly raised hand shielded his face from hot sparks that seared the skin of his wrist and knuckles. As he blinked past the smoke, he was gripped by the nightmare of O'Brien collapsing to the deck, his shoulder a matte of blood.

Sisko hammered the comm link on his chair. "Dr. Bashir to the bridge!"

"Yes, sir?"

He turned—Bashir appeared in the vestibule. Psychic? Or just luck when they needed it most.

"You needed me, Captain?" Dr. Bashir spilled out of the lift and waved at the smoke.

Sisko just nodded toward O'Brien, who was miraculously crawling back into his chair.

"Chief caught a piece of shrapnel," he called over the clatter and howl of battle. "Worf, shields aft!"

"Aft, aye."

Julian Bashir choked his way across the bridge, dazzled briefly by the sheer weight of occurrences the captain was fielding, and bent over Miles O'Brien, who was gasping his way through waves of pain. Bashir recognized that in O'Brien—the engineer was trying to set the pain aside so he could get back to work. The gash in his shoulder had other ideas.

"I can't leave you alone for a minute," Bashir commented as he applied pressure to the bleeder.

"Just fix it, Julian," O'Brien gasped. He reached up with his good arm and continued to work the panel in front of him, then winced in pain. "Careful!"

"Sit still or you're going to wind up with one arm shorter than the other."

The ship rocked sickeningly under them and for a moment Bashir had to stop what he was doing and hang on until the inertia turned him loose again.

"You'd do anything," O'Brien grumbled, "to beat me at darts."

"I haven't lost a game to you in months."

"I'm going to miss playing darts with you, Julian. . . ."

Bashir frowned through the smoke at his friend's blood-drained face. "What are you talking about? Your shoulder's going to be fine."

"I'm leaving *DS9* . . . going back to Earth."

Keeping a pressure pad on the wound, Bashir had a moment to absorb the shock. Had he heard right? Why would Miles go away?

"When?" he asked.

O'Brien coughed. "When the war's over."

Dealing with a wound of a different kind, Bashir dared the question whose answer he was afraid he knew. "Why?"

Sheepishly, O'Brien looked at him. "I've been offered a position at Starfleet Academy. Professor of Optronic Systems Engineering."

Bashir sank back a bit. That wasn't the answer to the question why.

"I see."

O'Brien was still watching him, harder this time. The smoke was making their eyes water. "Well . . . somebody has to teach you officers the difference between a warp matrix flux capacitor and a self-sealing stembolt. . . ."

"I suppose so."

Bashir no longer looked at O'Brien, but concentrated on treating the wound, a convenient excuse to avert his eyes.

"Julian?"

"Yes."

"I should've told you sooner. I couldn't find the words. It's just that Keiko—"

"Please, Miles. Let me take care of you." Bashir felt his expression harden as he tried to supress his emotions like a man. Tersely, unable to stop himself, he added, "While I still have the chance."

A hard bolt slammed the ship from nearly dead ahead. O'Brien winced hard, bleeding from an artery.

"This is no good," Bashir decided, tightlipped. "I'd better get you to sickbay."

"I'm a little busy right now," O'Brien resisted.

"That's an order."

"Look, Julian—"

On the main deck, Ben Sisko had been only half-listening, sifting for important words, and he caught the right ones. He cast his own words over there without looking at the two officers. "You heard him, Chief."

With a sagging tone, O'Brien moaned, "Yes, sir. . . ." at the same time as Nog reported, "Another Jem'Hadar to port!"

"Dodge them," Sisko muttered. Would Nog be able to move fast enough? Could the ship wheel out of the way before that Breen got them targeted?

"Diverting auxiliary power to port shields," Worf quickly attended.

"Dax," Sisko called, "we need some support from our attack fighters."

Another hit struck them from the wrong angle—Breen.

"Breen ship off the starboard aft!"

The Breen ship wheeled up on a wing, seemed to have them targeted, and then kindly exploded into a ball of roiling energy.

Sisko gasped, astonished. Had the Romulans come in? "Did we do that?" he asked. Of course, he knew—

"Sir," Worf interrupted, "I am reading Cardassian firing sequences in the Breen wreckage."

On the heels of that, two Cardassian vessels veered in and blasted furiously at the Jem'Hadar pursuers, damaging one severely and blowing the other from now to Christmas.

Odo fingered the sensor panel. "Sir, the Cardassians—they're attacking the other Dominion ships!"

Turning forward, Ezri stared at the big screen. "I think they've switched sides!"

"Yes!" Nog shouted.

Sisko cleared his throat of the raw chemical smoke. "It couldn't have come at a better time. Come about and head for the center of their lines. This is our chance to punch through."

Ezri frowned over her communications system. "From what I can pick up, it has something to do with a Cardassian city that was recently destroyed by the Dominion."

"Are they sending those messages?"

"I'm not sure who's sending them," Ezri said. "I'm picking them up on Bajoran encoding."

"Bajoran?"

"Now it's switching to Starfleet codes. Does that make sense?"

"I don't know," Sisko said. "Seems like somebody wants us to get the message as much as they want the Cardassians to get it."

* * *

Grim realization came into the control room.

The Founder shuddered against her disease, but was more troubled by what she saw on the screens. Reports from space were changing in their tone, their results. At her side was Thot Pran, the Breen general, crackling with great disturbance. At the monitor, a stunned Weyoun gave the report he could not avoid.

"The ships are not responding to our hails," he said. "The Cardassian fleet has turned against us."

The Breen erupted into a violent hash of noise.

The Founder ignored his complaint. "Have our forces pull back and regroup at Cardassia Prime."

Weyoun turned to look at her. "But, Founder, we'll be completely surrounded. What if we have to fall back?"

"There'll be no falling back. No more running."

More rattling from the Breen.

She waited until he finished his ranting protest and avoided telling him what she really thought of him and all his kind, but on this issue she had to agree.

"We should've rid ourselves of the Cardassians at the first sign of rebellion. You're right . . . it's never too late to correct a mistake." To Weyoun she added, "I want the Cardassians exterminated."

The Vorta blinked as if he didn't quite understand. "All of them . . . ?"

"The entire population."

"That's going to take some time. . . ."

"Then I suggest you begin at once."

"Captain," Worf barked, "the Dominion forces are retreating to Cardassia Prime!"

A cheer broke out through the crew, briefly setting aside their busy damage control and their efforts to keep injured shipmates from dying if it could at all be helped.

"Sir, Admiral Ross and Chancellor Martok would like to speak to you."

Not entirely unexpected, though somewhat charming.

"I'm sure they would," Sisko huffed. "Onscreen."

The split screen appeared again, with the Klingon on one side and Ross on the other. Ross looked as if he'd been dragged through an engine feet first. His bridge was a smoky mess and one large piece of bulkhead material lay at an angle behind the command chair. Martok's bridge was shattered too, but somehow for Klingons that looked normal. Martok himself seemed charged with delight.

"I never thought I'd say this," Ross gasped, "but thank God for Cardassians!"

"It's as I predicted," Martok claimed. "The day is ours."

"Not yet it isn't," Sisko warned.

Ross seemed annoyed. "Ben, we've won a great victory! We've driven the Dominion all the way back to Cardassia Prime. We can throw a blockade around the entire system and keep them bottled up there indefinitely."

"What if they don't surrender?" Sisko pointed out. "What if they use that time to rebuild their fleet?"

Martok didn't give Ross a chance to say why that somehow wouldn't work. "The captain has a point. The Dominion has displayed an ability to build ships at an impressive rate."

"Gentlemen, do I have to remind you of our casualties?" Ross rasped. "We've lost a third of our fleet."

"And we must see to it," Martok told him, "that those soldiers did not die in vain."

"Admiral," Sisko offered, "if the Cardassians are joining us, we have an opportunity to put an end to this war once and for all."

Sisko wanted to sit down over a table and make everyone calm down and pay attention. Ross had spent a lot of years behind a desk, working with theories instead of real losses, and today's losses clearly shocked him. He would need time to absorb the meaning of a full-out fleet assault. Then he would have to be talked out of this wound-licking mentality.

"Admiral," Sisko began, trying to be temperate, "we have an opportunity here to put an end to this war once and for all. We should seize the moment."

"I agree," Martok said. "We must move on to Cardassia Prime and do it now."

Neither of them raised their voices. This wasn't the time for shouting.

Instead, they would have to count upon the hope that Ross trusted them for their experience, the fact that they had had more combined time in the field—in battle—than he'd had in Starfleet altogether.

Come on, admiral, I know you've got it in you. Give the hard order.

Ross wiped his bleeding lip, paused, looked from one to the other on his own split screen, and blinked his stinging eyes.

"All right, gentlemen," he said simply. "We press on."

Martok thumped his command chair. "My people will sing songs about this moment!"

Ross shook his head wearily, though he seemed to collect a strength even he hadn't thought he possessed. "Let's hope we're around to hear them."

The transmission was cut off at the source. The screen flipped back to a disturbing view of the shattered wreckage from the last several hours of unremitting siege.

"All right, people," Sisko said evenly, "you heard the orders. Let's finish what we started."

CHAPTER
7

On Cardassia Prime, everything had changed in an instant. Weyoun's blunder had rocketed around the planet like shockwaves rushing from pole to pole and back again stronger. Whole regiments of Cardassian troops were finding their way through the secret channels to the resistance. Ekoor had opened a hundred veins of communication that yesterday would have been suicide. Now they were filled with eager voices, soldier and civilian alike. The planet had had enough of the Dominion, its Founders, its hive-headed Jem'Hadar, and its ethereal spook Vorta.

Damar huddled with Kira and Ekoor around last-minute preparations for their assault on Dominion Headquarters. Their forces had swelled mightily in the last two hours. Just in this cellar were five more Cardassians, including two soldiers and three civilians, armed and ready.

Ekoor troubled over the schematic Damar had drawn of the Headquarters' interior.

"According to this map," he said, "it's a long way from the cargo door to the briefing room."

"That could be a problem," Kira agreed. "The explosion's going to alert everyone in the building."

"If I know Weyoun," Damar told them, "there'll only be a handful of Jem'Hadar on duty. He'll have sent the rest to hunt down Cardassians—"

The rest of his sentence was stripped away in the sound of an explosion, a resonant boom that came down through the walls. The floor trembled.

Kira tensed. "What the hell—?"

Garak rushed down the stairs and nearly fell. "The Jem'Hadar! They're leveling the city, building by building!"

"We have to go," Kira said, "right now!"

Damar stayed any action with a temperate hand. "Once we get inside Dominion Headquarters, we stop for nothing and no one until we capture the Changeling. For Cardassia!"

"For Cardassia!"

Kira Nerys watched as all the Cardassians dodged from the cellar, fired by the opportunity to take back their planetary pride, led by the rogue officer who had become a legend.

Damar? A legend? How things could change.

She waited until they were all out of the room. She wanted to make sure nothing had been forgotten which they could use. They wouldn't be coming back to this place.

As she put her foot on the bottom step, she cast one gaze to the least likely and most disturbing corner, the place where Mila's body had been tucked, wrapped in a tarp.

There, she paused. In the shadow, Garak stood mute over Mila's clumpy form.

Kira thought he'd gone up with the others. When Mila had been killed, Garak had shown only one moment of horror before returning to his typical self, casting off trouble like shedding rain from his shoulders. Now Kira could see the lie. And the truth.

"Garak?" she began gently.

"I'm coming, Commander," he said, as if expecting her to speak up. "I'm just saying goodbye."

Though she tried to leave, assuming he would want to be alone, Kira responded instead to an inner alarm that told her he needed something other than solitude. They'd known each other a very long time, had never really been friends, but had fought side by side long enough to have a certain bond of understanding that she felt very powerfully now. Here was Garak, as blithe and lubricated a salesman-spy as the universe could boast, this time with all his masks down. Kira understood that right now she was seeing the real Garak, a man displaced for years from the home he had once served honestly and with great energy. Today he was home again, and about to be again thrown out.

"During all these years of exile," he began without looking at her, "I used to imagine what it would be like to come home, maybe even to live in this house once again with Mila. But now . . . she'd dead. And this house is about to become nothing more than a pile of rubble. My Cardassia is gone."

Kira offered a sympathetic pause. "Then fight for a new Cardassia."

Another explosion rumbled closer than the one before. The walls rattled. Pebbles and dust fell upon the tarp covering the old Cardassian woman.

Garak watched the dust settle into the tarp' folds.

"I have a better reason to fight, Commander," he said. "Revenge."

"But Thot Pran, I have come to depend on having you here at my side. Your sage military advice has proven invaluable to me and to the Dominion."

The Founder struggled to hold her form, despite the cracking of her skin like old paint and the intense pain it caused throughout her body. Everyone around her saw the terrible plague eating her humanoid form on the outside. What they could not see was that all her form, inside as well, was made now of sharp-edged flakes, flintlike chips each cutting into the other moment by moment.

The staticky voice of the Breen general had grown shrill as he protested all her arguments. He was growing tired of her. Or perhaps he was coming to suspect that she was keeping him here in order to hold influence over him or eventually to hold him hostage. . . .

No matter. He was only a small cog in the wheels of her plan. If she could no longer deceive him, it was little loss.

"Very well," she accepted. "If you feel that the seriousness of the situation demands your presence on the front lines, I will not stand in your way. In fact, knowing that you will be leading our troops into battle is very reassuring."

He blathered another burst at her, then bowed and swung for the door, leading his Breen officers with him.

Near the monitor, Weyoun had been watching in silence. Now he spoke.

"I still can't help but wonder."

The Founder turned to him. "Wonder what?"

"What's under that helmet."

She moved in agony to the monitor. "A braver man than you. Though I do find the shrillness of his voice tiresome."

Feeling a wave of ghastly weakness roll through her limbs, she turned away from him. Holding this shape was almost as agonizing as knowing she could no longer dissolve from it. Somehow this illness trapped her between nightmare and torture. She could not alter, yet holding solidity took constant effort. What would she become if she gave up? If her form took its own route?

She tried to walk away, to go to her desk, when her legs folded beneath her and gravity came to pull her down. Would she puddle on the floor, a mass of crackled liquid? Would she crash into a million bits like shattering glass?

Weyoun's grip wrapped around her and held her on her feet.

"Founder! What's wrong?"

What an idiot.

"I'm dying, that's what's wrong," she told him, disinclined to spare whatever he had for feelings.

"Perhaps if you were to rest for a while . . . revert to your natural state—"

"I only wish I could. But I haven't be able to change form in weeks. Ironic . . . isn't it? That I might die as a solid. . . ."

"You're not going to die," Weyoun desperately insisted. "You're a god!"

"Gods are not always immortal," she said. Was she speaking to a child in fact? Very well. "You must see to it that the Dominion does not die with me. Promise me that."

As he shifted position, his pale face and colorless eyes took on a genuine fear. "But Founder, what can I, a mere Vorta. . . ."

Her hand, as if disembodied and possessing a will of its own, raced to his throat. The full power of her own will now took over, squeezing the life out of him that the Founders in their wisdom had given him in the first place.

"Promise me!" she growled.

Fighting for breath, Weyoun attempted a terrified nod. "I promise . . . gladly."

Even she was unsure what she was asking of him, how he would protect the Dominion without her in this quadrant to guide him. The Vorta needed guides.

"My loyal Weyoun," she went on, "the only solid I've ever trusted."

Overwhelmed, Weyoun managed to bow even in this awkward position. "I live only to serve you."

"And you've served me well. I don't mind dying . . . what's painful is knowing that my entire race is dying of the same illness and there's nothing I can do about it."

"I would give my life to save yours," Weyoun said with great emotional trouble.

"I only wish it were that easy."

Her hand—she must unclamp it. This took a great effort, though she finally gave him back his existence.

"Your loyalty is comforting," she said. She pulled out of his grip. Somehow her strength had been renewed for now, through the desperation of her concern for her fellow Changelings.

Weyoun let her go without further attendance. He rubbed his throat. He seemed surprised.

Was he also honored? She thought he should be.

She thought he'd better be.

The cap of the Kai spun into the abyss, taking with it all the symbolic devotion of a lifetime's meditation and trial.

Dukat watched the little cap whirl away into the fire and be consumed. How completely wondrous—a full Kai, shedding the shackles of the Prophets, casting her lot with the antiprophet Pah-wraiths, joining with Dukat in his cause to finally come out from under the pall of some alien power. At least this power was native to Bajor, native to the Alpha Quadrant. A much better platform from which to launch any plan, he believed.

Nearby, Kai Winn crossed the final path to the rejection of everything she had previously embraced. Solemnly, she removed her ceremonial cloak and pitched it over the edge of the abyss into the charged flames. With a gasp of consumption, the robe disappeared.

Now she stood only in a simple penitent's smock. Even the pin in her hair was plucked away. Her hair fell about her shoulders. She looked suddenly free, even younger.

"Finally," she breathed, "I rid myself of the Prophets! Once and for all! And shed a lifetime of hypocrisy!"

With the flames blazing behind her, she turned to Dukat and in a shock of boldness clasped him passionately and drove him into a long exuberate kiss.

Stunned and invigorated, Dukat gazed at her. "I've never seen you so radiant."

"I feel like a young woman!" she crowed. "Waiting for my lover to come and sweep me off my feet!"

"Do you give yourself willingly to the Pah-wraiths?" he asked, just to make sure she wasn't consumed by something that might distract her from their reason to be here.

"With all my heart!"

"Then . . . call to them."

Winn, no longer a Kai, broke the embrace. "Bring me the book!"

A shiver of hesitation ran through Dukat. To touch the book? The thing that had last blinded him when he dared invade its private and sacred envelope?

"I said bring it!" Winn insisted.

This last step had to be taken. Dukat realized that if Winn were to give up all her securities, he would have to show a willingness to do the same. Surely the Pah-wraiths would smile on him and not allow the book to hurt him a second time, to defy their healing powers.

He bent before the book, muttered an inaudible apology just in case. So many unexplained powers in the universe—who was he to suggest any might be silly? If the book itself had no particular power, surely something attached to it did and the book was the wand which channeled it, for he had felt the power himself.

He picked up the enormous bindings. He offered it to Winn with a hint of minor ceremony.

She opened the book, as Dukat cradled it against his chest. Standing at the brink of the flaming abyss, Winn began to chant again, slowly at first, then more rapidly.

MEEK RAK DORRAH PAH-WRAN
YELIM CHA ONO KOSST AMOJAN . . .
SHAY TA-HEL TER-RAH NO'VALA DE
RAM
AKA'LU FAR CHE . . .

And the flames grew higher and hotter. And the light grew bright with joy.

"Sisko to Bashir. Report."

It had taken him a few minutes to ask for this one. He didn't mind getting reports from O'Brien about the engineering status or from Ezri about hull damage or from Worf about the tactical situation, but asking Bashir to break off from tending the wounded belowdecks just to report on how many crewmates they'd lost—that was a hard one and it always would be, Emissary or not.

Sisko felt eminently human as Bashir's voice came up through the comm.

"Three dead, eight wounded, four of them critically." The doctor sounded strained in part, and somehow relieved in another.

That made sense. For a major battle, they'd been lucky.

"I need every able-bodied crewman at his post," Sisko challenged.

"I won't keep anyone here a second longer than I have to," Bashir promised.

Hopeful, at least. No one was trying to talk him out of pursuing the retreating Dominion forces and putting an end to this once and for all. Even Ross hadn't contacted him. The decision had been—thankfully—made.

Now they had to live with it.

"She did pretty well for a first date, don't you think, Captain?" Nog asked as he nursed his helm.

"I do, Ensign," Sisko offered.

He didn't stay near the helm, but instead moved to Worf and Ezri.

"Our phaser banks have been fully recharged," Worf said, with a measure of satisfaction that proved Sisko's assessment that they'd been lucky. "But we're down to only forty-five quantum torpedoes."

"That'll have to do," Sisko said. To Ezri he offered, "How're you holding up, old man?"

"All things considered, I'd rather be on Risa," she said with a little smile.

"That makes two of us."

He returned her smile, wondering how much comfort old Curzon Dax's life force could offer a young girl who had never been in a battle situation.

So far, so good. And that's what worried him.

He crossed past the repair crews and tried not to get their attention with his presence. On the other side of the bridge Odo was gazing uneasily into a monitor. Sisko didn't ask—the shapeshifter would speak up if there were anything to say.

For a moment Odo remained silent, but then voiced a genuine concern. "Have you seen the reports from Cardassia? The Dominion has begun destroying Cardassian cities . . . millions of people are dying. They're being dragged out of their homes and executed."

"Are the Cardassians fighting back?"

"They're trying to. But what chance to do civilians have against the Jem'Hadar?"

"I wouldn't count them out just yet, Constable," Sisko offered, "not with Kira down there."

Odo smiled reservedly, apparently taking the compliment as it was meant, trying to find some comfort in it that Kira was indeed still alive, that there might be a future for them yet somehow, somewhere. The bird and the fish might find a place where both could live, if only this single great struggle could be won.

"Captain," Nog interrupted. "We're approaching the Cardassian defense perimeter."

"Let's see what they have waiting for us." Sisko stepped down to the command area. "Onscreen."

The ship's company bolted to action, squaring away

the wreckage on the deck, clearing the walkways, taking positions. If anything wasn't repaired by now, time was up. They'd have to make do with whatever they had working. Positions of the dead and wounded would have to be covered. That was up to each individual department head and not Sisko's problem any more. He drove that concern from his mind as others came to clutter it.

Just then O'Brien stepped back onto the bridge, reading a padd as he approached the command area to make a report.

"I've cross-polarized the phaser emitters, which should give us a—"

Sisko didn't respond. No one did. O'Brien stopped talking as he looked up.

Together they all stared at the image on the forward screen.

Before them, a virtually impenetrable wall of Breen and Jem'Hadar fighting ships, defense installations, and weapons platforms orbited Cardassia Prime, a bristling net of destructive power, formidable and terrifying. Knitted like barbed wire, all enemy forces had taken an organized position—nothing seemed random at all this time. This wasn't just a formation. It was a nearly solid wall of killing energy waiting to be released.

On the main fleet channel, a broadcast came through which Ezri did not bother to announce.

"This is Admiral Ross to all ships. We all know what we have to do. All forces form up for Operation Final Assault."

Sisko turned to his crew, putting the horror on the forward screen behind him as he met all their eyes.

"You heard the man. Let's do it."

This was what the last two years of war had been building up to, what inevitably came if neither side of a conflict fell soon enough. This would be the one decisive upheaval, sink or swim, and neither side was thinking about tomorrow. There would be no holding back any more. Tomorrow, there would be nothing left with which to try again. The decision would be made today—here—and right now.

The *Defiant* led the way, as the strongest tight-maneuver vessel left in the Federation fleet. At their sides, Klingon and Romulan fighter wings pressed forward boldly. Backing them up were the remaining starships, support tenders, and any other vessel that could still hit and take some. The Allied Fleet was depleted by a third.

That figure did not change Sisko's now-or-never commitment or dull his determination.

"Hold your fire until proximity distance," he ordered. "We won't get any second chances."

"All systems ready, sir," O'Brien reported.

Sisko understood what that meant. All systems were up to their top ability for the moment, even if that only meant thirty percent. He had to be ready to lose things much earlier than in the first-wave assault.

That meant adjusting his thinking process and his orders to compensate and improvise.

On the planet below, countless thousands of civilians were absorbing the brutality of the Vorta and Jem'Hadar extermination teams. An act of desperation on the part of the Dominion, yes, but there was also the taste of bitter vengeance in such wholesale slaughter. On the planet, a horror was playing out.

In space, the second horror now erupted.

The enemy ships did not come out to meet them, but forced the Allied Fleet to spread itself thin and circle as much of the planet as possible—and it was a very big planet indeed. Even seven hundred ships couldn't cover so much area effectively, and within moments the sheer firepower of engaged vessels lit up space as if the Cardassian homeworld had become a nova suddenly torched in the night.

Defiant roared in slashing. Nothing was held back. No one was in the mood for restraint. The bridge exploded into an unrecognizable wreck and no one cared. Sisko barked orders and authorizations, letting them free from anything that might make them hold back. The everbalanced triangle of life, risk, and cause, generally rocking on its tip, finally turned and slammed down upon its base. Die if we must, but make it cost. Our lives for something bigger, much better, and everlasting—possession of our own quadrant for everyone who comes after us. That is the code of the military branch of any civilization, and today it was the banner of the *Defiant*.

Shrapnel spun across the bridge from port to starboard as a Breen hacker got its teeth into them on a blunt pass. Sisko took a dozen slivers in the arm, brushed them off in a patch of blood, and dodged from position to position, doing things faster than he could order them done. There weren't enough people left standing on the bridge to follow his orders anyway. All he needed was himself, Nog at the helm, Ezri, Worf, and O'Brien. The rest would have to be let go.

Every time a Breen or Jem'Hadar vessel veered into range, Sisko snapped, "Fire!" He didn't even wait for the targeting computers. Worf gave up trying to aim by sensor and simply blanketed wedges of phaser fire into space, hitting something almost every time, even if once or twice they grazed another Starfleet ship or an ally. They were getting their share of friendly fire—that was unavoidable. It seemed that everyone accepted the chance of getting killed by a neighbor. With phaser and disruptor fire crisscrossing intervening space, there was no way to avoid getting struck by somebody's something.

There was no sense or order, no coordination to the attack. In fact, that was an advantage. With all the wild-hearted Starfleet, Klingon, and Romulan captains bringing to bear their decidedly individual talents and experiences against the programmed uniformity of the Jem'Hadar and Breen, the Allied forces were almost impossible to predict and willing to be crazy.

"Worf, portside! Open fire! Ezri, compensate for the lateral shift! O'Brien, don't move!"

He kept the orders running for each consecutive surge, keeping off the bow of this enemy ship, hugging the tail of that one, shooting, dodging, twisting, ducking. His arms and shoulders quivered with energy as his body charged to the task. He felt none of the wounds he knew had been inflicted upon him. Not a bruise ached, not a scratch burned. They were there, but he couldn't feel them. That made him feel immortal, invincible. The fact that he could force by sheer will the acrid chemical smoke through his lungs as it poured from the ship's damaged bridge conduits made him even more powerful.

"Captain!"

"Coming, Odo."

Sisko made his way to the other side of the bridge, where Odo hovered over a flickering monitor.

"I may have found something interesting," the constable said. "So far, Mr. Worf has managed to score direct hits on eleven Breen ships, but only three of those suffered significant damage."

At tactical, Worf shot them an insulted glower. "It's difficult to penetrate their shields. They appear to use stochastic field emitters."

Odo peered past Sisko's shoulder to the Klingon. "I'm not questioning your abilities, Commander."

"What are you getting at, Constable?" Sisko prodded.

"All three ships that suffered damage were struck in the aft impulse manifold."

Halleluja. . . .

Sisko peered into the screen, making sure there hadn't been some missed detail that could explain better. There wasn't.

"Constable, you may have found a chink in their armor. Helm, find us a Breen ship. Mr. Worf, target—"

"I'll target their aft impulse manifold." Worf seemed both insulted and victorious. Not a bad combination for a Klingon.

Defiant veered hard over and whined in pursuit of the nearest Breen, locking onto its prey in seconds.

"Pull in tight, Ensign," Sisko directed. "Three more degrees port . . . that's better . . . z-minus two . . . fire!"

The weapons howled. Streaks of energy lanced through the Cardassian ionosphere like slicing the top off a cake, and drilled the back of the Breen ship. A few seconds—and *FFFFWOOSH*—obliterated.

Odo looked at Sisko, who looked at Worf, who was already looking at Ezri, who didn't have a clue what all this meant.

Well, maybe she had a clue, but she hadn't quite distilled it out of her memories yet.

"Dax," Sisko began, "send a priority-one message to all ships. Let 'em know what we found!"

Now she got it.

CHAPTER

8

There it was—the cargo door. Dominion Headquarters' rare weak spot.

"No guards," Kira observed. Damar, she hated to admit, had called this one pretty well. "Our own private little Achilles' hell."

"Heel," Garak corrected.

"No, I think I got it right the first time."

Ekoor squatted near her. "Where are the guards?"

"Like the commander said," Garak explained, "they're probably off killing Cardassians."

"Then this may be easier than we thought," Damar said from the other end of the assault team.

"I wouldn't count on that," Kira warned.

"We have a problem," Garak pointed out.

"Only one?"

"But I'm afraid it's a rather large one. That door is made of neutronium."

Kira felt her shoulders sag. "Then the explosives we brought aren't going to make a dent in it."

Garak's wide eyes rolled. "Now you see the problem."

"What do we do?" Ekoor asked.

"I don't know," Damar said, "but I'm done hiding in basements."

Garak rewarded him with a laugh.

"I fail to see what's so funny, Garak," Damar shot back.

"Isn't it obvious? Here we are, willing to storm the castle and sacrifice our lives in a noble effort to slay the Dominion beast in its lair . . . and we can't even get inside the gate!"

"We could knock on the front door," Kira suggested, "and ask the Jem'Hadar to let us in—"

"Or send the female shapeshifter out to us," Damar grumbled.

"Whichever's more convenient."

They looked at each other, and spontaneously laughed. It *was* kind of funny, right in the middle of this big ugliness.

"Well," Garak reminded, "we do have to think of something. . . ."

Kira nodded, but knew she couldn't honestly blame Damar for the murderous gleam in his eyes. She'd spent all her childhood sneaking around, hiding, lurking, becoming an expert at strike-and-fly assault missions, guerrilla tactics, and resistance thinking—and she was the first to admit that a person could become absolutely excellent at it, but could never learn to love it. Damar had spent his life as a Cardassian military officer. This running and hiding was new to him and somehow degrading.

"We can't stay here much longer," she told them. Now that they knew their explosives wouldn't scratch this door, they had to come up with another plan.

"What if I were to give myself up as a prisoner?" Damar offered.

"They'd kill you on sight," Kira canceled.

"And us along with you," Garak concurred.

She started to turn away, to find a route away from the Headquarters, or another less daunting portcullis to break through, when the cargo door abruptly slid open with a terrific screech. She ducked back into the shadows beside Garak. Damar and the others pressed into an opposite hiding place.

Together they watched as three Cardassian soldiers emerged from the Headquarters. In handcuffs!

"I know those Cardassians," Damar whispered. "They're part of Weyoun's security force!"

What a strange sight—Jem'Hadar pushing Cardassians in irons!

Kira pressed closer to the wall and squinted. Yes, here came two Jem'Hadar, pushing the Cardassians out at gunpoint. Their rifles had bayonets fixed. Why?

The question answered itself after the Cardassians made a few steps into the alley. The Jem'Hadar offered no pause for thought or confession, nor did they even allow their prisoners to turn and face death head-on. They simply moved forward and drove their bayonets into two of the Cardassians, then shared the third, spearing the helpless natives through the spines.

Damar leaped to his feet, enraged. "No!"

"Damar!" Kira tried to grab for him, but he was gone, rushing into the alley, blanketing the Jem'Hadar with wildfire. The two Jem'Hadar went down hard.

Damar rushed past them and stormed the open cargo door. But the door was starting to close! And their presence here had been compromised.

"Charge!" Kira shouted, and raced after him.

Garak, Ekoor, and the other Cardassian conspirators vaulted from their hideout and clambered after her. Nothing left to hide. She was relieved to hear their bootsteps hammering behind her, that they hadn't had a change of heart at the sight of the coldhearted slaughter exacted on their own people by the Jem'Hadar.

Kira and Garak, leading the group behind Damar, opened fire, blowing aside the shocked Jem'Hadar who appeared here and there in their path. The Jem'Hadar were built for space and clumsy on land, a factor which very swiftly washed in the resistance's favor.

They broke inside the cargo door, into a brightly lit loading dock, with Damar boldly leading the way. He was driven to blind fury, and this was enheartening for all who followed him. They *would* get in! They *would* turn the tables here somehow!

They would blast their way past the half dozen Jem'Hadars who appeared in front of them!

"Hah!" Damar shouted insanely, and opened fire.

The Jem'Hadar were instantly attracted by his shout and opened fire themselves, all aiming at the single target who had drawn their shots. In an amazing flurry, Damar took combined bolts to the chest. Driven backward, he slammed into a wall, his face plastered with shock and rage.

The resistance fighters spread behind boxes of cargo, clearly stunned. Kira covered Garak as he bent at Damar's side, his face crumpled and fearful.

"He's dead," Garak murmured.

She barely heard him. The news showed clearly in his astonished face.

Something happened to her—she recognized it. All Damar's rage, insult, devotion, and pride transferred itself, like a soul changing bodies. He'd gotten them inside and now it was up to her. She was suddenly charged with the drive to take back Cardassia as if it were her own. How was that for a story to tell!

She spun on the hiding resistance fighters. "Get up! Remember Damar's orders! We stop for no one!"

Shuddering with emotion, Garak rose to his feet, daring the fire from the Jem'Hadar, and turned to his fellow Cardassians.

"For Cardassia!"

Ekoor burst from hiding. "For Cardassia!"

Following the supercharged Ekoor, Kira and the others easily outmaneuvered the Jem'Hadar guards—and Damar had been right, there weren't as many as there should have been—freely blowing them to piles of flesh and plastic tubing all the way through the Headquarters.

None of this building was familiar, and Kira found it disconcerting to race through unfamiliar corridors with such directioned purpose—evidently Ekoor did know his way, for he led them at full tilt without so much as a pause at a corner or a hesitation to remember the right way.

Alarms began to ring. *Security alert.* They were aware of the breach now. She knew the sound of that. So much for subtlety.

She kept firing, trying not to hit Ekoor, who continued to roar through the corridors, blind with fury. He was firing wildly, hitting every Jem'Hadar he spied. At that imprudent rate his weapon would be drained any second now and he'd be helpless.

"Get the explosives, Garak! Ekoor!" she called. "Come forward here, get ready—"

"We're ready," Garak called. In both hands he held not his weapon, which he had handed to Ekoor, but the grenades.

"This door!" Ekoor shouted. "This one! Hurry!"

Ekoor fired foolishly at the door, causing a dangerous backwash of energy from the shielded panel.

"Stop!" Kira shouted. "Garak, the grenades!"

"Coming!"

"Take cover!"

They spread out. Two seconds, and a concussion blast nearly took their heads off.

Kira shook away the blur and dove through the smoking wreckage where a moment ago there had been a door. She opened fire even before she had a target, and felt the hot buzz of shots whizzing by her. In a cloud she saw one Jem'Hadar fall. Another, though, got his weapon up and fired, killing one of Ekoor's Cardassian recruits. Following the trajectory she thought she'd seen,

Kira fired again. The second Jem'Hadar crashed to the floor.

She plowed into the briefing room and leveled her weapon joyously at the flaky face of the female shapeshifter who had so often compromised Odo. Ah!

"Contact the Jem'Hadar fleet!" Kira ordered. "Order it to cease fire!"

Garak stepped forward, again holding his weapon and aiming now at Weyoun's astonished glare. "And order the Jem'Hadar troops on Cardassia to lay down their arms immediately."

"He'll do no such thing," the female shapeshifter said. At her words, the Vorta dutifully regained control over his expression.

Kira moved to a position allowing her to cover both Weyoun and the shapeshifter in one shot. "Garak, check the monitors. What's going on in space?"

Garak was as comfortable with the Cardassian mechanics as he had become with the workings on Starfleet ships. Instantly he had the readouts displayed on three monitors.

"I'm not reading any Breen ships in close proximity to the planet," he said. "There's a trail of Breen exhaust leading out of the solar system. Looks like the Allies have them in retreat."

"Cowards," the female shapeshifter commented bitterly. "First the Cardassians, now the Breen. This proves what I've said all along—solids are not to be trusted."

"The Jem'Hadar haven't abandoned us," Weyoun claimed. "They'll fight to the death."

"There aren't enough of them on the planet," Kira told him. "We're here, aren't we?"

Weyoun glared coldly at her. "Tell me . . . where is my old friend Damar?"

"Damar's dead," Garak announced before Kira could stop him from speaking up and tipping any hand they had in their favor.

"A pity," Weyoun said.

Garak's bitterness got the better of him. "He died helping to free Cardassia."

The Vorta tilted his head. "What's left of it."

Garak's anger boiled over. He raised his weapon to Weyoun and fired at point-blank range. This time Kira had no inclination to stop him at all.

As her loyal follower collapsed to the floor, the shapeshifter regarded him unemotionally. "I wish you hadn't done that. That was Weyoun's last clone."

Garak sneered, "I was hoping you'd say that."

Kira stepped forward. "The war's over. You've lost."

"Have I?" the shapeshifter challenged. "I think you'll find the Jem'Hadar don't agree with that assessment. They'll continue to fight to the last man."

"What will that accomplish?"

"Isn't it obvious? To make sure your 'victory' costs you as many ships and as many lives as possible. When the next Dominion fleet comes through the wormhole, there'll be no one—not the Federation, not the Klingons, not the Romulans—who'll be strong enough to stop us."

Kira pressed down a shudder at the prospect. "That's an empty threat."

Clearly weakened by her sickness, the shapeshifter

sank into her chair. She seemed too tired to argue. She leaned back in her chair, her demolished face strangely content.

"Is it? . . . We'll see," she uttered. "In the mean time, more of your ships will be destroyed, and your casualty lists will continue to grow. By the time it's over, you will have lost so many ships, so many lives . . . that your victory will taste as bitter as defeat."

"We'll launch a three-pronged attack," Admiral Ross explained. "The Romulans and our new Cardassian allies will engage the Jem'Hadar forces. The Klingons will target the Breen, and the Federation will take on the orbital weapons platforms. Any questions?"

Only one question slapped back and forth in Ben Sisko's mind, like tide knocking on rocks. "When do we go?"

"As soon as everyone's in position."

"It will be a glorious battle," Martok claimed on his half of the split screen.

"But a costly one," Ross said unhappily. "Estimates project our casualty figures could be as high as forty percent. And God knows how much higher they'll go once we send in our ground forces."

Fearful that Ross might be talking himself out of this offensive, Sisko quickly said, "The Dominion's beaten and they know it. But they're going to make us pay for every kilometer of that planet."

He hoped his tone communicated that he was willing to pay, and to take out of the enemy forces every pound of flesh they exacted from his own side.

"Yes, they will," Ross said, then did not make any further complaints or voice any doubts. "Godspeed," he added.

Chancellor Martok wrapped up their session in what might be the last word they would ever hear from each other.

"*Qa'pla!*"

In the flaming cavern, waiting for their great reward, Dukat and Winn joyously poured wine from a flask into a ceremonial goblet. Dukat watched the dark liquid flow and thought of Federation blood.

"What is it?" he asked, still holding the Kosst Amojan.

"This?" Winn raised the goblet. "This is the most important part of the ceremony."

She held the goblet high above her and chanted . . .

*TARNA PU-ONO ULL-KESS PAH-RAN
LANO KA'LA BO'SHAR LANU. . . .*

She lowered the goblet, preparing to drink, and as the warm brass touched her lips she stopped and turned instead to Dukat.

"After you," she offered, beaming at him.

Gently Dukat set the book down, quite frankly glad to be rid of it, and bowed before her. "I'm honored."

The wine was sweet and warm, with an exotic pungence that coiled its way down his throat and seemed to effervesce. He had never tasted anything like it and suspected it had been part of the Kai's private cellar for many years. Certainly this was a special enough occasion . . .

"Now you," he offered.

Winn smiled, took the goblet, and smelled the wine indulgently.

Rather than drink it, though, she leered at him and poured the remaining liquid to the bubbling cavern wall. It sizzled in the heat from the flaming abyss.

Dukat stepped back from her. Why would she refuse to share the sacrament?

Raw pain bolted through his intestines. The wine burned its way deeper and deeper into his body. He choked, nearly heaved, but nothing came up. Reaching for Winn, seeking support, Dukat slipped forward and fell to his knees. Shock gripped his throat. He could no longer stand!

Winn backed away from him, refusing him any support. Why did she look like that? What was that glow in her eyes?

"Why—" he gagged.

Winn outstretched her arms, but not to him.

"Because," she began, speaking loudly, "the Pah-wraiths demand a sacrifice! Someone worthy of them . . . devious and cruel . . . twisted and corrupt . . . whose soul lusts only for power and vengeance!

"Who better . . . than *you!*"

She smiled.

As Dukat's insides began to wither, he stared in horror at her joy and fulfillment, the pure love and unmatched hatred jousting in her face.

"That's why you were sent to me," she told him, "so

that darkness could feed on darkness, hate on hate! Your death will be the key that brings forth the Restoration of the Pah-wraiths!"

The hot ground came up and embraced him. He tumbled onto his back. Towering over him, Winn's form seemed enormous, elongated, stretching higher and higher into the vaulted flames which lit her wide face. He reached for her. The fires rose higher. His hands burned, withered to black, blew to cinders. As a searing curtain closed slowly around his vision, Dukat saw through his paralysis the last moments of sacrifice, and heard the last words of the depraved life he had so abused.

"I offer you this life for your nourishment! This martyr to feed your hunger! May it fuel the fires that will set you free! Kosst Amojan! I am yours! Now and forever! Now and forever! Now and forever . . . now and forever . . . forever. . . ."

CHAPTER
9

Odo held his silence with great difficulty, as he watched Kira Nerys make her report on the viewscreen to Captain Sisko. What torture it was to keep his emotions in check! She was alive, she was alive . . . the bird and the fish—was there a place for them to live together?

"I'm very glad to find you in one piece, Commander," Sisko was saying to her.

"Very glad," Odo murmured.

He hadn't thought he'd spoken very loudly, but Kira looked at him and seemed relieved to see him clean of the Changeling disease. Her kind smile emboldened him, and he smiled back.

The ship rocked from another hit—yes, they were still in the middle of the battle, but somehow it seemed less consequential now that he knew Kira was alive and in charge of Dominion Headquarters.

"What's your status?" Sisko asked.

Kira shrugged meagerly. "Only three of us made it to the briefing room."

"What about Damar?" Odo asked.

"He's dead."

Sensing the subject changing, Sisko changed it back. "Is your position secure?"

"I don't think the Jem'Hadar will attack. They won't risk endangering the Founder. She's in pretty bad shape . . . she won't speak to anyone . . . just sits at her desk, deteriorating."

At tactical, Worf spoke for the first time. "If she dies before ordering the Jem'Hadar to surrender—"

"They'll fight to the last man," Sisko finished.

"There's another problem," Kira offered. "When the Jem'Hadar realize what's happened, they'll storm the building. They'll try to rescue their 'god.' "

"We'll beam you out of there."

At the engineering console, O'Brien turned from where Bashir was still cauterizing his shoulder wound. "I'm not sure that's a good idea, sir. I've locked onto their biosignatures, and according to these readings the Changeling won't survive the trip."

"I agree," the doctor said, looking at O'Brien's monitor. "Her morphogenic matrix is too unstable."

Odo stepped to the captain's side. "Sir—Captain, I'd like to beam down as well."

Sisko watched the screen. "I understand you want to help Kira, but—"

"It's not that." Not *all* that. "I want to talk to the Founder. I might be able to reason with her."

"You haven't had much success reasoning with her in the past," the captain rightly reminded him, courteously holding back the fact that, actually, Odo's attempts had turned out to be downright disasters.

"I'd still like to try." He refrained from pointing out that things had changed—that the female was dying, which would alter anybody's outlook, and that he had things in mind which Sisko would not find particularly comforting.

The ship shook again, saving him from having to explain.

Instead he quickly added, "Think of the lives it might save."

"Point taken," Sisko said. "Good luck, Constable."

Sisko shrugged, not about to be put off at this late hour. "Commander, tell the Founder that Odo would like to pay her a visit."

"The more, the merrier," Kira accepted.

The ship rolled again, then pitched forward. Another hit. The Jem'Hadar weren't giving up. In dismay Odo watched as the comm screen cut off the view of Kira and went again to the view of space, showing relentless Jem'Hadar ships sweeping around them at all angles.

Sisko turned to Ezri. "Contact Admiral Ross and tell him we need to secure that facility."

"I'm on it," she responded.

Odo hurried to the transporter room, collecting six Starfleet security guards on his way through the ship— and given the casualties and the action still going on, it wasn't easy to get the department heads to give up manpower. Six guards with phaser rifles would be sufficient to guard the facility until more could be available.

"We'll have to beam down in two waves, sir," Ensign Bremerton told him as they crowded into the *Defiant*'s little transporter room. "Systems are damaged and we don't want an overload."

"Very well," Odo accepted, and started for the pad.

"Sir—" The ensign stopped him by stepping up there first, having the common sense not to actually touch him. "With your permission, sir, I think three guards should go down first, and secure the situation before you have to go down."

Odo surveyed the young man's bruised face. "Ensign, I have been for many years the senior security officer on board a fully armed deep-space outpost. Are you telling me I can't handle the first wave of a landing party?"

The young man came suddenly to attention. "No, sir! It's just that . . . we just all thought you might . . . want somebody else to have a look around down there first."

So. His situation had not been a secret among his security teams. He had underestimated the intimacy of life at *Deep Space Nine*.

His instinct to lash out and claim his prowess and self-control subsided as he studied the young security man's expression and the deep sympathy he saw there. In it was reflected their loyalty to him, their sorrow that they couldn't protect him perhaps as he had always tried to protect them by indeed going first into every situation.

"Ensign," he began, "yes, thank you . . . but whatever is down there, I cannot shy from it. I will lead the first wave. You follow me, and beam directly to the outer perimeter of the building. Signal us when you believe the entrances are secured."

Bremerton nodded sadly. "Aye, aye, sir. Whatever you say."

Odo led two other beefy guards into the transporter and steeled himself for the nauseating process of beaming. Unlike with solids, the transporter usually seemed a bit fitful and confused at trying to rearrange the molecules of a Changeling, and he always had to fight to hold form just as he was being reconstituted.

Using the coordinates supplied by Kira, he was able to beam directly into the corridor outside the briefing room.

Kira was there waiting for him, and charged into his arms with a passion that drove him wild with joy and sorrow. He clutched her slim form against his and wished she had more meat on her bones so there would be more to hold. The fear of her death came to its full flowering and broke to the wind. He hadn't let himself think she might be gone until finally he saw that she wasn't. The sensation of victory nearly overwhelmed him.

When his head stopped swimming, he noticed that the two guards had dutifully taken positions outside the briefing room door.

Kira drew back from a heart-drowning kiss and gazed at Odo happily.

"Nerys," he murmured.

"It's been a while," she said, not quite joking. She lowered her voice. "Watch yourself . . . I don't trust her."

He looked down at her. "But you trust me, don't you?"

"Of course!"

"That's all I need to know." Odo peered down at her, cupping her knobby shoulders in his hands.

Yes, he was sure. All his decisions had been made. He had weighed all the consequences both larger and smaller than himself, and he knew what he wanted.

In the briefing room, Garak stood with another Starfleet guard. "Constable," he greeted tightly.

Odo nodded. "Garak."

And there, in the chair, was the female of his own kind with whom he had shared so many dreamlike moments.

She looked up to see him. Her face was a demolished mask of illness and dessication. He pitied her deeply. She must be in indescribable pain, yet there was serenity in her eyes. Whatever her fate, she was taking it courageously.

"You're looking well, Odo," she said. Her voice was tight.

"Thank you for seeing me," he said sincerely.

"It's always good to see you. But don't think even you can change my mind. I have no intention of surrendering my forces. If I did, it would be a sign of weakness . . . an invitation for the solids to cross into the Gamma Quadrant and destroy the Great Link."

So that was at the bottom of her stubbornness—expecting others to act with the same ruthlessness she and their kind had shown.

"Believe me," he told her, "I'm well aware that the Federation has its flaws, but a desire for conquest isn't one of them."

She offered him the smallest of shrugs. "And what of the Klingon and Romulan Empires? Can you make the same claim for them?"

He glanced at Kira. "The Klingon and Romulan Empires are in no shape to wage a war against anyone. Besides . . . the Federation wouldn't allow it."

The female shuddered momentarily, then regained control. "The Dominion has spent the past two years trying to destroy the Federation . . . and now you're asking me to put our fate in their hands?"

"Yes."

A very simple answer . . . the one word communicated all his faith in the civilization in which he had lived for so many more years than the last two.

She paused, reading his eyes, but in the end she rejected what he said.

"I can't do that, Odo. I don't share your faith in solids."

For that, too, he was ready.

With one final glance at Kira, at the bird who should be free to fly, Odo reached for the female of his own kind.

"Perhaps I can change your mind. Link with me."

CHAPTER
10

"Odo, what are you doing!"

Though Kira's protest certainly did have its effect upon him, Odo had not a thought of changing his mind. He knew she didn't understand yet what was motivating him to dare the heretofore tricky and threatening link with this dangerously enticing creature from his own world.

Until now he had been the child, always at risk, drawn by the intrigue of the adult who tempted him away from his safe street corner. This wonderful day, for the first time, things were very different.

Kira, who loved him and wanted to protect him, had no way of knowing that. She had no way of knowing the depths of his conviction this time. He could never hope to explain it to her in simple human words. There would have to be another kind of understanding between them.

Before this, in every Link he had attempted, he had always been thinking about himself, the mystery of his origins, the otherworldly nature of his abilities, and the differences between himself and the solid beings who had embraced him as one of their own. Exploring the vast clutter of fantasies allowed him when he discovered what he was—a Changeling, a shapeshifter, part of that great merged Link of millions of other souls that freely intertwined. The revelation had been shocking, and had filled him with questions.

Since he could remember he had been a single entity, alone in his unusual body, just like all the other people around him. All at once he had been told he wasn't alone, that he could blend, share, flow with a whole civilization, that instantly they would know him and he them. An extended family beyond anyone's idea of extended families, the shapeshifters were an entire race that could freely merge, separate into individuals, then merge again, giving a whole new meaning to the word "alien."

After a lifetime alone—individual, vulnerable—Odo now knew that he could merge with them and not lose his singular personality. He would keep his private self. They could never drive him to the blended ecstasy of artificial togetherness and make him forget who he was. Never again.

So he wasn't afraid or hesitant. This time he would merge on his own terms, and he would be the one in charge.

"I'm afraid I can't Link with you," his counterpart said. "This disease prevents me from changing my form."

He offered his hand. "If we Link, I think I can cure you."

Garak didn't step toward them, but did say, "That's a very bad idea, Constable."

Kira, on the other hand, did come closer. "I'm afraid I have to agree with Garak."

Odo glanced at Kira. "Nerys, I know what I'm doing."

And there isn't time to make you understand. People are dying.

"Take my hand," he said to the other Changeling.

"And if you do cure me? What will you ask in return?"

"All I ask is that you Link with me."

Garak brandished his weapon again. "I'm warning you, Odo—"

Imploringly, Odo looked at Kira. Would she have faith him, as he had asked?

Kira stepped back and motioned Garak back also. "Lower your weapon, Garak."

"I don't think so," he refused.

Moving sideways, Kira simply put her hand on his rifle and pushed it down. "I said put it down."

"Why?"

"Because I trust Odo."

Overwhelmed with affection and gratitude, Odo was warmed with confidence. He lifted his hand to the female Changeling. He was giving her no choice. She would accept this, but on his terms. They were for the first time on completely equal terms. No—better than that. He, for the first time, was superior in ability.

After a few seconds she summoned the strength to

raise her hand to his. With ease that surprised even Odo, he wished a blending and it happened. His hand liquefied and engulfed hers, assisting her in morphing the sickened flakes and the mottling of her diseased limb. Starfleet had the cure and had given it to Odo, and then quite wisely and bravely elected not to share it with the ugly culture of the beautiful Changelings.

Why?

Because they didn't deserve it. They were using their abilities to conquer and repress others, a decidedly less noble cause than their lofty super-ideal of themselves should have embraced. They could not be superior if they would not treat others with mercy and respect. Starfleet had been right. Odo was going to show her what the "lowly" Federation had that the Changelings had not been able to develop for themselves.

The disease crawled into his cells as his arm flexed and molded with hers, losing structural integrity and flooding each to the other. It tried to overwhelm him. It was strong and tenacious as any cancer, but this time science and determination had learned how to turn back its insidious tide.

Odo closed his eyes and concentrated on all his personal and professional victories, the pride he had in the people he knew were really *his* people—his shipmates, stationmates, and all of the Federation who had stood by him for his individual self while the Changelings merely tempted and crowed at him to lose that self, as if that were somehow better.

With the force of mental and physical will, he pushed the regeneration up his arm into the milky substance that was both their hands, and farther into her body. Gradually she learned to take over, to possess the wondrous cure that could beat the disease. He felt her strain and confusion, the momentary loss of control, but he helped her continue to find the trail of health and dismiss the disease.

When he opened his eyes, the female Changeling's face was no longer a cracked plaster of near-death. Once again it was smooth as mercury.

She looked wonderful. She looked peaceful.

The cure wasn't all he had given her. He had lifted the responsibility away from her and taken it upon himself. For the first time, he felt strong enough to bear it.

"Odo!"

Kira had apparently had enough. When she'd seen this before, it hadn't gone well.

"Move away, Odo," she ordered.

Both Kira and Garak now had their weapons raised and aimed at the female's face.

"That won't be necessary, Nerys," Odo told her. He looked at the female. "Will it?"

His hand returned to his own body and let the female go. She was cured—beautiful, passive.

With a nod of what might be regret—he couldn't tell any more—the female Changeling took one step toward Kira. "If you'll step aside, I'll order the Jem'Hadar to cease fire."

Kira hesitated and looked at Odo. He gave her a reassuring nod. For the first time in his relationship with the female of his kind, he was in control. He had given her a gift she did not deserve—her life. She would, for a change and from now on, do what *he* wanted.

Lowering her weapon doubtfully, Kira allowed the female to approach the monitor and begin working the console.

Garak and Kira clustered around Odo. He felt wonderful and superior, confident and proud at their expressions of respect and wonder.

"Very impressive, Constable," Garak offered.

Odo was looking now at Kira.

"Did you know the Link would cure her?" she asked him.

"I was hoping it would. Thank you for having faith in me," he said to both of them.

Garak flared at him. "Now that the Founder can shapeshift again, perhaps it would be wise to secure her in a containment field?"

"Don't worry, Garak. She won't try to escape. She's agreed to stand trial for war crimes."

Kira looked impressed—and doubtful. "Whatever you said to her in the Link must've been very persuasive."

Garak not only looked doubtful, but downright disbelieving. "I'm surprised she didn't insist on returning to the Gamma Quadrant so she could cure her own people."

"There's no need of that," Odo told them sadly.

"Why not?" Kira's eyes narrowed.

He offered her the kindest gaze he could manage. "Because I'm going in her place."

The blow was encompassing. She didn't seem to fully understand what he meant. "You're leaving?" she asked. "For how long?"

He turned to her, trying very hard to be gentle and strong. She was the bird, she must fly, and not be dragging a fish who belonged near an altogether different island. With him in the Great Link, there would be no more invasion, no more imperialism from the Changeling civilization. He was not going back to be one of their vague children, lost in a dream. He was going back to teach them what it meant to be an individual.

Could she see that? Could she take it?

She would have to.

"Nerys," he began, then paused. "It's time I rejoined my people in the Great Link."

How could he explain it to her? He wanted to be with her, not with them. The weren't really "his" people. They were physically like him, but that was the end of it. They had sent him out as an infant to go among the solids and learn. If they didn't want to know now what he had learned—they were going to hear it anyway. There was no inherent good or bad in Changeling or solid. The Changelings could merge from now until eternity and still only be a million individuals.

Why had it taken so many millions of deaths of his own people—yes, the solids of the Alpha Quadrant— before he understood that?

He had to make them see it. In their way, they were just liquid solids, each to himself ultimately. They were born single, and they died single. How could the middle be any different?

That was what he had learned and he was damned well going to make them understand if it took the next century. This foolish war against all solids—it was the Changelings' lack of understanding that had caused their fears. As the solids had once hunted them out of fear, they now hunted the solids out of fear—and that was simply primitive.

Shameful.

He felt supremely confident, even eager. He had his own conquest to exact. Go be with his own people? No. If he were to be with his own, he would stay here. If he were to do the best thing for himself, he would stay.

Even as the temptation fluttered within him, he knew he would go to the Link. His friends here still needed him . . . they needed him to be in the Gamma Quadrant, guarding their future, doing the best he could with all his strengths as a Changeling, not as a solid.

He would go, he would stay, and he would teach all the other fish how to be birds.

CHAPTER
11

The capital city was in ruins. Around the planet other cities were burning as well, through the days and into the nights. Fires billowed with ironic beauty against the horizon of obliterated buildings, collapsed homes, and burned-out shells. Bodies by the dozens were strewn along the street like paper litter.

"Eight hundred million dead. . . ."

Julian Bashir looked out over the city from the window of the briefing room. He'd been assigned here to triage the wounded, but there weren't any. Long-range scans showed that the Jem'Hadar had been superior in their efficiency. Who they had set out to kill, they had killed.

Beside him, Garak looked over the ruins of his native planet. "And the casualty reports are still coming in. My exile is officially over, doctor. I have returned home for good. And what have I found awaiting me? A wasteland."

Bashir gazed at him thoughtfully. "Wastelands can be made fertile again," he offered.

How hollow it sounded.

"It's easy for you to be optimistic. They're not your dead."

Bashir held back pointing out that all dead were his dead, that it was patently racist to think that somehow the suffering of strangers who *looked* alike was closer suffering. Yet, he knew that was how some people thought. No point arguing surface moralities right now, was there?

"You must have some hope for the future, Garak," he pointed out instead. "Otherwise you wouldn't stay."

"You have it backward," Garak told him. "I have to stay, even without hope. So I'm afraid this is goodbye. After seven years, you're going to have to find yourself a new lunch partner and a new tailor. I'm afraid I've hemmed my last pair of pants."

Bashir offered a meager smile. "Tinker, tailor, soldier, spy . . . I wonder what's next for you, Garak."

"Who can say, Doctor?" his Cardassian friend said. He seemed reluctant to say more, except finally to add, "We live in uncertain times."

They looked at each other, without the typical jovial sparring that usually went on between them. This was a time to lose loved ones, to lose friends. Bashir felt his chest grow hollow with the fear that big changes were coming, that the family they'd built over the past seven years, sometimes the hard way, was about to get a whole bunch of reassignment orders.

But what else? How long could a given condition

go on? Children grew up, people died, relationships came and departed, things changed, and without those alterations there would be no sense to cherish the precious.

"I hope all goes well for you, Garak," he offered. "The galaxy is going to get very big for a while, after seeming very small lately . . . there's going to be a great deal of rebuilding. Much sorrow, I suppose, but there are things to be learned from all that."

"You optimize too much, Julian," Garak said with a little chuckle. "Of all of us, you've had the steadiest life over the past several years. Somebody gets a cut, you patch it up. We've all gone through major changes. You've managed to hold onto your anchor most of the way."

Bashir sighed. "I suppose I don't like changes very much, Garak. Usually I just sit back and wait, and things settle down again. This time, I don't see the settling any time soon. There's not going to be any more time at anchor for me."

Garak smiled and his eyes flared. "Ah, but when one is in love, one doesn't want to be held down. Does one?"

Bashir managed a laugh. "No, one doesn't really. Oh, my goodness, I feel so terrible thinking about that while looking out at . . . all this."

"We Cardassians brought this upon ourselves. Intrigue eventually turns upon the intriguer."

"And you would know."

"Yes, I would." Garak held out his hand. "Good luck, Doctor."

Though there was a sadness, Bashir felt a rush of hope

as he clasped Garak's hand. "Good luck to you . . . citizen."

"This is a moment worth savoring. To victory—hard fought and well earned."

Chancellor Martok drained his glass, as he stood with Ben Sisko and Admiral Ross on the balcony overlooking the ravaged city which now stood in the possession of the Allied force.

Sisko glared out at the carnage. The people had been dragged from their homes and slaughtered, dumped in the street, and their homes torched. The tortured landscape closed his throat. He could no more take a drink than bring those people back to life.

This was victory?

He told himself it was nothing to the carnage that would have taken place if the Jem'Hadar hadn't been stopped.

Still. . . .

"Suddenly I'm not thirsty," he muttered.

Ross put his drink on the balcony rail. "Neither am I."

Martok poured himself a second glass. "Before you waste too many tears," he said, "remember those are Cardassians lying dead out there. The Bajorans would call this poetic justice."

Sisko bristled. "That still doesn't mean I have to drink a toast over a million dead bodies."

He put his own glass down and followed Ross back into the briefing room, leaving Martok alone to gaze at the devastation with his own Klingon sensibilities. To Martok, those people had paid a price they'd set themselves up to pay. The Klingons had dealt with retribution for centuries uncounted.

Well, they could have it.

The men collected their various convictions and all the pall of winning at such cost, and gratefully left the crushed hulk of Cardassia. The voyage back to *Deep Space Nine* was solemn and lacked conversation. Everyone seemed to prefer that.

Sisko certainly did. What more was there to say? If there was one person left on either side, in any faction, who didn't know why they had been fighting, he was living in a shoebox and knitting spiderwebs.

He entered the station to a blaze of fanfare and applause. He led his crew onto the Promenade, met Kasidy and Jake and their embracing arms, saw with deep satisfaction Odo and Kira walking together, Bashir and Ezri, O'Brien and his family . . . even Worf seemed placid.

Within an hour, a short blip of time, the wardroom was crowded with dignitaries and representatives for the formal cease-fire.

The female shapeshifter was here, looking smooth as ever. Two Vorta, three Jem'Hadar Firsts. When he arrived, they were all seated around the curved table, official surrender documents layered on its surface.

Sisko joined Admiral Ross, Chancellor Martok, and High Centurion Lar of the Romulan delegation. Among the witnesses filling the room were all Sisko's close command family, other Starfleet officers he didn't know well, and several more Vorta and Jem'Hadar.

The female shapeshifter signed the documents—he

would have to look later to see if she had a name or had simply squished an X—and looked up at them. She looked unusually . . . happy?

"The war between the Dominion and the Federation Alliance is now over," she announced without holding back.

Admiral Ross surveyed the documents, then looked up.

"Four hundred years ago, a victorious general spoke the following words at the end of another costly war. 'Today the guns are silent. A great tragedy has ended. We have known the bitterness of defeat and the exultation of triumph, and from both we have learned there can be no turning back. We must go forward to preserve in peace what we've won in war.' "

A moment of silence ushered in an appreciation for the rightness of vigilance.

Sisko nodded at his guards. Two of them stepped up behind the female shapeshifter. With her usual dignity she stood up and unashamedly headed for the door.

As she passed Odo, however, she paused. That made everybody nervous.

"It's up to you now, Odo," she said.

What was that supposed to mean?

Sisko watched, but there was no signal of clarification.

Odo simply nodded, and the female continued out of the room without another word.

The Jem'Hadar filed after her, and the Vorta after them, all flanked by Starfleet guards. There would be no more trouble. It was really over.

The significance of the fact that all this had started at

Deep Space Nine and now was ending here was not lost on Sisko. He felt a shining pride that history had just been made on his doorstep. Maybe there should be a plaque.

He met the eyes of his friends, one by one, and gradually they filed from the room, everyone overcome and unable to make casual conversation.

With a gesture, he escorted Martok and Ross out onto the Promenade for the final brilliant moment of this day.

People nodded politely at them as they walked, but kept their distance. As Sisko and his colleagues chose one of the wide Promenade viewports on the wormhole side, other people moved away to other windows, letting the three men have the best view and a bubble of privacy from which to enjoy it.

There, in space, was the Jem'Hadar armada of warships, escorted on each side by Federation starships. The armada approached the wormhole without signal or declaration. As the unexplainable maw opened, sparkling and swirling, the Federation ships peeled away, clearing the armada to be gulped down by the giant spacial causeway to the Gamma Quadrant.

The wormhole accepted them, then drawstringed itself closed and disappeared. Hard to believe it was still there, just invisible. Would it remain for a year, or a million years? No one could tell. They still didn't really understand how stable it was, or whether it was a plaything or repository for the Prophets who lived inside.

Sarah? Are you watching?

"Gentlemen," Ross began, "for the first time in two

and a half years, there isn't a single Dominion ship any-where in the Alpha Quadrant."

Sisko shook his head. He actually hadn't thought of that.

"Now, that . . . is worth toasting," he said.

"Finally!" Martok looked around and saw Quark's bar just over there, saw a Ferengi waiter carrying a familiar bottle and some glasses to a table of Klingons. "Waiter! Bring over that bloodwine!"

The waiter didn't even pretend to argue. His simply came out of the bar, crossed the Promenade and fumbled for a moment about how he was going to hold the tray, the glasses and the bottle without ditching the whole affair.

Martok saved him by pouring the wine himself and offering glasses to Ross and Sisko. "I'm glad we agree there's something worth celebrating!"

Ross raised his glass. "Let's hope this is the last war we see in our lifetime."

"You call that a toast?" Martok roared. "To a glorious victory!"

They drank, and grudgingly, after he got his toast, Martok offered a grudging shrug.

"Though," he added, "I admit the cost was high."

Sisko sipped his bloodwine, and gazed down to another level, where he saw Odo and Kira walking slowly together.

"And I don't think we're quite done paying it."

"You're coming to Vic's tonight?"

"I will be there. But I will not dance."

"Who's asking?"

The conversation between Ezri and Worf was almost cute as Ben Sisko strode up behind them, feeling a little voyeuristic for having heard. He could only be so polite—he had Martok and Admiral Ross with him. Amazing that Worf hadn't heard them approach, or that Ezri hadn't just sensed their eyes on them.

Better not to embarrass them.

"Commander Worf," he called, and they stopped to wait. "Can you spare a moment?"

Martok didn't seem bothered by Ezri's presence and boldly said, "We've been discussing your plans for the future."

Worf looked at him, then at Ross. "I wasn't aware I had plans."

"Commander," Ross took over, "how would you feel about being named Federation Ambassador to Kronos?"

Worf gawked at them, waiting for the punch line. At his side, Ezri contained a smile.

When nobody started laughing, Worf screwed up his resolve and announced, "I am not a diplomat."

"And I am not a politician!" Martok shot back. "But sometimes fate plays cruel tricks on us. Come, Worf! Kronos needs you. And what's more, I need you."

Completely stunned, Worf turned to Ezri as Sisko bottled up his own grin and waited.

Ezri's eyes glittered happily. "You helped him become chancellor . . . you can't very well turn your back on him now."

Disarmed by that, Worf looked at Sisko. "My first loyalty is to you, Captain!"

Sisko blushed inwardly at the idea that he could stimulate more devotion than a whole empire waiting in the wings. "I'll probably regret this in the morning, but if this is something you want, then by all means. . . ."

He offered a little shrug that clinched the deal.

Absorbing too much too fast, Worf caved to the pressure of all those surrounding him, but kept his eyes fixed on Sisko and held his breath. "It has been a great honor to serve with you, sir," he offered sincerely.

Sisko nodded to him. "The honor was all mine."

After a pause, Worf turned to Martok, still holding the same breath. "I accept."

Martok bowled forward and embraced him in a big Klingon way. "An ambassador who will go targ hunting with me! Maybe being chancellor won't be so bad after all!"

And he broke into a fierce laugh.

Ezri touched Worf's arm. "Congratulations, Worf."

Sisko watched as her eyes filled with tears, then she almost immediately regained control over herself. She went up on her toes to kiss Worf on the cheek and give him a hug—as friends.

It was good to see. And Sisko needed something that was good to see.

"When will you be going?"

Kira was warm and tender on Odo's arm as they strode along as if nothing were wrong.

"In a day or two," he told her, hoping it sounded wise.

"You could come back," she suggested carefully, "after you've cured your people. . . ."

"Nerys," he said, stopping that line of thought, "I hope you know my feelings toward you haven't changed. But my people need me. They need to know what I know, learn what I've learned from living among solids. It's the only way they will ever learn to trust you."

"You don't have to justify your decision to me, Odo," she said.

He appreciated her for that. She wasn't dismissing herself from loving him, or claiming that she wasn't a big enough part of her life to deserve an explanation. She was telling him, in her way, that she knew he had a good reason, something beyond his own personal satisfactions.

Strange, but he knew she would have protested before this, because she was worried about the effect the Link would have on him. This lack of protest proved that she understood, or at least suspected: it would be Odo affecting the Link from now on, not the other way around.

"There's only one thing I ask," she added.

"Name it."

"That we spend your last few days as a solid together. I want to take you back to your homeworld."

Her bravery and bittersweet faith in him almost knocked him over. She was giving not only her love, but her blessing.

"I'd like that," he said, and almost couldn't speak. "I'd like that very much."

Heat, flame, ecstasy.

The Fire Caves burned and swam with concoction. She

could hear her own voice, but as if disembodied, louder and louder, echoing now.

*DOORA TOLKA BRE-TRI PAH-WRAN
DOTTA TOLKA O-CHEN DOORA TOLDA
WEY-DAY SHAYHAL!*

She was half insane, her voice cracking, her skin slimy with sweat, her clothing damp and hanging, but the chant rose within her with a power she could never have imagined before! Over there, Dukat's lifeless body lay in sacrifice to the Pah-wraiths. They would come! They would come to her! She had done everything they could possibly want!

The flames! The fires of the abyss rose over her head into unnatural spirals! The Pah-wraiths! They were hearing her!

*Kos'se nusso ma'koran kajnani
preen dah-ono uka'lamor eye anu!
Kosst Amojan!* I await you! Come to me!

The energy spiral gained speed, raced, flew, ran, surged over her head. She stretched out her arm to it, seeking the blessing of the Pah-wraiths, whom she herself had freed from their prison.

They would adore her! They would favor her! Energy spears darted all around the vaulted ceiling of the Fire Caves, all at her bidding. She was the greatest conjurer!

A spear of flame came down like a javelin and struck

her in the heart. Their power was too great—the javelin slammed her backward into the hard wet sizzling wall.

Plastered there, she was helpless to raise her arms again. Her unblinking eyes saw the flames take on a living shape, springing and darting in their exuberance. But they were making a mistake.

The javelin vectored away from her, denying her the power.

Instead, it went to Dukat and drove itself into his open mouth, surging, surging into his body. But *he* was the sacrifice—she had brought him to them!

They were making a mistake. A mistake!

As her shuddering legs betrayed her and she began to slip down to the cliff shelf, Winn's burning eyes remained open and her brain remained aware, though her limbs were leaden and her heart had seized up.

Before her, on the shelf at the brink of the flaming abyss, Dukat's body shook from within. Its eyes flew open with unworldly power. There, in his eyes, she saw the life force of the Pah-wraiths.

They had chosen him and not her. They had come, they were here. They were free.

CHAPTER
12

Vic's Lounge, inside Quark's Lounge, a little bit of unreality inside a place of, some would argue, equal illusion. Eh, well, the 1960's had their charm—didn't they?

Barbie Dolls and cars with fins, beatniks and bongos, and something called go-and-go boots.

Quark entered the bar-in-a-bar and was greeted by Vic Fontaine.

"Hey, pallie! If you're here for another game of go fish, I'm a little busy right now."

"Actually," Quark told him, "I'm here for the end-of-the-war-goodbye-Chief-O'Brien-goodbye-Odo party."

"Over there, at the bar."

"Thanks."

Yeah, there they were. Sisko, his wife Kasidy, Kira with Odo, Worf more or less by himself in a crowd, O'Brien, Dr. Bashir, Ezri Dax, and Jake Sisko. Nice bunch of bananas. They all looked perfectly content, even happy. Well, except Worf. He wasn't howling yet.

"I'm serious, Miles," Dr. Bashir was saying as Quark approached, "I envy you. I really do. San Francisco is one of my favorite cities on Earth."

"Earth's got lots of wonderful cities," O'Brien said. "Every city on Earth has its own personality. Now, just let any other planet make that claim. And country! Do we have country. Canyons and grasslands and forests and redwoods and—"

"Miles, have another drink."

Quark muscled his way between Sisko and Ezri. "May I have everyone's attention please? Attention, please! In appreciation for all that you've done to end the war and save the Alpha Quadrant, the Promenade Merchants' Association has voted to pay the costs of your holosuite visit this evening."

The crowd of DS9ers cheered at themselves and Quark got a few good slams on the back.

"That's very generous of them," Ezri said.

Jake Sisko leaned forward. "Who are they paying, Quark?" he asked.

"Me, of course! And since they're being so generous, I'm charging them double."

Nobody seemed surprised. After all, he knew it was a great idea. Maybe he could market it.

Hmm. . . .

"So," he went on, "eat all you can, drink even more, and stay as late as you like."

Sure—the more they ate, the more they drank and the later they stayed, the bigger the bill.

"Don't worry, Quark," Bashir said. "It's going to be a long night. There's a lot of good-byes to be said. To Miles and Odo and Worf—"

"Worf?" Quark swung around to the Klingon. "Where are you going?"

"It does not concern you, Ferengi."

Ezri smiled and patted Worf's enormous hand. "Worf's been made Federation Ambassador to Kronos!"

"You?" Quark swung around again. "A diplomat?"

Worf scowled, then decided to admit, "That was my first reaction."

Ben Sisko beamed at his favorite hunk of granite and raised his glass. "But Admiral Ross and Chancellor Martok wouldn't take no for an answer."

Quark bothered to fill all their glasses as long as they weren't really paying attention, and distracted them by asking, "Anybody else leaving that I should know about?"

O'Brien reeled back and proclaimed, "I didn't know you cared, Quark."

"I don't. If you want to spend the rest of your life on that rotating ball of boredom called Earth, that's fine with me. I just don't like change, that's all."

Bashir laughed aloud, as if that meant something.

"Well," Sisko said, "you better get used to it, because things are going to be pretty different around here."

Perhaps he hadn't meant it heavily, but his words threw a pall over the occasion. Suddenly they all seemed to realize they were celebrating the breakup of long-time acquaintances. Quick—pour more drinks before they all get depressed!

Odo broke the threatening mood. "What ever were we talking about before Quark showed up?"

Kasidy caught the ball. "How much Julian loves San Francisco."

"That's right," Bashir plowed on. "The Bay, the bridge, the restaurants, the painted-lady houses, Big Sur, Monterey, the antique street cars, all that history . . . you're going to love it, Miles."

"I sure will," O'Brien said. "But it's going to be a bit of an adjustment at first—"

"Nonsense!" Bashir cut off. "You'll have your students, your family—think of all the quality time you can spend with Molly and Kirayoshi . . . the long, romantic walks with Keiko through Golden Gate Park. . . ."

Kasidy gazed at Sisko. "Sounds wonderful," she uttered.

"It *is* wonderful!" Bashir proclaimed. He pressed a hand to O'Brien's shoulder. "You lucky devil. Bartender! Another round for my friends here!"

When the bartender didn't respond right away, Bashir drifted off down the bar to hail the service in person.

O'Brien watched him go, appearing happy and content about the break-up.

"He's taking it better than I thought," he mentioned, knowing he was probably about to jinx the whole attitude. "My leaving and all. . . ."

Ezri, typically, found the truth much more comforting than a fluffy deception. "Are you kidding? He's dying inside."

Sadness pressed in on O'Brien no matter how he tried to pretend it wasn't there.

"I know how he feels," he said.

But did he? He was going off on a new adventure. Teaching, Earth, home life, safety . . . yes, these had their kind of adventurous nature. They had their attractive wonderment. There was challenge in making things work, showing young minds how to make things happen, in raising a contented child, providing security for his wife and kids. He was starting to feel a whole other kind of intimidation and anticipation: stare down the barrel of a thirty-year mortgage and say that guy's not a hero. A good honest job, leaving the glory-mongering to the young upstarts. He *did* like the idea. There *was* a challenge there and he was looking forward to it. He knew the captain and Ezri Dax and the others would be all right without him, despite the fact that he'd been taking care of them all these years, making sure they had air to breathe and propulsion when they needed it . . . only Bashir worried him.

Julian was hiding something, burying his real feelings—Ezri was right about that. Even a new love couldn't replace the security of old friends. O'Brien knew he'd been wrong to hope so. He knew, and felt awful, that Bashir was determined to be happy for him and not make him feel bad.

"Ladies and gentlemen!"

Vic Fontaine raised his hands and gained everyone's attention from where he stood at the front of the jazz band.

"This is a very special night for some friends of mine," he began. "They've been together a long time, but like the man said, nothing lasts forever. Gang," he added, looking over to them, "this one's from the heart. One . . . two. . . ."

The tune was jazzy, cheery, yet the words gripped O'Brien and most likely all of them with the firm hand of melancholy. They really were breaking up. Until now, it hadn't seemed so imminent.

Well, this couldn't go on.

He pushed away from his seat, went around Ezri to where Julian Bashir was watching the band play.

"Julian? All right?"

"Oh, Miles . . . it's good music, isn't it? I think it was written in the fifties, though. It's got that little swing about it—"

"I'm not talking about the song, mate."

Bashir glanced at him. "No . . . I suppose not. Don't worry about me. I've got my work cut out for me . . . we're going to be helping to rebuild Cardassia, after all, and—"

O'Brien put a hand on his arm. "Julian, stop. No job is going to come between us. Not yours, and not even mine. Is that perfectly clear? You get leaves, I get leaves—there's only so much that distance can do to keep us apart, and we're in charge of that. This is the age of warp speed. Understand?"

Realizing perhaps for the first time that his looming loneliness wasn't going to dominate their lives, Bashir met O'Brien's gaze with a glint of genuine—not pretend—hope and gratitude.

"I understand," he said.

O'Brien nodded. "You know the first thing I'm going to do when I get to Earth?"

"Take a trip to Texas."

"And visit the Alamo."

Bashir smiled. "You'll send me a souvenir?"

Shaking his head, O'Brien did his best to look offended. "What do *you* think?"

A round of applause broke their conversation, and they realized the song was over. Thank God.

Captain Sisko's glass was held high. O'Brien and Bashir turned to meet their commander's toast.

"To the best crew any captain every had," Sisko offered. When they had all lifted their glasses, he continued. "This may be our last night together, but I know one thing. No matter what the future may hold, no matter how far we travel or where we end up, a part of us, a very large part, will always remain here . . . on *Deep Space Nine*."

Neither the most poetic nor the most profound speech ever made, but there wasn't a one of them who didn't believe every word. It was a promise between them, an extension of Bashir and O'Brien's, that even those they would never see again would remain with them somehow.

O'Brien raised his glass to Sisko, then, before actually drinking, made sure that he and Bashir were looking at each other and had a private moment amid the public farewell.

Yes. It was time to move on—together.

"Are you sure you want to leave without saying good-bye?"

Kira Nerys walked beside Odo to the airlock, where the runabouts were stationed, fueled, and ready. Odo seemed pensive as he walked at her side, but he seemed also serene and in control. There wasn't a bit of doubt in him.

"Quite sure," he said. "I'm not very good at good-byes."

No, he wasn't, she had to agree, and there was some sense to his refusal. If a goodbye was focused upon too much, then that would be all anyone would ever remember.

He was smart.

She beamed at him. "A lot of people are going to be disappointed."

"If they don't know how I feel about them now," he pointed out quite rightly, "a few parting words won't make any difference."

At the threshold of the airlock, they had almost gone in together when a voice cracked at them from back in the corridor.

"I knew it!"

They turned—first mistake.

Quark was rushing toward them.

"When I saw the two of you slip out of the holosuite, I said to myself, 'That no-good misanthropic cantankerous Changeling is trying to sneak off the station without anyone's noticing!' "

Kira smiled.

"That was the idea," Odo confirmed.

Quark rushed up to them and wheedled around between them and the airlock. "Well, it's not going to happen!"

"Apparently not."

"So now that I'm here, isn't there something you want to say to me?"

Odo peered down at him. "Such as?"

"Such as, 'Goodbye, you certainly were a worthy adversary,' or maybe something with the words 'mutual respect' in it—"

"No." Odo straightened sharply.

"No? What do you mean 'no'?"

"There's nothing I want to say to you."

Quark huffed, insulted. "You're telling me that after all these years, after all we've been thorugh, you're not even going to say goodbye to me?"

Clasping his hands behind his back, Odo raised his chin. "That's right."

Kira held her breath while the two men stared at each other for a long—and longer—time.

When that snapped, Odo looked at her. "Nerys, I'll be on the runabout."

With a final dismissive glare, he disappeared around Quark and into the airlock.

Quark shifted his weight a couple of times. "I guess that's it, then."

Kira nodded. "Don't take it so hard, Quark."

"Hard? What are you talking about? That man loves me! Couldn't you see? It was written all over his—back!"

The Ferengi turned on a heel and wheeled down the corridor without turning even once to look this way again.

Of course! It wasn't over! Kira smiled, then let herself actually laugh. Nothing was over, not at all. They were the kind of friends who could see each other every twenty years and it would be as if nothing had changed! Why hadn't she realized that before?

And a lot could still happen, couldn't it?

Sure it could. The future was big. She was looking forward to it.

The Fire Caves roared their full-fledged hellfire. Winn slowly regained control over her eyes, her arms. She looked and finally saw.

At the edge of the abyss, standing strong and straight, Dukat had been transformed back into a Cardassian—his born form, his birthright—and he seemed thrilled with himself.

Winn crawled to her knees. The Kosst Amojan lay discarded a few steps from her.

"No . . . no . . . not you . . . it was supposed to be me!"

Disgust and terror ran through her body. Pah-wraith Dukat's victorious smile bored into her mind. His eyes were the orbs of a demon.

"Did you really think," he began slowly, "the Pah-wraiths would choose you to be their Emissary? They hate the Bajorans. *All* Bajorans."

Encased in bitterness, Winn understood she had been used.

Pah-Dukat glared down at her with his red-ringed eyes.

"Soon the Pah-wraiths will burn across Bajor," he said, "across the Celestial Temple, the Alpha Quadrant . . . can you picture it? A universe in flames! Burning brightly for all eternity! Can you see it? Can you see it? Burn . . . burn . . . burn!"

"Ben? Ben, what's wrong? Ben?"

He had stopped dancing. He saw fire in his mind.

Kasidy took his hand, leaned before him, tried to bring him out of what he saw.

He would not come out of it.

"I understand now. . . ."

His voice—but strange.

"Understand what?" Kasidy prodded nervously.

"What I have to do . . . what I was meant to do. Kas . . . I have to go."

He heard his own words, and knew his life would never be the same, from this moment. A bizarre serenity came over him. This had been a long time coming. She would have to accept it.

"Go?" She followed him as he broke from the table. "Where? Ben, where are you going?"

"To Bajor. To the Fire Caves."

"Right now? Can't it wait until morning?"

She didn't understand. She didn't see what he saw.

"In the morning," he told her, "it'll be too late."

Fear came into her eyes. "I'll go with you!"

"No."

Even through the flames in his mind he found the strength to turn and look at her. He owed her that, for after this night nothing would be the same. She would have to be strong. She had it in her to survive, to get through, to accept that . . .

"I have to do this alone," he said.

CHAPTER
13

His head swam with fire through the whole voyage.

He was concentrating, steeling himself, preparing for what must come. His hands and legs tingled. Soon he would have no more use for this body. He did not answer the sensation, or even think about it after the first moments. He'd issued himself a priority-one phaser rifle and kept it on the copilot's seat the whole way.

In his mind all he saw was the caverns. Already the smell of moist walls, steam, and the guttural snarl of volcanic action filled his nostrils and ears.

When he was finally beamed to the maw of the Fire Caves, his mind and soul were already inside. He walked inside, armed with his rifle, lit by his palm beacon.

"Dad . . . ."

His son's voice called to him from the walls, the cathedral ceiling that had no top, but only darkness.

"Jake?"

Ben Sisko felt the pull of his humanity as he turned to see his son standing among the stones.

"You've got to come back to the station with me."

"How'd you get here?" he asked.

"It doesn't matter," Jake claimed. "If you stay here, you'll die."

"He's right, Ben," Kasidy said.

Clasping his rifle, he swung around. She was there, standing by the wall on the other side of the cavern. She looked so peaceful, so beautiful . . . he hadn't realized how lonely he had been since his wife—

"You're not real," he told her. "Neither one of you."

Kasidy seemed hurt. "But what we're saying is real.

"If you try to stop the Restoration," Jake said, "you'll be killed."

"And you can't defeat the Kosst Amojan," Kassidy explained. "They're too powerful."

"Come home, Dad." His son's face crumpled with worry. "You don't belong here! It's not your fight!"

His wife—"We're trying to help you!"

"No," Sisko rejected. "You're trying to make me doubt myself. I won't let you."

He turned his back on them as Jake held out a hand. "Dad, please!"

In his periphery, Kasidy's face was tortured. "Ben . . . don't."

He moved on without them, turning his back on the two—no, three people he cared most about in the universe. Something bigger, more magnetic drew him forward, a purpose, a responsibility so powerful that he never hesitated another step.

"Their beloved Emissary . . . sent forth like an avenging angel to slay the demon."

Who was that?

Sisko blinked his eyes. Burning sweat poured into them, snapping him back to his physical body with very real pain.

"Dukat . . . ."

"The Prophets have sent me a gift!"

Moving forward toward the glowing form of the Cardassian, Sisko squared his shoulders. "I should've known the demon would be you."

Dukat raised his arms. "Go on. Kill me if you can."

Sisko raised his rifle, but before he could take aim, the weapon vaulted from his hands and dashed itself against the rocks. He hadn't entirely expected that to work anyway.

"Come now, captain," Dukat crowed, "you'll have to do better than that."

The Cardassian stretched out a hand, discharging an energy bolt with no weapon at all.

Sisko felt the hard zap and tried to relax as he was blown to the ground.

"This is too easy," Dukat complained. "I want to savor the moment."

Bruising quite humanly, Sisko climbed to his feet. The cobwebs of hypnotic awareness fled, leaving his head clear. He climbed back to the ledge where Dukat stood.

"That's right," the Cardassian tempted. "Come closer."

Sisko willingly did that, determined to show Dukat that he had not ever and did not now scare Benjamin Sisko.

"Now bow to me."

Ridiculous.

"I said . . . bow."

A force of fury blew across the ledge, knocking Sisko to his knees. Didn't count. Wasn't voluntary.

He shook his head at Dukat. "You're pathetic."

"Am I? Then why are you the one on your knees?"

"First the Dominion," Sisko began, "and now the Pah-wraiths. You sure know how to choose the losing side."

His reward was a crass bolt of agony from the Cardassian. Somehow that was satisfying. Even in immortality Dukat was still a superficial guy and Sisko could get under his skin with a couple of insults.

"Benjamin, please," Dukat began again. "We've known each other too long. And since this is the last time we'll ever be together, let's try to speak honestly. In the past, we've both had our share of victories and defeats, but now it's time to resolve our differences and face the ultimate truth . . . the only truth: I've won and you've lost."

Sisko looked up at him, leering fiercely, with a damnable satisfaction that wouldn't go away.

Pah-wraith or not, Dukat was still Dukat, skin-deep and easy to prick.

"If you think," Sisko challenged, "the Pah-wraiths are going to do any better than the Dominion, you're sadly mistaken. They're not going to conquer anything. Not

Bajor, not the Celestial Temple, and certainly not the Alpha Quadrant."

"And who's going to stop us?"

"I am."

"You? You can't even stand up."

"Then *I'll* stop you!" A shriek of threat rose from ten feet away.

Sisko spun around to see Kai Winn—or a ragged phantom of her—rise out of the dust and steam, holding the Kosst Amojan text high over her head. She reared back to throw the book into the flaming cavern.

"Are you still here?" Dukat mused.

He raised his hand. The book rushed out of her grip and flew into his own.

A tendril of bright energy, clearly not just another lick of flame, snaked out of the abyss, coiled around her body six times, a dozen time, then burst into searing electrical fire.

While it consumed her, Dukat clutched the book. "Farewell, Adami."

In that last moment of snide vulnerability, between god and lowly creature, Sisko seized his chance. Whatever this creature was, the real Dukat was enjoying a last bit of crude pleasure. He had to be in there somewhere.

Sisko launched himself in a running tackle and thundered into Dukat's all too solid form. Dukat was merely an obstacle. Sisko had aimed not at the Cardassian, but in his mind and with his body he had aimed at the cavern beyond, like a high-diver charging off a cliff in some tropical paradise. Paradise would come, he could reach it, and he wasn't about to leave Dukat behind to plague the natural worlds Sisko had so long protected.

Together, their forms wheeled and turned through the skyscraper-high flames, down, down into the endless depths of the Fire Caves. White limbo wrapped around them. . . .

Cool mist cradled his sweating face, taking his body in its gentle fingers and rocking him as if in a hammock. He heard his own heartbeat, the breathing of his lungs. Sweet, cool air, moist with fresh rain, drew into his lungs and spread its droplets on his face. No more fire. No more burning.

"Sarah?"

He felt her presence, and many others.

"Are you there?" he asked her. "What happened?"

"Congratulations, my son. The Emissary has completed his task."

"But the Pah-wraiths?"

"You've returned them to their prison within the Fire Caves."

"The book. It was the key, wasn't it?"

"To a door that can never again be opened."

"And Dukat? Is he dead?"

"He is where he belongs. With the Pah-wraiths. Your time of trial has ended. You may rest."

"I will . . . as soon as I get back to *Deep Space Nine.* . . ."

"You won't be going back there, Benjamin. Your corporeal existence is over."

He heard his own voice now as an echo, not as sound. He said something else, but there was only music.

Before him, the mist took shape. Many other Prophets gave him the gift of belonging. There, within reach of his mile-long arms, they took the forms he wanted to be near. Kira, Worf, Ezri . . . Martok, Ross . . . Odo, Bashir . . .

And his mother. He saw her as Kasidy and as Jake, and with them the child of the future.

She spoke to him in a voice like harp strings.

"You are one of us now."

CHAPTER
14

"A sea of Changelings. . . ."

The whole planet seemed wrapped in gold. Not the
yellow gold of a child's crayon nor the jaundice of envy,
but the deep chamois gold that artists dream to make,
milky melted honey with that oily slick that makes it
soft . . . and there was a whole ocean of it.

How many souls rolled and surged out there? How
many *people* was she seeing in this seemingly uninhab-
ited expanse? Was there one to a bucketful? One to a
droplet? She couldn't begin to judge.

This was the most alien of alien worlds, and Kira
Nerys could not even begin to imagine how it would be
to live out there.

And she could stand here on this atoll for the rest of
her life and all other conceivable lifetimes, and still
never be part of that civilization. They would have to

change to an unnatural state in order to accept her, and that would be unfair.

She would not stay here and tempt them to embrace a person who had no business wanting to stay. She had nothing in common with them physically and—far more importantly—nothing in common with them morally either.

Why was she so peaceful at the idea of Odo's staying here with these million or billion strangers? He wasn't one of them, not really. They weren't "his" people. They just looked like him. They loved each other, and she was losing him—yet she embraced with a strange passivity that this was the goal he had been seeking so stressfully all the time they'd known each other.

Odo had always been a man out of place. He'd been here before, though, and knew this wasn't his place. He could've stayed the other times he met the Link. These weren't really his people, not by the heart, by the cause, or by the spirit.

He wasn't staying for these Changelings. He was staying for himself, and for the Alpha Quadrant. His personal generosity and sense of right and wrong would keep him content here, for he had a purpose here like none other he had ever faced on *Deep Space Nine*. He had a reason.

He thinks I don't know why he's coming back to them. I'll let him keep his secret. I won't make him explain. Nobility shouldn't have to comfort its own sacrifice.

The gelatinous golden ocean, rolling beneath a golden sky, provided a romantic backdrop for their final moments. Somehow Kira had no inner turmoil, which surprised her. Being strong . . . she'd expected it to be harder.

He was so happy, though, standing at her side, gazing out at those other creatures without the slightest selfconsciousness at his solid condition or the life he had led as a solid. She was happy too.

"I didn't expect it to be so beautiful," she told him.

Odo indulged in an all-too-solid sigh. "It is, isn't it? You know, Nerys, I *am* going to miss them all . . . the captain, Chief O'Brien, Dr. Bashir . . . Worf, Dax. . . ."

"And Quark?" She grinned up at him.

He grinned. "And Quark." He turned to her now, and looked into her eyes. "But most of all—"

"I know." She pressed her hand to his lips.

They drifted into a kiss, long and heartfelt, a full escapade not into passion, but compassion. They were sharing, not adoring, not craving, saying the last things they couldn't really think of in words.

They were being watched, of course. What would the Changelings learn from them in this minute? Hopefully, the one thing they couldn't have between them, no matter how much they merged and read each others' minds—unconditional trust.

When Kira broke back from him, he was "wearing" a full dress-black tuxedo with a satin bow tie in place of his pretended uniform.

She laughed. "What's that for?"

"You always said I looked good in a tuxedo."

"You do!"

"Then that's how I want you to remember me."

She smiled again and straightened his bow tie. In a

way, she really was sending him off to the prom of a lifetime, where he would be the center of attention and all would listen to his proclamations. He would give them no alternative, she knew. His resolve fairly pulsed with a supreme self-confidence she had never witnessed in him before.

It was contagious.

"I'll remember this moment for ever," she offered. "I'll remember all our moments."

"As will I."

Oh, he was getting uneasy. Time to break off.

"Goodbye, Nerys," he told her, probably sensing the same sudden urgency.

She squeezed his hand. "Goodbye, Odo."

Wisely, he simply turned and strode into the mercurial sea. As the searching tide of his fellow Changelings lapped at his knees, he turned and waved one last time.

As Kira waved her own hand, before she lowered it, Odo released his humanoid form and melted into the golden sea.

She stood alone on the atoll, but not alone at all.

Kasidy Sisko sat on the couch in the quarters she had shared with her husband and knew that things had changed irrevocably. The room, normally so sprawling and empty, was filled with friends and colleagues who desperately wanted answers. In fact, they were rather more desperate than she was. She already had part of the answer they were seeking. She knew this was a turning point.

"Thanks, Jake," she murmured, "but I'm not hungry."

Jake Sisko had hovered over her for hours now, bringing her tea, now a tray of food, muttering hopeless reassurances, promises, and vows to search endlessly, suffering the troubles of a young man who really hadn't experienced much of the vagaries of life in space. He had always been safe, living his life pretty much on this station, protected by those around him.

Kasidy was a space captain. She knew better. She knew this feeling of dread, an instinct laden deep within on her long tour of merchant duty. Some losses couldn't be grabbed back.

She had that feeling now.

"You need the nourishment."

Dr. Bashir.

She looked up at him from her couch. His sympathy was very moving.

"Those are doctor's orders," he added with a pathetic attempt at a smile.

"Something's happened to Ben," she said. Everyone in the room turned at that one. They stopped pacing, quit moving, quit talking, and simply held still in that terrible realization that this was something they couldn't fix, despite all their combined ability and technology—or the wonders of modern anything.

"I can feel it," she added. "Something bad. . . ."

Ezri came and sat beside her. "We don't know that for sure," she offered weakly.

"We've searched all through the Fire Caves," Worf spoke up, his frustration like all his other emotions, right on top for all to see. "There's no sign of him."

"Here," Julian Bashir appeared at her side again with a hot mug. "Tarkalian tea. Very soothing."

"Better keep it coming," Ezri quietly told him.

Jake was confronting Worf. "You're not calling off the search are you?"

"Not until we find your father."

"What about the Kendra Province?" Jake suggested. His desperation also showed, but had reached neither a peak nor the resignation Kasidy already felt. "Where he bought all that land . . . maybe he went there for some reason."

"Colonel Kira and Chief O'Brien have just completely another scan of the planet. As far as they can tell . . . he's not there."

"But his runabout!" Jake protested, swinging to O'Brien. "You said you found it orbiting the planet!"

Poor O'Brien, standing there helpless, gazing into the fearful eyes of the captain's son—"I wish I had an explanation. . . ."

"We will keep looking for the captain," Worf filled in when the engineer faltered. "I promise you that."

They could look forever, Kasidy realized as he said that. They could actually do that—pass on the search to generations to come, to enhanced technologies, better science—and they still wouldn't find him. He wasn't anywhere that living corporeal beings could possibly look.

Why did she feel so light? As if she were floating.

"The Prophets warned us . . . they said we'd know nothing but sorrow. . . ."

She leaned her head back against the rim of the couch.

The people around her faded into the wall, the wall drifted into the corridor, the Promenade and its many levels dissipated, and she was gazing at clouds as white and fluffy as Earth's beautiful northern mornings.

She blinked. Suddenly frightened, she felt her bearings falter. Her balance—was she standing? She hadn't been.

Yes, she felt her feet, her legs.

"Hello?" she murmured. "Is anyone there?"

Her own heartbeat bumped reassuringly. One of them was alive, at least.

The wind blew gently, touching her ears, running like fingers in her hair, down her shoulders.

"Ben? Is that you?"

Was he calling to her?

His voice, deep and resonant, as if he were speaking inside a cave—

"Kasidy."

"Ben!"

She turned, found him in the mist, and ran into his arms. Her husband!

He was solid, real. His arms—she felt the muscles, she felt them bend to hold her, warm and secure.

Whatever this was, it wasn't death.

"Where are we?" she asked, as if the answer would make all this be real and right.

"At the entrance to the Celestial Temple."

Oh . . . that told her too much.

She backed away. "The Celestial Temple . . . then I'm having a vision."

"That's right," Ben told her. He wasn't going to tell

her any false wishes or treat her like a child. At least that.

"This is scaring me, Ben," she attempted. "I want us to go back to *Deep Space Nine*."

Worth a shot, wasn't it?

Even as she said it, she knew the answer.

"I can't," he told her immediately, without frills.

It was the destiny he had been born for, the mysterious truth that had been masked by his human existence. How the cloudy beings who called themselves the Prophets would have a link to the living, breathing worlds they could only observe.

"Oh, my God," Kasidy breathed.

"It's difficult to explain. It isn't linear . . . . My life, my destiny—the Prophets saved me so that I could be with them."

"Be with them?" she repeated.

Ben took her arm, then her hand in both of his. "They have so much they want to teach me."

She felt like she was frozen—she could barely force out the words. "How long will you be gone?"

"It's difficult to say . . . ." He hesitated. "Time doesn't exist here."

A terrible breath rattled through Kasidy's body, proving to her that she was alive and really here, not imagining all this in a muddle of grief or fatigue. What was all that supposed to mean? Time doesn't exist here?

What was he trying to say?

"Then this is the sorrow the Prophets warned us about?" she whispered.

She wanted him to say it.

He smiled. His dark eyes were soft beacons for her.

"Kas—I'll be back."

"When?" she persisted.

"It could be next year." He smiled suddenly, with an understanding she didn't share. "It could be yesterday. But I *will* be back."

She heard the grim determination in his voice and knew he would find a way to make it true. "I'll be waiting," she promised.

She thought he took her in his arms once more, but now she was back on the couch, her arms tingling from his touch.

"Kas?"

That sounded like him.

No, the voice was . . . younger. . . .

"Can you hear me? Kas?"

Jake bent over her, looking relieved as she blinked at him.

Everyone else was looking too. Worf, O'Brien, the doctor, Ezri—

She was back with them. Had she ever left?

"You seemed pretty far away for a second," Julian Bashir said, bending over her.

"Not that far," Kasidy told them. She looked at Jake, and for some reason she found herself smiling. An unworldly contentedness came over her. Like the wives of a million space captains and adventurers and great men of past times, she would find herself called upon to raise his children and be their guide alone, benchmarked by the high standard Ben Sisko had set for them.

She could do that. As she gazed at Jake, she saw in his youth the bright hope of the child within her, a new chance for the future, and somebody to be with.

"I was talking to your father," she said.

They would wait for him.

CHAPTER
15

"Today's duty roster, Colonel."

Kira Nerys looked down from *Deep Space Nine* at the distant orb of Bajor, and noticed that it was morning over her home province. Everything was dawning. A whole new day, a new life.

She took the padd from Nog and scanned it. Everything was back in order. The day-to-day procedure of station activity was the best therapy she could imagine, not only for herself but for everybody here. The military had something, she decided, in its order and sense, in the strict utility of rank and process. Somehow it helped everybody to have duties, watches, purpose.

"Nice work," she told the young Ferengi. "And congratulations on your promotion, Lieutenant."

Nog seemed a little small and uneasy to be carrying such a big rank.

"Thank you, ma'am," he said. "I guess putting me in for promotion was one of Captain Sisko's last official acts."

"I'm sure he's very proud of you, Nog."

"I'd like to think so, ma'am."

Kira deliberately didn't say "was." She didn't believe Sisko was dead. Nobody did.

Was he watching them? Now, there was a disturbing thought: no, he probably wasn't acting as some kind of mystical voyeur. They were free to have privacy, and to make mistakes without a big daddy watching over them. He wouldn't have wanted that for himself and she was betting he wasn't eying them from the ethereal plane. He probably had his own duties out there, somewhere, teaching the Prophets a thing or two about life.

That made her smile.

But back to work. "Now, about the cargo inventories—"

Nog stepped back. "I'll get right on it!"

He raced out of the room, delighted with his new job as station adjutant. A big job, a mighty station, very busy and getting busier as the sector stabilized. Starfleet was actually enjoying itself, and so was she. She too was proud of her own promotion—to station commander, carrying the authority of both the Bajoran military and Starfleet Command. It was a singular honor, and she was gratified by their faith in her.

They were showing faith in Sisko, too, she recognized, by giving her this post. He had trusted her, and that was good enough for Starfleet.

She appreciated their judgment. She *could* do the job.

—Well, not from here. . . .

Ops. She suddenly wanted to be at the pulsing heart of the station, to spread her wings and really take over, to make sure they all knew that she was here to catch the ball.

The ball!

There it was—Captain Sisko's little dutiful baseball, sitting on its stand where he had left it, giving a whole new meaning to the phrase, "You can't take it with you."

She plucked the ball into her hand and tossed it in the air and caught it a couple of times. With that, the mantle had shifted fully to her. She'd never dared to touch it before.

He must approve . . . she thought he was smiling on his cloud someplace out there in a universe much bigger even than it seemed to be.

Managing to hold herself down from a run, she strode in amiable satisfaction to ops and plunged right in to the bleeping, humming center of activity that made *Deep Space Nine* a living place. In her hand the baseball was warm and solid. She rolled it in her fingers and scanned each post, taking solace in the steady information streaming from all over the quadrant to this single beacon in the darkness.

All around her at every station were new faces, young officers and trainees ready to tackle the next chapter in the conquest of the final frontier. Over there was the new chief of engineering. Beside him was the new tactical sergeant, and speaking to the new life sciences coordinator was the new chief constable of station security.

They nodded a polite greeting to their commander as they noticed her watching them. This was their time, and hers.

"What do you think?"

Julian Bashir had babbled away the morning after spending the whole evening transferring the Alamo from the O'Briens' old quarters to his. And a bloody tight fit it was.

Despite a decidedly sour note to the move, the Alamo's presence in his quarters somehow galvanized the idea that he was on his own for a while, without Miles.

Across the table from him in the replimat, Ezri was picking at her breakfast, with her mind obviously on something else. Her short dark hair reflected the overhead lights, separating them into the spectral colors green, blue, red, and yellow and making her eyes seem bright.

"What do you think of my new medical supply system?" he asked. "I've reworked the whole storage process."

She blinked up at him. She hadn't been listening. "I think maybe tonight, after dinner, we could go to Quark's . . . maybe spend some time in the holosuites."

Bashir thought about that. "I wouldn't mind a little trip to Vegas."

"Actually," Ezri corrected, her eyes crinkling, "I was thinking about the Alamo."

Sounded like a nice idea. Obviously she was trying to help him through this, working on adjusting the future to be as full as the past few years had been, even generously trying to replace the close friend who was no longer here with him.

But he shook his head. "We can't go there."

"Why not?"

He thought about coughing up some excuse, but the truth kept bubbling up and ultimately would do just as well. Probably because she already knew it.

"That was something Miles and I did."

Would she understand? She was the repository of more than a dozen life forces, all those memories, relationships . . . she'd understand, more than most, wouldn't she, that one person, no matter how loved, simply could not replace another?

"But," he said, brightening, "we could try my new program. The Battle of Thermopylae."

She gawked at him, her fork in midair. What? No human lifetimes lurking around in there?

Of course not. She hadn't heard of that.

"You know," he attempted, "where a small band of Spartans led by King Leonidas defended a mountain pass against the vast Persian army?"

"What happened?" she asked.

"For two days, the Spartans put up a heroic struggle."

"Until they were wiped out."

"How'd you know?"

"Lucky guess. I take it we'll be the Spartans?"

"Fighting to the last man!" Bashir proclaimed.

"Just like the Alamo?"

"Exactly!" He thumped the table.

Ezri put her fork down and sat back. "Julian, have you

ever talked to a counselor about these annihilation fantasies you seem to have?"

Bashir blinked. Hadn't thought of that one.

"You think I should?" he asked.

"I'll set up a session for us tomorrow."

Hmm . . . how very enticing. A doctor and a Trill getting together to discuss annihilation . . . oh, that was better left alone . . . but why was she leering that evil glare at him?

He leaned forward. "And tonight?"

She smiled broadly, her eyes crinkling with unshielded happiness and commitment.

"Tonight . . . we defend the pass!"

Commander Kira of *Deep Space Nine* strode the Promenade with a purpose and vectored into Quark's bar, feeling somehow fulfilled at the mundane duty she was about to discharge.

Over there. Quark.

He was arguing with Morn. He had his back to her, so she strode up without announcing herself and listened to the last couple of blurts.

"That'll be ten strips of latinum—I know, I know, I'll put it on your tab. Don't worry! It's guaranteed to grow hair within a week! If you ask me, your dome's hairy enough as it is. Besides, hasn't there been enough change around here already?"

"Quark!" Kira swung around in front of him and wagged a padd in his face. "Do you mind explaining this?"

Quark's knobby eyes flashed. "That's this week's betting pool."

Kira huffed with insult. "You're taking bets on who's going to be Bajor's new Kai?"

He spread his arms. "It's a wide open field! Just between you and me, the smart money's on Vedek Ungtae."

Lowering the padd, she scowled at him. "Well, just between you and me, all bets are off."

"What are you talking about!"

"As of this moment," she said, "betting pools of any kind are illegal on this station." Oh, that felt good! "I catch someone placing a bet, *you'll* spend fifteen days in a holding cell. Is that clear?"

Quark looked shocked, then leered at her suspiciously. "Holding cells? Ah . . . let me think. Fifteen days . . . can I brink my own pillow?"

"Quark!"

"It's clear, it's clear."

"It better be."

Quark shook his head as he strode away. "It's like I said. The more things change, the more they stay the same."

Kira smiled. She let him go back to work. It felt good to do something so mundane and normal as chewing out Quark and telling he couldn't do something. Anything. After a few days, she'd let him take bets again, but *after* the new Kai was appointed. Some things shouldn't be matters of lot.

Strolling out onto the Promenade, Kira experienced an overwhelming sensation of peace and satisfaction. This alien station, once the very exemplar of despicable for her—a Cardassian outpost in claimed space—

was now itself the embodiment of how things could change for the better. Despite its Cardassian design, this was a Starfleet station, a Bajoran holding, and a supreme victory for them all. They'd taken it, they'd lost it, they'd regained it, and now it was secure. The presence of *Deep Space Nine* secured the whole sector, indeed the quadrant. She believed now that it would never again fall.

She paused on the walkway overlooking the lower Promenade. Below, people freely roamed the shops, paused to talk, smiled, cried, comforted each other, and went on their ways. They all knew things were unconditionally different, but that somehow this was the brink from which they would all leap to the better.

There . . . that was where she and Odo had walked on their way to their last voyage together, where they had linked arms in a way that his native people could never imagine or know how to enjoy.

Over there, on the second level, Worf and Ezri strode together with Chancellor Martok, on the path to the docking pylon where the Klingon ships were serviced. Martok was doing all the talking. Worf and Ezri were looking at each other in silence. Worf carried his duffel bag. His bat'leth was slung over his shoulder. Kira imagined what Martok was saying—enthusiasms about the future of the Klingon Empire . . . great hunts and good songs . . . but Worf wasn't listening. He turned instead, gazed at Ezri as he never had before, and all of them, even Kira way up here watching, began thinking about Jadzia.

Somberly, Worf removed his bat'leth from his shoulder and handed it to Ezri. A parting gift—to her who knew what it was to be his wife.

Kira shivered with emotion, and had to look away.

As her eyes scanned the vast sweeping walkways of the station, they fell upon another quest for the future—Chief O'Brien shooing his family down the ramp toward Airlock Four. His own bags were slung on his shoulder, together with several more bags that must belong to his children. Before him ran Molly, while Keiko carried the baby and nipped orders at two yeomen who were carrying still more bags and boxes.

Kira watched the little face of Kirayoshi and tried not to remember what she had promised herself she could forget—the undying tie between herself and the O'Briens. That was a family she had helped build. She had to force herself not to call out to them before Keiko and the children disappeared under the walkway she was standing on. Now there was only O'Brien, shuffling along with all his burden—

Oh, there was Bashir, catching up to him, taking a couple of the bags from him. Then the doctor caught O'Brien by the elbow and stopped him.

They were too far down there for Kira to hear what they were saying—not much, judging by what she saw. In fact, they seemed to be having trouble speaking at all to each other.

She understood. After years here together, what words could be enough? She thought of Odo.

Bashir was making O'Brien put his bags down for a moment. Kira squinted as the doctor put something into O'Brien's hand. What was that? A good luck charm?

Then she recognized it . . . it was one of those little figurines from the Alamo model they'd worked on together. O'Brien had showed it to her proudly—little Colonel Travis, the brave commander of the losing side.

O'Brien smiled and his cheeks reddened. He didn't know what to say, so he was saying nothing. Shoring up his resolve, he nodded, and extended a hand to shake. Bashir put out his own hand and clasped O'Brien's. See ya.

Kira shook her head and smiled at them scoldingly, but before she could shout an interruption that would embarrass them both, they had done her job—they were locked in a bear hug.

Much better.

She settled back and turned away to the other side of the walkway, letting them have their last moments in privacy.

There were other people to watch, people who were staying on *Deep Space Nine*. Putting one hand on the rail, she gazed downward custodially at the customers coming and going from Quark's and the other shops below. They were hers to protect now, hers to understand. She would help them if she could.

As she scanned the Promenade viewports, windows that showed the open panorama of space, she saw something that did disturb her—one of the people here she probably couldn't help.

On the second level, Jake Sisko stood at the viewport, staring out into open space where the wormhole lurked in its other dimension. The boy stared out into it.

A man looked back, but it was his own reflection in the viewport permaglass.

Kira moved quietly to stand beside him. Together they watched as the wormhole magically burst open, its giant drain swirling and rushing, and a messenger ship from this side effortlessly slid inside.

The first of many. A whole new realm of possibility.

They stood together, thinking the same thoughts, two small beings on a great station—only a dot of light on the ceiling of the space cathedral, but a star of hope for all who looked.

Look for STAR TREK Fiction from Pocket Books

Star Trek®: The Original Series

Star Trek: The Next Generation®

Star Trek: Deep Space Nine®

The Search • Diane Carey
Warped • K. W. Jeter
The Way of the Warrior • Diane Carey
Star Trek: Klingon • Dean W. Smith & Kristine K. Rusch
Trials and Tribble-ations • Diane Carey
Far Beyond the Stars • Steve Barnes
The 34th Rule • Armin Shimerman & David George
What You Leave Behind • Diane Carey

Star Trek®: Day of Honor

Book One: *Ancient Blood* • Diane Carey
Book Two: *Armageddon Sky* • L. A. Graf
Book Three: *Her Klingon Soul* • Michael Jan Friedman
Book Four: *Treaty's Law* • Dean W. Smith & Kristine K. Rusch
The Television Episode • Michael Jan Friedman

Star Trek®: The Captain's Table

Book One: *War Dragons* • L. A. Graf
Book Two: *Dujonian's Hoard* • Michael Jan Friedman
Book Three: *The Mist* • Dean W. Smith & Kristine K. Rusch
Book Four: *Fire Ship* • Diane Carey
Book Five: *Once Burned* • Peter David
Book Six: *Where Sea Meets Sky* • Jerry Oltion

Star Trek®: The Dominion War

Book 1: *Behind Enenmy Lines* • John Vornholt
Book 2: *Call To Arms . . .* • Diane Carey
Book 3: *Tunnel Through the Stars* • John Vornholt
Book 4: *. . . Sacrifice of Angels* • Diane Carey

Star Trek®: My Brother's Keeper

Book One: *Republic* • Michael Jan Friedman
Book Two: *Constitution* • Michael Jan Friedman
Book Three: *Enterprise* • Michael Jan Friedman